HIDDEN PATH

ELENA FORTÚN

HIDDEN PATH

Translated by Jeffrey Zamostny

With a Foreword by Nuria Capdevila-Argüelles

SWAN
ISLE
PRESS

Chicago

Elena Fortún (pen name of María de la Encarnación Gertrudis Jacoba Aragoneses y de Urquijo, Madrid, 1886-1952) is the author of the classic twenty-volume saga *Celia and Her World* (1929-1951). Her work created an essential link between pre- and post-Civil War generations of Spanish women writers, although her novel, *Oculto sendero*, was not published during her lifetime.

Jeffrey Zamostny is associate professor of Spanish at the University of West Georgia. He received his Ph.D. in Hispanic Studies from the University of Kentucky.

Nuria Capdevila-Argüelles is professor of Hispanic and Gender Studies at the University of Exeter. She received her Ph.D. at the University of Edinburgh.

Swan Isle Press, Chicago 60628
Edition©2021 by Swan Isle Press
©Herederos de Elena Fortún
Translation©Jeffrey Zamostny
Foreword©Nuria Capdevila-Argüelles

All rights reserved. Published 2021.
Printed in the United States of America
First Edition
25 24 23 22 21   1 2 3 4 5
ISBN-13: 978-0-9972287-8-6(paperback)

Originally published as *Oculto sendero*. Translation is based on *Oculto sendero* by Elena Fortún, 2016©Editorial Renacimiento (Seville, Spain)

Cover Image: "Two Women Embracing" by Egon Schiele (1913); Medium: Gouache, watercolor, and graphite on paper.
    The Metropolitan Museum of Art, New York, and The Frederick and Helen Serger Collection, Bequest of Helen Serger, in honor of William S. Lieberman, 1989.

LIBRARY OF CONGRESS CATALOGING-IN-PUBLICATION DATA
Names: Fortún, Elena, author. | Zamostny, Jeffrey, translator. | Capdevila-Argüelles, Nuria, writer of foreword.
Title: Hidden path / Elena Fortún ; translated by Jeffrey Zamostny with a foreword by Nuria Capdevila-Argüelles.
Other titles: Oculto sendero. English
Description: First edition. | Chicago: Swan Isle Press, 2021. | Includes bibliographical references. | Translation is based on Oculto sendero by Elena Fortún, 2016, Editorial Renacimiento (Seville, Spain). |
Identifiers: LCCN 2020042052 | ISBN 9780997228786 (trade paperback)
Classification: LCC PQ6611.O78 O2813 2020 | DDC 863/.64--dc23
LC record available at https://lccn.loc.gov/2020042052

The translation of *Oculto sendero*, *Hidden Path*, has been published with a generous grant of subvention from the Ministerio de Cultura y Deporte de España.

Swan Isle Press gratefully acknowledges that this book was made possible, in part, with the generous support of the following:

THE UNIVERSITY OF WEST GEORGIA-The Office of Research and Sponsored Projects

THE GOLDEN MERCER CHARITABLE GIVING FUND

THE EUROPE BAY GIVING TRUST

AND OTHER KIND DONORS

A todos los que equivocaron su camino…
y aún están a tiempo de rectificar.

~LA AUTORA

To all who missed their path…
and still have time to change their course.

~THE AUTHOR

CONTENTS

Nuria Capdevila-Argüelles

Hidden Path was probably finished between 1940 and 1945 and start-ed in the mid-1930s. Elena Fortún (pen name of Encarnación Ara-goneses, 1886-1952) did not date it. She also used a different alias, Rosa María Castaños, to sign this Sapphic autobiographical novel: a novel about lesbianism without the word but with ideas on sexu-al inversion, gender unorthodoxy, androgyny, and more generally not wanting to be and not being a woman in the heterosexual and feminine sense of the word. Significantly, she gave it a title in tune with more contemporary views of the notion of the closet, the most important contribution of gay studies to the exploration of identity in modern times, a field highly relevant to feminist cultural historians like myself. The protagonist, María Luisa, and the women in *Hidden Path*, how-ever, do not use notions of identity to perceive themselves in the same way as people today, and they do not understand homosexuality in the contemporary sense either. The story of the two manuscripts of this autobiographical *bildungsroman* or novel of apprenticeship is too long and geographically complex to be dissected now. It extends from the 1940s to the autumn of 2016, when it was published in Spain for the first time. By the spring of 2017 it had become a best-seller. That year I frequently spoke to the media in Spain and abroad to discuss the im-portance of the novel and the story of Fortún's authorship coming out of the closet. My introductory essay was exhaustive. It explained, or so I hoped, everything that was necessary to understand the importance of the text for Hispanic audiences. British and American audiences are familiar with *The Well of Loneliness* by Radclyffe Hall (1928) or with

Henry James's *The Bostonians* (1886). Hispanic audiences received the text when different closets were being opened in culture: the closet of historical memory, firmly sealed to cover a violent civil war and the hard decades of dictatorship; the closet of Spain's lost feminist legacy to which I have dedicated my research career, a legacy of memorialistic literature like this book, kept in archives or printed in rare editions; the closet of gender, hiding not just lesbianism but bisexuality and other experiences undermining the heterosexual norm and the universal archetype of the self-sacrificing housebound mother.

People often asked me, "Didn't you feel bad for telling the secret?" My answer was and is clear: the voice of the secret was screaming to be let out, and translating its history into English continues that process. Furthermore, the story had been typed up in a book that was finished and bound. At the time of Fortún's death, one manuscript of *Hidden Path* was in Orange, New Jersey. Another one was in Buenos Aires. Both were brought back to Spain in the late 1980s by Marisol Dorao, a lecturer from Cádiz University who felt unable to approach Fortún's lesbianism. There were other materials making up the archive of an author who had written a saga of twenty books with a storyteller girl called Celia and her family as protagonists and Spain and its troubled twentieth-century history as background. That nobody knew much about Fortún is not strange: she belonged to a generation of female writers and artists turned into ghosts by the pact of oblivion that became the foundation of the Spanish transition to democracy after Franco's death in 1975. It was felt that the wounds of the past would be better left untouched. In order to do so, obliterating the dictatorship, the civil war, and the Second Republic was fundamental for Spain's society and politics to move on in the last third of the last century. Wiping the slate clean implied letting go of the mothers of Spanish feminism. This was an impossible task: they had a story to tell, and their time would come. As ghosts, they started to haunt us historians. What could not be discussed in the political arena got recessed into the closet of a denied historical memory. Too heavy a burden to be hidden forever, too important a discourse to be silenced when it was not silent, it could never be fully removed from reality. That was my explanation for the frequent presence of mute grandmothers and orphaned girls in the culture of Spain's transition to democracy. As I grew up, nobody taught me about recent Spanish history at school. Celia did. My only connection with a narrative of Spanish twentieth-century history was her. For a long time, she signalled a crack in the otherwise rather solid façade of the new Spain I was growing up in. She made me inquisitive about the generation of my grandmothers, sometimes annoyingly so, as one of my teachers told me when I was fourteen.

Recent legislation on historical memory has opened the Pandora's box of Spain's feminist past and has created the perfect climate for *Hidden Path* to appear and be well received. Elena Fortún was never pretentious but rather modest and discreet. She just wanted her texts to be loved and enjoyed. The 1980s were the decade of Spain's second attempt at genuine democracy. Franco had died in 1975; the new constitution came into force in 1978. But Spain had a first attempt at genuine democracy in 1931, when the Second Republic was proclaimed. A nation used to having military declarations as a mechanism for political change could not suddenly acquire democratic praxis. A violent climate prevailed. That climate existed too beyond Spanish borders, fuelled by the post-1929 economic recession. Progress was not a positive term anymore after the roaring 1920s, and a key emblem of progress, the emancipated woman with her income and shorter hair and skirt, started to see her recently acquired rights eroded. Just then, when the flapper was being questioned as perhaps nationally unhealthy and a threat to the family, the Spanish modern woman was legitimised by new Republican legislation on women's rights. The implementation of equality was controversial. Tradition and modernity continued to clash. The former started to win between the two World Wars. The feminist movement had indeed flourished, but conservative values undermined it too. This tension between the modern and the traditional and this new female identity merged in the life of a Spanish woman nearly in her forties who made the most of that time of acceleration of modernity precisely when other European nations were starting to slow it down or reverse it altogether. Elena Fortún had been born.

As mentioned above, she belonged to a generation of Spanish feminists active before the Spanish Civil War (1936-39). For the first time in Spanish history, those feminists were aware of being a group. They founded clubs and associations, were very active in the press and in the cultural and political spheres, and generally believed that the regeneration of Spain, no longer an empire after the loss of the last colonies in 1898 and therefore no longer a great European nation, could only be achieved if a regenerated, new, and modern woman contributed to the task, separated herself from the domestic sphere, and became by work and education the best version of herself. It is a world we see in *Hidden Path*. These women gradually entered the public sphere as parliamentarians, lawyers, doctors, anarchists, journalists, artists, writers, telephone operators, and many other occupations. While they did so, they were disdainfully scrutinised by eminent misogynists such as Nobel Prize Dr. Ramón y Cajal or his famous disciple, the endocrinologist Marañón, on whom Fortún probably modelled the character of the physician María Luisa visits as an adult woman artist who finds heterosexual sex repulsive. Important men feared the advancement of this new androgynous female and got either concerned about or genuinely interested in the gender unorthodoxy these women displayed in their public activities in traditionally masculine domains, activities that weakened the bond between woman, motherhood, and domesticity and forced men to share public spaces, authorship, power, and work.

Celia was fun and so were the other characters in her saga. But the story of *Hidden Path* is a very different affair, despite some comic episodes in line with the typical *Fortunian* dialogues so many Spaniards recognise and love. *Hidden Path* is about authorship and sexuality, both key components of human identity, the former as vocation and work, the latter as inclination and desire. Both important; both, essential. Terms matter to contextualise the book in relation to the tale of the tense Spanish modernity. The world in which Encarnación Aragoneses turned into Elena Fortún was regenerationist and essentialist: obsessed by grasping and controlling essences, keen to modernise and regenerate Spain. The Spanish black legend consolidated itself, an antimodern country on the edge of Europe: Spain as a problem. One word became leitmotif: regeneration. The Second Republic (1931-39) was regenerationist. It is therefore no coincidence that it gave legal legitimacy to this Spanish *New Woman* with legislation on salaries, maternity rights, and divorce and abortion laws meant to accelerate the achievement of equality between the sexes. It was a tense modernity, more so than that of other Western nations. The *mujer moderna* achieved a remarkable consolidation in the 1930s. The protagonist of *Hidden Path* reaches her anagnorisis, a present of awareness from which to revisit the past and have this story told, precisely in the avant-garde Madrid of the Second Republic, a world that existed and was not fictional, a world Francoism would destroy.

The essence of man, the essence of woman, the essence of the nation, whatever they were, if there were any, needed to be restored. Reality was saying they were lost. Science, technology, and the avant-garde were providing new understandings and new processes of knowledge acquisition. There it is, the most basic of narrative quests, the baseline of the novel of apprenticeship: follow a hidden path and find an essence, some sort of pristine truth about the 'I' and bring it to light for life to make sense and perhaps, one day, achieve some sort of harmonic completion. Or, if shocked by the discovered essential truth about the self, hide it forever. This is what Fortún did with her sexuality, covered by an unhappy companionate marriage she never dared to end. Her husband was an army officer and also a very mediocre man of letters, hurt by the success of his unorthodox wife, so keen to wear shirt and tie and such a busy bee with her writing and her studies and thirst for knowledge. He was probably unaware of what she wrote inside the closet. Nevertheless, it was he who wrote in 1922 a novel called *The Thousand Years of Elena Fortún*. Two years later she adopted the name and used it to sign her articles, books, and most of her letters, so much so that she hardly used Encarnación, her real name. The Elena Fortún of the novel travelled throughout different historical times changing sex and gender, adopting different guises, a bit like Virginia Woolf's *Orlando*. The *nom de plume* Elena Fortún came then from a character that cross-dressed and experienced transsexuality. The initial premise of the book is that woman is second to man and therefore the female body is a prison from which anyone, in this case Elena Fortún the character who travels through history, may wish to escape. Escaping, though, is impossible; hence the act of fantasy and fiction that the historical novel is. Still, one cannot escape the body and one cannot be a time traveller. But if the body is a closet, a material exterior with revealing truths inside, that exterior is as protective as it is restrictive. Inside the closet of Elena Fortún, externally protected by the stories of Celia, her brother Cuchifritín, her cousin Matonkikí, and her sisters Teresina and Mila, eclipsed by their fame, Fortún wrote *Hidden Path*. In it, she reflected on sexuality and authorship via another very unorthodox girl narrator and character: María Luisa.

As the writer Fortún in pre-civil war Madrid and the adult character and narrator María Luisa in *Hidden Path* embrace modern spaces, the *new woman* or *flapper* is endlessly debated as perhaps unavoidable but scarily detrimental to the welfare of society, condemned to a democratisation of the sexes, i.e., to a world in which men would not be men, women would not be women, and inversion, intersexuality, and other new selves would proliferate, eroding the family unit and by extension society. This was to be feared. Luckily, the conventional family with its traditional gender roles got the validation it needed in the conservative years of Francoism and post-war Europe. No more eroding tradition, considered by many as some sort of essential and eternal value that made individuals feel secure rather than alienated as the modern woman felt by it, and eroding even, as Elena Fortún the protagonist of *The Thousand Years of Elena Fortún* did, official narratives of history founded on values considered wholesome and eternal, not new. This antifeminist terrorism might make us laugh nowadays but was unfortunately highly influential. As a little girl a voice from inside the closet spoke to María Luisa and scared her while in bed. Never sure whether it was real or whether she was dreaming it, the message, told by the adult María Luisa recounting her childhood, was both invitation and command: "Want to see how I draw back the curtain? Look at the door, pay attention." The girl character was terrified. However, it is not difficult to picture the author writing this scene in serene dialogue with her life experience of her secret. Safe in the closet behind the amazing tales that made her work profitable and successful, she probably empathised with María Luisa's fear of herself, fear of the spectacle of her gender and sexuality hidden behind the curtain, hidden on a hidden path. María Luisa does not want to grow up to be a woman. María Luisa hates conventional femininity but likes girls. She anticipates the fracture between sex and gender underpinning contemporary views on these two concepts, views that had hardly been formulated in the essentialist times Fortún lived in. The voice that invites the little girl to recognise herself in whatever lies hidden behind door and curtain is part of the same mind that feels embarrassed by frills and ribbons and struggles to eat and digest. This happened to the real Fortún too, who eventually died of lung and stomach ailments: the mouth and the stomach revealed symptoms of a body that felt its inside essence had been raped and disturbed.

Celia is to this day the most famous child and teenage character of Spanish literature. Her books have been present in Spanish bookshops and libraries since the 1920s, having hardly been affected by Francoist censorship. In the 1980s children like myself at the time bought the latest editions of the Celia books, laughed with the incredibly witty stories, and enjoyed the beautiful illustrations. Celia lived in Madrid. She went from being a sort of Spanish Pippi Longstocking, Huck Finn, Anne of Green Gables or Just William to being a teenager living through the civil war and a young woman going into exile in Argentina, like Fortún did. Fortún's friends there, a feminist network made up of Argentinian women and Spanish Republican feminists forced to go into exile, looked after the manuscript of *Hidden Path*. Eventually, Celia returns to Spain and gets married. It is not a happy end, but reads like a symbolic death. Fortún herself returned to Spain to die too. In *Hidden Path*, María Luisa knows marriage for her will be deadly. The same voice that invited her to contemplate the dark spectacle of her gender unorthodoxy warns her not to do it, but she does. It is far too difficult to be unconventional, strange, *queer*, like María Luisa is. Fortún's abundant correspondence testifies to this too. Celia does not seem to be much in love when she gets married. She is gone and reads absent from reality when she is narrated by her little sister Mila in *Celia Gets Married* (1950). She does not become a writer, a lawyer or a librarian, as she expected to be when she was younger. She becomes nothing. However, by the time she drifts into a resigned silence, María Luisa already existed, somewhere, hidden. And by then too the voice of yet another girl storyteller had taken over the last volumes of the series in the external successful authorship of Fortún. The cheeky voice of Mila, Celia's fearless little sister, protagonist of the last books of the saga, is a robust storyteller in the making, proof that the voice of women's history always exists even in a world in which a very patriarchal censorship carefully monitored and tried to silence her. Mila's disregard for gender conventions and her total inability to do her gender right and even her hilarious capacity to make gender look nonsensical and alien make her have one foot firmly inside the closet of Fortún's authorship. And in that secluded space another female voice, sadder than funny Mila, walks a hidden path and tells us about it. Free, vagabond Mila is an open end and a symbol of hope. María Luisa is too.

Generations of Spanish children and teenagers had in Fortún's books a crack in the façade of oblivion that formed the pact on which our democracy was built. But can you ever really forget? Can you ever really lay the past to rest if the past has not been incorporated into the narration of the present? Freud would have said no. Repression, the psychoanalytic equivalent of oblivion, might be the most basic mechanism in the construction of the self but, at the same time, it is predicated on never being totally achieved. *Hidden Path* proves that in what lies repressed the truth is written and indeed that looking for the truth, being on a hidden path towards it, is the opposite of oblivion.

PART 1: SPRING

THE DRESS

When I got home from school, mother was crocheting by the balcony overlooking the Plaza de Matute.

"Your dress just came from Justa. It's precious," she said. "I laid it out on your bed."

She saw me race out and shouted behind me.

"Now don't you go staining it!"

I saw it from the hallway, all stretched out, with open arms, as if it had fainted. I don't know why I didn't faint myself. Lord, what a disaster! It wasn't the sailor suit I'd been promised.

The anguish that burst in my chest sprouted spines and rose into my throat, filling my eyes with bitter tears that streamed down my cheeks onto the dress and the rug at my feet. I went back to the sitting room sobbing. Mother was still crocheting, unaware of the terrible catastrophe she'd just provoked. I collapsed onto an armchair in a fit of burning tears.

"What's the matter with you?" asked mother, flatly. She was accustomed to scenes like that one and didn't budge from her seat.

"The dress, the dress," I bawled in despair. "The dress wasn't like that. I don't want it; I'll never wear it. I don't want it!"

"What?" mother protested. "What did you say? You will wear the dress, and I'll hear no more of it! You're nobody here, understand? In my household, I give the orders… And your father, naturally."

Much to my good-natured father's amusement, mother would assert her rights only to remember she was merely the queen consort of the house. At that time of day, he must've been behind the shop counter measuring out bolts of madapolam and gingham for the coming spring.

Still sobbing, I murmured, "But I said … I said … that it had to be a sailor suit … with the cap and all, and you said … 'fine' … and now …" I couldn't go on. My pain had grown new barbs and could no longer fit in my body, which trembled and doubled at the knees.

I couldn't see mother, but I knew she'd set her crocheting aside and was squinting down at me. Her voice was harsh and cutting.

"You quiet yourself down this instant. This instant, girl! You'd better watch out. If you keep it up, tomorrow I'll send you packing to a boarding school. You hear? Quiet down! I'd better not hear you again. Off you go!"

Rising shakily, I stifled my whimpers in a handkerchief and took refuge in my bedroom, where the sight of the navy blue dress with thick lace frills running down its lantern sleeves sent me into another fit of fury and despair, forcing me to the floor like a madwoman.

I cried myself to exhaustion, maybe even to sleep, for when I opened my eyes it was dark out and I could hear the key turning in the latch. My father and brothers had closed shop and were coming home to supper.

"María Luisa! Where are you, child?"

It was father, who was used to me coming out to greet him.

I approached him with the handkerchief soaked in tears and my heart sad and aching.

"What were you doing in the dark?"

"She was crying, the little missy," laughed my youngest brother Juan. He was six years older than me and had a different mother.

"Leave her alone," exclaimed Ignacio, who was already much older. He too was father's son from a previous marriage. Father had been married to a very lovely lady who'd left him a widower.

"Crying! What's wrong, child? Tell me, dear, what's the matter?"

"The new dress…"

"Did you tear the new dress?" Father never had a clue about household affairs.

"No, but I don't like it. It's got lace trim!"

"Ring-a-round the rosies,
a pocket full of posies.
Ashes! Ashes!
The brand new dress!" sang Juan.

"Won't you leave the little girl alone?" grumbled father.

At ten years of age, I was already a big girl, but he hoisted me up and I nestled my head onto his shoulder.

Mother's voice blared through the dark hallway.

"Don't pay her any attention, she's just being fussy. Of course, it's all your fault."

I was comfortable against father's strong chest, his sturdy arms around me and his wiry beard grazing my face. He carried me like that into the sitting room, where mother refused to drop the issue.

"Look, it's like she was going to have a fit when she saw the dress Justa made her. But you'll see, it's precious."

Without lifting my head from father's shoulder, I could tell mother had gone for the ill-fated dress, and I whispered bitterly in his ear, "It's got lace trim!"

Father tried to nudge my face away to look at me.

"What's the matter with that?" he asked.

"I don't like it!"

By that time, he must've been looking at the dress, for he was talking without much conviction.

"It's fine! What more could you ask for, silly?"

Father's ignorance brought back my original anguish, and once again my pain grew barbs and I broke into uncontrollable sobs. Father was surprised to feel my body shaking. He struggled to separate my head from his shoulder.

"Let's see here... Let me see you... Look at me, dear!" He took me by the chin against my will. "Aren't you ashamed of getting upset over such a silly little thing?"

"No, it's not silly."

"Yes, it is," insisted father. "It is, and a ten-year-old like you shouldn't throw a fit over a dress. If you don't like the lace trim, then we'll have it removed."

That's when mother unleashed her full fury on him.

"What? What did you say? Remove the lace trim? But it came from the cream tulle dress I made for myself when we got married—the dress from my aunt's house!"

There could be no good response to such crushing words, but father in his innocence replied, "That's why we can get rid of it, dear. It must be very old."

Mother was on the verge of a breakdown over father's stupidity. Old! But didn't he know the value of lace grows with age? Besides, Tía Teresa was the most elegant woman in Burgos and, when it came right down to it, in all of Spain. She'd chosen the lace for the dress, and all the local newspapers had sung its praises.

Mother belonged to a long line of Castilian aristocracy, never mind her parents had lost the whole family fortune or she'd grown up a charity case in her aunt's house. Mother regarded that aunt as the leading authority on matters of elegance and distinction.

Not saying a word, father clutched me nervously to his chest as the domestic storm broke over him.

"And most importantly," continued mother, after a short pause, "I'm her mother and she'll wear what I want her to wear. And that's that. I'll hear no more of it! To think this little troublemaker should give orders in my household!"

I'd already submitted to mother's will, and the unfairness of her insult brought more tears to my eyes.

"Really, dear! Forgive the girl, and don't make her cry. You're going to obey your mother. Won't you, darling? Won't you?"

"Yes," I assured him, renouncing one of my dearest aspirations. Oh, to dress in sailor's attire!

"Do you hear that, dear? And as a reward for her obedience, I'll get her a little hat."

"Yes, yes; spoil her," said mother, getting mad again. "But don't be daft. She doesn't need a new hat. I'm getting alterations on the straw one we bought last year. They're going to give it two ornamental birds."

At the news of the misfortune, a fresh bout of sobs left me shaking.

THE FANCY RESTAURANT

The same day as every year, we went out to eat at the restaurant of an elegant hotel.

That had been a tradition of my parents ever since they got married. It was there they ate on their wedding day; it was there they would eat on every anniversary. My brothers Ignacio and Juan attended the wedding when they were little and never failed to recall what fun it was.

"The food was never-ending," Juan would marvel. "That day there were over two hundred people."

"How would you know? You were five years old," mother would reply.

"I swear, I remember. They gave us a dining room just for us."

I preferred to eat in the dining room where we were seated at the moment. To me it seemed incredibly luxurious, with its paintings and mirrors, its potted palms, its crystal vases and fresh flowers on every table, and its hotel guests, who descended from their rooms on a

8

grand marble staircase, not once stepping off the plush carpet.

Even though it was a workday, father and mother had exchanged their usual attire for their Sunday best. Me and my brothers, too; I was debuting my spring dress. Ugh! That horrible dress with lace trim.

"Little missy is mad she has to wear her new clothes," taunted Juan. He knew full well how much I hated that dress.

But the instant we were around the table, the only thing we could think about was the menu. It was printed on a card held upright by what appeared to be a silver brace. Everything in the place was so up-scale!

While everyone else was reading the bizarre names of the dishes, not understanding a word, I peered around timidly, breathing in the perfume of roses and truffles. Behind us a man sat alone in a black suit—black and white, in fact, for his vest opened to reveal a large swath of white. What an elegant gentleman! I'd never seen anyone like him in father's shop. The man, who was bald, took tiny sips of a golden liquor.

At another table a lady with snow white hair sat eating with two boys the same ages as my brothers. Seated beyond them were a man and a woman, followed by a lone pair of women and, on the opposite end of the room, a blond youth and a striking *señora*.

I couldn't keep looking because the *hors d'oeuvres* had arrived. That was what mother called them, emphasizing her words. Mother was the most refined of our lot; not in vain had she been raised by Tía Teresa, the aunt from Burgos. The waiters placed little silver soup bowls in front of us. Not a thing in the place had silver plating, for all was solid silver. The bowls had an egg and pieces of various other things I couldn't identify.

Everyone agreed it was very good.

"It's scruuumptious," joked Juan, rolling his eyes.

The others were all too absorbed in the contents of their bowls to pay him any attention, and I was the only one who laughed.

Suddenly my surroundings went blank and I only had eyes for two girls who were coming down the marble staircase. Two *señoritas*, I said to myself, and Lord, what *señoritas*!

One was dark-skinned and wore her hair like a man's, slicked down like my brother Ignacio's, except her head was small and round, her eyes big and velvety, and her lips an intense shade of red. Her outfit was entirely original, a source of great envy: gray jacket with lapels just like a man's; silk shirt; tie; short, snug skirt. It was something unheard of at the turn of the century.

The other was a blonde. Her blue velvet dress must've been lovely, but I remember only her milky white skin and the curls cascading over her ears.

They crossed the dining room and waved two or three times to the diners before taking their seats at the table across from me, behind father and Ignacio. We'd tried to sit there, but the waiter told us it was reserved. That table was theirs and had two place settings and a bottle of mineral water.

A delicate perfume wafted around us. I breathed it in eagerly and felt like I was floating on a cloud.

What fine hands they had, the two young ladies. Their hands were like pale flowers, pure white with an azure glow and lustrous pink nails.

They unfolded their napkins and glanced distractedly in our direction before looking quickly elsewhere, then gazing at each other and smiling. They were speaking so softly, I couldn't hear their voices.

I saw their feet under the table. The blonde's were nestled in exquisite high heels with diamond studs, a wonder to behold. The dark woman's were flat, small, and strong as a man's, but nothing at all like my father's and brothers'. Gray silk stockings stretched over her strong, muscular legs.

"This little missy isn't eating," blurted Juan, who was sitting beside me.

"Girl," exclaimed mother, "why aren't you eating?"

"Don't you like it?" asked father, talking with his mouth full.

"If you don't want it, I'll eat it," proclaimed Juan.

"That's what you think! Half is for me," answered Ignacio.

They were making such a commotion, the women looked over at us. I don't know what thoughts crossed their minds seeing a family all dressed up on a workday, but they smiled at the corners of their mouths and went on chatting.

The blood rushed to my face, and when I thought I couldn't blush any more, yet another wave of heat broke on my cheeks.

"She's embarrassed to eat," laughed Juan.

"Come on, child. Eat," father prodded. "If you don't eat, you won't come back here again with us."

Try as I might, I couldn't eat.

"I'm not hungry."

I said it so softly, nobody heard me. Father made me repeat myself but still didn't hear.

"I'm not hungry, I'm not hungry."

"What's that, girl?"

"I said, I'm not hungry."

"Ah! She says she's not hungry," shouted Juan.

Now the ladies wouldn't stop looking at us. Under my lace-frilled dress, I felt all the shame and humiliation of a sinful wretch beheld by cherubs.

My brother Juan looked at the table behind father and froze with his fork halfway to his mouth.

"Hey, Ignacio! Look, a boy wearing lipstick. That's some kind of chap!"

Ignacio turned his head and was equally astonished.

"Father, look! Take a peek behind you. Do you see *that*?"

Father stole a glance, and mother too, then they both looked quickly away.

"The things one sees," mused mother.

Their looks and especially their words stung me like a personal offense. The young ladies were already mine. I'd seen them first, I knew they were two *señoritas*, and I admired and adored everything about them, from their ethereal fragrance to their divine fingertips.

"They have to admit everyone in these places," said father. "Those people don't have to pinch pennies."

"But what is *that*?" mother asked again. "It looks like a woman in disguise, but without hair or earrings. Lord, the things one sees!"

The waiter cleared the soup bowls, changed the plates, and hustled to and from our seats while my parents and brothers did their best to steal glances at the next table over. They thought they were being sly, but the two young ladies finally felt their prying eyes. It seemed to me they couldn't care less.

The fish arrived, and my family forgot about the ladies and left them just for me.

My brothers had sopped up the rest of my silver soup bowl, which left the table as clean as the others. Now they were watching as mother poured white sauce over my sole fillets. Those too would be for them, they thought.

"Let's see if you like this, picky," said mother.

At the next table over, they were nibbling daintily as if eating were some deliciously useless pastime. As they drank, their red lips on the fine crystal made me tremble with emotion. They laughed quietly and spoke in hushed voices. Sometimes they looked at each other without saying a word, and something in their looks was new and puzzling to me.

They finished long before us, and the dark-skinned woman pulled a cigarette case out of her jacket pocket, offered a smoke to the blonde, and lit a match. They were smoking!

Their fingers nimble and white, their nails gleaming, the cigarettes in rose-colored holders; they tilted their heads back and puffs of smoke issued from their red lips and delicate nostrils.

"Hey! Those two are smoking," said Juan, and everyone looked.

"People today are going to hell in a handbasket," warned mother.

"Have a look at those calves," whispered Juan to Ignacio.

The four sheer-stockinged legs captivated my brothers, who couldn't stop sneaking a glance while my parents weren't looking. That was a time when women wore dresses down to their feet, and no decent woman crossed her legs in public.

But the blonde was crossing her legs, and the dark woman had hers pressed together, perfect and still.

"The boy's wearing shorts and silk stockings," said Ignacio. "He's a…"

Out of respect for my parents, he hushed something horribly naughty, no doubt.

Now the two ladies were talking, smoking, and sipping coffee. Everything about them was delightful, charming, unlike everyone and everything. It was like they belonged to another race from a wondrous, bewildering world.

Surely, those marvelous hands had never gripped a broom like the one I used to sweep my room on the orders of Casiana, Juan's brutish former wet nurse. Those alabaster hands were used only for holding a book or a cigarette or filling a vase with flowers or stroking each other as they were doing now. Because the dark woman was gently caressing the blonde's hand as it rested on the table, almost translucent.

"This little missy isn't eating! I don't know why you threw away money on food for her," grumbled Juan. He was in the process of wolfing the sirloin off my plate, and he snapped me out of the reverie I'd been living with the ladies.

"You can't bring children to places like this," said mother. "Look at what's happening. She's always staring, can't seem to mind her own business. Why don't you eat something, María Luisa?"

With great effort I looked away from the other table and tried to eat what Juan had left me. We were quite the family! Father, poor father, he was always just *there*. The boys couldn't have been any more savage, and as for mother, she was the most refined of our lot... Except that now she didn't seem so elegant. Had she been truly sophisticated, had Tía Teresa been anything like the ladies beside us, she wouldn't have said certain things.

Father and mother were talking quietly and kept on glancing at the other table. When the waiter came by with the desserts, father called him aside.

"Who are they? I can't believe they're allowed in here."

"They're distinguished people, very rich."

"That's all fine and dandy, but what about that boy wearing lipstick and women's stockings?"

"That's a woman, sir. I believe she writes coplas. Poetry, I think. She's an American, and the other one's her secretary."

"The things one sees," exclaimed mother. "And why does she dress like that?"

"I don't know... Whims," said the waiter. He didn't want to say any more around strangers.

A little while later, the two ladies got up and crossed the dining room, once again smiling and waving.

"She's wearing a skirt! But look how short it is. It's indecent," said mother.

They paused for a moment at the table with the white-haired woman and two boys, who rose to greet them. The four of them laughed, remarking on something, then separated shaking hands. The ladies ascended the marble staircase and disappeared onto the second flight, which must've led to that marvelous world that I couldn't see and perhaps never would.

"Look at her, father! Her mouth's hanging open."

Mother made me look her in the face.

"You aren't going to eat your strawberries, either? Get going, girl. You haven't eaten a thing, and the food they served was so good!"

"Those two women are to blame."

"They were nothing but trouble," father declared. "Wearing men's clothes and a calf-length skirt! Painting their faces and smoking in public! Two girls, so very young, no family in sight… It's just not right! There are things I can't stand for."

"Me neither," agreed mother. "I don't care if they're from America. Going against public decency like that, it's no good at all!"

I was furious. I wished I didn't have a family, to be alone, an orphan. What use were my brothers, who were always teasing me? Father was good, but he didn't understand anything I liked. And mother wouldn't let me wear a sailor suit. Right then I hated them all for being vulgar and ordinary, and most of all for having spoken so badly of the two ladies who'd smelled so good.

Their perfume had already faded, and we were practically alone in the dining room.

Father was puffing his cigar, and because it was a special occasion, my brothers had permission to smoke their cigarettes around us, which they did like true novices.

Mother was studying the rings on her fingers—her hands passed for being pretty—and was getting bored.

The waiters took up the linens and reset the tables with miniature cups, saucers, and dainty utensils.

"For five o'clock tea," said Ignacio in English, showing off his studies. "But it won't actually be served until seven."

"Let's go," signaled mother. "They've got to set this table, too."

Father griped a bit before finally giving our marching orders, and after taking our coats from the waiter, we went out to the street.

It was midafternoon, and the sun was shining on the rooftops, but the narrow, bustling street was dim in the shade. A drunkard with a jacket covered in medals and crosses was staggering down the middle of the road, drool dripping down his chops.

"Long live Garbaldi! Long live me… Giddy-up, old mare!"

My brothers laughed themselves silly, and father and mother smiled smugly. They were standing on the edge of the sidewalk in the crowd of curious onlookers who'd stopped to take in the spectacle. A wave of disgust and fear swept over me.

"What's he got on his face?" I asked mother, latching onto her arm.

"Nothing. A chafed, red nose. The poor fellow's always drunk."

He'd managed to stumble to the end of the street, where he was shouting senseless insults amidst a throng of boys.

"Why do they let him walk the streets, mother?"

But neither father nor mother answered me.

THE GIFT

t was eleven o'clock, and the middle grade was taking dictation when they called for me.

"María Luisa Arroyo!"

"Out you go," said Doña Margarita, the headmistress. "Your father came to pick you up."

I stowed my knapsack and pen in the desk and paraded out of the room, much to the envy of my classmates, who still had another hour of class. I met father in the lobby.

"We're going to buy your mother a gift," he said, helping me into my coat and beret. "You know better than me what she wants, don't you?"

"I'm not sure."

"Yes, child," father insisted on the street. "You must've heard her talking about something. She refused to give me any ideas. Try to remember. Hasn't she told you anything she'd like?"

I tried to think back…

"Ah, yes! The day we ate at the hotel, she said later on, 'Those ladies smelled so good! I wonder what scent they were wearing.' You could buy her a bottle of perfume."

Father looked skeptical.

"Hmmm, I don't know. I'm not sure your mother likes that kind of stuff."

"Yes she does!"

We were walking briskly because we had to get home by the time school let out for lunch. Hand in hand, we reached the perfume shop on Calle de Sevilla.

What a wonderful smell! I was back in the magical world of the hotel dining room. One lady was buying creams, another was looking at bottles of fragrance. But could it really be? It was the poet's secretary!

"Look, father, look! It's her."

"Who?"

"The *señorita* who was eating at the other table."

"What are you talking about, child? Are those the bottles you were wanting?"

Father never had any idea what I was talking about, as if we inhabited two different worlds or he were blind to our surroundings.

He walked up to the bottles where the blonde was standing and started to look at them, changing their places.

"Sir, would you like to see the perfumes?" asked a clerk.

I couldn't look away from the lovely blonde. Was it her? Now I was thinking that maybe it wasn't, but she was just as pretty and smelled just as nice. Surely she lived at the hotel and also smoked. Lord was she gorgeous! She'd slipped off a glove and was picking up bottles to examine them against the light, lifting them to her nostrils. She couldn't decide which one to purchase and was wavering between one with a white rose and a longer one with a green crystal serpent in coils.

Finally, she settled on the one with the rose, and they put it in a little box for her.

"María Luisa, pay attention," said father, who might have been talking for quite some time.

"Tell me, which one do you like most?"

"The one with the snake."

The young lady paid and left while father was forcing me to listen. Now he was negotiating over the price of the bottle, which turned out to cost a small fortune. But I didn't like any of the others.

We had no time to lose, so father quit haggling and told them to wrap up the bottle. Resting it carefully on a bed of cotton in a little box, they made a pretty parcel with wrapping tissue and gold ribbon. Father handed over a ton of money, and the clerk took a bottle from a drawer and gave it to me as a gift.

The bottle was tiny, but the fragrance filtered through the leather-covered cork and made me feel truly euphoric.

"I'd have liked to get your mother something else," said father after we left the shop. "That was expensive and impractical. How about we get her some stockings? What do you think?"

It sounded good to me… Oh, dear little bottle of mine! … We entered a luxury boutique and father asked to see their finest stockings. They brought out a pair with lace insets… The second I got home, I'd pull the cork!

"This isn't at all what I want," complained father. "They need to be high quality, but without all that lace. Right, dear?"

"They're very pretty," I answered, just to say something.

"Your mother doesn't wear that stuff! I long for the day you grow up and understand these things!"

I was still thinking about the bottle hidden in the palm of my hand when father finally bought some stockings without lace, emphasizing they were for a married woman. But of course! Who else would they have been for?

Back at home, father went into the sitting room where mother was sewing. Casiana was setting the table, and Juan was reading the newspaper by the dining room balcony.

"Where are you coming from, missy? Why did father pick you up?"

"Just because… Look what I've got."

"What's that? Perfume? Wow, what a luxury! A whole bunch of perfume and dirty hands."

I had ink-stained fingers. From taking dictation, of course! I remembered the blonde's immaculate hands and went to scrub mine, but the ink wouldn't come off.

"Come eat, girl. Hurry up," yelled father.

I ran down the hall without having opened the bottle. Drat, the soup had those thin noodles I hated! Before long the daily struggle had begun.

"But child, aren't you going to eat?"

"I'm not hungry."

"That can't be," said mother, anxiously. "This girl will be the death of me! Why aren't you eating?"

"I don't like it."

"You don't like noodles?" asked father, though he'd sat through the same scene a hundred times over. "Have them make you something else, then."

"That's right," mother roared. "We've got plenty of money to satisfy her every whim! Let her eat noodles like me and her brothers. I've had enough of her being so picky. Start eating, and don't make me say it again!"

I started to cry with my head on the table, intent on not eating.

"Don't be stubborn, child," said father, trying to sound stern.

Casiana was bringing the platter of garbanzos, and I hadn't even touched my bowl of soup. Mother declared she couldn't keep eating with me in her sight.

Then father did something unexpected after treating me that morning like a grown-up. He came at me, snatched me from my usual high chair, and whisked me to the sitting room, dropping me on the rug in front of the balcony.

"You, young lady, are a stupid little girl!"

And he slammed the door behind him. I'd have never thought father was capable of such a thing. God was I unlucky!

I was taking my handkerchief out of my pocket, when the bottle fell to the ground. Seeing it, I forgot all my troubles. How lovely it looked, and that smell! That perfume transported me to a world free of noodle soup, of anxiety-ridden mothers and fickle fathers. What a delicious smell!

The door opened, and in came Casiana.

"Come on, come with me to the kitchen. Let's see if you'll eat something. Why are you so picky? I don't know what's to become of you when you grow up. What you need is to experience hunger and some good spankings like the ones my mother used to give me."

Grumbling resentfully, she made me sit down at the kitchen table and set a plate with a fried egg in front of me. It was the one thing I could stomach with my constant lack of appetite.

I was grateful to Casiana for the crude consolations she offered me at times like that one, when everyone else was scorning or mocking me. On those occasions, if my heart was attached to anyone in that house, it was surely to Casiana.

She'd already eaten and was bustling in and out of the kitchen with plates and glasses. Then she left me alone, saying she was going to help dress mother while the water was heating to wash dishes. I didn't dare move for fear that father or mother would come barging in. They must've been very angry. Maybe they were talking about sending me to a boarding school the very next day and I'd never come home again. What a terrible tragedy!

Once more the perfume bottle comforted me, and I decided to remove the stopper. It was a difficult task, for there was a piece of white leather stretched tightly over the cork and tied to the throat with a golden thread.

I heard footsteps in the hallway, Ignacio coming for me.

"Come on, let's get back to school. It's nearly two. Did you end up eating, you rascal? You make more trouble… Let's go."

We went out holding hands without meeting anyone from the family in the hallway, much to the relief of my tightened chest. Arriving at school, my brother dropped me off at the front door like always.

"Be good!"

Surrounded by girls and with the precious little bottle in my pocket, I was quick to forget about the trouble at home. I even seem to remember the afternoon flying by and the girls admiring the perfume bottle. I didn't let them touch it, only look at it in my hand while I praised the wonderful thing father had bought for mother.

The shop boy picked me up at five and left me at the doorman's post at home. By the time Casiana let me in, I'd forgotten mother was angry at me. Like any other day, I asked, "Is mother here? Where's mother?"

"What do I know? She must be out somewhere idling about."

She was out! I held out hope Casiana was pulling my leg like other times. I liked to have mother at home when the sun went down and the bedrooms filled with strange shapes.

"Mother," I shouted from the hall.

"You just keep right on calling! She's sure to answer right away," muttered Casiana on her way to the kitchen.

She wasn't in the sitting or living rooms, or in the dining room. She was out!

"She said you were to eat a snack and not to make trouble," said Casiana, handing me a piece of bread and a square of chocolate.

Then she sat down in a low chair by the dining room balcony and started sewing socks and humming.

I ate the chocolate without touching the bread and rummaged

through my toy box for the lovely storybook mother had given me when I was still little. On the cover was Princess Elisa with a white tunic and a golden ring to pull back her flowing hair. She was contemplating a swan feather on the shore of an azure lake.

Sitting in a little chair across from Casiana, I delved into the pages of the only book of my childhood. Like a bed of fine sand channeling a nascent spring, it had shaped the figments of my overactive imagination.

"When the wind rustled through the rosebush by the door, it whispered to the roses, 'Who is more beautiful than you are?' And the roses answered, 'Elisa!' And when the old woman sat on Sunday on the porch, reading her prayer book, the wind turned over the leaves and said, 'Who is more pious than you are?' And the prayer book answered, 'Elisa!' And what the prayer book and the roses said was the simple truth."

My budding soul soaked in the genuine poetry of Andersen's brilliant book, which forever filled my thoughts with beauty and emotion.

"Where'd your father take you this morning?"

At a single blow, Casiana's gruff voice jarred me out of the story, back into the reality of my sordid living room.

"This morning? Ah, yes! We went shopping. Have a look at this bottle," I said, just then remembering I had it in my pocket.

Casiana snatched it in her clumsy hands and took a whiff. I'd already managed to open it at school with the tip of a pair of scissors. It smelled so good!

"This would be better off with me," replied Casiana, as usual.

"No," I protested. "They gave it to me, and I don't want you to have it."

"Well, you can go shove it," she roared. "What use have I got for it?"

I felt overcome by bitterness. I knew for a fact I'd wind up giving her the bottle. That was how it went with the little Virgin Mary father brought me from Lourdes, and the gift box of shells from my godmother, and the Mason jar pincushion filled with souvenirs of the beach at San Sebastián.

"I said, where were you this morning with your father?" asked Casiana, insistent.

"We went out for a bottle of perfume for mother, a really pretty one. It cost an arm and a leg!"

"What was today?"

"I don't know. Nothing."

"It must've been something if your mother got a gift like that. Lord knows, I don't get any," she grumbled. "Was that the perfume in the package your father was carrying?"

"No, those were stockings. Really good ones! We got them for mother, too. They gave me this bottle at the perfume shop, and it didn't cost us a dime. There was an elegant lady who bought another one with a rose inside."

Casiana kept quiet. After a moment, she rose to her feet, kicked over her chair, and left in a huff for the kitchen. She didn't come back till it was getting dark out, when she gathered her sewing and stormed off again, slamming the door behind her.

I kept on reading till I ran out of light. As the lampposts lit up and shadows crowded the corners, I made my way to the kitchen. Seated at the table, Casiana was still sewing socks to the light of a kerosene lamp hanging from the wall.

"Would you mind telling me what you're doing here? There's no getting away from this little troublemaker! Off to the dining room with you. The kitchen is just for us maids."

"It's dark in there!"

"You don't need light for what you've got to be doing. You'd better get going or I'll take the lamp to my bedroom! Either get out now or face the consequences."

I imagined her capable of all sorts of evil deeds and went out to the hallway without daring to make a move in any direction. I was barred from the kitchen, and who knows what horrors awaited me in the foyer's shadows. It wasn't the first time I'd been cast out of the light and into the pitch-black hallway. As usual, I was crying inconsolably. When would mother get back?

Casiana heard me crying and didn't say a word. I tried crying louder, but it was useless.

"Casiana, let me in!"

Silence. Not a sound was to be heard in the kitchen, but I was hesitant to take a peek lest she hurl something at me.

"Let me in, Casianita! I promise to be on my best behavior."

Dear Lord, what a dismal existence, so different from the story of Princess Elisa! Even the villains had an aura of magnificence. Take the queen who put the three toads that turned into poppies in the princess's bath. She was wicked, but between her and Casiana there was no comparison, not with the queen's ermine cloak.

With the fear once again tightening its grip on me, I remembered the bottle of perfume. She'd let me in if I handed it over, but it was so pretty, and I liked it so!

"Casiana, let me in. I'm really scared!"

I heard her clattering dishes and cleaning the burners on the stove. I put my ear to the door. Maybe she had her back turned and wouldn't notice if I peeked in. I was about to do it, when *thud!* The door slammed in my face, leaving me in absolute darkness. How horrible!

I covered my eyes to block out my vision and cried until I got tired. I thought I felt a hand on my shoulder. Frightened out of my wits, I cried hoarsely, "Casiana, take it. I'll give you the bottle, just let me in."

It took a moment for the door to open, but open it did.

"Come on, silly, get in here already!"

I left my precious offering on the table and cried all the tears in my eyes, broken-hearted. Meanwhile, Casiana stashed the bottle deep in a pocket and went back to fighting with the dirty dishes, cursing all the while.

"I wish I would die this instant!"

I too would've liked to breathe my last.

LOOSE WOMEN

That morning I'd just witnessed a horrendous crime. It was a day of ill omens!

Over the course of a month, a big fat spider had taken up residence in the intricate ironwork of our balcony railing. Every day it would spin its web in a corner, and every day it would have to start over because I destroyed its work in the morning.

Defying mother's orders, I'd sneak out onto the balcony at the break of dawn, when my parents were still in bed and Casiana was sweeping the dining room. Mother kept the balcony strictly off limits because some loose women lived in the house next door.

She never explained why those women were bad or why I wasn't allowed to see them. In my imagination, they were always getting into cat fights, clawing and pinching each other, shouting out loud, even spitting over the balcony—terrible, abominable acts!

But the day before the crime, mother offered another detail to feed my suspicions of their depravity.

Talking to father, she said that those wretches—they were loose *and* wretched—were very superstitious and wouldn't call the snake by its name.

"Huh?" I exclaimed. "What would they say if they had a bottle of perfume like yours?"

"They wouldn't say a thing. Besides, they wouldn't have one, wouldn't like it. Now hush your mouth! Little girls shouldn't butt in on grown-up conversations."

I kept on thinking. Truly, those women weren't worth a dime. How could they not like the glass bottle with the coiled serpent and the transparent caramel-colored perfume? The bottle sat among the white draperies on mother's vanity, admiring itself in a mirror with a plush frame of pink silk and speckled tulle.

The vanity also had other flasks and a crystal powder compact embossed with the image of a fair-skinned girl wearing a bustle and leaning on a parasol to support the weight of the enormous bulge hanging from her waist.

But the bottle was the prettiest thing there, and I could look at nothing else when I went into mother's sitting room. And the loose women didn't like it! I thought about them as I gazed at their balcony, which was always closed at that time of morning. It was then that I witnessed the horrible crime, trembling with emotion.

A botfly had gotten stuck in the spider's web and was desperately struggling to work its way loose. I watched it with my young eyes opened wide as a pair of magnifying glasses, not missing a detail of the fly's plight. I was waiting to see if it would escape on its own. The potbellied spider emerged from one of the railing's iron filigrees and scurried towards its web, where the fly intensified its struggle. Was the spider going to help it?

Seeing it get closer, I thought it would, but it mounted the fly's black abdomen and the fly made an extraordinary racket. Surely they could hear its buzzing from the street. Then the spider sank a fang into its head, and the fly went absolutely still. The spider had killed it!

Terrified, I dashed back into the dining room, where Casiana was senselessly banging around the furniture.

"It killed it," I shouted, but she wouldn't listen. "Casiana, the spider killed the botfly," I insisted.

"Leave me in peace, you imbecile!"

For several days, Casiana had been in a constant state of rage, bandying about the house with her lips pursed and a familiar scowl on her face.

"What's up with her?" father asked one day when he got home for lunch.

"I don't know," mother answered. "She's been like this for a week. She's already broken two of my glasses and the salad bowl. What a woman, constantly making me suffer!"

"Only till I've had enough of her," answered father.

But it seemed he'd never had enough. In fact, they let her do whatever she wanted on the excuse she'd been such a fine nurse to Juan, taking him to her village when his mother died and he was still a wee little infant.

Casiana continued to wield her broom against the dining room floor, refusing to be my confidante. But I was by nature too talkative to keep the horror I'd just witnessed to myself.

"Listen, the poor fly was trying to get loose, and I didn't help it because I thought it'd be able to on its own. And then the spider…"

"Spare me your nonsense! A ten-year-old girl ought to know better. Then again, you've got everything you want and won't have to work to put bread on the table. When I was your age, I was already harvesting olives in the winter and weeding and gleaning the fields in the summer. I went out gleaning like a grown woman, and sometimes I brought home a whole sack of barley for the hens. And garbanzos! Mother and I made it through the winter on the ones I gathered."

That was a long speech compared to what little she'd said over the preceding week, and it gave me the courage to keep on talking without bringing up the crime, which apparently left her indifferent.

"Did you go gleaning alone?"

"Alone or with others, it depended. More than once I crossed paths with a bull or a lizard in the bushes."

"Oh my!"

"What did you think? That we all see life the way you do? No, dear, no. Schools, dresses, gifts—there ain't never been none of that for poor folk."

I could've reminded her that even if she hadn't gotten presents as a child, now she took all the ones I got. But I let it go, glad she was opening up for a change.

"They didn't give you gifts?"

"Who would've given me gifts, silly?"

"I don't know, your father or your godmother."

"I didn't have a father, and as for my godmother..." She tilted her head back, laughing harder than I'd heard her laugh in a long time. "The old crone was just the one to give presents! She promised to give me a mortar and pestle when I got married, but seeing how that hasn't happened..."

"But when you get married..."

"Sure, but now I've got myself a beau, so she doesn't have to give me much more," she joked. All of a sudden, she got serious. "Of course, I won't ever get married. But if I did, I'd never have a husband like your father, who spends his money on such stupid things."

"Stupid?"

"Yes, that's right. You've got to be swimming in money to shell out for such a lousy bottle. As far as I'm concerned, it's not worth a penny!"

"You don't like it?" I was astonished. "But it's beautiful. A pretty lady was going to buy it, but she chose one with a rose."

"If I ever got such a stupid gift, I'd throw it in the trash," said Casiana, the brute. "What a gift!"

29

That infuriated me. Who was Casiana to say what was ugly or beautiful? She was utterly ignorant! I took everything she said about the bottle as an insult to the lovely blonde who'd held it in her hands, hesitating a moment before choosing the other one. Not knowing how to express my fury, I shouted, "You don't like it because you're a loose woman like the ones who live in the house next door!"

Casiana froze in her tracks, leaning on her broom. For a moment she looked at me with eyes ablaze, as if she were preparing for the kill. Then she ran out of the dining room and shut herself in her bedroom in a fit of shouting. I'd just made a terrible mistake!

She was shouting so loud, father and mother must've heard her. Still buttoning his pants, father opened the sitting room door and emerged into the adjoining dining room.

"Who's doing all that shouting?"

"Casiana."

"Casiana? What's wrong with her?" Without waiting for a reply, he went into the hallway with me in tow.

Father rapped at the door, which she'd locked from the inside.

"What's the matter, woman? Speak up. What's going on? Are you in pain?"

She kept on shouting and wouldn't answer even with father pounding at the door. He called for mother.

"Juanita, honey, get up and see what's the matter with this madwoman. Good grief!"

Still terrified, I didn't dare say what had happened. My heart was beating out of control, full of regret for the tragedy I'd provoked with my imprudent words.

Mother got out of bed and came to knock on the door but didn't get a response, either. Casiana had quit shouting, but now she'd broken into terrible sobs.

It was time to open the shop, and mother had to light the stove and make breakfast. Ignacio and Juan were waiting at the table.

"Were you out of bed when she went off like this?" asked my brothers. "What happened to her?"

"I don't know. She was sweeping the dining room, and I went out on the balcony. And then I told her... Well, the spider killed a fat old fly, and I saw it."

"You're dumber than a doornail," taunted Juan.

"But what exactly happened to Casiana?" asked Ignacio.

"I'm telling you, she was sweeping the dining room, and she said she didn't like mother's perfume bottle, that if she got it as a gift, she wouldn't want it."

"This house is a loony bin!"

What I'd never tell them was the terrible insult I let slip. Why had I said such a thing?

My father and brothers went out after breakfast. Since school was cancelled for the headmistress's name day, I stayed home and helped mother clear the table. She bustled back and forth putting everything in order. Once in a while, she'd pause to listen to the sounds coming from Casiana's bedroom. I too kept on passing in front of her door, till it opened and I peered in.

Seated on her bed, Casiana was carefully combing pomade into her hair. She didn't give any indication of having noticed me enter; still, I was sure she was watching me.

Having finished her hair, Casiana put on a new pair of heels, a starched petticoat I'd seen her crimping one afternoon with a curling iron, and a black silk skirt.

"Where are you going?" I asked.

She stayed quiet for a while, perhaps hoping I'd insist, but finally she cried, "I'm going to kill myself!"

The blood froze in my veins. How horrible! I ran in search of mother, who was still scuttling around in the kitchen.

"Casiana's going to kill herself and is getting dressed."

"What did you say?"

"I said, Casiana's going to kill herself. She told me so."

Mother dried her hands and went to the bedroom. Casiana was already dressed and had nearly finished buttoning her tulle-collared jacket.

"Where are you going, pray tell?"

She paused for a moment and looked away. "To the Viaduct!"

"Don't be insane, woman! What's the matter? Bad as it seems, there's got to be a solution. First and foremost, it's not Christian to take one's own life. Tell me, what's got you so upset? Go ahead, you can trust me."

Casiana finished adjusting her collar in silence. She was going to the Viaduct! I'd never seen it, but I pictured it as a kind of machine in the street for killing people.

She opened the chest and put away her clothes. Now that she was going to die, she could return everything I'd given her! But I didn't dare tell her so...

"I can't stay on in a house where I've been called such a dirty word. And it isn't true," she shouted. "Perhaps I made some mistakes, but I've always been a decent woman!"

"Of course, dear. But who called you..."

"The girl. It was her, and if she said it, then others must be saying it. No, no, and no! I'm not going to put up with it!"

Mother looked at me, and I started to quiver.

"You? But what did you say? Where did you learn to say swear words?"

"I... She said she didn't like... And I said..."

Furious, mother grabbed me by the arm, gave me a thorough shaking, and thrust me into the hallway, where I collapsed to the ground in tears. Then Casiana came to pick me up and take me into her room.

That's adults for you! Always so fickle and absurd around children.

"She's not to blame, just the person she heard it from."

"But what did she say?" insisted mother.

With fits and starts, all the morning's foolish words were being repeated.

"The girl had no idea what she was saying," assured mother. "She doesn't know the full meaning of the words… She's heard us say the next-door neighbors are… But she doesn't know what…"

The long lecture that followed had the virtue of arousing my curiosity about *loose women*, but since mother mixed in constant gibes against me, I kept crying with my face buried in Casiana's bed. Now she was defending me.

"Foolish girl, always wagging her tongue, always making trouble!"

"Leave her be, ma'am, leave her be," said Casiana magnanimously.

"Absolutely not! We've got to get her out of the habit of running her mouth. Little brat, what does she know? You ask Casiana to forgive you, young lady. Come on, ask to be forgiven!"

"Leave her be, ma'am, leave her be."

"No, she's got to ask your forgiveness. It's the least she can do!"

The humiliation to which mother was forcing me made my cheeks burn with shame and my heart fill with gall till it burst out in sobs, the poor thing.

Mother pulled me off the bed and forced me to my knees, her hand on my shoulder.

"Repeat after me, 'Forgive me, Casiana, for what I said.' Say it!"

"For … for … for … gi …" I couldn't finish on account of my heart racing.

Casiana stood up and gave me a kiss on the brow, brushing aside my tear-stained bangs.

"Yes, child, yes; I forgive you."

Then she took off the clothes she'd put on to kill herself and went with mother to the kitchen, where they chatted merrily all morning long.

I alone was left gasping for breath, as if the air in my chest were heavy with tears!

BILBAO: THE SEA

Mother and I got to Bilbao on a rainy July afternoon.

"You're going to see the ocean," mother had been saying ever since we made plans for the summer holiday. "You'll see just how big it is, no end in sight. And the waves are tall as houses!"

I saw what I thought was the ocean in the sunset as the train passed Pozuelo and in the sunrise over the fields of Burgos.

"Look, mother, look! It's the sea!"

I spoke softly so only she would hear me.

"Hush, child, that's not the ocean," said mother loudly, smiling at the passengers as they scoffed at my ignorance.

Stupid grown-ups! What's the use of humiliating a child who already knows she's ignorant and is ashamed, to boot?

As the train neared Bilbao, I smelled something new and unknown in the air, something fresh and salty that filled me to my core, enveloping my body and making me light and happy as an angel on a cloud.

But I didn't ask questions and was forced to seal my mouth by other people's ignorance.

A coach drove us down damp streets lined with gray façades to the house occupied by mother's godmother. Nana had invited us to visit for a few days. She was a friendly old woman who lived with an enormous maid in a white apron and a parrot tethered to a perch by one foot.

Judging from their ardent greetings, mother and Nana must've been very close, but I couldn't pay attention to anything but the parrot. I've never seen anything prettier than that mirador with the parrot on its perch.

"A parrot's reign, for Portugal and Spain," I managed to understand it saying. Then it sang a hymn to the Sacred Heart of Jesus and repeated the word *druuuunk!* over and over.

The old woman said the parrot's bad manners came from living on a ship and hearing swear words. She'd managed to teach it a respectable vocabulary, but she couldn't break its habit of saying the word *drunk*. And sometimes it had gone without chocolate or food for an entire day!

"Girl," it screeched, suddenly taking fright.

I was even more startled than the parrot. I dashed out of the room, leaving it behind with my beret in its beak.

"Don't get close or he'll bite you," warned Nana. "He's a jealous little guy, and he saw that I like you."

She and mother were sitting on rocking chairs, gossiping about people I didn't know.

"And Don Juan Antonio, what's he doing?"

"He got married, is what. At his age! And to a hearty young lass, very pretty."

"Is Doña Manolita still alive?"

"Yes, dear, alive and kicking. She went to live with her niece Juliana. Luisa is the one we lost track of. Have you seen her in Madrid?"

"No, but I saw Cayetano the Amurriano."

And so on and so forth until they noticed me watching the parrot, not daring get close for fear of its hooked beak. A bite on the finger would be horrible! Later I found out that one of Nana's nephews got his finger bitten in half for making it mad. How did you make a parrot mad?

The windows of the mirador were all misted up, and the droplets of water formed glistening paths.

"She's itching to see the ocean," said mother, looking at me. "She's got a wild imagination, that one. The second the train left Madrid, she was seeing the ocean all over the place. She got herself so worked up, I bet she got a fever just thinking about it. You can't imagine the headaches she gives me. Come here, young lady!"

She put a hand on my forehead, soothing me greatly. Only then did I notice my head was burning and something like a vise was squeezing my temples.

"What did I tell you? She's running a temperature. Feel, Nana, feel."

Nana too put her wrinkled hand on my brow and my cheeks.

"Bah, it's nothing. Don't worry, just a touch of fever. The ocean air will get rid of it. Palmira," she shouted, "come here!"

The overgrown maid appeared with her immense white apron, and Nana ordered her to take me to Las Arenas. There was plenty of time before dark for the trip there and back and a stroll along the beach. Hurrah!

I let Palmira take my little hand in her giant grip, and together we crossed streets, boarded trams, followed a route that seemed to go on and on, until finally…

The ocean! Nobody told me that was it, and I neither saw it nor believe myself to have seen it. Instead, I felt it on my skin, drew it into my lungs, heard its roar of tearing silk, entirely new in my ears. We walked along the sandy beach, and I communed with the afternoon mist and the ocean's scent and sound, not a thought in my mind, in a perfect state of nirvana.

"Shells, there are shells! What do you think?" blurted Palmira, who hadn't said a word the whole time.

I thought it was fine, and since she was bending over to pick them up, I too started collecting, though I couldn't care less about the shells. On the contrary, the task was ruining the supreme happiness of the moment. The sea! For many years afterwards, the word conjured in me the rustling of silk, a brine perfume, and happiness under the canopy of an umbrella, pressed against a white apron.

When we got home, it was already dark out and mother and Nana were still chatting away in the light of a lamp.

"Did you like the ocean?"

"Yes, ma'am."

"Was it how you pictured it?"

I couldn't remember how I'd pictured it, only mother's words: "It's so big you can't see the end of it, with waves tall as houses." No! It wasn't like that!

How was it? The old woman was asking me with dogged determination.

"Come on, now, tell us. What did you think of it?"

I kept quiet. I had no intention of putting words to the salty sensations in my nostrils, on the roof of my mouth, on my skin, in my ears. Only my sense of vision had not been impressed. How could that be? I hadn't seen the ocean!

"Answer, girl," said mother. "Don't be daft, dear. You liked it a lot, didn't you? Say so to Nana."

"Yes, I really liked it."

"I'm glad," said Nana. She looked so satisfied, it was as though she'd made the ocean herself.

Finally they left me alone and I could study the headless parrot, who'd tucked his head under his wing to sleep. Nana told me all about him while we were eating dinner, making up for her obsession with asking me impossible questions.

The parrot had traveled to and from America many times on a merchant ship whose crew had gone out of its way to teach it pranks. Nana's husband, who'd passed away years ago, bought it for her as a gift for twenty duros.

Back then, she was very ill and would never leave the house. She and the little parrot would spend days on end in the mirador. What patience it had taken to clean up its foul language! It called everybody a drunk, and still did, of course. But in those days it said even more dreadful things, and she'd managed to substitute its repertoire for pleasantries and pious devotions. Wasn't it charming, saying "to your knees, gentlemen, the King of Heaven draws near"? It was enough to eat it up!

One time, Nana decided to go out for a stroll.

"Farewell, Panchito," she bid him goodbye. "You be good now. Farewell, dearie."

When she got to the entrance, the parrot had flown down from the balcony and was waiting for her on the sidewalk.

That seemed extraordinary to me, and I thought about it long and hard. I liked Nana's tale as much as a storybook.

The next day was Sunday, and we went to mass and for a stroll around town. I was hoping the parrot would do something out of the ordinary when it saw us leave, but it didn't say a thing or wait for us on the sidewalk. Maybe the balcony was closed or it couldn't free its foot from the chain.

I despised strolling down the streets, for mother considered it wrong for me to walk at her side, listening in on her conversations. I had to stay in front of her, turning my head with every step to see if we had to cross the street or change sidewalks.

After lunch, Palmira came in with some slips of paper and handed them to Nana. They were tickets to the circus. It had been forever since the old woman had gone to a show, but as a treat for me and mother she was breaking the vow she made after the death of her husband, the same man who'd given her the parrot to keep her entertained in the mirador.

I'd never been to the circus. At home they didn't spend a dime on fun and games, and I had no idea what was in store for me. All the same, I shook with excitement when we sat down in the stands among the crowd, hearing a rollicking march.

The music went quiet, and a man stepped forward with a top hat, out of which he pulled over a hundred colorful kerchiefs, two doves, four rabbits, and ten flags. What an extraordinary man! He had the ability to produce something unexpected wherever he went. I saw him take an egg out of a young woman's nose and a watch out of a light bulb. In that way he'd always have anything he wanted.

Then came a family of little dogs acting out a horrible comedy that forced the poor animals to walk on two legs and let out dismal whimpers. That crushed my heart and filled my eyes with tears.

But what amazed me the most was the *écuyère*. She came out dressed as a ballerina, balancing on a single foot on a white horse. Every time she leapt to the ground, her long blond hair would float in the air for an instant like a flash of gold.

I held my breath watching her routine, and it went on for quite a while. When she disappeared with her horse behind a curtain, it seemed to me the circus had fallen dark.

And that was true in a sense, for there was an enormous balloon hanging over our heads, in the process of inflating and blocking out the sky completely. All of a sudden, it started to rise. A man in a silver bathing suit clambered into the hanging basket. The balloon rose and rose and finally disappeared.

Mother and Nana kept chattering about that. It was what they'd liked most in the first half of the show, though I thought the man looked ugly and ordinary when the basket went past us.

"Mother, will it reach the moon? No, not the moon, that's not what I meant. Will it reach the clouds?"

"And higher. The balloon will go up and up, and then it'll go down somewhere. The important thing is for it not to fall into the sea."

Oh, if it were to fall into the sea! Maybe that's why the man was wearing a bathing suit. Nana said he'd drown if he fell into the open ocean.

That had me so worried, I didn't enjoy anything else. Never mind that there were dancing monkeys and long-leaping Chinamen and a man who sang flamenco and two ballerinas, or that the white horse made a second appearance. This time its rider was not the lady from before, but a young man wearing breeches, a jacket, and a wide-brimmed hat.

"Why didn't the blonde come back?" I asked, disappointed.

"That is her, dressed as a man. Don't you recognize her?"

No, that couldn't be her. Maybe it was a woman, but another one, not the one from earlier. This one was smaller and thinner. I put all my soul into watching the graceful young woman, who was leaping back and forth from the ground to the horse with the animal at a canter. She passed through a paper hoop held out by an elegant horseman and brought the horse to a gallop with a single shout.

All of a sudden, the horse came to a halt, and the young lady took off her hat. Her golden hair had been gathered inside it, and now it was spilling down her back, to everyone's applause.

The show went on long after that with performances by gymnasts and skaters, but nothing could take my mind off the *écuyère*'s blond beauty. I left the circus without saying a word, lost in my thoughts of the dazzling image.

"Did you like it, child? What did you like most?"

Again with the never-ending questions, ruining my happy silence!

Getting into the bed I shared with mother at Nana's house, I saw she was in a good mood and ventured to tell her that the most beautiful thing of all had been the lady riding the white horse. I would've liked to learn how to ride a horse, but I'd never put on a tutu, only men's attire. When I grew up…

"You're a foolish little girl. What'll you do when you grow up?"

"Dress like a man and ride a horse," I solemnly vowed, adding that nothing else mattered to me.

Mother claimed she could never take me anywhere without me talking nonsense. That young lady we'd seen must've been … a good-for-nothing! Something bad, no doubt.

"I don't care if I'm a good-for-nothing," I exclaimed, with utter disdain for society's prejudices. "I want to be just like her, and I will be. You'll see."

"Silence!" ordered mother. "Quiet down and say your prayers like a good girl."

TÍA TERE∫A'∫ PALACE

Only in the illustrations of storybooks had I seen a marble staircase like the one at Tía Teresa's palace on that moonlit night when we arrived. And marvelous things must've happened in that dense park lined with leafy trees that were swaying just then in the wind.

I couldn't fall asleep in the vast bedroom where a cot had been placed beside the tulle-curtained bed reserved for mother. I heard voices talking in the distance, the moonlight streamed through the trees onto the shiny parquet like a lake of silver rippling in the breeze, and my wild imagination made me see visions.

Surely there were fairies in those woods! And maybe even black-clad witches with pointy nails! An infinite terror passed over me, constricting my throat. Why wasn't mother coming?

She'd tucked me into bed and organized the contents of our luggage in two closets, and I'd had a glass of milk and some sponge cake served on a platter with an embroidered cloth. The maid was wearing a bonnet and struck me as the height of elegance. While I ate, mother was at the vanity running a comb through her splendid, flowing hair. I saw her in the mirror, wearing powder and a white dress I didn't recognize. She looked like a different woman.

"You go to sleep, and be good," she'd said on her way out.

"Why are you leaving now?"

"We're going out to dinner, dear. You'll go to bed like a good girl, and you won't make trouble. Tomorrow, the maid who brought the milk will come early in the morning to dress you for you to play in the park. Her name's Aurora."

I loved to get up early. The moment a ray of light slipped through a crack in the balcony, I had to get out of bed. For me, every breaking day was an unspoken promise of happy, extraordinary new adventures, and I was eager to get started.

Mother had given me a kiss, switched off the electric light, and left the room.

What a fright! Through the large windowed door adjoining our room to the next, I saw a faint reddish glow that wasn't from the moon. The creaking of the furniture and the parquet floors sounded like the blasting of gunshots in my head, dazed as I was with sleep and exhaustion.

It seemed like hours were passing, an eternity of terror and solitude. When at last I fell into a restless sleep, I woke up every few minutes. One time, I opened my eyes to see mother undressing for bed.

"You still haven't fallen asleep?"

"I was scared!"

Mother had come back saturated in an atmosphere very different from the one back at home in Madrid. She got mad at me for no reason.

"What were you afraid of, silly? Apparently I've got to go to bed at seven o'clock to keep the little girl happy. Foolish girl!"

I hadn't told her to go to bed any other time, and as always the injustice of her words dug into my flesh and filled my eyes with tears.

43

I hid under the sheet, cried without her hearing me, and didn't take off my covers till she turned off the light. I was very sad, but since my safety was assured in mother's company, before long I'd fallen asleep.

When the maid Aurora got there in the morning, I'd already spent a long time examining the bedroom's opulent details, eyes open in the soft light of the closed room.

She tiptoed up to my bed and whispered softly, "Would you like to get dressed, miss?"

Nobody ever called me *miss* except at school and when mother was angry, and that made me puff up with pride. Yes, indeed, I wanted to get dressed and go down to the garden immediately.

But Aurora objected. First she had to wash me and comb my hair, then there'd be time for everything.

That made me realize that despite the courteous treatment, I'd made little progress down the path to my freedom. Everything was done just as Aurora had decided, and I was given a conscientious scrubbing with cold water in the white and nickel bathroom. Aurora explained that it was very early and the cook hadn't heated the stove yet.

Hand in hand, we went down to the garden surrounding the house. The sun had come up, and the perfumes of roses, honeysuckles, and heliotropes exchanged greetings in my heart. It smelled so good out! My nostrils were fluttering like butterfly wings.

"Would you like us to go see the tiger, miss?"

The tiger! I said yes, ready that very day to undergo a marvelous initiation into the mysteries of the park—or the woods, I said to myself, remembering that Princess Elisa had crossed a forest. With a mild shiver of fear, yet trusting in Aurora's guiding hand, I let myself be ushered down privet-lined paths and lanes of rosebushes, on staircases that led to honeysuckle arbors and reflecting pools. Leaving behind the garden's sandy paths and trimmed hedges, we walked through green meadows to a spacious square, where there were pens with thick vertical bars like the ones I'd seen in Madrid at the Retiro. Vague shadows were stirring within.

"The wild boars," said Aurora. "The tiger's in the last one."

Mother hadn't told me Tía Teresa's park had animals like those, but I found the whole thing too extraordinary to forget.

"Before there was a lion," said Aurora, "but it was so old it died of rheumatism this past winter. The same thing's going to happen to the wolf."

I was disappointed to learn the skinny dog in the cage beside the tiger's was a wolf, just like the one who devoured Little Red Riding Hood.

The tiger was enormous. It rose from the spot on the ground where it had been sleeping and opened its terrible jaws in a yawn. Then it set about pacing the walls in search of the door. It went round and round but didn't get tired of looking. I asked if it had ever escaped.

Aurora ignored me. Still holding my hand, she peered into the woods with a worried look, and I got scared. Was there a tiger on the loose?

"What's wrong? What's going on, Aurora?"

"Nothing, it's just that them girls are picking strawberries for breakfast. Other days I'd be helping them, but since I've got you to look after…"

I knew she'd rather pick strawberries with "them girls" than be with me, so I told her I wanted to pick them, too. The sounds of laughter and conversation grew louder as we drew near, and after leaving the square and descending through the woods to the stream bank, we saw three women and a boy bending over the ground.

"Have you picked a lot?" asked Aurora. "As for me, just look. Right now I've got too much on my plate to do anything else."

The other women straightened up to look at me. They didn't say a word, but I understood plain as day they were alluding to my arrival with mother and didn't much care for guests.

"You know what summers are like," said the fattest one. "So long as this is it. Last year we had to handle forty, enough for a grand hotel!"

"Shush," warned Aurora, pointing at me. "Kids repeat everything."

That was a minor disappointment. Those maids were better dressed than Casiana, prettier and cleaner, but ultimately they were all the same. In the following days, I realized they were even worse.

I gave up listening because the boy who was with them picking strawberries asked me where I was from and what my name was. His was Mateo, and he had over two hundred crickets.

"Where?"

"In my room. I'll show you."

Then he asked if I'd seen the tiger. His name was Caiphas, and the wolf was Suleiman, and he was pure evil. Soon they'd be bringing another one, and Tío Felipe had laid a trap in the forest to capture it. That one would definitely be a good wolf!

"How do you know it'll be good if they haven't caught it yet?"

Mateo studied me scornfully upon realizing my ignorance. All the shepherds had already spotted the wolf, and it was big and dark, "with a snout like this," said the boy, opening his arms.

I didn't ask any more questions but listened zealously to his zoological lectures. Aurora had given up looking after me to pick strawberries and chat with the other women, greatly contributing to my state of happiness. I managed to slip away with Mateo to take a second, more careful look at the tiger and the wolf. According to him, the latter had rheumatism.

But what really interested the boy were his crickets. Did I happen to have a cigar box? I didn't? Well, that was a pity, because he only had one, and the crickets barely fit.

Mateo was the cook's son, and in time he'd be a priest. The lady of the house was paying for his studies, so one day he'd be like Father Sinforiano. Did I know Father Sinforiano? He had lots of butterflies mounted with pins on a board.

46

"Alive?"

No, they were already dead. Mateo didn't much care for butterflies or strawberries. If only they'd been barberries! Did I like barberries? He knew where there were lots of them, and crabapples, too. They had tough skin and were tart and delicious.

We were wandering so far from the maids, I started getting nervous.

"You don't ever get lost around here?"

"Me? I know all this like the back of my hand."

That set me at ease, especially when I found out there weren't any tigers or wild boars or even wolves on the prow. There were in fact roe deer and some larger deer, but not so close to the palace. They were thirty minutes farther away on foot, where the park met the forest. Mateo had seen them when he went hunting for crickets. That was his specialty, and no other boy could capture so many.

He could also pick out all the different birds by their songs. The one we were hearing just then was a swift. Swifts don't have legs, and if they fall on the ground, they're done flying for good. Mateo was throwing rocks at a tree when he said this, which I took as a sign he was quite a bully.

"See, there's a nest over there," he said.

"But if you knock down the nest, you'll kill the baby birds."

He wasn't paying attention and kept on throwing stones. What a boy! He was going to hit me in the head if he didn't look out. I moved away a bit and saw sunlight streaming into a clearing in the trees. It was a square with a statue and a fishpond in the middle. The water was falling from a stone seashell in the nude woman's hand into a basin where birds were drinking.

Without warning, the birds took flight, and I looked up. My heart skipped a beat, so great was my astonishment. A princess clad in white, curls streaming down her back, was making her way up a promenade on the other side of the square, reading a book.

Mateo had abandoned his barbarous pastime, and I felt his hand on my shoulder and let out a shout.

"Scaredy cat!"

"Look," I said, pointing out the princess in white, who was also looking at us.

"That's Señorita Sweetname. She got here the day before yesterday from the school in Bergara. Come on, let's go. She's already spotted us."

No! I didn't want to go. An irrepressible sense of shame was holding me back in the shade of the trees, and a terrible, uncontainable desire was forcing me to look at her.

"Well, I'm leaving," said Mateo. "If you want to stay behind…"

The fair young lady had taken a seat on the edge of the pond and from there was motioning for me to approach.

"Come here, dear, come."

I approached her slowly and timidly. She wasn't a princess, but she almost looked like one, with her black hair divided in tresses by a part like a cord of white silk. Closer up, I saw she had green eyes in the dark shade of her lashes.

"Are you María Luisa? I didn't see you last night because you went straight to bed. You know we're cousins, don't you? Didn't you know that?"

"No, ma'am."

"Don't call me ma'am. My name is Sweetname. It's strange, isn't it? It was a whim of Mama Teresa. Won't you say anything?"

She was almost a girl, and her eyes and her voice made me trust her, along with her hands holding mine.

"What's your name?" I asked, perplexed.

"Sweetname, I already told you."

"You've got a different name, but you don't want to say it," I risked suggesting.

My cousin gave a small, silvery laugh.

"What an idea! Tell me, dear, why would I keep it to myself? But you're right, and the same thought has crossed my mind many times… Sweetname isn't a name but the description of a name that other people have to guess and whose secret rests with me… I too would like to know what the sweet name was, but I don't know it. Do you?"

I thought it could've been Elisa, but I didn't dare say so.

Sweetname led me by the hand to a formal flower garden. Strolling among trimmed myrtles, she asked me where I went to school, how many brothers I had, and whether I'd taken First Communion. She'd gone to boarding school in Bergara since she was eight years old, but now she was sixteen, and there was a possibility she wouldn't be going back.

"Do you know everything there is to know?"

I immediately felt embarrassed for asking.

"Of course not," she laughed. "But father went to America, and he might send for me, because mother passed away a couple of years back."

Everything about my cousin was something out of a different world, and I quivered in admiration at her sight. What was it like, that boarding school where she'd lived for so many years? Would she sail across the ocean alone in search of her father?

She told me a lot about the school. It too had a park, though it wasn't as big as Tía Teresa's, and its chapel was lovely. Had I seen the garden and the rose-covered pergola? Few gardens and parks in Spain could complete with the one we were in. What had I liked most?

Sweetname shared the mania for asking one's impressions. The hardest thing for me was that I could never put words to the sense of elation that the sounds and smells of nature awakened in my young soul, still barely separated from Mother Nature's divine embrace.

"Did you see the wild animal cages? And the pond with the swans? Yes? And the birdhouses? And the path with the French roses, bursting in bloom? I saw you with Mateo. Surely he showed you a nest. Tell me, what did you like most?"

"You!" I said, and all my blood rushed to my cheeks.

49

SWEETNAME

Mateo's crickets were stuffed like sardines into the cigar box, and he had to pluck out the finest specimens with his fingertips for me to admire them.

"This one's a prince, and this one, a king. You can tell from their wings. This one's worthless; it's a female and doesn't have legs because the others ate them."

After making their acquaintance, I could tell they were all more or less mutilated, missing antennae, short one or two legs, wingless, or even with body half eaten. The inside of that cigar box was a constant battle.

"They're real fiends," explained Mateo. "Get two of them together, and in no time flat they'll be gobbling each other up till there's nothing left. And since I've got so many of them…"

Maybe they were hungry, I suggested, but he took it as a personal offense.

"Hungry! I give them over ten leaves of lettuce a day! No, it's just that they're little devils. I have yet to meet a person as evil as a cricket."

We were in the garrets, where Mateo and his mother lived in two big rooms with windows overlooking the slate roof. There was a small basket hanging from the ceiling, and the boy said a stock dove came in the window at night and slept there. Now that was exciting!

"Why does it come inside?"

"Just because. Mother is fond of it, so we leave the window open at dusk so it can come in. One time we forgot, and we found it huddling against the glass, all soaking wet, because it was raining buckets."

The garrets were almost always deserted, and Mateo and I liked to play hide-and-go-seek in the long hallways lined with empty rooms. Those halls had twists and turns and dark, scary junctions that gave me a little chill whenever I dashed through them.

One day, a door opened at the end of a hall, and Sweetname appeared in a dazzling rosy light that illuminated the gray walls and the old, crumbling floor tiles.

"Why are you two raising such a ruckus? It's time for the siesta, and Mama Teresa is resting. Mateo, your mother called for you a while ago, and you, María Luisa, where did you leave Aurora?"

I didn't know what to answer because I hadn't left Aurora anywhere; on the contrary, she was the one who was always leaving me at the drop of a hat.

"Come with me," said Sweetname, leading me into a room that I thought looked magical.

The light was pink because it streamed from the skylight through a rose-colored curtain. Like in pictures out of a storybook, there were tapestries hanging haphazardly in the middle of the room, half covering sofas and chests.

"It's a studio I put together out of odds and ends. Do you like it?" she asked. Then, changing tones, "It's not right, you playing like a tomboy with that awful Mateo! Why don't you play with Pilar and Catita?"

Those girls, very calm and mild-mannered, had arrived a week after us and were the daughters of one of mother's cousins.

"Tell me, why don't you play with them?"

"Because I get bored."

Sweetname looked at me, surprised.

"You really are a troublemaker, dear. You've got to straighten up. That's enough playing for today. Just look at yourself in the mirror. See what a state you're in? It's very hot out, and you've been running and jumping like a lunatic. Sit where you like or have a look around. I'm going to paint."

It wasn't till then I noticed a table with a little basket and two doves that were barely moving. To one side was an easel with a canvas on which the doves were gradually appearing.

Sweetname started painting. She was wearing a beige smock that covered her all the way down to her feet. In one hand she held a palette and in the other a long brush she was using to mix colors. She made a stroke on the canvas and took a step back.

I was watching her in rapture. Her hair was jet black; her brow, pure white. Her delicate silhouette stood out against a velvet drape, and my eyes feasted on her perfect beauty.

"You're still here?" she said out of nowhere. "Goodness me, I didn't even notice the time going by. Did you get bored? It must be time for an afternoon snack. Come, dear, come along."

She took off her smock and picked up the basket with the doves.

"Let's go set them free," she said. "Right now their legs are tied."

And we went downstairs.

I took hold of her hand and passed it over my face in a feline caress that left her astonished.

"Aren't you strange! Rowdy one moment, calm and affectionate the next. Did you like watching me paint?"

"A lot!"

"Well, you can come to my studio whenever you want, as long as you're good like today."

That permission was the key to my happiness and, on many days, a constant source of agitation. Sometimes, running through the garden or singing ring-around-the-rosie, I'd slip off to the studio, trembling with emotion. I'd push on the door, first gently, then stronger. Afterwards, I'd peep through the keyhole. There was nobody there, and it was all shut up!

That was because Sweetname spent a lot of time out of the house, on trips with girl friends or making lunch visits to Burgos. She kept the studio locked whenever she was out.

Pilar and Catita were slightly older than me and always wanted me to play with them. They'd try to lure me to the honeysuckle arbor to play at taking vows.

"I don't want to. I don't like that game!"

My cousins had seen one of their sisters take her vows at a convent, and the ceremony made such an impression, they didn't want to play at anything else.

"Come on, it's very pretty. Look, you'll be the novice and we'll put the veil on you," they said, showing me a shabby piece of muslin. "Then comes a crown of white flowers. And you'll keep your hands together and your eyes looking down."

"I don't want to," I grimly refused. "I don't like that game."

"Good grief! Well, what do you like to play?"

"Hide-and-go-seek or cops and robbers or duck, duck, goose. Running games. I don't like to sit still."

"That's because you don't go to a good school," reflected Catita. Her pity for me was tinged with pride. "If only you went to Sacred Heart like us!"

One day we were having our usual dispute, when Sweetname came up to us from her stroll in the woods.

"What's going on?"

"María Luisa never wants to play at taking vows."

I felt myself turning bright red.

"Girl," chided Sweetname, "go along with your cousins, just this once. I'll play with you, too, if you play. You'll be the novice, and I'll be the abbess. Wouldn't you like that?"

Yes, of course! Now that Sweetname was playing, I was fully capable of strolling through the garden with the phony veil and the honeysuckle crown.

"Good, I like it this way, but we're going to do it for real, completely for real, and for that we've got to go to the Lourdes grotto."

There was a misty grotto in a half-hidden spot of the park, tucked away in thickets and leafy trees. It was always cool, even on the hottest days, and there was a pink marble Virgin in a niche in the rock. More than once, I'd seen the mannered composition and thought it was lovely.

Catita and Pilar were ecstatic that Sweetname, an actual sixteen-year-old, was descending to our level to play a game that would almost be the real thing.

The abbess and the two girls sat on a stone bench in the grotto to weave the crown, which didn't take long to finish.

Then Sweetname made me kneel before her, parted my wild hair from my brow with her cool hands, and spread the veil over my head. Her hands moved to and fro, placing and replacing flowers in the crown, which she used to secure the veil. She was making me feel a delightful touch of dizziness, a sweet bewilderment that forced me to close my eyes, shaken and happy all over.

"Look how pretty she just got," said Catita, amazed. "She looks like a new woman."

"It's the state of grace," said Pilar, who claimed to know a lot. "Isn't it, Sweetname?"

Yes, that was it, my cousin confirmed. Like an automaton, I said and did everything they ordered, never leaving the state of grace, which came to me through the hand of the abbess.

"See how nicely we played?" Sweetname asked afterwards. "Why didn't you want to, silly?"

Her calling me silly elevated me anew to the state of grace, leaving me a little light-headed.

What was bad were the days Sweetname was nowhere to be found, and I felt driven to commit the most terrible atrocities.

"Leave her alone," said Catita to her sister. "Leave her alone, she only likes to play with boys."

Mateo would accompany me through the woods to pick barberries and crabapples. Once in a while, from our place in a treetop, we'd spy a charcoal black stag crossing our path and quickly disappearing. We'd jump across brooks from the widest bank and hop the fence to other estates, and at night I'd get home with my linen shorts in tatters and my legs ravaged by thorns.

But on the eve of our departure, I wound up without a single playmate. It was the first of September, and Mateo left for school in the morning with a satchel hanging from a strap. I watched him go from my bedroom balcony.

Aurora was calling to me from the garden, where she was with Pilar and Catita. I'd better get down there, we were going to recreate a religious procession. Those girls and their pious imaginations! I snuck up to the garrets, where they wouldn't find me.

Sweetname was out, and the studio was locked. The painting of the doves had been hung in the hall on the ground floor. Mateo and his mother's room was open, and the cigar box was in the corner with its mangled heroes, still fighting ferociously to the death.

Carefully, I opened the box. Almost half of the crickets had already perished, and the others were devouring their remains. Those critters were real brutes! Next to the cigar box was a pile of jacks and foil wrappers. The cook saved the latter for Mateo from the household's used chocolate bars, and they were meticulously smoothed out and folded. What a lucky boy! There was also a little box I'd given to Mateo to keep his picture cards.

There were trading cards from the chocolate wrappers, holy cards with saints, and even some paper lace prayer cards he'd gotten at school. He refused to let me examine them as much as I would've liked, fearful I'd ask for one.

I heard a creak in the hallway and jumped. I listened... There wasn't a sound to be heard, but by then I'd been seized by fear of the empty garrets full of hiding places and shadows. I would go down to the garden, where my cousins and Aurora would be parading around a square.

Taking the boxes of crickets and picture cards, I went outside through the small door off the lower gallery, running as far as I could from the palace to where nobody would find me. I spent the morning sitting beside the brook that fed the strawberry beds, where I emptied the crickets out of the box. They stayed perfectly still, unable to move; not one of them still had its legs.

Among the picture cards was one that was bedazzlingly beautiful. On the outside it looked like a shell, but it opened in two to reveal a garden with promenades and silk-paper flowers that also unfolded like tiny lanterns. A little girl dressed for her First Communion was going out a golden door. No other work I've ever seen since has made me feel so indescribably ecstatic.

Maybe that's why I lost track of the time. When it was time for lunch, mother and Aurora had to search all over for me. Hearing my name being shouted through the woods, I went to see who was calling and left behind the boxes out of fear they'd take them away from me. It was Aurora.

"Lord in Heaven! You gave us quite a scare! Where were you this morning, if you don't mind me asking?"

I found mother in a rage.

"You'll be giving me trouble to the bitter end! Foolish girl! Why don't you play with your cousins? Mateo's going out of his mind, saying you stole I don't know what. You'll never learn, will you dear?"

I was starting to get really frightened. I hadn't considered what was going to happen when Mateo noticed his boxes were missing. I saw him when I came onto the terrace, but he didn't dare approach me because mother had me by the hand. His face was red from crying. He looked in my direction and shouted hoarsely, "thief," then scampered towards the kitchen doors.

Aurora always served me and my cousins lunch in the dining room off the lower gallery. That day the girls were already sitting at the table. Seeing me enter, they gave me a look and whispered as if the two of them were in on a secret. I grew more wary by the minute.

"They're going to punish you," blurted Catita. "Why did you steal Mateo's picture cards?"

"I didn't steal a thing from him."

It started to rain, and water was pounding furiously against the windows, filling them with rivulets. Alas, the picture cards were out in the meadow!

We finished eating and went out to the gallery with Aurora. Maybe the grown-ups didn't care what had happened! Time was ticking by, and my cousin's looks and whispers were the only things reminding me of Mateo.

Out of the blue, mother burst in on us, grabbed me by the arm, whisked me into our bedroom, shook me by the shoulders, and let me fall into a chair.

"Naughty girl! You'll spend the afternoon here, reflecting on what you did. That's just what I needed, for Tía Teresa to get me all upset. Scoundrel! Where are the cards?"

Sobbing, I stammered that the cards and the crickets were beside the brook with the strawberry beds. But not in the brook, in the meadow.

"It doesn't matter," declared mother. "At this point, there's been so much rain, everything will be soaking wet. If only you weren't such a tomboy and played with your cousins like a good girl!"

When she finally got done yelling at me, she went away locking the door behind her.

I cried myself to exhaustion, then kept busy studying the blue rug with white roses in the middle of the room. The rainy afternoon already smelled of autumn, and I felt cold gazing out onto the damp, gray park.

I heard the key in the lock but didn't turn my head, assuming it must've been mother.

"María Luisa, what are you up to?"

It was Sweetname.

"I can't believe what they told me. You didn't steal anything from Mateo, did you? Answer me!"

"The crickets didn't have legs," I began. "And that's why... That's why I let them go!"

"And the picture cards he's going on about? You wouldn't have!"

I couldn't bear the stern look of her green eyes any longer and broke into tears. Then I felt Sweetname's arm around my shoulders, and I rested my head on her chest, sobbing so violently she started to get alarmed.

"Come now, dear, hold yourself together. You're a strange girl, but not a bad one. I've always thought you were a good girl. Come with me to my room. Come along, dear."

Hugging me tight, she carried me to her bedroom, where she sat me down beside her on a sofa. She wiped my tears with her batiste handkerchief and lavished me with kisses. Little by little, I told her everything I'd done that morning.

"But that wasn't right, María Luisa. It wasn't right to go out to the garden with something that didn't belong to you. And all that about the crickets. Goodness gracious! Why did he have them all caged up?"

It was a delightful afternoon. I thought the whole palace was against me, but tucked in that refuge, nestled against Sweetname, feeling her hand run through my hair, nobody would dare come in search of me.

She was talking to me, telling me about a girl at her boarding school who was just like me, just as fidgety, rowdy, and impulsive. One Sunday, all the girls said a prayer for her at communion, for God to touch her heart.

"And guess what? I heard she's on her way to becoming a saint. You see?"

Then we looked at a book in English with lovely illustrations of kings and princesses. Sweetname left me holding the book to rummage for something in her vanity drawers. It was a small white box from which she revealed a gold bracelet with a tiny heart bearing her name.

"A gift from me to you. You're leaving tomorrow, and when we're no longer together, you'll see it and remember me and this afternoon, when you promised me you'd be a good girl. Won't you?"

Yes, I'd remember!

I kissed Sweetname's hands with such passion, she pulled back.

"Don't be a madwoman, child! Heavens me, you're excitable! What's to become of you if you keep this up?"

FATHER'S VILLAGE

Perhaps mother had taken it upon herself to civilize those humble villagers in Ávila province where grandpa lived. He was father's father, and that was where our summer vacations met their end.

She resorted to all sorts of measures, from advising the women about how to raise their kids, to shrouding the newborns who died every year during the harvest (as if up in Heaven they too were filling their granaries with pure little souls), to handing out meat and bread to the poor on Sundays. And since there was something those people needed even more than meat and bread, mother saw to it they had that, as well. Claiming to toughen up the little ones, she convinced the mothers to give their kids nine days of showers to leave them clean as a whistle.

If the mothers were up for it, she would take care of everything herself. So at seven in the morning, she was standing on a bench in the kitchen, pouring a stream of cold water over the head of each of her victims. I showed them the way, being the first to receive the terrible frozen downpour.

The second was Lucrecia, the cleaning woman's daughter, who was also forced to set a good example. She offered her skinny brown body as a valiant spectacle to the other village girls. Because it was always girls who came over, as mother wouldn't admit of promiscuity.

"This is very healthy," mother would insist from atop the wooden bench. "It raises strong girls who don't catch colds."

Since it didn't take long to test that claim, and the girls all caught a cold right away, the lines for the shower dwindled after three or four days. Before the nine days were up, Lucrecia and I were the only ones whose water cure had no end in sight.

That cast something of a shadow over my usual happiness in the morning. The instant I opened my eyes, mother would be waiting with watering can at the ready. There was no choice but to jump from the warm bed into the zinc tub, to tremble and shiver my way through the five obligatory liters of cold water. Afterwards, the cleaning woman Deogracias would wrap me in a sheet and return me to bed, where a few minutes later another package would arrive containing Lucrecia, who'd poke her little purple face out from the folds in the sheet.

Ready for their morning chores, mother and Deogracias would put a candy in each of our mouths before setting off to clean the chapel of Nuestra Señora de los Remedios and put oil in her lamp. It was an hour-long trip to and from the shrine.

The front door would clatter shut, leaving me and Lucrecia all alone, still shivering. Well, not completely alone. In the bedroom next door, grandpa was still snoring, a source of much laughter for the both of us.

Sometimes the warmth would begin to overtake us, plunging us into a sweet sleep, but other times we'd chat on and on, even if that was getting harder by the year. It annoyed me that Lucrecia didn't understand any of what I was thinking.

"In Tía Teresa's park…"

"What's a park?"

"A ginormous garden, one that never ends. Anyway, there was a tiger."

"What's a *triger?*"

"A huge animal that gobbles people up."

"Like a bull?"

"No, not at all. And there were also wild boars, which are like pigs with big, long tusks."

"You're pulling my leg!"

"I'm not, it's the truth. There's a zoo in Madrid. Think that's a lie, too? And it's got lots of monkeys. I saw dancing monkeys in Bilbao."

But Lucrecia didn't know what monkeys or a circus were and had never seen a parrot or a mirador. She went so far as to deny there was sand on the beach. What a piece of work!

I ended up turning my back on her in a huff. Since then, I've realized conversation is an exchange of allusions, making it difficult and unpleasant between people whose lives and circumstances are so different.

Still, Lucrecia knew more than me about life's fundamentals. She knew when to sow the wheat, when to plow the fields, and how to thresh the grain. And she also knew other things...

"Macaria's getting married," she reported one day.

"Good for her."

I was indifferent to all talk of weddings.

"Anyway, they've got to marry her off because she's going to have a kid."

"Huh? How can that be?"

"Aren't you ignorant! Just because she's going to..."

And she let out a cynical laugh, completely inexplicable.

"But how are they going to bring her a baby if she isn't married yet?"

"You claim to know a lot, but you haven't got a clue!"

I'd never considered where human beings come from, having accepted mother's explanations without a second thought. God sent kids to married couples, and babies came from Paris.

"Well, in Madrid…"

"In Madrid and all over," said Lucrecia, "women carry babies in their bellies. Just look at my sister Lorenza. But you'd better watch out if you let slip I told you."

Of course, I wouldn't make a peep.

The revelation made me feel sick to my stomach. Over the following days, Lucrecia went about filling in the gaps in my knowledge, which never became clear, perhaps because her own understanding was spotty. In any case, it was deeply disturbing to find out I'd been in mother's belly and father and mother led an unsuspected, disgusting life when nobody else was looking.

But I forgot about it quickly because my games filled my every thought. I was captaining a gang of the naughtiest boys and girls in the village, and around that time we'd discovered that a steep slope in the drainage ditch was perfect for sliding down on all fours on a plank of wood.

We'd spend the last few hours of the evening playing at that pastime. Often we'd tumble down the slope without the plank, ripping our hands and knees to shreds. I lost whole patches of skin, and the blood stuck my socks to my legs. Getting undressed at night, I'd grit my teeth to keep mother from hearing my moans, which would doubtlessly have prompted her to ban me from leaving the house the next day.

Lucrecia, who was much gentler than me, only joined in my games because she was fond of me.

"But why in the world do you behave so badly? Are all girls from Madrid the same way?"

I didn't know what to say.

One evening, returning home with Lucrecia just before nightfall, we found our street full of women kneeling, their heads covered with cloth and satin mantillas.

"What's going on?" I asked one of them.

"They're giving your grandpa his last rites," she said. Then seeing the look of surprise on my face, "His Last Communion, child."

So that was it! For days grandpa hadn't sat at the door in the armchair mother and Deogracias used to drag out of the house for him.

"Is he going to die?" I asked Lucrecia.

"Obviously, he's really old."

We waited for the priest, the altar boy, and two rows of men bearing candles to come out of the house and head for the other end of the street, with all the women in tow. Or not all of them, because there were so many people inside, we could barely enter.

The house was tiny and made of adobe. Thanks to mother's zeal it had red brick floors in place of the dirt floors of all the town's other houses.

All night long, I heard people coming and going through the front entrance. Once, I woke up in a fright to hear mother's voice saying something very slow, very long, and very solemn. Impressed by her tone, I went barefoot from my bedroom into the living room.

Nobody saw me. There was a crowd of people, but they all had their eyes fixed on the door to the bedroom. Within, mother was still admonishing the demons to disperse from the dying man's pillow and explaining what the angels had to do in order to deliver his soul to God. She was speaking so energetically, it was as if she'd been named master of ceremonies for Heaven and Hell.

Later on, I found out the Recommendation of the Soul is a long prayer that comes standard in prayer books, and that mother was reading it to the shock and awe of the humble townsfolk.

The next day there wasn't a shower. The moment I got up, Deogracias whisked me to her house next door, where I ate breakfast with Lucrecia and her married sister, Lorenza. We hadn't finished eating when father barged in.

How he embarrassed me! I don't know why, perhaps on account of

Lucrecia's revelations, but in my head I'd stopped picturing father like I always had, and I blushed bright red when he kissed me.

I wished he hadn't come and barely brushed his stubbly cheek with my lips. I didn't calm down until after he left, telling me to be good and to stay put where I was for the day.

Lucrecia and I played push-pin and told each other riddles, exhausting our repertoire of ways to entertain ourselves without leaving the house. Then we started singing but were told to be quiet. I was quite pleased grandpa had died, because now they would dress me in mourning and mother would strip the lace trim off my blue dress and wouldn't make me wear the hat with the birds.

The next day a coach came from Ávila, and the three of us departed with our trunks and suitcases. Deogracias and Lucrecia stayed behind crying at the front door. I felt embarrassed, annoyed, and mistrustful sitting opposite father, who wouldn't stop looking at me.

"She's done a lot of growing this summer. I don't know what, but there's something about her, she's different."

"You wouldn't believe the trouble she's been," mother complained. "At Tía Teresa's I saw neither hide nor hair of her all day long, off playing with the cook's boy. She's a tomboy, this one! And the same here. She'd go out in the morning and return for lunch all out of breath, her hair a mess, covered in bruises. Ask her to show you her hands. Just look at what she's done to them!"

Covered in scratches and scabs, my hands were forced to expose their naked palms, bucking opposition from all the rest of me.

"Leave me alone! They don't even hurt!"

"In any case, the summer holiday has worked wonders for the girl," said father, releasing my hands. "And for you, too, Juanita. You look healthier, prettier…"

They gave each other a look I'd never noticed, and I realized everything Lucrecia had told me was true, and I was left out of a dirty, terrible secret they kept to themselves.

I gazed out the carriage window onto the fields and the yellow granaries. I hated my parents and everything awaiting my return to Madrid: Casiana, Doña Margarita's school, my brothers…

Father had decided we'd spend a week in Ávila because he wanted to rest. His father's death had been too harsh a blow to go back to the shop the following day.

The inn was in a narrow street, and there was a view of a square from the balcony of our room. It was a spacious suite with two bedrooms, one with two beds for my parents, and a smaller one with a single bed for me.

Starting the next day, we began the absurd life of summer vacationers in a small town during the first chills of autumn. I started getting up at the crack of dawn, as usual. I had permission to go down to the street provided I didn't bother my parents, who didn't get up for another two hours.

Without wandering far from the entrance to the inn, I'd walk up and down the street and linger near a fountain where the women would fill their pitchers and dip their aprons in the basin to wash their faces. With a broken comb taken from a pocket, they'd take turns crouching and combing each other's intricately braided buns.

That was my favorite time of day, and I felt free and happy. Then mother would call me from the balcony, and I'd go upstairs for her to wash me and comb my hair. We'd eat breakfast in a dining room buzzing with flies and spend all day at a café on the square.

The café was also frequented by some gentlemen and lovely young ladies who were staying at the same inn and ate at the same big table in the dining room. *Artistes de théatre*, every one of them.

Why did they make friends with my parents, so bourgeois and so prosaic? Maybe because people who call themselves artists tend not to be overly artistic. They'd come to Ávila to give three performances, and they wanted my parents to attend closing night.

"No, no," declined mother, mounting a weak defense. "That can't be. It hasn't been a week since we buried our father."

But father insisted. He never went to the theater, but staying at home would be an insult to those friendly folks.

"Nobody knows us here, dear, and it's not as if we're going to have fun. Just think, an Italian opera! It'll probably put us to sleep."

Everything happened just as he said it would. I was the only one who didn't fall asleep, though I was used to going to bed early. I'd always seen the ladies in street clothes, and now they were wearing extraordinary dresses with plunging necklines. From that I could tell they didn't have flesh like everyone else's, for theirs was a lovely shade of porcelain or rose petals. I thought they looked simply gorgeous!

They sang nonstop, and I couldn't understand a thing that was happening, but I could tell from their sad expressions they were enduring terrible tribulations. One of them could barely sing, her voice was so choked in tears.

I looked to my parents for an explanation, but they'd nodded off. Father was even snoring a little, much to the dismay of the gentleman seated beside him.

"The theater's no place for a nap," he grumbled.

But I knew my parents had indeed gone with the intention of falling asleep.

They woke up and ate chocolates in the intermissions. They'd bought them that afternoon, so I thought eating chocolates was part of the show.

Unfortunately for me, the performance came to an end, and we went out to the street, where we waited a while at the door for the actors to exit. Father thought it was his duty to greet them, but they closed the theater, turned off the lights, and left us in the street all alone. At that point, we figured they'd already gone home.

I couldn't fall asleep that night. My hyper-sensitive ears kept replaying the harmonies of the opera and the laments of the lovely young ladies. In the end, I fell into a deep sleep from which I didn't emerge until well into the morning.

By then, dawn had passed and sunshine was streaming in through the cracks of the balcony shutters. My parents must've gone down to the dining room for breakfast and left me to sleep.

I slipped out of bed and went to their bedroom. Father's bed was empty, and there were clothes strewn on the floor. They were both in the other bed, gaping at me in shock and confusion. Their heads rose together from the pillow to see me, and I left without saying a word… And all the shame that can fit in a human child rose up to my throat to strangle me.

THE GIRLS AT MY SCHOOL

Big changes were in store for me at home after the summer holiday. The house had been fitted with electric lights, the girls at my school had grown and changed their hair styles, and my grade was now the oldest at the school, which put us on a pedestal in the eyes of the younger classes. But most important of all, at one fell swoop we'd lost our immaculate innocence catching dirty glimpses of the original sin.

Encarna and María Aycart were always trying to befriend me, but it was no use; I was dead set against making friends. The two pretty sisters told me that a girl in the dance class where they were learning Sevillanas had advised them to proceed with caution around men. Just sitting next to one in a tram was enough to get a swollen belly and a baby in no time flat.

No, that's not how it worked. Lucrecia had told me something different. Still, their revelation kept me worried for days. Maybe it was less complicated than Lucrecia said.

Sole was who knew the most. She was a short, plump girl whose hands were covered in blisters every winter from shopping for groceries, lighting the stove, even scrubbing the dishes before school.

The other girls looked down their noses at her because she didn't have a maid and walked to school alone. I practically ignored her despite her devotion and sheepish humility. She was constantly begging me for a look or kind word.

"I know all about it," she said. "If you want, I'll whisper it in your ear."

"It's a sin to talk about such things," I replied, well aware that listening to the secret would bind me to that girl who was willing to do anything to be my friend.

As for me, I wanted to be friends with Emilia Ontiveros, the new girl. The whole class admired her, but nobody more than me.

At twelve years old, Emilia was tall and slim, with light brown hair and an arched white brow. But that's not what made her worthy of our adoration. There was something indefinable about her, and it was hard to say if it came from the elegant way she sat, or the grandiose gestures she used to underline her words, or the original and absurd way she talked.

"Last night we went to see *Juan José*. 'Twas a lovely play, very good… My father's a socialist and my mother's from the *borrzh-wa-ze*, and they got into a fight on the street… When I grow up, I'm going to open a flower shop."

Seeing how Emilia was friendless like me, I tried to befriend her by talking about Tía Teresa's park and its path of French roses. Apart from the social issues that brought her parents to blows, botany was her only interest. She knew dozens of herbs and wildflowers by name and would describe their colors and aromas in a style all her own: "It's like a star with a red kite flying in the middle, and it smells of venom and breadcrumbs. A wonderful smell!"

I gave Emilia all my picture cards, but she'd barely glance at them and didn't give me anything in return.

But one time she did tell me a secret that I heard in a state of angst and excitement, like the Virgin Mary receiving the visit of the Archangel Gabriel.

"Guess what? I'm a woman! It happened last night. Mother didn't want to let me come to school today, but I get bored out of my mind at home. Don't tell a soul, it's a secret."

A nasty voice interrupted us.

"María Luisa Arroyo and Emilia Ontiveros, punished for talking in class," said Doña Margarita.

The punishment consisted of thirty minutes of after-school detention. Following the extraordinary revelation, I was happy to think we'd be left alone together.

Meanwhile the headmistress separated us, making Emilia sit near her and me stay in my usual place. I studied Emilia from across the classroom and couldn't detect anything new in her face, her hands holding the geography textbook, or the green wool dress peeking out from beneath her white apron. What did it mean to be a woman?

"María Luisa, where's your mind gone wandering? Come here and recite the lesson, and speak up now if you don't know it. We've got no time to waste."

But I knew it by heart. I wouldn't have been able to say the same for my dreaded arithmetic, but geography was my forte. Looking at a map, my surroundings faded away and it wasn't long before I was trekking through mountains and rivers, forests and plains. In fact, I'd devoured the geography textbook at dawn in the first few days of school with the same delight as a storybook. So what if it gave the surface area of each nation and province and statistics about their inhabitants?

For that reason, I suspect I knew more in that geography class than Doña Margarita, who, for her part, had the decimal system down pat, those ghastly numbers that were ruining my life.

At the end of the school day, Emilia and I stayed behind alone in the dark, empty classroom. It was already November and they still hadn't turned on the lights.

Emilia was protesting under her breath. The second her mother found out she'd been punished, she'd be there to pick her up. Her mother was a wonderful woman! And with all she was going through…

But what was it? I didn't understand. How had she suddenly become a woman? You wouldn't know just by looking at her.

"Lord, what a girl! You really don't know, do you? But it's a matter of common knowledge!"

She brought her lips to my ear and whispered something terrifying.

"Good heavens! And that's something all women go through?"

"All of them, obviously."

"Well, I don't want that to happen to me."

"Like it or not, it's bound to happen, and you aren't a woman till it does."

"Then I don't want to be one. I want to be a grown-up, but not a woman."

Later, Emilia told me about her parents' garden in the province of Lérida. A royal jasmine had climbed up to the upstairs balcony and could be smelled from a mile away. Its flowers were white spiders, five legs apiece, and smelled of lemon and curdled milk with a slight hint of rats. That made it impossible for me to imagine their scent.

She opened her arms to show how the jasmine climbed the garden wall, then brought them to rest on her lap, her white hands cupped together with fingers laced like in prayer.

"Do you want to be my friend?" I asked out of nowhere.

"No," she answered calmly, "because they're going to withdraw me from school. Mother said so this morning."

That made me sad, and I said I'd leave school, too, if she was going. I knew all too well that whatever I wanted or said on the matter was completely useless, but we all liked to boast of the great importance attached to our decisions at home.

Emilia didn't come to school the next day or the following one or the one after that.

I was still keeping her secret like my most prized possession when María Aycart blabbed, "She isn't coming because she's a woman."

"Who told you that?" I asked, indignant.

"She did, but it's a secret, and you can't tell anyone else."

It turned out the entire grade was in on the secret, and I alone had kept it strictly to myself. Oddly enough, that wasn't enough to break Emilia's spell over me, and her charm grew exponentially a few days later when she came back to class dressed in mourning.

"Emilia Ontiveros just lost her father," said Doña Margarita. "I trust you girls won't bother her with chit-chat."

Emilia took a seat and started crying. The pained look on her face moved me so deeply, I too burst into sobs and had to be removed from class so I could cry to my heart's content in the closet with all the girls' coats.

In the following days, Emilia continued acting sad and slightly aloof.

"Tomorrow's my saint's day," she told me one afternoon, "but I'll come to school like any other day because this year we won't be celebrating. Don't tell anybody!"

I vowed to keep quiet and, getting home, went straight to looking for a gift worthy of my beloved classmate. I'd already given her all my picture cards, so I thought about taking a little notebook with filmy white covers and gilded letters advertising El Ramillete Europeo, the perfume shop on Calle de Sevilla where mother had bought a powder box the week before.

"May I have your notebook?" I asked her.

"What are you going to do with it? Lose it, like all your other gifts?"

Everything I'd lost was in Casiana's trunk, but I wouldn't have dreamt of saying so.

"No, I want to give it to a girl at school. Tomorrow's her saint's day. She's pretty as a picture and very well-behaved."

"I don't like you girls always exchanging gifts," said mother.

"But she's so well-behaved! She just lost her father, and she cried and cried."

Perhaps this sentimental flourish stirred mother's emotions, for she started rummaging in the top drawer of her dresser, where I imagined her keeping all the world's wonders.

"I'll give you something, but not the notebook you asked for," she said, rifling through the drawer. "Don't you see? The notebook's an advertisement for a store, not something you can give as a gift."

She took out a scent bottle consisting of a hollow walnut with a metal neck and a screw-on cap. She cleaned it with care and filled it with perfume from her bottle. After testing to be sure it wouldn't leak, she wrapped it in tissue paper and made a cute little bow out of pink ribbon.

I was watching her every move, not missing a detail, touched and grateful. Emilia would be thrilled! Now she'd have no choice but to be my friend and prefer me over all the other girls.

I had a bad night's sleep, waking up constantly to make sure the scent bottle was still under my pillow. If Casiana found out, she'd make me hand it over! I'd been sleeping in her room for a while now because I was prone to dreaming and getting scared at night.

That night was one of my worst. I couldn't wait for the following day, and the anxiousness set my nerves on edge and made me fall into frightful nightmares.

I dreamt as I had on other restless nights that I was entering a vacant church. My footsteps produced deep, hollow echoes as if I were in a cave. I was terribly scared, but something made me press forward.

Once I got to the center of the church, gangly black puppets wearing hoods and moving at the will of invisible hands emerged from the altars and confessionals. The terror of it froze the blood in my veins and the voice in my throat, and I wavered between sleep and wakefulness before crossing the magic circle separating me from reality. Waking up, I was terrified and sweating.

"Casiana, Casiana! I'm having a bad dream!"

She didn't answer.

"Casiana! Let me get in bed with you. I'm frightened!"

She finally woke up and sighed. Half-asleep, she felt around for the light and said, "Come on, get over here, and leave me in peace."

I jumped out of bed clenching the bottle in my fist and ran to Casiana's bed just as she opened her eyes.

"What've you got there?"

"Nothing!"

"I said, what've you got?"

"I haven't got anything. See?" I opened my hands, having slipped the little package under the pillow.

Casiana propped herself on an elbow and yanked up the pillow.

"What do we have here?"

But before she could look, I'd snatched it away.

"It's nothing, silly! It's just something I happen to have. You can't see it."

That was exactly what she was waiting for! She shook herself awake and demanded I show her what it was or go back where I'd come from.

"And if you're scared, you can tough it out, just like I do with other things."

I hesitated for a moment, I was so terrified of dreaming. God knows the willpower it took to go back to my bed. Casiana cut the light before I got under the covers. Once again, the witches were lying in wait, ready to swoop down from the altars and confessionals the instant I shut my eyes. What a fright!

Mother had advised me to pray when I had bad dreams, and I said every prayer in my repertoire, from the Confiteor to the Salve Regina.

Casiana was awake. She must've been waiting for me to cry for help, certain it wouldn't take long. But that time she was mistaken. A mystical spirit of sacrifice was calling me to face up to the nightmare instead of handing over Emilia's gift.

To rally my spirits, I played through the scene of the following day. When I got to school, Emilia would already be sitting at the desk in front of mine. I'd give a gentle tug on her white apron and wish her happy saint's day as I handed her the parcel. Then, mildly surprised, she'd lift the lid on her desk drawer, as was our custom when we wanted to hide something from Doña Margarita. And she'd unwrap the paper...

What a wonderful surprise! She liked it so much!

She turned to smile and offered me a hand.

"Do you want to be friends?"

And all the girls at school who'd not won her friendship would see us leaving the classroom arm in arm, whispering secrets, and laughing over inside jokes.

I fell asleep, and the awful dream came crashing back down on me from the bedroom's dark corners: the solitary church, the hooded witches dancing an infernal sarabande in skeletal hands.

It was a long and agonizing night from which I emerged feeling sick and exhausted. Knowing Casiana would get up at dawn, I threw on some clothes and slipped the parcel in my school bag with its pink bow already coming undone. I felt sick to my stomach, and my head spun when I looked down. If the others found out, they'd keep me home from school and make me take castor oil!

I tried to study because we had to know the lesson by heart, but I felt worse looking at the book and had to give up.

I struggled to feign good health till it was time for Casiana to take me to school and do the shopping. After dumping a cup of coffee with milk down the sink, I went into the kitchen to hurry her along.

"Shouldn't we leave? Doña Margarita told us to get to school early today."

"Have you looked at yourself in the mirror?" complained Casiana. "You look like death warmed over. Dirty girl!"

As usual, she left me at the school's front entrance, and I took the stairs at a bound. Emilia was nowhere to be seen!

I emptied my bag into my drawer and sat down to wait, giddy with excitement. I'd already forgotten about the morning's ailment. There came Emilia! She approached gingerly, with her usual elegance and restraint, and sat in front of me without looking at a soul. Suddenly a torrent of parcels, boxes, and picture cards rained down on her from every direction.

I looked at the other girls, dumbfounded. Until then I'd ignored them altogether, unaware that they too had their eyes on Emilia and had brought her a gift. Every one of them had been told in secret about her saint's day.

With a sense of bitter disillusion, I too tossed my parcel into the open desk while Emilia took her time carefully untying each and every knot and ribbon. Doña Margarita hadn't started class because it was still a few minutes before nine, and the girls crowded around Emilia to watch her reactions as she opened the gifts. I occupied the seat behind her and could see without changing places.

Wrapped in two or three pieces of paper, the parcels opened to reveal picture cards, colored pencils, pencil sharpeners, dime novels, and an empty box of sore throat medicine. Emilia thanked each of her benefactors with a kiss.

"Very nice, it's very nice," she repeated. "You really shouldn't have."

It was finally time for my gift, and she was already unwrapping it when María Aycart pointed out hers and said she'd untie the ribbon so both gifts would appear to Emilia at the same time. From the other parcel came a little notebook from El Ramillete Europeo whose white covers and gilded letters sent the birthday girl into raptures.

"How precious, I absolutely love it! What a brilliant idea! And it comes with a pencil! Look, I'm going to write your name so I'll always remember it was you who gave it to me. María Aycart... A gift on the tenth of December of the year..."

She still hadn't said anything about my gift! I held out hope.

"And who gave me this walnut?"

"Me, it was me. It's a scent bottle full of the most wonderful perfume. Go ahead, open it."

Emilia said she didn't want to smell it because perfumes made her dizzy.

"But look at this precious white notebook," she repeated, leaving the bottle in the bottom of the drawer. "It's got ivory covers and a silk ribbon on the pencil. It's my favorite present."

Doña Margarita came in, shouting.

"Everyone to their seats! What's going on here? Let's see, María Luisa Arroyo to the board. Write what I say: If a worker makes four pesetas and fifty cents per day and works four days one week, three days the next, and five days the week after..."

Between my bitter disappointment over the gift, the terror-filled night before, and something sickly circulating in my veins, I was feeling feverish and delusional. Even so, I took the teacher's dictation. Afterwards, I looked at Emilia and saw she was still holding the notebook. And she hadn't even thanked me! I couldn't hear what Doña Margarita was saying, and her image blurred in the distance. The classroom was spinning, and I raised my hands to my head.

"I'm going to be sick!"

They rushed to my aid and escorted me out of the classroom, then sent news to father's shop. He picked me up at school and carried me home in his arms. Seeing me gave mother a terrible scare, and before very long it was off to bed with me.

CARNIVAL

When I got out of bed, I was yellow and thin as a rail and it was nearly Carnival.

Mother had fallen ill around the same time as me, so it was Tía Manuelita who stayed at my side and cared for me day and night through two weeks of measles and all the ensuing complications.

Tía Manuelita was mother's elderly aunt. She made herself out to be refined and modern, but even after all her travels, she still said things like *talephone* and *dientist*.

I didn't much like her because she was always complaining to mother about my poor manners and lack of class, inexcusable in someone from a family of our standing. Our great grandfather had been a viceroy in Peru!

"Today I saw your daughter coming home from school, gloveless and hopping down the middle of the street on one foot. And your stepson was talking to some vulgar chap. I can't say I was surprised, knowing where the poor thing came from. His father's a good man, but the son of farmers and merchants, and his mother was a dressmaker. But your daughter's got no excuse. That school she goes to, I don't like it one bit. Not a single bit!"

My illness was long and solitary, for anything lacking the gravity of mother's condition lost all importance in those days, but Tía Manuelita was a tender and sensible caretaker. She was so modern, the poor dear didn't close the balcony even when she was frozen stiff, and she slipped me cool water with orange juice when the doctor and Casiana weren't looking. She also told me about her trips, bringing me a happiness beyond comparison.

"One time when I was in Paris," she had a habit of starting.

And even if what happened to her in Paris was of little interest, I could picture the streets, the great department stores, the Opera, the Louvre, Versailles… Afterwards I had magnificent dreams, light-filled and joyous.

Besides, Tía Manuelita kept Casiana at bay, aware that the maid hated her heartily.

"The lady of the house is sick as a dog, but sick as a dog, you hear? And as I've always said, the dead to the grave and the living to the loaf, but it's easier to say goodbye to a child."

"What a stupid woman," said Tía Manuelita. "What gives you the right to come around here with stories of imminent death?"

"Stories?" shouted Casiana in a fury. "I don't think the truth's a story. Besides, the girl's better now, and she ought to know what's going on with her mother. And she shouldn't have her hoofed feet sticking out from under the covers to catch cold."

Indeed, I'd poked out my burning feet in search of a little cool air.

"What did you say?" asked Tía Manuelita, angry. "My niece doesn't have hooves. You might, though, vulgar as you are! You'd better watch your manners!"

Casiana gave a jump and stormed off to the kitchen while Tía Manuelita went on and on about the coarseness of the lower classes and my parents' stupidity for allowing such a lunatic to come into the house.

I saw father two or three times a day and Juan almost never. Only Ignacio took the time to sit with me during my long hours in the chair by the balcony in the days of my recovery.

"I brought you a storybook," he announced one day, "but don't lose your marbles like you usually do! It's called *The Singer in the Woods*, and it's about a nightingale who lives in the garden of the Emperor of China. Listen, I'll read it out loud."

But my brother's reading was so labored and monotone, I got bored right away and said I preferred to read it on my own. Besides, there was no way the Emperor's palace was actually made of a porcelain so fragile it couldn't be touched.

"Anything can happen in a story," said Ignacio.

"So what if it's a story? The part about the nightingale is true."

I devoured the book in a single sitting, transported to the Chinese forest where the little kitchen maid heard the nightingale's sublime singing. I reread it the following day and dreamt about the Emperor and his little bird made of diamonds and emeralds. It was only a music box, but it replaced the real nightingale!

"Wait and see, Tía, it's a beautiful story! There are two nightingales, one real and one fake."

But my aunt lacked imagination and refused to go along with anything in the book.

"That stuff's nothing but hogwash written to derange simple minds. If you're good and don't get excited and stay calm so your fever stays down, I'll dress you up as a Dutch peasant with the costume left over from my Julianito. Would you like that?"

Yes, yes; would I ever! I was so enthusiastic, I lost my appetite and couldn't sleep, and I woke up early with a fever. Later I fell into a fitful sleep that lasted until Casiana placed a big cardboard box next to the bed, a recent delivery from Tía Manuelita.

"That's your costume, but you won't be putting it on anytime soon. You're sick again, and you can congratulate that crazy aunt of yours, driving you insane with her tomfoolery. She'd be better off saying the rosary or meditating on death, not getting your hopes up. No good ever came from dressing up for Carnival."

I covered my ears to drown her out, thinking only of the costume. I couldn't wait to see myself in the mirror as a Dutchman!

The box was fastened with thick knotted twine, and Tía Manuelita was running later than ever. When she finally came in, she was gasping for air from having bounded up the stairs.

"I'm late! How are you? I went out looking for a piece of satin to make a sack for the *confitti*"—her attempt at *confetti*—"but I couldn't get a hold of what I was looking for. Madrid! You can't find a thing here! Now Paris, that's a different story."

She talked and talked, unpinning her veil and folding it neatly. In the meantime, I was chomping at the bit.

"Tell me, Tía, what does the costume look like?"

"You'll see soon enough. And by the way, how did your mother make out last night? You don't know? I'm going to check on her for a minute. I'll be right back! Wait just a moment, and we'll open the box."

She came back at once, not wanting to go into the bedroom while the doctor was visiting, and started leisurely untying the complicated knots. After removing all the twine, she even took the time to wind it into a ball.

"What color is it, Tía?"

"You'll see in a second, dear. But you'd better not catch a cold. If you get any worse, they'll blame me. That terrible maid already told me you had a fever last night."

The box opened, and my room filled with the smell of new cloth and a hint of mothballs mixed with the unmistakable aroma of the scented confetti from Casa Thomas. The smell of Carnival!

Piece by piece, Tía Manuelita let me feast my eyes on the costume's various components.

"These are the pants. They flare out, just like they wear them in

Dutch villages. I saw pants like these on the docks of Holland. Here's the vest and the cap… Here's the pipe… It's all brand new because Julianito only wore it once."

There was a portrait of Tía Manuelita's deceased grandson in the living room.

I doubt the preparations for Carnival in Nice could be any more exciting than what I experienced in the following days. Tía Manuelita adjusted the costume over and over to fit it to my scrawny frame. Casiana came and went on various pretexts, spying on my aunt out of the corner of her eye and making nasty faces.

One night when Tía had gone, the maid took me aside.

"Your mother's simply thrilled with your costume! You'd think, she says, that with her being so sick… She's better now, but she could've died. You and your aunt haven't got a lick of common sense!"

Casiana's words fell like the first bitter drops of a downpour over that happy limbo where my thoughts had taken refuge in the days of my convalescence. But I was used to keeping her insults to myself and didn't say anything to my aunt, who kept on sewing without a worry in the world.

"Today we're going to try on your outfit in your mother's sitting room. We'll have a mirror there."

Wrapped in blankets, mother was napping beside the fire. She barely opened her eyes when she heard us come in. The pants and the vest were a good fit, and the shirt was ready to go. I blushed with joy.

"What do you think of your daughter?" asked Tía Manuelita, admiring her work. "See how much older she looks? She's like a genuine miniature Dutchman. Well, what do you think?"

Mother finally opened her eyes and sat up to look at me. Not bad, she said, but my mourning dresses for grandpa suited me better. They might as well have been for her, too.

Tía Manuelita accompanied me back to my room without saying a word.

"Your mother," she cried when we got there. "I've never met a worse spoil-sport. Lord, what a woman! There's no having fun when she's around."

I didn't make a peep, but my eyes were full of tears, and I had the feeling Carnival wouldn't be as happy as I'd originally hoped. Nevertheless, I'd placed such high hopes in the Dutchman costume, nothing could shatter my illusions: not mother's disapproval, nor Casiana's complaints, nor a few extra degrees on the thermometer the second I got worked up.

One afternoon before Tía Manuelita's arrival, Casiana showed a girl into my room. It was Sole!

"I told her not to come in," said Casiana, "that you were down with the measles, but she said she had to, absolutely had to. Oh well, if you like the scratching, then you don't mind the lice."

Sole and I looked at each other not knowing what to say. When Casiana had gone, she talked to me in her street urchin's Spanish. She'd told her mother she was off to play in the Plaza de Santa Ana. It was Thursday, after all… But would you get a look at me! I was skinny as a beanpole!

"At school they said you were going to die, and I was the only one who cried, for your information."

"They're going to dress me up as a Dutch peasant," I said, ignoring her. "Tía Manuelita had a lovely costume."

Sole would also be changing sex with her outfit, as they were going to dress her up as a bandit with a shawl and a blunderbuss.

"I'd rather be a *chula* from Madrid, but mother kept the costume from a brother who died."

Apparently we were bound to inherit our costumes from dead kids.

Later Sole told me María Aycart would be dressing up as a French garden maid and Encarna as an old woman, wig and all.

"What about Emilia?"

"She doesn't go to our school anymore. She and her mother moved far away, and she cried and cried when she came to say goodbye. María Aycart said she'd die of pain if Emilia never came back, but she's not dead yet and now she's got Rita for her best friend and Julia Maestre for her second best."

She told me Doña Margarita had been out sick for many days and had left her cousin as a substitute teacher. Señorita María had a brilliant wit and was much nicer than her cousin. One afternoon, she'd even told stories.

"And Pilar Fernández is embroidering slippers for her father, who's a bullfighter and makes lots of money. Rosario's going to make a lace kerchief, but she never knows the lesson for the day. Nobody can compete with you in that department!"

"I can't wait to get back to school! I'll be back after Carnival."

Why didn't they take me to the Plaza de Santa Ana, Sole inquired. Make no mistake, there were plenty of ladies and gentlemen there.

"And there are lots of yellow flowers. You'd really like them, coming from such fine folk. Things like that don't matter to me."

We talked about the garden at Tía Teresa's palace, about its pastel roses, the hydrangeas on the terrace, the tiger…

"Just think, there was a tiger and a wolf and some wild boars in cages."

"Well, isn't that the cat's meow," said Sole, who always knew the phrases of the day. "A tiger! And why were they raising beasts like that? To serve them for dinner, or what?"

She went out promising to return the following day. Tía Manuelita had arrived in the meantime and saw her to the door.

"What a vulgar girl," she said, coming back. "So that's how you learn to say such things. I should've known as much!"

Tía was right. I was dying to have an excuse to say "the cat's meow." The first chance I got, I said it to Casiana, making her laugh with delight.

"Good Lord, girl! You know the new sayings the moment they come out. You're a funny one, you!"

And we were friends for a while, because only the most vulgar part of my soul fit in easily with the people around me.

The Sunday of Carnival I woke to overcast skies and eyed the clouds anxiously from my balcony windows. If the weather was bad, I wouldn't dress up as a Dutchman.

Tía Manuelita arrived around noon, all decked out in a lace mantilla and yellow gloves.

"Are we going out?" I asked her, nervous.

"Yes, it's cloudy, but the rain's holding off and it's not very cold out. How's your mother?"

"Does she know I'm going out?"

"Yes, dear, she knows. She's not happy, but she's keeping her mouth shut. She wouldn't dare cross me. Don't you worry about her qualms, there's nothing to them. Your father doesn't mind. Look here, you see?" She showed me a bundle. "It was he who sent for a scrap of fabric to make a sack for the *confitti*."

It was a piece of brown satin with velvet flowers, and I thought it was beautiful. How very soft! With their sensitivity heightened after months of inactivity, my fingertips sent a new, unknown pleasure up my nerves, something distinctly sensual.

I hadn't gone back to eating at the table, so Tía Manuelita served me a poached egg and a cup of coffee with milk that I couldn't finish.

"Get going, dear. Hurry up! If you don't eat, you won't be able to dress up and take a stroll this afternoon."

The sack was made in a minute, and I got my hair combed into a single braid to be hidden under my cap. Only my bangs were to show, and Tía cut them with scissors. My underwear was reinforced with a second pair for the cold, and finally I slipped my legs into the loose Dutch breeches.

The costume's aroma wafted around me like a new soul hugging tight to my own. I studied myself in the mirror. I was a Dutchman with his pipe, a genuine Dutchman! I put my hands behind my back and strode in front of the mirror, but Tía Manuelita still hadn't given me the final touches.

"Sit still, dear! You can barely see any hair under your cap. You've got nice blond hair, and it's better to show some! The Dutch are blondes. Too bad you don't have blue eyes. You're awfully pale, but I brought… Just you wait and see. But won't you sit still?"

She took some cotton balls from her purse and applied rouge to my cheeks and lips, blue eyeshadow to my eyelids, and powder to my nose and brow. I made for a most handsome Dutchman!

Tía Manuelita took me by the hand and presented me to my parents and brothers just as they were finishing their meal at the dining room table.

"Good heavens! What have they done to you?" snarled mother.

"She's all made up," exclaimed Juan. "They gave her rouge!"

"You saw the devil in the mirror, didn't you? Because that's what happens to little girls who use makeup," continued mother, peeling an orange.

For his part, father motioned for me to approach him.

"What a handsome girl! Anyway, she's not going out, so why all the fuss?"

Tía Manuelita said we would indeed be going to the Prado for a short stroll. After all, I was all bundled up.

"No, definitely not," objected mother. "She can't go out. Her first day out of the house in two months and the skies clouded over, not even wearing a coat. Nobody would ever think of such a thing!"

"Well, I did," said Tía Manuelita, "and I've raised more kids than you."

I followed the argument back and forth with my heart in my throat, choking back tears.

My brothers were also against me, and even Casiana had her say.

"Just think how ridiculous she's going to look, out on the Prado on a day like today!"

"And who gave you permission to speak?" asked Tía Manuelita, livid. "A little more respect and decorum, that's what we need here."

Father made the final decision.

"If you promise to be back soon, you might as well go. María Luisa's already got her hopes up, and it's no use upsetting her over a trifle."

"There she goes again, getting her own way, the little rascal!"

Tía Manuelita wasn't ready to leave yet. She followed mother to her sitting room.

"I say, do you happen to have any white gloves? She can't go like this."

Mother had the gloves from my First Communion, but besides me having outgrown them, she didn't think it was wise for me to wear anything I'd worn in such a transcendental act.

Another argument over the gloves, and our outing was back on the chopping block. Naturally, there was no way I could go out with Tía Manuelita with my hands exposed.

"Fine, take the gloves," mother fumed, "and enjoy yourself while you can. You just might get back to find your mother dead."

My legs wobbled on the staircase, and my heart was beating out of control, not only after months of being sick, but mostly on account of that violent scene that had spoiled the day's long-awaited happiness.

It was cold out on the street. Worrying what would happen to me, Tía Manuelita decided we'd drink hot chocolate at a café on Carrera de San Jerónimo instead of going to the Prado.

Inside it was warm and there were lots of girls wearing costumes like I was. They thought I was a boy! In all my excitement, I did everything I could to mimic boyish postures, opening my arms and straddling my chair.

"Don't be vulgar," warned Tía, seeing me struggle to remove my gloves. "Stop it! Leave them on!"

"But it's just to drink chocolate."

"And who said you've got to take your gloves off to drink chocolate? Distinguished young ladies eat with their gloves on at the grand hotels of Paris and London. They most certainly do! I've seen it many times with my own eyes. You've got to get used to being a proper young lady."

It was hot in the café, and the gloves were too small on me. They were squeezing my hands like instruments of torture. With my hands in that state, it was practically impossible to cut the sweet bun and dip it in my cup. But since Tía Manuelita didn't give an inch when it came to good manners, I ate with the white leather gloves on, sticky with sugar and soiled in chocolate.

Back at home, Casiana told us a nervous breakdown had forced mother into bed right after we left. Tía Manuelita and I went into her bedroom.

Mother was sitting up on a pile of pillows and clutching father by the hand.

"You came close to finding me dead," she said, looking at me. "That's what you get for being a bad daughter and having fun while your mother's sick. But you're not to blame, just the person who put ideas in your head. Don't give me those looks. You think you're so handsome! But you're ugly, my dear, and try as you might, you always will be."

Tía Manuelita couldn't keep quiet any longer.

"Enough of your nonsense," she erupted. "You're nothing but a raving egomaniac who always wants to be the center of attention. God forbid anyone else have fun when you're bored."

Mother started crying and saying she was very ill and didn't have the strength to face our blows. We'd teamed up against her!

"Calm down, dear," father intervened. "And you, Tía Manuelita, keep quiet. We don't want her to get any worse. Just a while ago she gave me quite a scare."

"Exactly! That's exactly what she'll do, give you a scare. And you take the bait every time! There's not a thing wrong with her, believe me. She's like any other spoiled woman, always wanting all eyes on her. And you men are so idiotic, every last one of you."

"Oh dear," cried mother, "I'm going to be sick! I can't breathe, I'm out of air!"

She fanned herself with the fold in the sheet.

"Shut your mouth right now, woman," shouted father at Tía Manuelita. "And keep it closed. Just because you're getting on in years doesn't give you the right to offend her!"

Tía glanced in the mirror, hastening to put on her mantilla.

"Fine," she conceded, "have it your way. No need for me to offend anyone. But remember, the next time you're sick and need someone to spend the night, you'd better find somebody younger. And you can all go to Hell!"

She left without looking at me. Father comforted mother, who was acting like she was suffocating, Casiana brought a basin of hot water, and I went to my bedroom, took off the Dutchman costume, and put on my mourning.

That was the last I saw of the lovely costume, which was returned to Tía Manuelita the following day. I watched the rest of Carnival through the balcony windows while mother dozed by the fire.

Tuesday afternoon I saw the kids across the street climb into an open carriage.

"Mother," I gushed, unable to contain myself, "mother, look. Those kids are coming out of the house and getting into the carriage dressed in Carnival costumes. One girl's wearing white from head to toe. She's a fairy. No, no; she's a little Moorish princess."

Mother didn't reply.

The fairest girl was wearing a strawberry-stitch mantilla, and the smallest one had on a black satin bodice with open batiste sleeves. The boy was dressed up as a Pierrot. They were all laughing, and their mother climbed into the carriage and took a seat among them.

"There's a Pierrot, mother, in black with white buttons!"

90

"You'd be better off thinking of your mother," came the angry reply, "of your mother who's so very ill. Blasted Carnival!"

The carriage still wasn't leaving. Another girl was missing, the eldest, and just then she came out dressed as a gypsy with a frilly red polka-dotted skirt.

"What a lovely dress! Mother, look, it's…"

"Shut up!" she shouted. "Do you think I care what those girls are wearing? Is it so hard for you to understand your mother's ailing and might die any day now?"

I looked out the window and wept. I wept for myself, alone, isolated from everyone, not a single direct response to any of my observations. As for my mother, she could die already.

"I'll be happy," I thought, in a rage.

SPRING

Back at school, everyone had been working since January on an end-of-term show of our needlepoint. There were frames and hoops and stands for embroidery, stretched satin and mesh, fine Filipino *nipis* and thick tatted lace, and little brunette and blond heads knelt over their work, absorbed or distracted.

Seeing me return from my illness to the bustling classroom, Doña Margarita pondered whether to let me stay or send me back a grade in view of my limited dexterity with a needle. Finally it was decided I would make a scented sachet to put in my clothes.

"It won't take much work, and if you can't figure it out, we'll all pitch in."

At home they gave me a silk cord and a piece of light blue satin, from which mother made a neat little bundle for me to take to Doña Margarita together with an embroidery frame, a needle and thread, and a pair of scissors.

And one morning I arrived at my place by the balcony in the upper grade's classroom to find the blue satin stretched tightly over the frame. The teacher had drawn a bouquet of daisies and pansies on the cloth, and somebody had started working on a green leaf using three shades of thread to imitate light and shade.

"María Luisa Arroyo, come here and I'll show you," called Doña Margarita.

I approached her with the frame and listened attentively.

"The center will be darker, the edges lighter. Try not to pull on the needle because the fabric will bunch… See? That's right. Go slowly and stay in the lines… Vary the stitches to mix the colors… This is called needle painting. Got it? Good. Back to your seat, and we'll see how you manage to botch things up."

By the time I got back to my place I'd forgotten what she said and had no idea where to make the first stitch. Oh, what terrible despair!

"Señora," said Sole, ever mindful of my worries. "Señora, María Luisa doesn't know what to do."

"You're going to change places," said Doña Margarita. "Take a seat next to Pilar Fernández. She'll show you. But don't make a racket!"

The warning was entirely called-for, as I would've gladly traipsed across the classroom with my chair and my frame held on high, shoving and tripping and making the girls laugh as they worked. But everything happened in a quiet, orderly fashion under Doña Margarita's stern gaze.

Pili Fernández was the tallest girl in my grade. She was twelve years old and had blue eyes and rowdy blond curls. She always wore the latest fashion and exuded a faint, unidentifiable aroma. Her scent mingled with her embroidery thread, writing paper, and everything she touched with her porcelain hands lined in blue veins.

We were in the last days of April, and for the first time I felt something vague and languid in the springtime. Before long the fragrance from Pili's house had permeated my needlepoint; to tell the truth, she was the only one working on it. And so my pressing need to love and be loved found a ready object of adoration.

"I love you, Pili, I love you," I told her one day. "I love you so much, I could cry."

"Lord, what a girl! What a thing to say! Tell me, is it true you lived with the king and queen?" she asked out of the blue, undoing a knot.

"No."

"Well, that's what Sole said, the liar. And that you played in the woods and had a tiger."

"That was at Tía Teresa's palace! I did spend a summer there."

"Ah, that must be it. And your uncles are counts or marquis."

A keen intuition told me my family's importance elevated me in Pili's eyes.

"Yes, indeed," I replied, "and my cousin Sweetname's a princess, and Catita and Pilar go to Sacred Heart, and one of mother's grandfathers was King of Peru. And we've got a red damask quilt of his that only comes out when somebody's dying."

"Lower your voice and don't look at me," warned Pili. "That way the headmistress thinks we're talking about our work. You're my best friend, and Lolita, my second best."

The thrill of it kept me from answering, and I gazed at her little head bending over my embroidery, her wild curls gathered into two braids that met somewhere down her back.

"Solfège students to music class," announced Doña Margarita.

Pilar and I were in that class, and with the May devotions to the Blessed Virgin starting the following week, we had to rehearse the Salve Regina and the daily Marian litanies.

Surrounded by a semi-circle of girls, the piano teacher would bang on the keys and sing:

"Hail, Virgin of virgins,
mother of flowers,
of nightingales
celestial queen."

And we would sing, going terribly out of tune and intoning incongruous lyrics that we thought were poetic and sublime. All the girls at the school would repeat the four lines like a chorus, after which we'd sing another four, and the supremacy we felt as leaders of the song would fill all that year's solfège students with a childish pride.

The piano was moved into the big classroom that belonged to the middle grade, and a long table with a lace runner was placed against one of the walls under a large copy of an Immaculate Conception by Murillo. Serving as a make-shift altar, the table had vases full of roses and mock-oranges, and candelabra that were lit at the hour of the devotions.

The month of May kindled mystical emotions in all of us, between the scent of roses drifting through the classroom, the happy songs only slightly off pitch, and the candlelight casting movement and life onto the Virgin's perfect face.

But as far as I knew, nobody had entered like me into an extraordinary world full of adventure, wild joy and sudden heart-wrenching sadness, light and shadow. Pili occupied my every thought, my entire life. Pili, the blue satin sachet, and the Murillo kept me awake at night tossing and turning. By then, they'd moved my bed into mother's sitting room because Casiana was complaining she couldn't sleep. Father would wake up several times a night to comfort me.

"What's wrong? Why are you undressing? What did you say about flowers and Pili? Who's Pili?"

Mother stayed in bed and was the one who got angriest.

"That girl will be the death of me! And all because of some blasted needlepoint that's costing us a fortune and won't ever be finished. And she isn't even making it herself. Lord, what a foolish child!"

The school day was too short for me to tell Pili everything on my mind, and our conversations were awkward and scattered.

"I wanted a sailor suit, but mother refused… We have a little alcohol-fueled curling iron, and the other day it overflowed and soiled my kerchief. Have you ever smelled alcohol? It smells so good… Princess Elisa had to stop talking until she finished weaving the tunics for her brothers. Would you have done it? I would have."

"Me too, for my mother and father."

"And for me too, right?" I asked longingly.

"No, you're only a friend."

I fell silent, feeling the bitterness of her words slowly working its way into my ingenuous soul. But the need to tell my secrets, always so stifled by the ignorance of adults, made me go on.

"I'm never getting married. Haven't you seen how newlyweds start fighting?"

Pili was in complete agreement on that point. Her older sister had married her boyfriend Paco, and Pili saw with her own eyes how he used to kiss her every chance he got. Now he refused to leave the house with her, and her sister was constantly crying.

"Sweethearts love each other so much, but then what?" said Pilar disappointedly.

I knew all about the love between sweethearts. In the winter when I was sick, I'd spent entire hours watching a pair of lovebirds who talk-ed every evening right there on the street corner opposite our dining room balcony. They were so in love!

"They're so in love, they can't bear to part, and they take each other by the hands, and when she turns to go, he stays behind, and they say goodbye over and over. And she looks back over her shoulder with every step… They love each other just like I love you!"

"Lord, what a girl!"

That was Pili's response to all my sentimental outbursts.

"Nobody loves me at home. They only love mother since she's always sick," I confided sadly.

Pili was indeed loved. Her father smothered her in kisses before each of his bullfights, and her mother loved her even more, not to mention her older sister.

"I love you over everyone else," I said, clasping her hand under the embroidery frame. "Before I wanted to grow up and find a boy to adore me, but not anymore."

Pili put me in third place after her mother and father, and that sufficed to make me happy for a whole sleepless night.

I felt a burning desire to compare my own preferences and beliefs with those of my friend.

"Do you believe in gnomes? They're tiny little men with beards who live in village wine cellars. Casiana's heard them playing cards and swears they're real."

"Yes, and my nanny says there are witches in her town. It's a sin to believe in such things."

"Do you tell everything in confession, absolutely everything? I keep some things to myself... Do you like to get up early? I like it a lot... And do you like flowers? At my house right now there's a pot of white carnations with thirty blossoms... And we've got the blinds closed since it's about to be summer, and there's such a pretty light in the dining room! What do you like more, when the blinds are down or there are no blinds?"

"María Luisa Arroyo! On your knees for being a chatterbox. That girl doesn't stop running her mouth," Doña Margarita would shout two or three times a day.

I had so, so much to tell Pili, I couldn't shut my mouth for five minutes straight when she was around.

Sometimes I pretended to be embroidering, only to undo Pili's work and ask her for help again.

"Pili, it went and made a knot on me."

"Lord, what a girl! Could you be any clumsier?"

And with her skilled little hands she'd undo the knot and embroider a little more, while I looked on in awe of her prodigious talent.

"Look! You're just like a fairy. A fairy goes and says, 'Here where there's nothing, I want to make a daisy appear with long white petals and a bright yellow heart.' And whoosh! With a touch of her magic wand…"

"But I don't have a wand."

"So what? You've got a needle, and yours doesn't rust like mine but shines in the light. That's your wand."

"Fairies are very pretty," she'd say, sensing an opportunity with her feminine instinct.

"And you are, too. Your blue eyes are as pretty as the Virgin's in the painting, prettier even."

"Quiet! Doña Margarita's watching us!"

But that time it was Pili who spoke up again first, fascinated by our conversation.

"Tell me, do my eyes sparkle like the Virgin's? Nod yes or no so we don't get in trouble."

"Yes, they do; they do when you look at the sky. Tell me, am I your best friend?"

"Of course, I already told you, and I like it when you talk to me like this."

"Well, you're my best friend and my second best and my third best, because I haven't got any others!"

"María Luisa Arroyo," shouted Doña Margarita again. "What in the world are you telling Pilar? You'd better get down to work! She's making the whole thing for you."

Now all the girls wanted to be friends with me, and not a day went by without me rejecting a new proposition. There were even girls like Sole who could live with being my third or fourth or last best friend.

"No, no; I've already got a friend."

Much to my surprise, Pilar would take their side.

"Silly girl! Ritina's such a doll, she could be your second best friend. Mine is Lolita."

I was well aware, and it pained me to see how easily she doled out her friendship.

When my eyes weren't on Pili, I saw other girls spying on me from around the room, and there were already classmates copying the way I sat and talked. Even Doña Margarita took notice.

"Would you look at that! María Luisa's all the rage. You girls could've chosen a better role model!"

"You grew so much in the winter," explained Pili, "and you're in mourning and talk like someone out of a book. That's why. Yesterday Lolita started imitating you, going on about Princess Elisa and the fairies and saying all kinds of nonsense. She has no idea."

My success mattered little to me, for Pilar was the blaze that blinded my eyes and set my soul aflutter like a moth around a flame.

One after another, the needlepoint projects were nearing completion, and mine was no exception thanks to my friend. Doña Margarita unstitched it from the embroidery frame and sent me back to my usual place in the classroom, a thousand miles away from Pilar.

In those same days, Pili started to replace her rather lukewarm friendship with a condescending indifference. The change started small but filled me from the outset with an overwhelming sadness. Later, Pili was outright nasty to me.

"Leave me in peace! Don't be a bore! You're always talking, and then I'm the one who gets in trouble with Doña Margarita."

One morning at the end of May, Pili brought a new girl to school and sat with her. The other girl was a plain Jane, a mildly cross-eyed brunette with a pimply nose. Her embroidery frame was all set up to make a dainty kerchief. With Pili's help, it would be in the show just like my sachet… I hated the brunette with all my soul.

"Her name is Paulina," said Ritina, sounding very prim and proper, "and now she lives with Pili because their parents are good friends. Don't worry, silly, I'll be your new friend if you want."

I let out a snort and retreated into my grief, emerging only to give Sole the boot when she too tried to console me with her friendship.

I'd never talk to Pili again! When I grew up, I'd move far away and never see her face!

"María Luisa Arroyo," called Doña Margarita, "do you have any size ten needles? Yes? Then walk them over to Pilar and Paulina."

My heart beating hard, I crossed the room with the packet of needles and went up to the two girls, who were whispering furtively.

Paulina was studying me with her malicious crossed eyes and sticking a pinky finger through the eyelet of the handkerchief she was embroidering.

"Look! See this?"

The lewd gesture wasn't lost on me.

"Filthy pig," I roared.

"You're the pig here," answered Pili.

Doña Margarita ordered me back to my seat, and I felt a furious anger against everything and everyone. If only there were a fire in the school, a bolt of lightning! If only someone were to hang the teacher!

I sank into a sullen despair and didn't speak to anyone for several days. Pili came and went with Paulina, who refused to look at me and grew more cross-eyed and odious every time I saw her.

One afternoon we ran into each other leaving school. Pili was talking to Lolita, and Paulina was hopping on the landing of the staircase. My brother Ignacio had come with a friend to pick me up, and they were already reaching the bottom of the stairs when I approached Paulina.

"Are you staying at this school for good?"

"What do you care? But if you must know, yes, I'm here for good because we're moving to Madrid, and I'll always be with Pilar."

"Pili's my best friend," I answered gruffly. "Hasn't she told you?"

"That's a lie, I'm her best friend."

"That's what you think! Ask anyone, they'll tell you."

Paulina jumped to the edge of the landing.

"Lies," she shouted, not looking at me. "You're full of big fat lies!"

And without giving it a second thought, she started singing while she hopped:

"Little Bo-Peep has lost her sheep,
and doesn't know where to find them.
Leave them alone, and…"

Before she could finish, I pushed her from behind and sent her head over heels down the stairs with a clatter.

Ignacio shouted from the front entrance, "Did you fall, María Luisa? What's taking so long?"

I leaped down the stairs past Paulina, who wasn't getting up, and met my brother at the door.

The next day Pili and Paulina weren't at school, and the morning wore on through lessons and Marian devotions. The Virgin was gazing heavenward with her moist blue eyes, and I contemplated her passionately, a vague worry in my heart.

All of a sudden, Doña Margarita left class, and the air bubbled with giddy laughter and rapid conversations as if someone had popped the cork on a champagne bottle. The maid Pascuala appeared in the door and tried to talk over the ruckus.

"What's that? What's she saying?"

"She talking to you."

"María Luisa, she's talking to you!"

Sure enough, she was calling for me. Out in the hallway, she said mother was waiting in the lounge. Mother? Why had mother come?

The lounge had a gilded mirror and white upholstered furniture. Doña Margarita was sitting on a chair, mother on the sofa. The two of them looked at me, and I quaked at the knees.

"Is it true?" mother asked me. "Did you push another girl down the stairs? Answer me! Was it you? Answer!"

"The thing was… She was the one who said…"

"I'm asking who pushed her." Mother stood up and came closer. "Was it you?" she raised her voice.

"Yes, but only because..."

And all at once, my pain broke into sobs and mother's anger into two resounding slaps across my face.

"Goodness gracious, Doña Juanita, goodness gracious!" The teacher put herself between us. "Please don't hit her."

"Surely you brought me in for some reason," said mother, furious with Doña Margarita.

But suddenly remembering her numerous ailments, she collapsed into a chair in a fit of self-pity.

"As ill as I am! Ten different heart conditions! And the doctor forbade me from getting upset. This is sure to be the end of me!"

Doña Margarita looked stunned. I kept crying into the back of a chair while the conversation went back and forth between mother's laments and the teacher's excuses.

She hadn't wanted to cause trouble, but given the circumstances... Pilar Fernández's father was the owner of her apartment, and he was threatening to keep his daughter home from school as long as I went there.

"You know how damaging a landlord can be. What if he decides to blame me for this? The rent on my room's really low."

Mother moaned louder when she realized I was being kicked out.

"My Lord, what a disgrace! And on the eve of the Ascension, no less. I'll remember it to the end of my days. So, you're saying... Jesus, Mary, and Joseph! In other words, I've got to take her with me?"

"It's not so bad after all," said the headmistress. "She's very bright, and she can finish her studies at home with a private tutor. I really do regret it. Believe me, it's a terrible disappointment."

She was wringing her shriveled hands in the hope we'd vanish out of sight. In that moment, I hated her with every fiber of my being, as on the days when she locked me in a dark room and left me to entertain myself imagining horrible forms of torture. I hoped that rats would eat her, that her enemies would flay her piece by piece with sharp-pronged forks, impale her on a stake, drag her by the hair...

Mother stood to end the conversation, and never again did we set foot in that school where I'd spent six years of dazed and tumultuous childhood.

"Lord, what a woman," said mother in the street. "Always putting herself first, and the rest of us can go to Hell. I never did like that snake in the grass!"

"If only you could see her temper with the girls," I ventured to add.

"Shut up, stupid! Did you know you broke two of the poor girl's ribs? You'll have God to thank if we don't cart you off to jail. As ill as I am!"

HIS HONOR THE JUDGE

The doctor prescribed baths for both of us, sea water for me and a spa in the north for mother.

That time I definitely saw the ocean! My eyes drank in the maritime horizon, green and blue, mysterious and supernatural, serene and scary like a terrible, almighty God. My heart skipped a beat, and I felt an urge to cry.

It rained a lot in that first week at the baths. Shut in the room at the inn, mother prayed the rosary and wept over her ten conditions, all of which spelled *certain death*, as she was now fond of saying.

Meanwhile, I explored every inch of the dank garden, even venturing beyond the gate to the promenade of towering trees and the puddle-filled grotto with its mineral spring. The promenade was solitary and sad on rainy days. I would suddenly get scared of being alone and hasten back to the garden, the tree swing, the henhouse, and the storage shed. The latter had been a happy discovery.

It consisted of a wooden shack leaning against a sturdy garden wall behind the hotel. It was there that the owners kept their food reserves:

wineskins, salt cod, cured ham, sacks of rice and garbanzos. One day I found the little door ajar and tiptoed in.

The place smelled of moisture and cod. On a shelf of empty bottles shrouded in cobwebs was a worm-eaten, mold-covered book titled *The Blue Tailcoat*. I read the first few lines.

"If you have a blue tailcoat with gilded buttons, throw it out now, don't keep it. On account of such a coat I fell victim to countless misfortunes I mean to tell you about in this book. It was over twenty years ago…"

Thus began a story in long paragraphs and boldface type in which the author fell in love with a lady in an apricot velvet dress. In his eyes, she was pretty as an angel. In the illustrations she wasn't half so good looking, but perhaps the portraits didn't do her justice. I didn't doubt for an instant the lovely Elvira's unparalleled beauty.

Seated on an old chest, I was reading with the book on the table where the hotel owner kept his accounts, when I heard talking nearby. It was coming from the other side of the wall, and standing on the trunk, I could just reach a little window and see into the neighboring garden.

There was a fourteen- or fifteen-year-old boy sitting atop a wall between the two yards. From there he was talking with a girl not much older than me who was standing in the garden below.

"I was watching you, and you didn't even turn to look at me," he complained.

"I was distracted. Besides, I was with my cousin," she answered, batting her eyelashes.

"I know. You're always with a boy."

"But of course! I get very scared."

"Poor little thing! Maybe they'll gobble you up. The beach is full of sharks who like to munch on little girls."

What a sublime dialogue! I clung to every word and vowed never to miss the delightful afternoon rendezvous. But the following days were sunny, and mother insisted I accompany her to the beach.

"María Luisa, dear! Where are you?"

The beach was a constant and marvelous symphony, one that spirited me out of life and all the known world. The only unpleasant note was the cold bath at the crack of dawn. A lifeguard in flannel shorts and a rubber jacket made me dunk my head under water two or three times.

I was pleased with my wardrobe that year. Mother had made me three little button-down blouses, complete with cufflinks and a black neckerchief.

In combination with a gray or black skirt, these shirts marked my transition out of mourning. They gave my thin, lanky frame a slightly androgynous look that I liked without knowing why.

Deep down, I pitied mother for always being bored. Other than the beach, the garden, and the hotel room, she'd only been to the Café de Castilla and the promenade where people strolled at dusk. But what did she know of the pine grove, the ducks' secluded bath, the fenced path leading to the cow pasture, the storage shed with its smell of moisture and cod, the little window from which I spied the divine idyll?

Grown-ups undoubtedly get very bored for want of curiosity about hidden corners or the places that lie behind houses, and they don't dare venture into difficult spots, which were just the ones that I liked most. I was dying to climb the wall and hop over the gate between the two hotels.

When mother deemed I'd taken enough baths and breathed in sufficient sea breeze to last me through the winter, we departed for her nine-day water cure at the spa.

"And we won't see the ocean again until next year?" I asked sadly.

"That's right."

I watched it from the train window until the last glimmer of silver-plated water disappeared between two mountains.

The spa was across the river from the inn, and mother crossed the bridge several times daily: in the morning to take a bath, at eleven to drink a couple glasses of water, and again at five and at seven. She returned from her morning bath all bundled up and got back into bed to *sweat it out*, to use the phrase in fashion.

I didn't go with her and usually stayed behind on the hotel terrace, where the other girls my age would put on airs by imitating their mothers and gossiping about maids and convent schools and their father's latest luxury carriage.

Before long I'd tired of their company and was seeking adventure in the vicinity of the hotel, which had two stories facing the road and five stories over by the river. There was a pigsty with a young sow and eleven grumpy piglets deep in the valley. It was there I met Rufa, a poor devil of a girl who was younger than me but could identify all the trees on the riverbank.

"See that great big one near the bridge? It's got delicious walnuts. You know by the leaves if they're ripe or not. Those over there are chestnuts. I know one whose nuts are sweet as honey."

She called the sow a mama pig and the piglets grunters, and she knew which springs would make you sick and which had water cold as ice.

Through her I met Teresuca and Marichu and Julianuca the blacksmith's daughter. One afternoon we went down to Castle Crag, where there was a grotto from the time of the Moors and water so pure even the king would be amazed.

The four of us were talking about that when we saw some boys approaching us.

"I'm stopping here," said Julianuca. "Those guys are nothing but trouble."

"Me too."

"What? Just because of some boys we're not going to make it to the spring? And what are they going to do to us?"

"You don't want to find out," said Teresuca, full of rustic wisdom.

I insisted that nothing bad could happen because there were three of them and four of us. If they were looking for a fight, we'd defend ourselves.

Still hesitant, the girls accompanied me and Rufa to the spring at the mouth of a cave. I peeked inside and saw what looked like an enchanted palace.

"From the time of the Moors," repeated the girls.

But that wasn't true. Mother Nature had made that place without the aid of human hands. I'd seen an illustration with a caption in my geography textbook: "Cave with stalactites and stalagmites."

The boys were coming closer, laughing and saying dirty words.

"Let's get out of here," urged Rufa.

But I didn't want to leave without filling the canteen mother had given me. The boys closed in on me, always laughing, with a laughter that twisted their mouths into a smirk.

"This little lady is mighty fine down there," said one of them, lifting my skirt when I was filling the canteen and couldn't defend myself.

"Go away!" I shouted.

Another one slipped his rough hands up my thighs and tried to get into my pants. I fought him off kicking and hurled the canteen at his head. Then I ran and ran till I lost the boys at the first houses on the road. I got back to the inn shaking and scared.

Mother was on the terrace with some other ladies, and she got mad when she saw my torn blouse. And where was the canteen?

"No more roving around like a tomboy. For now on you're to stay put at the inn, you hear?"

Yes, fine; what did I care? The boys had given me such a scare, I had no desire to leave the hotel.

Mother had made friends with a pair of old women with an equally elderly brother. According to her, they were saints, the poor darlings. When they were young (had they ever been young?), they went bankrupt and couldn't pay the rent on their shoe store, so the two of them learned to embroider. Every night after closing shop, they'd each embroider a family crest on a bed sheet. The linens store would pay them ten reales apiece for their efforts, a duro in total, enough to make their rent on the store. And they never got married so they wouldn't have to separate.

"And they're really ugly!" I added.

"Dear, you're so foolish! They're not ugly. It's just their eyelashes fell out from embroidering so much. Now they're very rich and own a shoe factory and over ten stores all across the province."

Among mother's other friends was a married couple with a daughter and a niece. The two young ladies danced Sevillanas, and when they couldn't remember a step, they'd practice in the hall while the adults kept time clapping. Mother would watch them but wouldn't applaud.

She also talked a lot to the judge. I don't know his name because everyone called him Your Honor. He was alone at the spa, no family in sight, and was fat with a pointed beard. It was very black, but the embroiderers said he dyed it.

His Honor the Judge was very fond of me and would often call me over to praise my wit.

"Would you like to be my girlfriend, dove?" he had the habit of asking.

I would blush, not sure what to say.

"See, I'm all alone, not a friend in the world. Won't you be my sweetheart? Speak up!"

"Fine," I said, telling him what he wanted to hear.

Why do adults ask so many stupid questions?

"If you'll be my girlfriend, we'll take strolls and drink coffee and play billiards. Come here, I'm going to teach you."

Some gentlemen were taking cannon shots in the billiards room and were amazed to hear the judge say I wanted to learn.

"Who would've thought? Fine then, let her learn. Women these days have taken it into their heads to copy us."

And they all launched into explanations of how to hold the cue and line up a shot. I listened attentively and followed their instructions without hesitation. And I tried so hard, before long I could make a cannon shot.

"What an intelligent girl!"

I was just as delighted as the three men. The game was fun and easy, and the gentle clacking of the ivory balls gave me a new kind of pleasure. I spent half the day playing with the gentlemen, who claimed to have never met a girl as smart and serious as me.

"And cute as a button," added one of them. "Look at the foreshortening of her arm when she stretches it. Pretty as a picture! She's at that ambiguous age when girls on the way to womanhood look like boys."

The following day during the siesta I went downstairs to play billiards with the men. Later I lied to mother, saying I beat them all.

That state of affairs lasted for two or three days until one afternoon I found myself alone with the judge in the billiards room. The other men had finished their water cures and had returned to the station on the two o'clock coach.

"Today we'll play just the two of us," said the judge.

It was his turn first, and on his way to the table he kissed me.

"Your turn, beautiful."

And when I took my shot, he came over and kissed me again.

"And now on the eyes, your lovely eyes," he said, already kissing them.

Another shot, a lot more kisses… By that time he was panting, red as a beet, and blowing bad breath in my face. The longer the game wore on, the more his interest centered solely on me. Finally, he pinned me against the wall and pressed his fat lips to mine, kissing me greedily and practically stuffing his mouth between my teeth. Meanwhile, his gross, bloated tongue was searching for mine, nearly to the point of gagging me. His body was crushing my chest, and one of his knees was wedged between my legs.

"Mother!" I managed to scream, feeling the terror of something horrific.

His Honor the Judge drew back for a moment, giving an obscene laugh that contorted his face. I crawled under the table and tore up the stairs to the room, where mother was taking a nap. I locked the door and slumped into a chair, dazed and shaking and terribly nauseous. Mother sat up in bed.

"María Luisa, is something the matter? What brings you up here? Didn't you know I was sleeping?"

I couldn't answer. My teeth were chattering out of so much disgust.

"Speak up, dear," continued mother. "Did something happen?"

In the end, she got up and took fright seeing me tremble.

"What happened? Do you have a temperature? Answer me!"

"It was the judge. He..."

"Well?"

"He was kissing me..."

Mother opened the balcony shutters to get a good look at me.

"Well? Tell me, dear," she ordered, a crazed expression on her face.

I told her to the best of my ability.

"And what else? Tell me," she said whenever there was a pause.

"That was all."

"Tell me the truth, dear, the whole truth. What else did that swine do to you?"

"I already told you. Then I escaped."

"But there wasn't anything else?"

Apparently, mother would've liked for him to have eaten my tongue; anything less was too little.

I stayed with her all afternoon. She went downstairs several times and asked to speak with the hotel owner, which she did so quietly I couldn't hear them. That night after dinner I went to bed as usual, and mother skipped the lounge to write letters at my bedside.

I was already falling asleep when the two Sevillana dancers and the embroiderers barged into the room with their arms flailing.

"Heavens me, Doña Juanita, we heard about the judge! Is it true?"

I pretended to be asleep while mother repeated what I'd told her. Like her, the old ladies couldn't get enough.

"So that's it? There wasn't anything else?"

"No, *señoras*, fortunately that was all. He must've been afraid somebody would walk in on them."

"Lord, what a man, a veritable satyr. Just awful! At least he didn't disgrace her for life. Poor darling!"

"Just imagine if my husband had been here. There'd have been a tragedy, no doubt. Not to mention the girl is an innocent, an absolute innocent! You think she looks all grown up? Think again, she doesn't know the first thing about... She's always been with me, you know?"

With my eyes closed, I felt those women studying me and, forgetting about the judge's dirty mouth, was satisfied I'd acquired such importance.

The next day I went with mother to the baths and ate breakfast in the room while she rested, wrapped in her blankets.

"I want to go down to the terrace."

"Don't be silly. Didn't you learn your lesson yesterday? To think what could've happened!"

My thoughts were muddled on that point. I knew what had happened, of course, but not what could've happened. The judge and I had been standing up, and certain things only happened in bed. And what to make of the idea that he would've disgraced me for life? Still, I didn't dare ask any questions.

I was starting to get bored when one of the dancers arrived with news that the judge had departed with his suitcases. All the men in the hotel had gotten together, and the owner had begged him to depart.

Mother too was proud of the unexpected importance that had just accrued to us. She spoke to the girl a moment longer and let me accompany her to the terrace.

That's when I knew for sure I was someone. Everybody at the breakfast tables turned to look at me.

"It's her," they whispered, "she's the one."

"She's not pretty," said one man, "but there's something about her. She comes with a kick. Don't you sense it, gentlemen?"

"Quite right, quite right."

The girl at my side was also proud to be holding my hand and didn't let go of me all morning long.

Meanwhile, the shoe dealers' brother was sitting on a bench under the awning, watching me without saying a word or losing me from sight for an instant. He was a quiet man, but at the hour of the siesta, when everyone was sleeping in their room, he paid me and mother a visit.

"So you're telling me that the judge... Caramba! How old is the girl? Just twelve? But she's cute as a button!"

"No," shouted mother. "That's enough about buttons! She's an ugly little thing, the worst of her father and the worst of me. But she's an innocent! If only she weren't such a tomboy!"

"That's exactly it," said the man, with the same obscene laugh I'd heard from the judge. "No wonder she's so attractive! Two or three years from now, you'll have to marry her off or she'll be a public menace."

"I don't see the danger," said mother, grumpily. "On the contrary, I think it'll be hard to find her a husband. We're not wealthy, and she's not good looking."

"Wait and see," he insisted. "We'll chat again then. You ladies will be coming back, won't you? I'm not an old man, and I have a little money in savings... Who knows? In any case, I'm glad things have settled down for you two. I've got to go before my sisters start missing me. The poor dears, they really are a handful!"

And off he went.

"Stay away from that man," ordered mother, alarmed. "You'd better watch out. We don't want a repeat of what happened with the judge. Lord help us, the men around here!"

But her warnings proved unnecessary. The sisters looked away when mother addressed them at the table and no longer wanted anything to do with us. They'd noticed their brother's new fondness for me. The following day they were nowhere to be found. They'd departed without finishing their baths!

THE PAGE BOY LUIS

The autumn ushered in many changes. Casiana no longer lived with us because father had dismissed her over the summer. In her place came Felipa, blond, freckled, and no less brutish than her predecessor.

My bed was moved into the closet off the hall that used to store our dressers, and which mother had furnished with a chest of drawers, a washbasin, and an altar to baby Jesus with some vases of artificial flowers.

Every day from ten until twelve, Doña Sacramento would hear me recite my lessons and teach me to embroider and play the piano, continuing my deficient education. To that end, my parents had bought a second-hand piano and put it in mother's sitting room opposite the vanity with batiste draperies.

And there was yet another development. After dinner, once father left for the café and my brothers for the academy, mother would read a long novel with red covers. I was allowed to stay and listen while Felipa darned socks by the lamplight.

The novel was titled *The Heroes* and was about the conquest of the New World. There was a pretty indian girl who dressed up as a man to serve as page to Don Lope, one of those heroes with feathers in his cap, a breastplate, and a satin band across his chest.

In those days, the page boy Luis was my greatest interest. I wanted to be like her and dress like her, and for the duration of the readings, I thought I really was her. Mother would read slowly and pause to make comments.

"She's got a lot of nerve! I get the feeling she's headed for trouble!"

"Maybe not," Felipa would reply. "Women are braver than men. In my town, when there was a noise in the yard, I was the first one out of bed with a lamp to investigate. My brothers, on the other hand, were full of hot air, all talk and no action."

The page boy Luis was always on horseback alongside his master. He blazed through America's virgin forests, spoke native tongues to strike deals with the tribes, and fired his harquebus at just the right moments. Whenever his master got hurt in an ambush, he would hide him in a cave, prepare him a bed of dry leaves, hunt mud hens for cooking broth, and cure his wounds with a woman's able hands.

"There's no doubt in my mind she's in love with Don Lope," mother would say.

"Not true," I'd object, unable to contain myself. "She isn't in love."

"And what do you know?" said Felipa, smiling smugly. "You'd better believe it. You can see so a mile away!"

"You're wrong. She doesn't love anyone."

"Be quiet," ordered mother. "Lord, what a girl, always has to know everything. What do you know about falling in love? It's already ten. Enough reading for the night. To bed with us!"

And with my head burning under the sun of the tropics, riding on horseback between tribes with the page boy Luis, I'd toss and turn and not fall asleep until late in the night.

The following day I'd have to wake up early to study the lessons for

Doña Sacramento. Then came two hours of Clementi and Bertini in the afternoon, my dreaded needlework in the empty hours until dusk, dinner, and—finally!—the page boy Luis.

I didn't leave the house except to visit the park on Sundays, and those strolls through the Retiro in front of my parents were one of the week's worst tortures.

"Don't twist your feet when you walk, dear... Where did you stain your dress?... Don't hang your arms like a soldier... This child's driving me to an early grave!... Why don't you ever play?"

I couldn't fathom how they expected me to play on my own while walking in front of them.

One day father said, "My friend Paco Garcillán is in Madrid with his family looking for a place to live. In fact, you two should go and see them. They've got a daughter the same age as ours, and they could be friends."

Mother made a face.

"I don't like girls her age having friends. All they do is teach other naughty things they shouldn't know yet. A daughter's best friend is her mother."

Nevertheless, mother and I paid them a visit two days later. For the time being they were living in a modest room on Calle de la Ballesta. The father was out, and the lady of the house was identical to every other mother I'd ever met. The daughters, in contrast, had curly hair and powdered skin and ruffles like two overgrown dolls. To me they looked quite extraordinary.

They were much older than me. Later I found out that Rosalía was eighteen and her sister Nievitas was fourteen. The two of them greeted me effusively.

"Oh, María Luisa, aren't you a darling! But why don't you spruce yourself up a bit, dear? You'd be much prettier. Don't you at least use powder? Who would've guessed it? We thought you'd get more dressed up, living in Madrid and all."

Nieves played the latest music-hall songs at the piano, and Rosalía sang off tune with a raspy voice that I found delightful. Later they joined in on our mothers' conversation, and I noticed that their mother listened to Nievitas and laughed at her jokes, even though she was still little.

All the way home, I was mad with joy over my new friendship and couldn't stop singing the two girls' praises. My brother Juan interrupted me over dinner.

"Enough about your Nievitas already! They must be some primped up country bumpkins."

Mother wasn't far from the thinking the same thing, and I didn't bring them up again, wounded to the heart of my budding friendship.

That night before bed, I knelt to pray at the altar of baby Jesus.

"Thank you, dear Lord, for giving me a friend! I promise to cherish her dearly and not to tell her what anybody else says."

The days passed, and mother said nothing of making another visit. Meanwhile, the page boy Luis fell prisoner to the savages with Don Lope and did all he could to comfort his master. Mother and Felipa were increasingly certain she was in love.

"Definitely not," I protested. "That's not why. Besides, how could the page boy Luis fall in love with a man?"

"Because she's a woman."

"So what? She might as well not be."

They told me to be quiet, but I could tell that mother was secretly pleased.

"This daughter of mine will always be an innocent!"

When I least expected it, mother announced I was going out.

"Since you don't have to study on Saturdays, this afternoon Felipa will take you to visit Nievitas. I'll pick you up at six. Are you happy? And since grandpa died a year and a half ago, you can wear your new dress and blue hat."

What a pity! I'd have been happier wearing my black coat over a skirt and a button-down blouse, but I had to follow orders. In any case, Nievitas thought I looked better in the dress.

"See, dear? Today you're much prettier. Don't you ever curl your hair? It could really suit you."

Those girls knew what colors went best on one's face, what hairstyles to choose for any occasion, what creams made for a good foundation.

Rosalía was calmly crocheting by the balcony and had drawn the lace curtain to see the street. From time to time, she'd gaze out the window.

"She's making a lace trim for my doll's shirt," said Nievitas. "Do you have many dolls? Father brought me a lovely one from Barcelona."

Yes, I too had a pair of dolls. They had faces like fools but were sitting in two chairs in the living room. When their dresses got dirty with too much dust, mother made them new ones.

"I'd prefer to have a horse," I said, picturing the page boy Luis, "a cardboard horse."

They looked at me astonished, and Nievitas broke out laughing like I was the funniest thing in the world. I blushed when I realized she was laughing at me.

Just then Rosalía said, "It's him! He's out there!"

Nievitas ran over to her sister, put her head up to hers, and kissed her affectionately. Rosalía kissed her back, and for a while they were cuddling and acting lovey-dovey. They were such loving sisters! I was watching the scene of sisterly love, already surprised, when Rosalía's angry voice shocked me even more.

"Enough already! Don't be an idiot! I don't even know if he's still out there."

Nievitas came back beside me.

"It was just so he would see us," she explained. "He's dying to kiss her, but he can't!"

"Who?"

"That guy out there. He keeps following her around. Is he gone?"

"No," said Rosalía, "he's still there."

"I've got one, too," Nievitas continued. "Don't think I don't! Anyway, Rosalía drove two boys insane in Logroño."

"What?" I asked, astounded at such a strange case.

"They were crazy for her, but she didn't give them the time of day. Don't they follow you on the street? Of course not, since you don't dress up! I've already had over twenty declarations. Haven't you had any?"

I said no, I didn't know what she meant, and Nievitas broke out again laughing.

"You hear that, Rosalía? María Luisa doesn't know what a declaration is!"

"It's because she's too little."

"Little? She's almost thirteen. Let's see now, how many did I have by that age? You tell her."

"Leave me alone," raged Rosalía, who was still looking at the street and adjusting her hair for no reason.

Refusing to leave a doubt in my mind on the subject of declarations, Nievitas showed me a little box of letters, all of which began the same way: "Señorita, from the instant I first laid my eyes on you…"

They were dreadfully boring. And they were all from her boyfriends?

"Goodness, no! I stood up every last one of them. Mother doesn't want us to have a boyfriend until someone shows up with papers in hand, and whenever a boy makes a declaration, father looks into his social station and whether he comes with good intentions."

All that was Greek to me. I tried to ask about the papers in question, but they drowned me out laughing.

Didn't I know anything? Hadn't I ever read a novel?

Yes, yes; had I ever! In fact, every night mother read a wonderful book out loud. And feeling inspired, I gave them a detailed account of the page boy Luis and Don Lope, of forests home to wild beasts where the sun never shone, of savage indians and the brook that ran by the cave.

At first the two sisters stared at me in shock, then with malicious and mocking smiles, giving each other looks. That threw me off, and I started babbling, not knowing what I was saying.

"Your novel really is wonderful," Nievitas interrupted. "What's it called again, so I won't ever read it?"

From that moment on, I said nothing but nonsense. I tried to make up for the novel by telling them about my school and my classmates, mixing truth and lies in absurd combinations. The sisters wound up laughing like madwomen without making any attempt to hide their ridicule.

Mother finally came, and we left. My face and my ears were burning, and though the cold of the street calmed the flames in my blood, it couldn't keep the fire of my shame from raging on my brow with every new thought of the afternoon's laughter.

"Did you have fun?"

"Yes…"

I no longer had any girl friends! But I still had the page boy Luis, and we would meet again that night after dinner. With him as my friend, what more could I ask for?

A few days later, mother came in from the street saying she had run into Doña Inés and her daughter Rositina.

"Remember? The girl from the spa who wore her hair in curls?"

Yes, yes; I remembered. She was one of those girls who was always boasting about her dresses and her house in Madrid and her father's salary. She didn't interest me in the least.

"Well, they're going to drop by any day now. She's the cutest little thing. She gave me her hand and asked about you."

I don't know why mother found her so charming.

Sure enough, one afternoon Doña Inés and Rositina showed up at our house. We received them in the freezing cold living room, and mother sent for a foot stove to raise their hopes of warming up. Rositina sat on an armchair and flashed me a dimpled smile on her round little face.

"Look how pretty María Luisa's dolls are," pointed her mother.

Rositina stood, gently lifted a doll from her small rolling chair, and kissed her. Remarkable, I thought. I never kissed them.

"She's crazy for dolls," explained Doña Inés. "She's a genuine mother in miniature."

After they left, mother overflowed with praise for Rositina. What a charming girl! She made dresses for her dolls, helped her mother gather the laundry, and always kept an eye on the maids. And she was so clever, she never missed a thing that was said or done in the kitchen. No wonder her mother was always in the know. On days they had guests, Rositina even went shopping with their cook to make sure she didn't short-change them.

Mother wanted to try that with me, so she sent me shopping with Felipa the day before Christmas Eve.

"Pay attention to how much she spends on the fish and the cabbage, and don't go getting distracted!"

I promised to watch every detail, but it just so happened that Felipa went into the fish market at the same time as a man with a monkey on his shoulder. I couldn't focus on anything else. The man had the monkey tethered to a chain, and she was nibbling on peanuts with a daintiness that reminded me of Rositina's.

"What do you mean, you don't know how much the fish weighed or cost?" Mother was furious. "You're worthless, my dear! I give you one job, to check the price of the groceries, and you go off ogling a monkey. You'll never have any common sense!"

The Garcillán family had moved away, and that was the last I saw of Nievitas. On the other hand, mother became good friends with Doña Inés, whom we visited once or twice a week. Rositina was to be my role model.

Until then I knew nothing of feminine affectation, but Rositina showed me its purest essence. Everyone jumped at the chance to praise her.

"What a charming girl! She waters the flowers every day before school, helps her mother prepare tea, butters the bread, checks that nothing's missing on the table. One day she'll make for a delightful housewife!"

But I knew what was going on in her infantile soul and saw clearly in her girlish eyes. I understood that her mother's constant doting and father's coarse masculine ingenuity were forcing her more and more into the role of housewife and out of her true nature and tastes.

"What intuition God puts into a woman's soul," her father would gush. "It's marvelous! Even little girls have a spirit of sacrifice, a need to consecrate themselves to the family's happiness!"

Of course, Rositina *consecrated* herself even more to smoothing the tablecloth with her chubby fingers, and the feminine intuition gradually took form under her father's loving eyes.

But how could the grown-ups not see what was happening? Not even mother noticed the affectation behind everything she said and did. If the charming child had a feminine intuition, it was only for hypocrisy and deception.

One afternoon we were reading a picture book while our parents were talking. All of a sudden, Rositina covered her eyes and started crying.

"What's wrong?" I asked, not very interested because I already knew everything in her was false.

Her father came right away to give her a kiss.

"Rositina, dearest! We won't talk about that anymore. Come with me, won't you? I'm going to buy you a miniature bed with drapes for your big doll."

And he took her by the hand and escorted her out.

"See what an angel of a girl?" said Doña Inés to mother. "We can't say a word about her little brother, who died when she was only five. She gets like that at the slightest thought of him. She's got a heart of gold!"

A few days later, we were having lunch at home when father brought up a sister of his who lived in Galicia.

"She's horrible! Ugly as a devil."

"She doesn't look so ugly to me," I objected. "Isn't that her with you in the photograph in the living room?"

"Yes, but she's dreadfully ugly. When she was little my brothers and I called her old maid and sour puss."

"Poor thing! Well, she doesn't look ugly to me. Right, mother? She's very nice."

"That's right," answered mother with a look of satisfaction. Then she turned to father. "Don't talk that way about your sister. Can't you see? The girl doesn't like you to speak ill of her aunt."

"But why?" asked father, full of masculine innocence.

"Because it's not right. She's a blood relation, after all."

Then father tried making an affectionate joke, looking at me all the while.

"Like it or not, your aunt is the ugliest. She's bald and snub-nosed and…"

Some obscure instinct made me take a different tack.

"No, no; she's not! Your sister's not ugly."

And with childish ease, I burst into tears.

Father took me into his arms, beaming with pride.

"What a good and loving girl! I won't say another word about my sister. I'll even write her a letter so she knows how much you love her!"

I'd never met my aunt and didn't love her whatsoever. But thanks to my newly learned hypocrisy, mother and father were finally doting on me. My insincerity had just been rewarded, and it was an experience I'd never forget.

I detested Rositina with all my might, and I'm sure she didn't like me any better. Other girls went to play at her house, and they'd look at me, whispering and giggling. They were making fun of me!

"I don't want to see Rositina today. I've got a lot to study," I'd tell mother.

She'd let me stay home if I spent an extra hour at the piano.

"Felipa," she'd say, before going out, "check the clock when María Luisa sits down and gets up from the piano, and tell Doña Sacramento how long she practiced."

Those tedious hours of scales found consolation in the page boy Luis. If only mother didn't keep the key to the bookcase!

I always had to wait until evening. The six volumes of the novel were coming to an end. Don Lope was in love with the King's beautiful cousin, whom he married when he returned to Spain.

"See?" I said, satisfied. "He didn't marry the page boy after all."

But the following night a gigantic brute of an infantry captain realized the page was a woman and said he'd die if she refused his hand in marriage.

"Then let him die," was my solution.

The page boy, however, was sad and crestfallen, embarrassed to keep dressing as a man. One day he put on a dress from Don Lope's wife, Alicia, and married the brute.

I refused to hear another word. I lay down in bed, covered my head with the sheet, and cried inconsolably. Now I really was completely alone! I had nobody, nobody, nobody!

And I fell asleep repeating it.

MYSTICISM

Among father's clients at the shop was a family of actors who, incidentally, were always in debt to him.

Maybe that's why barely a week went by without them sending us an envelope with three slips of green paper good for seats at the theater. My brothers Ignacio and Juan took turns going with me and father, and mother never went because she didn't like going out at night.

The theater made me giddy for days after the show. The music, the costumes, the set bathed in spectral moonlight or bright sunshine, the bells of a distant shrine—all of it was a magical reality, and I refused to believe for an instant that the action on stage wasn't true.

Returning home long after midnight, I'd walk arm in arm with father, immersed in an emotional silence, the harmonies of the music still washing over me. My brother and father would smoke and say little, and our footsteps would echo in the solitary streets where watchmen were patrolling with lanterns and nightsticks.

One night passing one of the better illuminated alleys, I noticed a quiet rustling, shadows moving in open doorways, strange forms

126

on balconies, hisses and muffled laughter. A woman in a nightgown emerged from an entrance and started coming towards us.

"Come here, handsome," she said, tugging my brother by the arm.

Ignacio gave her a shove, and she staggered backwards and let out a hiss.

"What was that?" I asked, frightened. "What did she want?"

"Be quiet," ordered father, turning to my brother. "This is no place to be at this hour of the night."

"Or any hour," added Ignacio. "It's the same in every house!"

I pricked up my ears and gleaned just enough for my blood to run cold. How awful! So there were women who did *that* for money? And men who sought them out like they were going for coffee? God, what a fright! And everyone knew about it. Mother, father, my brothers: they all were in the know. Up until that moment, everyone but me was aware of it, and they went about their business, smiling and happy. They didn't die of shock and horror!

I barely slept, tossing and turning to find the coolness in my sheets. I wanted to die! Yes, to die and go to Heaven, which I pictured like the dazzling light that showed through puffy clouds in certain paintings. There'd be no end to the theater's music in Heaven, and the angels would take turns singing.

It was already Lent, and mother took me to mass some afternoons. We usually went to our parish church, but one day we took a tram to a convent in a distant neighborhood.

A tall iron grille divided the modern convent church into two sections. It was nearly empty when we got there, with only six or seven people in the area reserved for the public. But almost immediately two beautiful figures dressed in white emerged from the little doors on either side of the altar, their faces covered in veils. They reached the center of the altar with their tunics trailing behind them in harmonious folds of white fabric. Kneeling down together, they bowed to the floor, then rose to take their seats facing one another at the ends of two pews. Another pair repeated the same ceremony, then another and another. This went on until the pews were full of white-clad nuns.

"I counted one hundred and fourteen," whispered mother in my ear.

Organ music filled the church, and a nun rose from the pews to pray for a while in Latin as if she were singing. The others responded, then another nun rose to say her prayer. One by one, they all took their turn.

I was entranced. So this was a convent! Everyone in white, in lovely theatrical habits; everyone talking to God face to face in the sweetest of voices and the language of Heaven. And this was the world, on the other side of the grille, with its two-faced Rositinas, its stupid Nievitas, its horrible women grabbing men by the arm at night, its dreadful men and their obscene laughter. And even its page boys, who despite being handsome and good, ended up marrying barbarous captains.

There was no need to die to leave everything behind. All you had to do was enter a convent, live there for years like a ghost amidst organ music and clouds of incense, and one day continue the same life in Heaven. I couldn't wait to tell mother!

"I want to be a nun," I declared upon leaving the church.

"What?" asked mother, who had trouble hearing on the street.

"I said, I want to be a nun. When I grow up, I'm entering a convent."

"You don't know what you're saying! I can see it now. You'd make the perfect nun, so docile and obedient!" And cutting off the conversation, mother crossed the square. "I think they sell apricots over there, and your father just loves them."

That night after dinner, mother read the silly potboiler that had replaced the tale of the page boy Luis. Felipa was delighted because the novel featured a maid who stole her mistress's suitor and prompted her to enter a convent.

"Well done," I said. "I want to join a convent just like her."

"Enough nonsense," ordered mother. "What a silly thing to think! You don't have to be a nun to be a good girl. You can be good in the world."

"I'm tired of the world!"

Mother laughed, I was being so dramatic.

"You must be insane! Really, the things you come up with!"

Felipa chimed in, too.

"That's the type of thing people can say when they've already had their fun. Isn't that right, ma'am?" she asked mother. "But not a thirteen-year-old girl who's only glimpsed life through a pinhole."

"So what? I've seen enough to be tired of the world."

Mother told me to be quiet and went back to reading, but I was too caught up in my thoughts to listen. If they wouldn't let me be a nun, I'd still live like one, not going on visits or strolls. I'd pray and study and go with father to the theater, for I didn't doubt for an instant that the theater was an integral component of secluding oneself from the world. And I'd give up fighting with mother over dressing me this way or that.

I repeated the verses I'd learned from an image of Saint Teresa in mother's bedroom: "I live, I'm not living in me, and high is the life that I'm yearning..."

I decided to embark on my monastic life the following day. I'd get up at dawn, just as I always had, so that wouldn't be a big sacrifice, and I'd pray for half an hour at the foot of the altar and do penance crawling on my knees in the hallway until my kneecaps got sore and spurted blood and my whole body shook with a painful pleasure.

I did exactly as I'd planned, adding a white bedspread on my head. Dragging it behind me, it vaguely resembled a nun's pretty tunic. I went up and down the silent, shadowy hallway, behind whose doors my parents, my brothers, and Felipa were still sleeping.

Ten times I made it to the end of the hall, when all of a sudden I heard father's voice.

"What in the world are you doing, María Luisa?" He was looking at me dumbfounded from his bedroom door. "What are you doing up at this hour of the morning? Are you out of your mind? Go back to bed, dear!"

I stood up, scared and surprised, trudged back to bed with the bedspread under my arm, and pulled the covers up over my eyes. Heavens me! What was going to happen next? What would mother say, and how would I answer?

But nobody said anything, because before it was time to get out of bed, a telegram arrived from America to say one of my brothers' uncles had died and named them his heirs.

The news was so momentous, no one thought to ask what I was doing in the hallway at four in the morning wrapped in my bedspread. My parents and brothers spent breakfast talking, arguing, and making plans. By evening, it was decided: the following week, my brothers would depart for America.

The newly deceased uncle had left behind a publishing house that was to come under their management, and they'd probably have to stay overseas. Father was giving in to the idea. The boys had their fortune in America, and he had nothing to offer them but a mediocre life like his own. In the blink of an eye, a whole bunch of modern luxury stores had opened in Madrid, and our shop couldn't compete without big sacrifices and a new source of capital.

Starting the next day, a seamstress set up shop in the house to help mother make shirts and underwear for my brothers. The sewing machine was constantly humming, the shop boy came and went running errands, Ignacio and Juan tried on new suits at the sitting room mirror, and mother complained about me.

"This girl knows nothing! You're old enough to help us."

It made matters worse that I was completely unoccupied, as Doña Sacramento had moved to Valencia to live with relatives. I would read and make paper birds and wander to and fro, not knowing where I could go to remain mostly out of sight.

"It's hard to believe," said the seamstress. "In other households, the girls her age always lend me a hand, and this one, so tall and so serious, could be sewing on buttons."

There was a bookcase with glass doors in father's office. He never read, so it was mother who retrieved the novels that stoked her and Felipa's imaginations. One time I found the keys hanging in the lock and could peruse the titles at my leisure: *The Criterion, The Martyr of Golgotha, Mary, or the Love-Struck Queen, The History of Spain, The Bible…* There were small, unbound books on a higher shelf, and who knows how and when they'd found their way to my house. *History of the Religions…*

The title startled me. Religions? So there was more than one? I took down the book from the shelf and tried to skim through it. The pages were still uncut! Nobody in the house, neither my parents nor my brothers, had ever been curious to know what it said.

I went back to my bedroom with the book in hand and sat under the window overlooking the patio. The reading thrust me into a sea of turmoil. It laid out plain as day the origins of man's religious impulse, the legends and historical accounts forming the base and foundation common to all religions, the passage of symbols from one religion to another, their meaning evolving until only the forms remain. A luminous beacon had just lit up in front of me, and my eyes couldn't stand that light showing me a heaven and earth empty of divinities.

"Mother?" I asked her that night when the seamstress had gone and she was putting away her sewing. "Tell me, are there religions other than ours?"

"Yes," she replied, "but they're all lies."

"And the people who believe in them," I started saying.

"The people who believe in them are doomed. They go straight to Hell."

"But what if they don't know about Jesus's coming?"

131

"It doesn't matter, they're doomed," she repeated, fierce.

"That's not fair, because it's not their fault. It's atrocious! I can't believe that God would…"

"Look, dear, I've had enough of this foolishness. I've got more serious things on my mind."

Evidently, mother thought my brothers' underwear was more important than the soul's immortality.

For days before and even after they departed, I read and reread the book and felt it leaving a deep imprint on my spirit. So there weren't any saints or Virgin Mary or angels or demons. But in the end, there was a God. Of that I had no doubt regardless of what the book said. I felt his eyes watching over me and his almighty hand resting on my shoulder. I had nobody—Lord, nobody—in whom to confide my troubles, no kindred spirit to tremble together, no dear voice to echo my own, no friendly hand…

"Whoever has God lacks nothing; God alone suffices."

I repeated those words over and over. I'd learned them from a new prayer book mother gave me for my saint's day, from which I'd only been able to read a few poems by Saint Teresa and Saint John of the Cross. And my mystical soul, momentarily lost in the blinding light of historical truth, turned anew towards a God, but now to one who'd care for me like a compassionate, watchful father.

My brothers left home in those days of religious turmoil, and I didn't mind a bit. On the contrary, they were four fewer eyes to watch over me and misunderstand my life's inner logic. I felt my freedom grow, as if two strong, brash bonds that were pinning me down had come undone.

A young teacher named Señorita Clara replaced Doña Sacramento, and I took piano lessons from Rositina's teacher and French lessons from a little old French woman who came over twice a week.

Señorita Clara was shocked at the questions I asked the moment I started to trust her.

"But who told you Hell doesn't exist? In any case, the Holy Mother Church says there is a Hell, so we'd better believe in it without asking questions."

"Why?"

"Because we're Catholics."

All the same, Señorita Clara was much more intelligent than Doña Sacramento and tried to direct my attention to other topics besides religion. I studied literature and grammar, art history and natural history.

"Since you're so fond of nature, you ought to learn to identify plants and flowers."

Books were the one thing in life that interested me, and Señorita Clara was amazed at how easily I absorbed everything I studied. Well, almost everything. I showed the same ineptitude for arithmetic and geometry as when I was younger.

As for needlepoint and the piano, they too were still arcane and incomprehensible to me.

"Don't you see? Those are exactly the things you need to know, much more than the ones you like," said Señorita Clara. "The young lady who knows how to play the piano and embroider is much better off in *high society*. It's the only way for a well-bred girl to net a suitor."

"I don't want to *net* a suitor."

"But surely you want to get married," she insisted. "For a woman there's no other path but marriage." At that point she gave a deep sigh. "And in marriage, you'll have to keep the accounts, manage your husband's money, mend the used clothes so they last longer, tailor the new ones so they come out cheaper, and entertain your husband playing trifles at the piano."

"He can entertain himself," I protested. "I don't plan on ever getting married!"

"Oh, my dear, you don't know how bitter life is for a single woman. She's a constant burden, and everyone mocks her!"

"That's just what I tell her," added mother, who had the habit of coming in at the end of the lesson. "Woman's path is marriage, and everything she studies and learns should be with a view to the future, to make the man happy who chooses her as his companion, and to be a good mother to her children."

That all weighed on my heart like a marker on a grave. Some nights I had trouble falling asleep and would wrestle with the sheets watching the shadows creep across the bedroom walls.

Ever since my brothers had left for America, mother kept the oil lamp in front of baby Jesus lit at all times, and its flickering irritated my taut nerves and prevented me from dozing off.

"Dear God," I thought to myself, "I don't want to be a mother, don't want to get married or take piano lessons or sew or keep accounts! All I want is to read, to read all the books in the world. But I can't tell a soul because everyone gets mad and yells at me."

One night I was in the midst of my sad monologue when I heard a familiar voice in my head that would speak to me at times while I was lying awake at night.

"Want to see how I draw back the curtain? Look at the door, pay attention."

I widened my eyes and heard the metal rings scraping against the iron bar while an invisible hand opened the curtain to reveal the blackness in the hallway.

The terror left me paralyzed and sweaty, my heart pounding out of my chest.

"I'm scared! Help me, God, I'm scared out of my wits!"

And in the end, I finally fell asleep.

THE NOVEL OF MY LIFE

Señorita Clara discovered I had a knack for drawing and painting, and after teaching me what little she could, she honorably declared herself inferior to the talent she perceived in me.

"You should look for a teacher. I think María Luisa will make something of herself if she takes her time learning good technique. She's got more than enough imagination and sense of color."

But father would hear nothing of it.

"She's got no use for learning to paint. What a silly idea! She already knows more than enough to doodle on postcards like other young ladies these days."

Mother was of the same opinion, and I was confined to endlessly copying the ivy leaves and mouths and noses that came in the notebooks Señorita Clara bought.

Tía Manuelita was my aid in that struggle. One day she appeared with a lovely book of drawings.

"It didn't cost a penny. There are landscapes and figures, and you can copy them on this drawing paper, which I bought from a painter lad who lives in the main-floor boarding house."

"She'd be better off practicing the piano," said mother. "Rositina can already play three pieces. This one ought to be ashamed of herself!"

"But I haven't got an ear for it," I argued. "The teacher said so himself, I haven't got an ear for it."

"Nor have you shown any interest or good will or desire to learn," mother continued. "This child is a constant failure!"

What mother didn't know, and what she certainly wouldn't have liked, is that I wrote literary compositions. Señorita Clara was pleased with me, even if she did chide me on occasion.

"Theme," I wrote in my notebook, "Greek Civilization."

By the next day I'd filled several pages with painstaking descriptions of ancient temples and women's hairstyles, marvelous pleated tunics, marble fountains with drinking doves, and the prayers of the vestal guardians of the sacred flame.

"Where did you do your research?" asked Señorita Clara, marveling at my detailed knowledge.

"Nowhere in particular. That's just how I picture it. There's an almanac in the dining room with some Greek women descending a staircase to the sea."

"Better syntax and less inspiration," she'd say, making a correction here and there in my hurried account.

Still, I was glad I could write whatever came into my head. It was like something deposited deep in my soul had risen to the surface transformed into diamonds, like I'd shrugged off a weight that had been crushing me all my life, like I'd discovered the secret doorway to true liberty. I could say everything on my mind without some banal voice mocking my dreams.

Sometimes I'd make a sketch to illustrate my literary pieces.

"Theme: The Snow."

And I pasted a sheet of Canson into my composition book and drew our balcony with its intricate ironwork banister festooned with snow. An unlucky sparrow had frozen to death on the ground, its icy little feet pointing rigidly skyward.

"The girl's got a good imagination," said father when he saw it. "Too bad her brothers are so inept, because she's got no use for that kind of talent."

Tía Manuelita asked me for the drawing and carefully rolled it up to take it with her.

"You'll be able to put it back soon enough," she explained, seeing how it saddened me to remove it from my notebook. "It's for the painter lad to see."

A few days later she asked for more.

"He said to give me everything you've got, and he thinks it's a shame your parents won't get you a good teacher. They're so narrow-minded!"

But when in view of her good will I ventured to read her a literary piece of which I was especially proud, she turned out to be just as rigid.

"Enough gibberish! That's the last thing you should be studying. You girls, that literary hogwash makes you into romantics and ruins you for life. Your parents had better be watching the silly things you learn from that vulgar *señorita*."

Fearing an indiscretion on her part would put an end to my new-found pleasure, I didn't say another word about my literary projects. As for her, she seemed to forget them and didn't bring them up again.

Instead she set about nagging my parents over the painter lad.

"He's a real talent, that one! I think he'd give her lessons for free. He's so impressed with her drawings."

"In that case," said mother, always keen to take advantage of a hand-out, "who knows? Drawing comes in handy for embroidering and tailoring clothes. And if it's free…"

Father gave in after much discussion since it wouldn't cost him a penny for me to learn to draw. As for painting, there was no talk of the matter, nor did it so much as cross their minds. I had no use for it!

One afternoon, Tía Manuelita came over with the painter, a young man over the age of twenty. He was tall and slender and wore a loose shirt and black neckerchief. I'd never seen a man quite like him.

He greatly flattered mother with a kiss on the hand and greeted me with a handshake as if I were a grown-up. How embarrassed I was to see him leafing through my drawings!

"Not bad," he said in place of the praises Tía Manuelita had reported. "Not bad. Too much blending. The obsession of those who've not mastered the line. From now on you'll work entirely in pencil, even for the shading. Who's teaching you to draw?"

He glanced at Señorita Clara's reference drawings and smiled politely.

"She said this was all she knew," I said in her defense.

Starting the following day, Jorge Medina came over for an hour every afternoon. Besides teaching me how to draw, he lent me books and talked to me. That was the best part!

His voice was clear and youthful, his hands delicate and womanly, his gestures like mine, still those of an adolescent. There were even times when I was the stronger and more spirited of the pair.

He brought me a romantic novel that I liked a lot. A beautiful Jewess had been kidnapped by an Arab and was living in a harem in Baghdad amidst censers and perfumes.

"Jorge, what's a censer?"

"A piece of pottery that looks like this ... and this," he said, drawing while he talked. "You put the embers here and the incense or storax over them."

"And what's a harem?"

"Oh my! Aren't you full of questions! Well, it's a house where a rich Moor keeps his women."

Realizing I wasn't supposed to have asked that, I blushed to the roots of my hair.

Other times he spoke about his village. He was a Galician, and describing the inlets and valleys of his homeland, his face lit up with the flame of enthusiasm that was always burning inside him. I'd finally found a soul sensitive like mine to the beauty of nature! With Jorge I lost my timidity and constantly longed to know more. What were Galician granaries like? Why did the women go barefoot? What color was the water in the inlets?

He brought me novels by quality authors that had to be read carefully, without skipping the descriptions.

"Just wait for the second chapter. There's a sunrise in the Pas River Valley. It's the moment when the clouds turn pink and the trees outlined in India ink start to take on color. A painter must read a great deal. Sometimes an author sees things a painter wouldn't notice in a landscape. He's got a different view of life and color that completes our own."

I listened in awe and admiration. How well he said what I'd only ever thought! With him I dared to speak about my summer holidays, about the ocean I adored with a primal instinct and revered with inexplicable devotion, about my impassioned memory of Tía Teresa's park, to which I'd never gone back.

"But here we are, nothing to see but the Plaza de Matute."

Jorge said there was beauty in all things. In his landlady's house there was an authentic piece of Louis XV furniture. Nobody had a clue how it had ended up there. For his part, he'd sought solace from many a sorrow gazing for entire hours at its legs' perfect lines.

One day I told him, "You're the only friend I've ever had. Isn't it good to have a friend?"

"It is," he said, squeezing my hand.

And I realized how lonely I was before I met him and whenever he departed.

Sometimes he wouldn't come over for two or three days while he was painting in the mountains. When he got back, he'd tell me about his trip, about the landscapes he'd admired and his chats with the shepherds. The mountains of Castile had every tone of violet, from pale mauve to dark Lenten purple. One day when I was older, we'd go there together, and if that meant we had to get married, so be it.

No, I didn't want to ever get married. All I wanted was to travel and to read widely, to paint and not to have children.

We could speak frankly of such things, for there wasn't a guilty thought in our friendship.

Be that as it may, Felipa was spying on us, and once I caught her eavesdropping outside the door. She also took every opportunity to embarrass me in front of Jorge.

"Filthy girl! What could she possibly do in bed to rip her nightgowns right down the middle? What a strange child!"

Another time mother said there was smoke in the hallway.

"It's coming from the girl's room," said Felipa, mockingly. "Don't you know what she's got on her dresser? Wait and I'll show you."

And she came back with a little tin box I'd turned into a censer, filling it with ashes and embers to burn a bit of lavender. Until Jorge arrived that afternoon, my room was the Moorish harem owner's bedroom.

They all burst out laughing, mother got mad, and I heard a hint of mockery in Jorge's laughter and started to cry.

"What a girl," fretted mother, turning to Jorge. "You haven't got the slightest idea how I've suffered with her! She's been a tomboy since the day of her birth. Since I was so sick after the delivery, it was over half an hour before they could see to her properly. 'It's a boy! It's a boy!' they said, with all the bawling. How many times have I had to repeat it? 'It's a boy! It's a boy!' But then she goes and acts like a silly little girl. Why else would she make a fire in her room?"

With childhood's lack of perspective, I thought I'd die, they'd made such a fool of me. And it was my first time crying in front of Jorge. Dear Lord, why had I cried? How embarrassing! I didn't want to see Jorge ever again. That was the end of the drawing lessons.

The next day Felipa, loathsome Felipa, looked at me smugly. But Jorge came, I sat for my lesson, and at first he didn't say a thing.

"You mustn't imitate others," he finally explained while correcting a line. "Understand? Nobody, living or fictional. Instead, it's up to each of us to develop the most original aspects of our personality within our life circumstances."

I didn't understand him very well, though I did realize he was alluding to the events of the previous day. Instead of imitating the Moor in his harem or the captive Jewess, I had to be myself, María Luisa herself, to be what I was and to be it completely.

Yes, but I didn't much know what that was because I'd never viewed myself from the outside. For that I would have to imagine myself as the heroine of a story and see it in writing. Aha! I would write my novel.

"The Novel of My Life," I wrote on the first page of a notebook after ripping out a page that had already been used. And after that: "María Luisa lived in her parents' castle…"

Obviously, that wasn't true, but it didn't make a difference if I lived in a castle or on the Plaza de Matute, and the former was prettier.

Then I took a horse ride with Jorge, who told me about trees and mountains in that special way of his. I tried to remember his words as best I could, unable to find any better ones. A little later, in a dialogue I considered especially lovely, I told him how sad I'd been before meeting him because the other girls I knew were fools who thought only of marrying and being mothers. But not me. Then Jorge asked what I planned to do when I grew up. "Sail the seven seas," was my grandiloquent response.

Jorge said it would be best to get married so we'd never have to separate, and I agreed on the condition we didn't have children. I'd never do anything so filthy! Together we'd sail the seven seas.

In two or three days, I filled up half the notebook with my small, cramped handwriting. Our maidservant Felipa was a nasty tattler, and my parents barely loved me because mother had seven heart conditions. And I was extremely good looking, because that didn't make a difference, either.

It was nearly summer, and the preparations for our departure were underway at home. Mother had the complicated task of packing our trunk, and she protested whenever I brought a bundle of books or papers.

"There's no more room. Those things have to go in the bottom, and it's already full."

"But I forgot…"

"Well, there's nothing to be done. You'll have to leave it here."

But when nobody was watching, I managed to slip in the notebook, some drawings, and the story of Elisa. Mother wouldn't notice because I was careful to cover them with clothes.

But we got to the ocean, and unpacking the trunk, the notebook, the drawings, and the storybook were nowhere to be found. Had mother removed them?

For days, I dreaded the consequences of losing the notebook. Still, time went on, and since father said nothing in his letters and mother gave no indication she'd read my novel, I finally calmed down and even forgot about it. It must've been back in Madrid!

Twenty baths on the beach, a stay at the spa without seeing a soul from the year before, nearly two months in the town in Ávila province, and we returned to the city in October.

Jorge was highly complimentary of the sketches I brought back: a shovel and bucket on the sand, a rocky outcrop against the sky, the spa's façade, the bridge, the walnut tree.

"Well done, child, you've made good progress. Your lines are growing more confident. You're destined to go far, I know it."

I went back to having lessons with Señorita Clara, the piano teacher, and the little old French lady, and Jorge would come every evening an hour before dinner to correct my drawings at the dining room table. Then he'd talk to my parents, bringing us news of the latest debut at the Apollo or a recently published book or an exhibition that was still in preparation.

"If you ask me," said father, "he's an empty-headed snob! He never talks about anything serious!"

Felipa said something even worse.

"He knows the girl's an only child, and let's put it this way, he wants to see if he gets any nibbles."

Unlike me, mother caught her drift.

"He'd better not get his hopes up! Did he think I'd raise a daughter for a lowlife like him? That's the last thing I need!"

"Mark my words, he's trying to flatter her," Felipa insisted. "If only my place in Heaven were so certain!"

I listened in terror. If Jorge were to stop coming over, I'd end up friendless all over again.

"But mother, that's not true. He's not a lowlife, I promise!"

"Be quiet, dear. Really! That's just we need, a boyfriend for a fourteen-year-old girl!"

Felipa was looking at me, and something in her evil eyes sent a shiver down my spine. What was that wicked woman thinking?

The following evening, mother called me into her sitting room while I was studying.

"María Luisa, come here."

She was sitting at the hearth, resting her elbow on a nightstand where she had a notebook. She looked at me coldly and didn't say a word.

"Did you write this?" she finally asked.

It was "The Novel of My Life." I thought I felt the earth teeter under my feet.

"So the scoundrel said he wants to marry you. Wonderful! Fourteen years old and married to a bohemian! Isn't that lovely? And that's how you repay our sacrifices, giving you an education and spending beyond our means, all so you can find a proper husband and not have to struggle in life. That's why you raise kids, or so I was told. And you, ungrateful, what made you go on about whether you want kids? You're killing me blow by blow! Any day now I'll keel over."

I was dying of shame and sobbing too hard to respond. I clearly remembered the novel's every word. It was awful what was happening to me! Why hadn't they discovered the notebook till then? It didn't take long to find out. Felipa had been holding onto it since the summer, and she hadn't wanted to rattle my parents until she saw if the lousy artist got tired of waiting around for father's money.

It was already dark out, and it wouldn't be long before Jorge came for my lesson. Mother turned on the light to see the clock.

"He's about to get here. I'm going to leave you alone with the wretch, and you'll tell him not to come back, that you don't like him and are done taking lessons. Understood? I'll be in the closet and will hear every word."

Dear Lord! My heart ached over the injustice we were about to commit, and I pitied myself for losing the one friend of my short life.

The doorbell rang twice, and we headed for the dining room.

"You know what you've got to say," whispered mother before going into the closet. "And you'd better hope your father doesn't get home and see him, because he's liable to knock him down the stairs!"

She left me there alone, trembling and frightened. It didn't take long for Jorge to notice that I was acting strangely.

"Where's your mother? Did she go out?"

"No… Yes… I don't want a lesson. I don't want to take them anymore."

"But why?"

"Just because."

"Did something happen?"

"No, but I don't want to be your friend anymore, and I don't want to marry you because I'm too little."

Jorge started laughing.

"Of course not! How could we get married now?"

"Not ever, because I don't love you, not at all anymore. Go on, get out!"

Jorge realized something extraordinary had happened and turned to see the door where I was staring.

"Are they kicking me out?" he asked, growing pale. "Tell me, what happened?"

"I don't know," I said, looking anxiously at the door.

"They told you what to say, didn't they? Fine then, I guess this is goodbye."

He left without shaking my hand, and when the door shut, I felt myself getting sick and thought I was going to die. But nothing happened, and I went on living without Jorge just like before I ever met him.

THE ANCIENT ELDER

Father too got an inheritance from the uncle who died in America, a house in a town of La Mancha. One cold winter day, the three of us went to take possession of the property. The key was being held by the man who accompanied us from the station.

It was a big, sad town with yellow clay houses and narrow streets, more potholes than sidewalks. Every so often we came upon a house with barred windows, balconies, and a stone coat of arms above a studded door, and every time I whispered, "Don't let it be this one, don't let it be this one." But one time the man stopped in front of a door and announced, "This is it."

It was a large, run-down mansion, two stories tall, with bulky old furniture and stuffed cats and birds in every room. It smelled cold and dank, the floor tiles were wet and crumbling, and sheets of faded wallpaper hung from the ceilings. Cat eyes stared at us from every table, my parents' voices echoed in the inhospitable house, and the cold made me shiver, forcing me into the garden's faint winter sunshine.

The frozen branches of an immense elder tree spread out over the abandoned, weed-filled plot.

"It's over a hundred years old," said the man who came with us. "When it flowers in the month of May, you can smell it all over town, and the shade in the garden is simply divine. What's bad is that nothing else does well here on account of the tree. Vegetables need sunlight."

The yard out back had a henhouse and a rabbit hutch, the latter of which was home to a flea-ridden mastiff puppy.

"I brought him," explained the man. "My dog had a litter, and I thought you folks would want a puppy. A big house like this needs a guard at all times."

I saw that mother detested the gift and was keeping quiet just to be polite. As for me, I set about making plans for the dog. I would bathe him in the garden tank, give him milk from my breakfast, and make him wear a collar. Most importantly, I'd think up the perfect name for him. And when he got big, which doesn't take long for a dog, he'd follow me everywhere. I'd take him for walks around the town, and he'd be my friend and companion. A silent, good-natured friend now that I had no others.

I went back to examining the elder with its enormous trunk and rough bark. What a marvelous thing is an ancient tree! None of us knew the uncle who died in America; none of us, that is, but the tree. His mother must've come and nursed him under its shade when he was just an infant, and he'd taken his first steps clinging to its trunk and waddling like a duckling. And the tree had also met his parents when they were little, and it knew their names and the days when they died. Now that everyone had abandoned it, the tree was still there, waiting for its new owners and ready to shelter us in summer in its cool, protective shade.

"The girl likes the elder," said the man, seeing me stand in front of it all that time as if I were hypnotized. "It's a fine tree with quality wood.

The day you cut it down you'll get two carts of firewood, good money in the winter."

What a brute of a man! It was a good thing the poor elder couldn't hear him. But maybe it *could* hear, because nobody knows what a tree can understand.

We settled into the house, and Felipa arrived the next day with bricklayers, painters, and carpenters close on her heels. They started tearing down wallpaper, putting up partitions, laying baseboards, painting doors and windows, all without any rhyme or reason, upsetting the house's tranquil appearance with gold fixtures and loud colors that clashed with the austere simplicity of the floor tiles.

Mother was living from one surprise to the next.

"This closet has a dinner service! The door in the hall leads to the attic staircase! Come look what I found in the drawer of the big side table!"

But no one paid attention to the poor little puppy, who would've died of hunger and fleas if it hadn't been for me... Although I never could rid him entirely of the pests. Mother wouldn't hear a word on the subject.

"Leave me in peace! We've got to see if somebody wants him. If not, we'll have to figure out what to do with him. In any case, I don't want him in the house!"

The town's leading families came over to meet us: the doctor and his wife; the convent priest and his mother; the wife of the pharmacist whose shop was on the square, with four of their eight children; the coronel's widow, who had five daughters.

They all came to offer their services. If we needed anything at all, we knew where to find them. But what were we going to need? And could they really offer anything? Then they talked about maids, about the dire state of things, about the hardships and worries of bringing up kids.

"Is this the only one you've got? Aren't you lucky," said the pharmacist's wife. "I've given birth to twelve, and eight are still living. Thirteen mouths to feed! Pray you should never have to endure what we do at home. When one kid has shoes, another's missing socks. And then you have to pay for school and for books. My husband and I work like dogs. You'd better believe it, *señora!*"

Meanwhile her four kids had set about stripping the new black and gold wallpaper off the living room walls with their fingernails. There were three boys and a girl who was smaller than me. Later they fought over a ball of goat hair they'd ripped out of a chair and took turns sliding down the handrail on the staircase. The smallest boy hit the sphere at the end and fell face first on the tiles in the foyer.

Our mothers came running at the sound of his screaming and scooped him up off the ground. Sobbing, his siblings explained what had happened, and their mother grabbed them by the hair. She shouted louder when she saw the wound on her youngest son's head. Mother rubbed it with arnica and gave the boy a bandage.

Once the front door shut behind them, she threw her hands in the air.

"Lord almighty, what a family! If they take to coming over very often, they'll be the end of me. I'm in no condition!"

"Those kids are idiots," I added. "All they did was fool around."

Mother went back to the downstairs living room, where she was mending a tear in a lace curtain, and I joined her in the heat of the foot stove.

"Poor woman," she continued. "The poor dears are sacrificing themselves to raise all those children. I heard the husband makes copies at night because the pharmacy doesn't pay the bills."

At that point I remembered a pressing question that had often worried me.

"Tell me, mother, do parents have to sacrifice themselves to raise their children even if the kids are fools?"

"Of course, dear. The more foolish the kids, the more the parents have to work and suffer. It's only natural."

"And when those kids grow up, they'll get married and have children of their own? And struggle the same way to bring them up?"

"Yes, child. It's the law of God, and we must obey."

"So everyone just has to raise kids and more kids?"

"The things you come up with! Yes, that's right."

"Who knew," I exclaimed, deeply disappointed over the aim of human existence. "If that's all there is, then I don't want…"

But I kept on reflecting and found a solution.

"It seems to me there must be some point to it. Right, mother?"

Mother was so absorbed in her needlework, she didn't answer me. I could see out the window to the garden, where the elder was swaying in the harsh wind of a February day.

"Listen, I've got it. I know the point."

"Of what?"

"Of everybody raising so many kids."

"You do? Well, you'd be better off giving me those scissors that fell."

I picked up the scissors without changing the subject.

"I think people have kids because every so often, among all those who are born and raised, a baby is born who grows up to be a writer, a painter, a wise man, a bishop, or something of the sort. Of course, he doesn't have to raise kids of his own, and everyone born before him was just to prepare the way for his birth."

Mother's curiosity finally got the better of her, and she started laughing when she understood what I meant.

"Aha! So that's where you're going with this. And naturally, you think you're the bishop, and three or four generations of us were born just to raise you. Very good! You, on the other hand, can just slop around paint and read novels. Humble you're not, dear."

I shut my mouth, thinking that even if I weren't a bishop, there was still a good chance I could escape the terrible obligation of raising stupid kids like the pharmacist's wife.

Within a week we knew half the town, and the coronel's widow had even invited me over for lunch. Her daughter was in bed with a tumor and wanted to meet me.

Much to my surprise, mother consented right away.

"Yes, yes; run along. There's going to be a lot of bustle at the house tomorrow because we've got someone coming to lay out the garden, and there'll be carts of topsoil and sand."

The sick girl was my age, and her name was Sol, a very pretty name indeed. She was pale and thin after two months of not leaving bed. She was very beautiful but dumb as a doornail.

"Does she dress nicely?" she asked whenever we were talking about another girl.

Who knows what she thought of my outfits, which weren't particularly elegant. Surely when I left she told her mother I was a terrible dresser.

I told her about the puppy and the elder in the garden, but it was as if she didn't hear me.

"Have you seen Rosarito's coral necklace?" she interrupted. "You know, the pharmacist's daughter? Well, mine's got bigger beads. Ask mother to show you."

The day started to feel long, and I bid them farewell at suppertime. Walking alone on the street was new and extremely satisfying. From the square you could see the elder's bare crown over the garden walls. But how come today you couldn't see it?

They'd left the door open, and I crossed the foyer without being seen.

The elder was lying on its side on the broken earth! It looked bigger and thicker than when its branches served as a canopy. Father and the gardener were smoking atop the rough old bark of its trunk.

"What happened, father? What happened? Who knocked down the tree?"

They weren't paying attention, and the questions poured out of me ever more anxiously. What had happened to the ancient elder, the poor tree who knew the uncle from America when he was just an infant?

"What happened is we had it cut down," answered mother. "And it wasn't easy! They've been at it all day long. Tomorrow they'll be back to take out the roots."

"But why?" I asked, on the verge of tears.

"Because it had to be."

What immense sorrow! Without the old tree, the garden was no more than an ugly plot of dirt. What useless cruelty! If Jorge had still been my friend, he would've understood the pain that was tearing at my chest.

It had been father's doing, father who was born on the plains of Ávila, who despised trees with the ancestral hatred of the peasant who watches his harvest dwindle under a tree's cool shade.

I protested, devastated, but mother cut me short.

"I don't want to hear a lick of your nonsense. When you've got a place of your own, you'll do what you want, but this house is mine, or mine and your father's, and we'll do as we please with it. What a hopeless romantic!"

Teary-eyed and heartbroken, I made my way to the rabbit hutch in search of the puppy. Poor thing, he probably hadn't eaten all day long! What? Where was he?

"There's no dog here," grumbled Felipa, lighting the kitchen stove.

"Well, where is he?"

"He must've taken a trip," she mocked while she fanned the burner.

"Did mother give him away? Answer me! Where's my puppy?"

"What do I know? Out in the cold, I think, so he doesn't get moth-eaten."

"Is he roaming the street?"

"Didn't I tell you? He's out in the cold."

"What have they done with him?"

By then I was plagued by dark premonitions.

152

"If you really want to know, he's in the well. In the well to get rid of his fleas."

In the well! There were two wells, one in the garden with a pump to fill the tank, and another in the yard with a wooden cover and muddy water we never used. It was there they'd thrown the godforsaken dog to drown in my absence.

I sat on the kitchen doorstep and wept for the puppy in the mud and the tree toppled like a dead man on the broken earth. There was no one more miserable than me!

"Let's hope nothing worse ever happens to you," said Felipa. "Don't be silly. Crying over a dog!"

When father found out why I was upset, he got so angry with me, it was if he wanted to justify to himself what he'd done. Mother ordered me to bed.

"And don't give me any dirty looks. I can't take your nonsense, not with my conditions! Off to bed with you."

I held a grudge against my parents in the days following that bitter afternoon. I didn't go out to the garden or show my face in the yard or the kitchen. No, I stayed in my room reading a book I'd found in the attic about voyages and navigators.

Father didn't notice because he was occupied with workers around the clock. When we gathered at the table, he'd talk only about selling the shop and taking up permanent residence in the house. He'd left the business under the direction of an honorable chap to whom he could entrust it entirely if it didn't sell. I'd never seen father so happy.

Every day, he'd think up new ways to change the house and the garden.

"We're going to turn the upstairs living room into two offices. It's far too big… And we'll wall up the window in my bedroom so it stops letting in the cold… I ordered them to dig up the rose garden to plant beans."

Every project was a new blow I was better off keeping to myself. As mother was constantly reminding me, it wasn't my house. Nothing there was mine, and it was none of my business. One day when I was older, I'd leave that house and never go back.

One afternoon, father went to bed with a fever after watering the garden. He was shaking so hard, the whole bed rattled, and mother gave him hot water bottles and mustard plasters. The next day he got up and said he was well again. Two or three days later, he went back to Madrid.

Mother and I stayed behind because the painters hadn't finished the doors. The whole house smelled of fresh paint and glue. Felipa and mother would clean and tidy the newly wall-papered rooms, re-arranging the furniture, painting the floor tiles, and waxing the tables and chairs, and I would aid their toil from morning to night.

Often I got so tired, I'd nod off over dinner, and mother had to wake me up to go to bed. At that time I was sharing a bedroom with her.

One night I dreamt I was leaning out a balcony at our house in Madrid, but the hat shop and paper shop and dry cleaners across the street had been replaced by the elder tree with its bare branches stretching over the square.

A little door opened to reveal a mysterious black hole right in the middle of its trunk. Father walked through that door, and I heard the people accompanying him: "He's dead! He's dead!"

All of a sudden, green leaves and white umbrella-shaped flowers covered every branch. Then I saw Tía Teresa wearing black with a white tulle fichu, just as I'd seen her four years earlier. She too disappeared through the mysterious door, which closed behind her.

"She's dead! She's dead," I heard once again.

Mother heard me moaning and shook me awake.

"María Luisa, wake up! You're having a nightmare. What were you dreaming?"

"I dreamt… Heavens me, what a fright!"

I told her my dream.

"Nonsense," she replied. "You were lying on your left side, that's all. Lie on your other side and go back to sleep."

But the next day mother sent word to the workers not to come. She packed our bags, and we left for Madrid on the eleven o'clock train. Felipa spent the entire trip griping.

"All that cleaning and tidying, just to leave everything a mess at the last minute!"

When we got home, the doorwoman stopped us at the entrance.

"Señor Arroyo's been sick for two days. I was about to send for you because I can't take care of him, and he's almost always alone, the poor thing. I'm sure it's nothing, but just in case, I'm glad you came. He'll be glad, too."

I don't think father even realized we were there. He had a terrible fever and was constantly groaning, and the look on his face had changed.

"Your father's really sick," said mother, frightened, while Felipa went for a doctor. "I've never seen him this sick!"

In three or four days, father had two consultations and was seen by several different doctors. In the end, they all said there was nothing to be done and abandoned me and mother with Tía Manuelita, who'd come at once when she heard the news. Before long the three of us lost track of time. Since we were sleeping in our armchairs and not eating at our usual hours, we never knew if it was morning or evening.

The shopkeeper came over whenever he wasn't working. He brought a sprayer and made the whole house smell of rosemary alcohol, such that I was living in the throes of a rural tragedy.

On the fourth day, father died after a terrible battle between his healthy young constitution and the poison his swollen lungs were pumping through his blood. He'd barely recognized us since we got home.

Mother and I were escorted from the bedroom by the shopkeeper and some friends of father whom I'd never met and who came in his final hour.

Mother was weeping uncontrollably in one of the living room chairs.

"Here we are," she said when she could finally speak, "not a soul in the world to earn us a living! What's to become of us?"

I too was crying, for the spectacle of death is a terrible thing the first time you see it. But I didn't feel the helpless grief and rage of the afternoon when the dog and the elder both died. This new pain was mingled with a resignation to fate and a sweet and sorrowful serenity.

I understood that a part of my life was ending with my father. Until that very day, I'd lived under the protective shade of his arms, which had always put bread on our table. The innocence and joyous abandon of my childhood were over forever.

Tía Teresa died in the month of May, leaving us an inheritance of some four thousand pesetas, and we moved for good to the house in the town of La Mancha.

PART II: SUMMER

CLARA'S SWEETHEART

We got up from the table, and mother went to her bedroom for a nap as always. Señorita Clara and I went back to embroidering by the garden window.

We were in the month of August. The cicadas were singing their drowsy song in the vines, and the green blinds were dimming the entrance hall in their soft semi-darkness. Felipa was scrubbing and humming quietly in the kitchen, and I was nodding off over my needlepoint, just like every afternoon.

"Don't you go falling asleep, María Luisa," warned Clara, who was spending the summer with us. She was there as my friend, and we were already speaking as equals. "Don't you go falling asleep. When your mother gets up, she'll get mad if you haven't made progress."

"I'm sick and tired of embroidering. A lot of good it will do me!"

"You're right about that," agreed Señorita Clara. "You'd have been better off learning to paint with the fellow who started to teach you. What ever happened to him?"

"I don't know, I haven't seen him since. But I sure would like to paint or study for a degree. Anything! I've asked mother quite a few times, but she won't hear of it. That way I could've worked and made money for the house."

But Señorita Clara disagreed.

"Listen, dear, having to work is sadder than you think. Aside from the fact that other women look down their noses at a woman who makes her own living, you've got to put up with constant affronts from the men who hold the purse strings. I've been working since I was twenty, and nobody knows what I've had to put up with. A woman's best bet is to get married."

I kept on embroidering, straining to keep my eyes open. What a boring life! If it weren't for books… Clara had brought me some from Madrid, a series of works by quality authors and classics that nourished my inner life, but mother didn't let me read except for on Sundays.

"What day is it, Clara?"

"Today? Thursday, I believe it's Thursday. You're anxious for it to be Sunday, aren't you?"

"Yes, it's a day we don't sew, and I can read."

"And someone very interesting comes over," said Clara, with an impishness that took me off guard.

"Who?"

"Really, dear, who else would it be? Antonio."

Antonio was the shopkeeper. He was fifteen years older than me, double my age, and was short and stout, with the first signs of a potbelly. I jerked awake on hearing such a suspicion.

"Antonio? What do I care about Antonio?"

"Look here, dear, he's an honest man, a hard worker who adores you. That's worth a lot."

"Yes, but he doesn't like to read or know how to paint, and when we talk he doesn't say a thing. I've got to say it all myself. He's a brute!"

160

Clara got angry at that. So he was a brute, was he? True, he wasn't well educated, but he had a keen sense for business, knew how to make a living, and would make a happy woman of his future wife.

"Yes, but since I don't plan on ever getting married…"

"You're very young, that's why you say that. You don't know what life's like for a single woman. I'm telling you, she's a burden for everyone."

As always when we got on that topic, Clara launched into sad considerations about her own experience of being single. She could've gotten married on numerous occasions! But she fell for a man and shunned all the others. Truly, her sweetheart was very handsome, very intelligent, a very smooth talker.

"Why didn't you marry him?"

"What do I know? There were reasons. He married another woman." She lowered her voice. "I didn't want to say anything, and your mother doesn't know yet, but I'll tell you. That friend who's coming to see me this afternoon with his wife and kid? It's him."

"You mean the teacher?"

"Yes, that's the one. I paid him a visit after he got married, and when I left to come here I invited him to supper with your mother's permission. They'll get here at five," she said, examining her watch. "I've still got plenty of time to get ready and go down to the station."

While Clara primped herself in her bedroom, applying foundation for her makeup and slipping on a starched petticoat that rustled loudly under her dress, I gazed out at the sunny garden through the slits in the blind.

Had Antonio really thought about marrying me? I didn't think so. Who was he to imagine the intimacy of my body and my thoughts? How repulsive, dear Lord, how utterly repulsive!

And every atom in my body protested with a dark sense of rage.

Clara came out, dressed and powdered and all dolled up, and airing herself with a fan.

"I think it's still early, but I don't want to be late. They don't know where the house is."

"Look, Clara, be honest. Do you think Antonio has thought about being my boyfriend?"

"Of course, it's plain as day. The man doesn't dare say a word because you're still very young, but after your next birthday... You've seen how he comes bearing flowers and chocolates. Obviously, they're not for me."

"They're for mother."

"Sure! That's what he says, but he eats you with his eyes."

"Me?" I said, blushing to the roots of my hair. "Me? But why? What have I said for him to look at me like that? How disgusting!" I covered my face with my hands. "When he gets here this Sunday, I won't come out for lunch."

"Why? Don't be a child, María Luisa. The man comes with good intentions, and there's no reason to turn up your nose at him. I'm not saying you should get married right away, but eventually the time must come, and your best bet's to marry the man who's taking such good care of the family business." She checked her watch again. "All right, I'm off. God forbid the train arrive before I get there."

While she was closing the door, mother came out of her bedroom, frowning and in a bad mood.

"So much talk and so little consideration for the infirm! You girls haven't let me sleep all afternoon. What a commotion! Did Clara already go looking for her friends?"

"Yes, since they don't know the house, she wanted to be waiting at the station."

"I'm sure Felipa hasn't prepared anything to eat. No, if I don't take care of it myself..."

She went into the kitchen, where I heard her talking to Felipa.

"Look at the work that girl heaps on our plate," said the maid, livid and fuming. "If I had my way, she'd have stayed in Madrid."

Mother asserted her authority.

"That young lady is exactly where she belongs, and I've heard enough! I asked her to spend the summer with us, and it was I who invited her friends over. If you don't like it, you can leave whenever you want. I'm not holding anyone back."

They fell silent, and mother crossed the foyer in search of napkins and a cloth for the little table under the arbor.

"You're all out to make my blood boil," she said, passing by my side. "A house isn't complete without a man around! Without one that woman's been driving me mad!"

But I knew that wasn't true. Even when father was alive, he'd always put up with Casiana and Felipa, hateful and wicked as they were in mistreating me.

When everything was ready for the meal, mother came and sat in her wicker chair with her crocheting.

"Have you embroidered much?"

"Yes, but not very much, because I was tired and it was hot out."

"Excuses! You wanted to get away with doing nothing. You know full well that the only reason I invited Clara to spend the summer with us was to teach you how to embroider. But to really do it right, no mistakes! And you've got to have it down pat before she goes home. You hear? Do you think I'd put up with her foolishness otherwise? Because Felipa is right in the end. Who's she to ask her friends over for supper?"

"Mother! She told you about it before she even got here."

"I know, and I agreed to it. And don't think I'm upset about the cost, no sir. When the time is right, I know how to part with some money. But around here there's nowhere to buy decent food. Just to have something to offer them, I had to save what Antonio brought us last Sunday, and not have a sweet bun with my milk. I don't know what we'd do if it weren't for Antonio. And that's another thing, Clara could keep her thoughts to herself and not go spreading gossip. If the rest of us are keeping quiet, we must have our reasons."

I realized mother had listened in on our conversation, and the shock of it made my hands tremble so much, I couldn't stick the needle through the cloth.

"Because you won't find another man like Antonio, and the woman who marries him can count herself lucky. We all think we're so great, and in the end we turn out to be useless. When it comes to women, the humbler and less clever, the better. You don't need to read novels to care for your husband and children."

Had it not been for a knock on the door, mother's nasty downpour would surely have continued. But just then Clara came in holding a child, followed by a man and a young woman. So that was Clara's handsome, smooth-talking sweetheart! He had a pointy black goatee, was bald, and wore a shabby suit.

"My friend, Don Luis Rodríguez, and his wife," said Clara, introducing them to mother.

Mother, who a minute before had been complaining about their visit, greeted them, friendly and smiling. She invited them to sit, cracked the door to let the air in, equipped them with hand fans, and called for cold drinks.

As for me, mother's insults had left me speechless, and I could think of nothing else despite my best efforts to smile at our visitors. So mother wanted me to marry Antonio!

The little boy was snub-nosed, ugly, and teary-eyed. He wet his underpants two or three times, and another time he did more than wet them. Seated on a low chair I'd brought from my bedroom, the father washed him with a sponge and hot water, powdered his behind, and replaced his clothes with others from out of a baby bag. Meanwhile, the mother made him laugh calling him *sweet pea*, and Clara watched the group with tender eyes.

"How precious, look how precious!"

She was saying it over and over, and I wondered if perhaps she was referring to the father.

They ate, toured the house, and picked figs in the garden, and when the boy fell asleep, the man with the goatee lectured us about the world's corruption.

"You all did good packing your bags and moving to this town. These days, it's impossible to raise a daughter as God commands in a big city."

Mother was in complete agreement. She too knew just what God commanded, and I was starting to learn, as well. What God commanded was exactly what I didn't want to do.

"These days there's no religion, no home life, no family or good manners in that perverse Madrid of ours," Clara's sweetheart was saying. "People go to mass on Sunday to see the latest fashions, drag themselves to confession once a year, don't have a spiritual counselor, and send their kids to schools where the leaders aren't deeply religious. And what's the result? The boys flock to brothels, and the young ladies have frivolous friendships and conversations, not at all becoming of a virgin's rightful honor."

"Yes, yes; right you are," agreed mother. "I'll never be thankful enough for the moment I decided to move here. All the girls in this town study with the Augustinian nuns. They were born here, get married here, and I'd bet many of them have never set foot past the station. What's bad are the summer vacationers. Lots of women come here on holiday, and they always bring new fashions and ... mannerisms... You know what I mean. Some don't even go to mass."

Don Luis knew just the solution. He was a supporter of the Inquisition, and if he became Minister of Justice one day, which wasn't as absurd as it sounded at first, he'd force every Spaniard to make a profession of faith. Anyone who didn't, or who refused to live according to the strictest morals—Roman, Catholic, and Apostolic—he'd pack onto a ship and abandon on the open ocean.

What a loathsome man! He went on and on about the ideal Christian family and the duties of the wife and husband. Oh, what great difficulties he'd faced in his career! There were many envious people out there just trying to trip him up. But God in his infinite wisdom would give them their just deserts.

And he'd settle for nothing less than sending them to Hell for all eternity. Why else have God for an ally but to help him take revenge? I thought it over and hated that man with all my soul.

It was time for the train, and mother told us to leave for the station; Clara and I were to accompany our guests while she got ready for bed. It was already late, and her many conditions would never let her miss a night of sleep. We'd take dinner in a pail and have a picnic in the fields.

"How lovely," said Don Luis. "How very lovely! To dine out in nature, under the velvet dome of the heavens, alongside the babbling brook."

Nobody told him there weren't any brooks around, with us being out in La Mancha, nor that we'd eat dinner in dusty fields of stubble.

At the station, the kid woke up, threw a fit, and had to have his underpants changed yet again. His father did the honors sitting on a step at the platform.

The train was so late, it got dark out. We walked back and forth and had no idea what to say or do.

"Do you have girl friends in town?" asked the mother, coming up beside me.

"No, ma'am. I know lots of girls my age, but I don't go out with them because I'm in mourning. Right on our street are some other *señoritas* in mourning, but they're summer vacationers, and mother doesn't want me going anywhere near them."

"You must get terribly bored."

"No, not terribly, because I read on Sundays and sew every day."

"Women's lives are so sad," she sighed, and the two of us commiserated deeply.

We all cheered up when the train finally arrived. Clara and I stood on the platform, bidding them farewell with our handkerchiefs.

"What a man," said Clara, when the train was out of sight. "What a man! Did you hear how he talks? He's a wise man, a genuine sage. That simple-minded woman doesn't deserve him!"

I took care not to tell her that I found him loathsome, and she kept on singing his praises.

"And what honest sentiments! What Christian chastity!"

"Yes," I said, unable to contain myself, "but they had a kid, so at some point…"

"What's that got to do with it?" she snarled. "You can't grasp certain things because you're barely more than a child, but you ought to know everything in marriage is pure, holy, and legitimate in the eyes of the Lord. Of course, they've got to practice abstinence at certain times of year when the Church requires it, but apart from that… Goodness me, wouldn't that be something if it were a sin within wedlock!"

I didn't reply. Walking along the platform, we followed the tracks into the fields. We knew of some rocks a little farther down where we could sit and eat dinner.

Clara was nervous from the afternoon's visit and couldn't keep quiet for long. She told me about their romance. It had lasted for three years, the best of her life. He was the only man she'd ever kissed.

"Aha! So he kissed you!"

"Yes, sometimes. That's what they all do, and you've got to play along with a certain give and take, whetting their appetite but not giving too much. Otherwise, men over thirty don't marry. He would have, it's true, but I had pneumonia, and it left me anemic."

"And what did that matter?"

"Everything, I assure you. The doctor forbade me from marrying, and mother told him he'd have to wait another year, but he couldn't bear it. He was raring to go."

"Why?"

"Really, dear! Because men have their needs. And he's not the kind of man to frequent certain establishments, so…"

I realized what she meant and reeled back in horror. What a vile life! I felt a deep sense of sadness. Everything around me was ugly: the field of stubble, which I could barely make out; the sooty dirt at our feet; Antonio, who wanted to eat me with his eyes; that man with his *needs*; the child who wet himself every time you turned around.

"I wish I'd die!" I said all of a sudden.

"Nonsense," replied Clara, "nothing but nonsense! You're not living hand to mouth, praise the Lord, and you'll marry Antonio and have a bunch of kids."

"No, I won't, I swear! I told you, I'm never getting married. But married or single, everything disgusts me."

"I don't know why!"

We fell silent over our meal. The crickets were singing in the furrows, the stars shining overhead. I gazed up at the sky and felt a sweet peace descend over me.

"Are there people on another planet, do you think?"

"No, I don't think so. There's Syrius, look how it shines. It's a sun just like ours. And there's the giant, Orion."

"I don't see him."

"Yes, dear, he's got his arms open. Those three little stars are his sword belt. You see it?"

How wonderful is the sky on the plains! I looked and looked and never got tired.

"Come on and eat, María Luisa."

"I don't want any more."

My sadness had faded, and I thought out loud, "I'd like to be able to travel between the stars. Maybe after I die, for the soul is light as a feather. But really, if you ask me, the same thing happens when we're sleeping. Sometimes the soul leaves the body, and then it can go where it wishes. What's bad is I won't be able to remember later on, because they say that…"

The sound of an approaching train cut me short. It was the express, a luxury train that always breezed past the station. I don't know why, but that time it stopped before reaching the platform.

The sleeper cars stopped in front of us, and a pretty young woman peered out a window. Inside the compartment, the bright cheery lights cast reddish reflections on her dark hair, but she couldn't see us in the shadow of a carriage.

"Ricardo, look," she said, "look out the window. We're so far from the station! Why did the train stop here?"

By her side appeared a young man who leaned out the window and took her lovingly in his arms.

"Are you scared, darling? The station's right there. Do you love your honey bear?"

He whispered in her ear, and she let out a nervous laugh. Then he squeezed her tighter. The light struck his face, and I saw his eyes and his mouth come to life with the same gross, shameful laughter I'd seen on other men's faces. Honey bear! What a phrase! It sounded to me like an obscenity.

"They're newlyweds," said Señorita Clara after the train departed. "It's their honeymoon, and this is their first night as husband and wife."

We linked arms and went home, and I heard her crying, as was I. Flowing from the same source, her tears meant one thing and mine, the opposite.

ANTONIO

I n the winter, the popular girls in town would get together after
lunch. If the day was clear and sunny, they'd go to the station to see
the three o'clock train. If it was raining or too cold out, they'd gather
at the home of one of them who had a piano and a spacious hall for
dancing. The few young men who wintered in the town flocked to the
call of the dance and their flirting.

Mother detested anything that might entertain me, and for a long
time she used our mourning as an excuse to keep me from joining
them. But the colonel's widow was so insistent, she wound up letting
me go out on Sundays.

"Not on workdays. She's got plenty to do at home."

I left the house happy but was quick to realize that I was out of
place in those gatherings, an utter disaster. I'd either bore them with
the stories of novels I'd read or fall into a stubborn silence that made
them mistrust me.

I was possibly the youngest of the group, where the girls ranged from seventeen to over thirty. But despite their different ages, a single obsession united all of them but me: marriage.

How were they going to make their wedding dresses, if they hadn't started already? What colors best suited their skin tones? Should their nightgowns have low necklines or short sleeves? And where would be best to go after the ceremony, to a hotel or to a love nest they'd spent months preparing? The moment their mothers left them alone, the *first night* was an endless topic of conversation.

"A light blue silk nightgown, with lace here and there, just enough for some chest to show through. Picture it! A girl doesn't have to be pretty to look good in that."

"My sister wore a pink nightgown with black ribbons. Well, girls, the next day it was shredded to pieces."

"What did you expect? They go wild."

But when the conversations really heated up, when all their eyes burned bright, was when one of them brought news of a specific case or could tell something from her own experience.

"My cousin Rosa's back from her honeymoon! They got back last night and left again this morning. She told me everything!"

"Well? Tell us, girl, tell us!"

"Go on, tell us."

Then they huddled on the promenade or in a corner of the hall and whispered atrocities that lacked the modesty even to be said in a dignified fashion. Their half-words were dirtier than the acts themselves.

"Don't you want to hear?" said Sol, who was walking with the help of two canes. "Come on, dear. I'll make room for you."

"What secrets are you all keeping?" asked the boys, already suspecting them.

"You girls want to know something? Come straight to me. I'll even give you a practical demonstration."

That made them keel over laughing. The story of Merche's cousin had already worked them up without completely satisfying their curiosity.

"That's all she told you? There must've been something else."

"With it being her first time and all!"

"It's true, your cousin always was a crybaby. But she should've known what she was getting into, what we've all got to suffer on our wedding night."

"If it were just a matter of suffering," laughed Paquita, who was one of the plump ones. "But later on…"

"Of course," they all chimed, "but of course!"

They'd tell each other terrible things that left me in a fright.

One of Paquita's sisters-in-law went straight from the church to the country house where she was to spend her honeymoon. Nobody knew what happened on the road.

"Getting out of the carriage, she left a trail of blood that the maids had to clean up with sponges."

And all of them clung to her every word and didn't give the slightest shudder.

One day the pharmacist's daughter Albertina came with momentous news. She was just two years older than me.

"Beatriz gets here tomorrow with her husband, and they're going to be in town for a week. That's what the hotel doorwoman told me. Which of us will go for her story? Because she won't want to tell the whole group. Let's send Paquita; the two of them are closest."

I didn't know the Beatriz in question, but they were eager to tell me all about her mischief.

"You don't know her because she only comes in the summer, and you had to stay at home mourning, but she's really pretty and has always had a boyfriend. There's not a guy in town who hasn't played the part. She drives them crazy! Seeing how she lets herself be fondled…"

Paquita knew all about it because Beatriz had been her older brother's girlfriend.

"You can't imagine. When they sat together, she always had the slit of her skirt on the left, and you never could tell where my brother's right hand was. They were skinny as beanpoles by the end of the summer. Her mother never left them alone together, of course, but they French kissed through the bars on the window. She did it with all the boys in town."

Paquita made excuses for her.

"What happened was, she was almost thirty when she got married. And truth be told, a woman can only wait for so long!"

Sol told me in secret that Paquita said that because she herself was like a cat in heat, and there was a rumor she found ways to console herself.

"Understand? And it must be true if the priest's mother said it. He's her confessor, after all. If anyone would know, it's his mother!"

The nuns' spruce young priest was also spiritual father to almost all those girls, who took a voluptuous pleasure kneeling at his feet to confess the weaknesses of their unsatisfied flesh. His mother was a fat woman in mourning who had long conversations with mine after mass.

"Believe me, they've got my son completely fried. They don't realize he's a man! We'll have to move, and it'll be all their fault! The best and the worst of them are all in love with him and like to get him all riled up. God in Heaven, what women!"

Mother would keep her thoughts to herself until we got home.

"Women and men ought to marry young. As a Father of the Church once said, 'Better to marry than to burn with lust.'"

Because mother read the Church Fathers and Saint Teresa. Since father died, they'd been her sole distractions, making her more rigid and unforgiving of other people's flaws.

Sometimes she asked about my friends' conversations. What were they saying? What were they talking about?

"I don't know… About the dresses they're going to make for the summer, or Enriqueta's mother, who's sick."

But in reality any conversation not about *doing the deed* ended quickly for lack of interest. Those secrets made me terribly embarrassed, and little by little I was left out of them. They'd even fall silent when I was around, or look at me and whisper. And so I lost what little confidence I had in social situations and grew timid and indecisive. Nevertheless, I didn't give up on the gatherings completely. They filled my Sunday afternoons and spared me the domestic drudgery of Antonio's visits. Ever since Clara's revelation, I'd looked askance at him.

One afternoon, I was strolling with my girl friends and some of their male admirers. I hadn't inspired much affection with the masculine crowd. Men always saw me as a strange creature, not very feminine, whom they enjoyed humiliating as if they had a hunch we were in some sort of ridiculous rivalry. When it was I who envied them! Their freedom, their simple, unornamented clothes, their right to act naturally, without affectation!

Perhaps to make his girlfriend jealous, one of those boys pushed past the other girls to catch up with me.

"Do you know how to play the piano like the rest of them?" he asked, fishing for something to say.

"No, not much. It's been a long time since I had a teacher."

"And the *señorita* who spent the summer at your house? Wasn't she your teacher?"

"Yes, but she taught me other things."

He wanted to know what other things I was learning.

"Euclidian geometry, by any chance?"

"No, literature and natural history."

"Amazing," he mocked. "That's some strong stuff! I bet you've even read Calderón de la Barca."

"No, I know he wrote honor plays, but I haven't read any."

"Look at you! And what about the Quijote?"

"Yes, Clara brought it this summer, with the Iliad and the Odyssey."

"Smashing!" he shouted, going back to the others. "Boys, look what I found! The jewel in the crown. She's read the Quijote!"

They all smirked, and the girls swore they hadn't read it and didn't even know what it was.

"Isn't it some kind of newspaper?" asked Merche.

"Listen to the things she says! Girl, your ignorance is simply divine! That's just how I like my women. But that doesn't mean I'm not watering at the mouth for María Luisa, who's read the Odyssey. Just think, boys, the Odyssey!" Then coming back up to me, "I like myself a girl who can read and write! I heard you were a wise woman, but I never thought… It's enough to split your sides laughing!"

"Leave her alone already," said Paquita, coming to my aid more to get close to my assailant than to stop his mockery. "And you, don't be such a know-it-all!"

They all laughed and talked of nothing else all afternoon. A woman's job was to make herself up, go to mass, and care for her hubby. They were all of the same opinion. And I was aware of my inferiority in that group of silly *señoritas*, who scorned and made fun of me despite all their ignorance and lack of imagination.

I refused to go out with them anymore on Sundays, even when Sol and Paquita came to pick me up.

"Don't take it so hard. It was your fault they teased you. Men don't like for us to know more than them. We know plenty already for what they want us for," said Paquita, giving a devious wink.

"But he asked what I studied."

"That's just what I'm saying. Why do you study that nonsense? If your mother wants to throw away money on your education, at least learn to sing or dance. Sevillanas are pretty, and a girl who can sing stands out."

"I don't have a good ear. Besides, I like to read more than anything else… And to paint."

175

The two of them looked at each other and smiled, and I started to suspect they were poking fun of me.

"It's a pity," said Sol. "If you keep up like this, you'll be a spinster dressing saints. Because pretty you're not, my dear."

"But she's not as ugly as Jesusa," said Paquita to comfort me.

Jesusa was a hunchback and had the typical face of those with her condition!

Mother was thrilled I'd stopped going out on Sundays. That way I could spend them with her and Antonio, eating chocolates and chatting around the foot stove. The first-floor sitting room was right next to mother's bedroom, and she could lie down without leaving the conversation.

One cold afternoon when mother went to bed early, we heard her sleeping.

"She's snoring," laughed Antonio. "She's already fast asleep." Then out of the blue, "How old are you?"

"Sixteen."

"How slowly time passes! I wait and wait, and the day never comes for you to turn twenty."

I kept quiet and studied the patterns on the velvet tablecloth.

"So it's now or never," Antonio went on. "What would you think if I said I really loved you? Be honest, what would think?"

He'd grabbed me by the arm and was leaning towards me, blowing his smoker's breath right in my face.

"Let go," I recoiled.

"Shush! You're going to wake up your mother... Answer me, darling, do you love me, too?"

"Me? No," I said weakly.

"Ah! So you don't... Well, I thought..."

Shaken, he suddenly switched tactics.

"Of course, that's what you girls always say. 'I'll get back to you, I'll think it over.' But those coy little games won't work on me. Come on,

176

girl, tell me you love me. Say it, but only if it's true! Come on."

"Why would I say what I don't feel? I don't love you! There, I said it."

"Okay, let's assume that's true now. But you will love me… Look, you've only got to say *yes* or *no*. That's all I need. Everything will stay the same, but I'll know what to expect. I'll work and come on Sundays, and it'll be like nothing happened. So? What do you say? Answer me."

"I already answered you. No!"

"So it's a *no*, a resounding *no*," he said like he couldn't believe it.

"No, I don't love you now, and I won't in the future. It's not my fault."

"No, of course not. Well then, I'm going for a walk."

With that, he got up, threw on his hat and coat, and stormed out of the house in a rage.

Mother woke up to the front door slamming.

"Who just left? Antonio? Where did he go?"

"I don't know."

"What do you mean, you don't know?" she said, sitting up in bed. "Something happened. Did he say something? Be honest."

"No…"

"Don't lie to me. What were you talking about? Tell me the truth. Come here so I can see your face."

I couldn't deny it with mother right in front of me.

"It's just, he says he loves me, and I don't love him back. I wish he'd leave me in peace! That's right. If only he'd leave me…"

"Well, he's left you," said mother, returning her head to the pillow. "God himself will leave you, my girl. If you spurn this proposition, don't count on getting others. Wedding prospects are grim these days."

"Good. That way I'll never get married."

"As far as I'm concerned, you can do what you want. I'm going to mind my own business. No need for people to wonder if I married you off to my liking. But look closely at what we lose if we lose Antonio, because you can be certain we'll lose him. No more coming every Sunday bringing chocolates and cakes and books and other things the little girl ordered. No more saying, 'Antonio, get me this novel I want to read' or 'Antonio, I don't like this letter paper and want another kind for writing to my brothers.' And no more Antonio searching all the shops to bring you the most modern paper. As for me—poor little me, as ill as I am! Since the day your father died, I haven't paid a bill, answered a business letter, or spoken with a creditor. Antonio takes care of everything! And he'll be the arm to support my old age, my sole source of help and comfort!"

Mother cried, wiping her eyes with a handkerchief, while I studied the floor, eyes dry and teeth clenched, firm in my resolve to hold my ground.

"All you've ever done is give me trouble, from the day you were born, when I almost died. You and your boy's games, always refusing to eat or practice the piano, always picking fights with other girls. Why, they even threw you out of school! Then there was that story about the painter, and now this! Lord in Heaven, what did I do to deserve such punishment?"

It didn't occur to her that I'd borne the brunt of that troublemaking much more than she had, but I didn't dare tell her so.

"Get out," raged mother. "Get out! You're upsetting me just being here. When Antonio gets back, send him in to talk to me. And shut the door behind you!"

I closed the door on my way out and went back to my place by the foot stove with a novel in hand. As long as there were books, I could escape from that life, which was dreary before and was about to get painful…

Antonio got back half an hour before his train's departure and went straight to bid mother goodbye without looking at me.

"Antonio," I heard her say, "are you mad, child? She's a silly little girl, but don't worry. It's all just a matter of time. Just wait, and I promise you..."

She lowered her voice, and they spoke so I couldn't hear them.

Fed on literary tales, my fantastic imagination led me to envision a tragic course of events far worse than the circumstances merited. Surely they were plotting to lock me in the dark until I said *yes*! Those same days, the newspaper was reporting on a woman who'd been kidnapped by her family, and one of the photographs showed her as a skeleton. How horrible!

I decided not to give an inch even though the fear gave me gooseflesh. I'd rather die than marry Antonio. Yes, I'd rather die! And even though the idea of that death satisfied my romantic sensibility, its harsh reality sent shivers down my spine.

In the following days, mother didn't say another word about Antonio. On the contrary, she treated me kindly, consulted me about things around the house, and complained about Felipa.

"That woman is an oaf, and she just keeps getting worse. Who does she think she is, talking to you on a first-name basis? It's got to stop. You're a young lady now."

When Antonio came on Sunday, he brought me three books.

"I've got to admit, I don't know much about them. I told the bookseller to give me the best and the latest, something for someone *instructed*. Isn't that the word? Anyway, here they are. Tell me what you think."

I was happy. My fears had blown over, and I let him spoil and dote on me, basking in the warmth of his unexpected friendliness. In addition to the books, Antonio brought chocolates, cakes, an inkwell, and a notebook that mother had ordered for me.

The day went by pleasantly, without any reference to the events of the previous Sunday. We strolled down the road in the sun and went home for supper at dusk. Antonio told vulgar jokes about the women who shopped at the store, and I made myself laugh to get on their good side and keep the mood cheery all day long, fearful I'd lose their esteem.

Only Felipa was in a worse mood than usual, going around grumbling and slamming doors. I caught her looking at me a few times like she wanted to know what I was thinking.

"That woman spends her life listening," said mother. "It's a good thing we're not keeping secrets; otherwise..."

After Antonio left, the storm that had been brewing all day in the kitchen finally broke.

"You'd better watch yourself," said mother to Felipa. "You look like a madwoman, slamming doors. Lord help me, a house isn't complete without a man around!"

"That's what I say," muttered Felipa. "Exactly what I say! If only your husband were alive! What's happening here would be out of the question."

"And what exactly is happening here?" asked mother, getting mad. "You tell me right now what you're talking about."

"Why should I, if you know better than I do?"

"I told you to talk right now!" shouted mother. "Right this instant! I won't have that kind of slander in my household!"

"Slander? Is that what you call it? So it's slander to say you're buttering up the child to marry her off to that dirty upstart? Is that it?"

"What did you say? What, woman?"

"I'm telling the truth, nothing but the truth. He's a poor wretch like me who used to be a soldier and didn't even finish the first grade. But since it's better to climb the ladder than to be born at the top, he wants to marry the girl. And she doesn't love him, because birds of a feather... And she got a different sort of upbringing from that saint who passed away."

"You've got no right to speak of him," shrieked mother, who was turning bright red. "And if you didn't spend your life listening through doors, you wouldn't know about other people's business."

"It's my business, too. For years I've been eating the bread of this house, and I won't stand for certain injustices." Then she spun to face the wall and turned on me, too. "But really, you're absolutely right. I couldn't care less whether the girl gets married or goes straight to Hell. She never could stand the sight of me! It's over for all I care."

"Well, not for me," said mother. "Not for me. Tomorrow at the crack of dawn, you'll leave this house, and if I don't say right now it's because I'm not used to throwing people out at this time of night."

We went back into our bedroom and mother, not saying another word, ordered me to lie down in bed. Later I heard her sighing.

"Together, they'll all be the end of me!"

But I'd heard in Felipa's words confirmation of a vague foreboding to which I hadn't wanted to admit. The friendly treatment of the past few days was to marry me off to Antonio!

SUMMER

That summer we were joined by Tía Manuelita, who came to me worried after two or three days.

"What's the matter with your mother? She's acting all serious and talking as little as possible, especially to you. Did you quarrel?"

"No, she's always like that."

"That's not what I heard. When Felipa left your house, the little scoundrel came to see me on the pretense of explaining why you'd sacked her. She told me all kinds of gossip, said that Antonio... And that your mother didn't know how to coax you into saying *yes*."

"That was then," I sighed, recalling all the twists and turns I'd endured since the winter. "Yes, at first they gave me all sorts of gifts, and he and mother didn't say a thing. But then..."

I trailed off. Tía Manuelita continued crocheting in silence, waiting patiently for me to reveal my secrets. It pained me to think back on those long winter months, when I'd sailed alone through a tempest of outrages and tactical changes. There was the day he gave me the bracelet—not that I cared about jewelry—and the spring day when he found me alone in the garden at dusk and assailed me with a kiss on the mouth.

"Stop it, you're gross! Leave me alone! I told you, I don't love you."

"Ah! So you haven't changed your mind? So everything I've done for you I've done in vain?"

And then there was the afternoon at lunch when he proposed to mother that she sell the shop. He planned to get married, form a family, secure his future. He couldn't be a shopkeeper his entire life. He'd only have agreed to it on one condition…

That was the start of a monotonous new phase wherein mother was serious and Antonio, indifferent. He stopped coming every Sunday, and when he came, he went up to the living room and spent all day talking to mother. They didn't address me at meals, acting as if I were invisible, and Antonio would go with mother to the station without even bidding me goodbye.

In the meantime, mother's conversations with the new maid and our house guests were always full of snubs and veiled gibes against me.

"Children! You can't expect them to give you anything but trouble! At least if they're sons… But daughters, they shouldn't even be taught to read. The less they know, the better."

Eventually I couldn't take it anymore. At that young age, one lacks the moral fiber to face the soul's absolute solitude.

Little by little, in the midst of my tears, I was confiding all my sorrows in Tía Manuelita.

"What a miserable life!" I'd recently read the phrase in a novel, and it was moving to apply it to myself. "Truly miserable! If only I had the courage…"

"What? To do what? That's no way to fix things. I'll talk to your mother."

"No, don't! Lord save us! Just think, you'll leave in the winter, and I'll be here all alone again with the two of them."

"I'm sure they won't kill you," she teased.

"No, they won't kill me, but I'll still end up dying."

"All right, that's enough nonsense. Dry your tears. What you need is to have some fun."

"To have fun!" I scoffed. "I don't know how!"

"That's what I'm for," said Tía, with a surprising sense of confidence. And from that moment on, she thought of nothing else.

"Say, doesn't this girl have any girl friends?" she asked mother.

"How could she? She's so strange, she wound up all alone."

"They didn't get along?"

"What do I know, auntie, what do I know? Ask her about it."

Tía Manuelita initiated the interrogation gently.

"Don't you have any girl friends, María Luisa?"

"Yes, but they've all got a boyfriend and like to dance, and I don't know how."

"Don't be such a loner, dear!"

"Didn't I tell you?" said mother.

"It's just, I don't like them. They bore me."

"But surely there's someone nicer and more interesting."

"Yes, the judge's orphan daughters live right around the corner, Carmen and Teresita. But we only talk on the way out of mass, seeing as they're summer vacationers."

"And what does that matter? So you can only mix with the local girls? Who ever heard of such a thing!"

Mother didn't have the courage to say it was she who wouldn't let me near them. The next Sunday, Tía Manuelita herself led the charge to put us on friendly terms.

"My niece thinks very highly of you. She says you're the only girls she gets along with."

Carmen and Teresita were twenty and eighteen, respectively. They'd lost their father and mother in consecutive winters and were living with their guardians, an aunt and uncle. Teresita was a tall brunette,

Carmen was a smaller blonde, and both of them were elegant, distinguished, and slightly cultured.

"Yes," answered Carmen, "we're neighbors. We like María Luisa, too, but since we're in double mourning, we only leave the house for church on Sundays. Why don't the two of you come over?"

Tía Manuelita and I went and spent the whole morning with them and their guardians. Carmen was charming, her conversation full of wit and banter, but I couldn't get over my shyness and the fear they'd make fun of me. I barely spoke.

Tía chided me on our way out.

"Dear, you're unrecognizable! What happened to that talkative, self-assured girl from home? You turn into a bore when you go out. I'm warning you, you'll never make friends if you keep that up."

But I did make friends, and Carmen was my friend and the confidante of my sad situation at home on account of Antonio.

"Get married, girl! What you do is get married the second you've got a boyfriend who isn't the shopkeeper."

"But I don't want to get married!"

"Me neither! Isn't that funny?"

That was the first time I'd heard another girl say that, and our shared way of thinking drew us closer together.

No, Carmen didn't want to get married, but she and Teresita had it rough with their aunt and uncle, who were living large on their orphans' pension. In the end, she'd have to get married to claim her independence.

"It's hopeless," I'd say. "Is there no other way to be happy?"

"No," Carmen would answer. "The most we can do is get married, have a house, and be able to live comfortably."

"Yes, but the husband..."

"Bah! The husband's another story. A clever woman always does just what she wants at home."

One afternoon, around the time of the summer fairs, Sol, Paquita, and Merche came to see me. All three had a boyfriend and were in high spirits. They were expecting to have great fun at the festivities. And what was I going to do? Did I plan on staying home as always?

"It would be right foolish," said Tía Manuelita. "I brought her ribbons and brooches and pretty adornments to wear at the fairs and the dances. Let me show you."

She came back with a suitcase full of gaudy ribbons, garish imitation jewelry, and pieces of lace embroidered with gold thread and wax pearls. The girls were thrilled.

"Look how precious! With a bow in your hair, a ruffle at your neckline, and a gemstone brooch, you'll be a real sight at the bullfights!"

"You all will! If María Luisa's up for it, you can design something original and all dress alike. What do you think? There's enough here for a dozen of you."

"Come on, María Luisa, you can't say *no* now!"

Paquita's parents owned a farm and, like all the other farmers, stationed a cart in the square behind a barrier for the family to watch the bullfight. I was invited.

The following Sunday, a group of girls came to see Tía Manuelita, who helped doll them up with the contents of the suitcase. In spite of my protests, I had to give in to wearing a giant ribbon with a gemstone brooch.

"But I'm still in second mourning!"

"Exactly, that's why the black velvet ribbon's for you. Right, Doña Manuelita? It wouldn't be fair for you to go out looking plain when we get to dress up thanks to you and your aunt."

And thanks to the justice and magnanimity of my friends, I wore a lousy ribbon in my bun and was convinced I was hideous all afternoon.

The square was blinding in the sun and full of dust. You could barely breathe for lack of fresh air and for all the shouting and brutality. The poor bull was lanky and livid and smarter than a whip, or so all the others were saying. And my friends were there with their boy-friends. Paquita's was French, Merche's had mocked me over my studies, and Sol's was so tall he folded into thirds when he sat.

"María Luisa, someone's looking for you over here."

I went to the other side of the cart and looked. It was Jorge Medina! I put my hand up to the dreadful black ribbon as he greeted me. No, he didn't want to board the cart. Just then he was headed to make a sketch of the square from the balcony of town hall. He was studying for exams with the mayor's son, and they'd come to the town for the fair. He'd seen me by pure coincidence. For over half an hour he'd been watching me, fearful he was mistaken. How I'd changed! He'd left me a girl and found me a grown woman! And my family?

"Father died two and a half years ago."

"I had no idea! I'm sorry."

He sounded sincere. What he didn't understand was what I was doing in that town.

"We live here."

"Ah! And your mother? And your Tía Manuelita?"

It was hard to hear over the commotion in the square, so he stood on tiptoes and I leaned over the front of the cart. We talked about my aunt, about the shop and its keeper, about Felipa who no longer lived with us, about the books I'd read and the things I was drawing.

"Nothing these days. It's been over a year since I picked up a pencil. Mother doesn't like for me to draw."

Perhaps I let something slip that led him to guess I wasn't happy.

"We took different paths," he said, "and now it would be hard to meet again. I hope one day you'll be happy, my dear, and that you'll forgive me if I ever did wrong by you."

He was holding my hand, and we were shouting back and forth.

"But don't go without seeing Tía Manuelita. She's here, too, and I'll go and get her after the bullfight. We'll come to the square or see you on the way to the station."

"I'm leaving at seven."

"Look for us, and we'll try to track you down."

"Well, well," said Sol's boyfriend after Jorge left. "Look what she was hiding away! He looks like the leading man from a play. Any chance we can know the lad's name?"

How I hated each and every one of them! Now more than ever they were vulgar and odious. The second the last bull fell, I ran home in search of Tía Manuelita.

"Come on, Tía, let's go to the station. Jorge's in town, and he wants to see you."

"Jorge Medina?"

"Yes, I ran into him at the fight. Not a word to mother."

Mother and Antonio were playing cards at the dining room table and were surprised to see us heading out.

"Where are you going, auntie? There are people all over the place. You're too old to be out and about on a holiday."

"I'm going out with the girl. We'll take a walk and come straight home. I too get bored of never seeing anything; I'm not old enough to sit around the house all day!"

The square was full of people, but the carts had emptied out. We took the alley beside town hall and walked Calle Real twice for good measure.

"It's unlikely we'll see him," said Tía Manuelita, already tired.

So we sat on a bench in the gazebo and watched the passersby. It was nearly seven. We saw mother heading to the station on Antonio's arm, but they didn't see us.

"Us too, let's go to the station," said Tía. "Maybe we'll run into him there."

Sad and disheartened, without saying a word, we made our way through the river of people on the promenade that ended at the station.

"Doña Manuelita," shouted Jorge out of the blue. "Thank God I saw you! I've been looking all over since I ran into María Luisa."

They chatted happily. Talking about travel made Tía young again, and Jorge had spent a year in Italy. The two of them talked and talked. He'd painted a lot, but one could never know too much. And now, she asked, what was he doing in Madrid?

"I'm sitting for exams to get a teaching post, and the second I pass, I'm heading to a province to live in peace. I'm no good for life. I don't like people and keep more and more to myself. Books, brushes—they're the only things that matter, and nature. I'd gladly trade Rome and all its museums for a spot in the mountains outside Madrid!"

Tía Manuelita disagreed, but I listened in a state of ecstasy. I hadn't heard anyone talk like that for years, not since I'd stopped seeing Jorge.

My aunt and I had an unspoken agreement not to say a word about Jorge at home, but mother and possibly Antonio had seen us with him.

"So Jorge Medina's in town?" asked mother over dinner. "What a nobody! He'd be better off learning his place and staying away from people he's got no right addressing."

"I don't know why," roared Tía Manuelita. "The boy couldn't have treated you better, and nobody but you is to blame if you got suspicious. As for me, I plan to invite him over the instant I'm back in Madrid. I haven't got so many friends I can spare such an interesting prospect. He's traveled a lot and knows so much!"

Mother kept quiet after that. We heard knocking at the door and the banter of girls coming to pick me up for the fair.

"I'm tired and would rather go to bed!"

"Come on, what's that nonsense?" said Tía Manuelita, who wouldn't hear of me missing a chance to have fun. "Enough of that, off to the fair. And nobody has to stay up late for you. I'll come down later and open the door."

The gazebo had music and dancing and was decorated with paper chains and colored lanterns. Sol's family brought us some benches from their house nearby. The sweethearts were talking, the girls whispering gossip and flirting with the boys.

"You know the cave off the road where the beggar woman lives? Paquita's servants all went there this afternoon."

"All of them? Why?"

"Don't play dumb. You know why…"

"How disgusting!"

"And you know what José Luis told us? That with their skirt over their head, all women look alike."

One of Paquita's brothers had come from Madrid with a nice Peruvian lad with a voice sweet as honey. He'd already driven the girls into a frenzy. They would flirt with him brazenly, and he'd flirt back without making any commitments. He hadn't even looked at me.

On the second night of the fair, he sat down beside me.

"Do you know many poems? They told me you're always reading."

I retreated into my shell and held my breath, fearing his mockery.

"I like to read, too. Do you know 'The Fisherman' by Núñez de Arce?"

"No."

"What about 'Despair' by Espronceda?"

"No, I don't."

"But you must know about Bécquer's spring swallows."

I didn't feel like talking. I was sure he was making fun of me and the others were just waiting to burst out laughing.

The musicians started a waltz, and the couples rose to dance. Albertina and her little sister Caridad remained on the bench with me and the Peruvian.

"Want to dance?" he asked.

"I don't know how."

"All right, but at least stand up as if you were going to. We'll take a walk."

I stood, and we crossed the square, making our way through the dancers towards the promenade down to the station. The fragrance of honeysuckle was wafting through the freshly watered gardens, and there were couples strolling along the wall in the darkness. Overhead the stars were twinkling. Oh, how I longed to be alone!

"Do you have a boyfriend?"

"No."

"Would you like to be my girlfriend?"

"No, I don't want to ever get married."

He arched his brows and tried to look me in the face.

"Caramba! What a way to brush me off! You know, I never would have guessed it. The girls around here are chomping at the bit to get married."

"I know, but not me."

"So what are you going to do?"

"I don't know."

"Well, we're not going to be boyfriend and girlfriend, but we can be friends, if you like. I have a little sister like you in Peru, just as plain and homely. She says she'll never get married, either… You must be smart and get bored of those other girls. Me too, to be honest. Don't tell the others, but I get bored to death. They talk like little kids! Lucky for me, I leave tomorrow. Luis is my friend, and he's something else, but as for his younger sister…"

We talked about the town and the festivities, so loud and so dusty, and when the music stopped, we went back to the bench, where everyone was waiting for us in anxious anticipation.

"She gave me the cold shoulder," said the Peruvian.

"Listen," whispered Sol, "you didn't really believe him, did you?"

"No."

"It was just to have a laugh."

"I know."

Perhaps they'd gotten together to plot the whole thing, and even though their ruse hadn't worked the way they wanted, I resolved never to see them again.

"They make fun of me, Tía. I don't want to go back there!"

"But surely it's all in your imagination. I can't believe it. Anyway, they're all just a bunch of country bumpkins. You're better off without them. Nobody here's worth our time of day."

The following day, Tía Manuelita wrote to Jorge and made me add some words of my own.

"Send him warm greetings and sign your name."

Later at home, she said out of nowhere, "The Kaiser's sister is marrying a violinist. I think it's great. An artist is worth at least as much as an aristocrat. Don't you agree, Juanita?"

JORGE MEDINA

Summer passed, followed by autumn, and the short cold days of winter kept me and mother around the foot stove. And there was no more Tía Manuelita to cheer up the long, reproachful silences.

Still, there was a truce at Christmas. Antonio came and spent the holiday with us, and I tried to be merry and friendly, for my youth was freezing over out of solitude and lack of earnest affection.

In those days Paquita had gotten married in Madrid to her Frenchman. Her mother, an exaggerating Andalusian known in town as Señora Gimpy, was going around spinning yarns about the fabulous ceremony. The bishop of Sion had married them in the chapel at the marquis' palace, with two ministers and a banker as witnesses. The pharmacist's wife told us the Frenchman was the marchioness's hairdresser and the witnesses were more than likely the household servants.

Antonio and mother would die laughing whenever I imitated Paquita's mother.

"Look here, *madame*, I'll tell you how it happened," I would gesture wildly. "My dear little Paquita came into the church on the arm of Prince Chulalongkorn of Siam, and the organ burst out into the opening strains of the umbrella waltz, just the right thing for the occasion. And René—because my son-in-law's name is René, which despite how it sounds is no name for a pussy cat—René came in on the arm of the princess of Caraman-Chimay, a pretty princess if there ever was one, but no match at all for my Paquita."

And while mother keeled over laughing and Antonio stared at me, entranced, I'd string together names and extravagant characters in a speech that would last till mother ordered me to be quiet.

"Enough, enough already! My whole body aches."

Those days of living together and seeing me in a good mood spurred Antonio to make a second or third attack. On Easter he'd given me a wrist watch, a wax stamp, and two books of poetry. Every so often, mother would make me read a poem out loud after dinner.

One night she left me reading while she went to pay the maid. Antonio went on pretending to listen, though in reality he never paid attention. When I least expected it, he put his hand on the book.

"Say, María Luisa, when are you going to decide to love me? Don't you see how well we get along?"

I shut my mouth, and he mistook my silence for some sort of acquiescence.

"Or maybe you already love me a little. Is that it? Is it?"

"No, I don't love you."

He'd been getting closer, and I pulled away in such deep disgust that he got mad.

"Ah, so now I'm the bad guy," he muttered. "Really, I don't know what you're thinking. You must prefer that lousy painter. You've got your head in the clouds, girl."

When mother got back, she knew from our mood what had happened and said it was time to go to bed. I jumped at the chance to bid them goodnight and go to my room while they stayed put talking quietly. Who knows? Maybe they were talking about Jorge and mingling my name and his.

The following day, Antonio left for Madrid with barely a look at me, and mother was harder to live with than ever. We'd go for hours and days without speaking. The new maid was young and clever and looked at me with pity in her eyes.

"Poor señorita! People think girls like you are always happy, what with being people of means. But that's not true; you're always sad. It's hard to believe your mother treats you like that, with you being her only daughter."

One day walking past where I was embroidering, mother bumped into my chair and almost fell flat on her face.

"You're always in the way, always a bother!"

"Am I really such a burden to you?" I asked her, wounded by her tone.

"Yes, really! Didn't you realize? Well, now you know!"

Days and days passed with no other joys than the shreds I could scrounge from my seventeen measly years on this earth.

One day, Tía Manuelita came with Antonio.

"I ran into this thickwit at the station and had to put up with him all the way here. He's a real brute! I can't believe your mother wants to marry you off to him! By the way, look what Jorge gave me for you."

It was a little notebook with several sketches, some with a caption in pencil. Under a gnarled old holm oak appeared the dedication, "For you, María Luisa, who can hear the trees speaking."

"If you want to thank him, I'll give him the letter."

I wrote a little note that ended up filling two pages front and back. I started off complimenting and thanking him for the sketches, and closed saying I was dying of sadness and couldn't take it anymore. I didn't state the cause of my distress, but Tía must've seen to that.

"Is your mother still in a bad mood? Yes, I already noticed... And Antonio's stopped talking to you. So sorry to hear he's ill!... Ah, but he talked to you again, did he? I hope he goes straight to Hell! Who does he think he is, the mangy mutt? He doesn't deserve a whiff of you. You're practically a blue-blooded aristocrat. Yes, you've got your father's blood, but only a little, because there's always more of the mother's. Your noble stock for his gravedigger's blood, I shudder to think of it!"

At the table she gave us her personal account of our family crest.

"It's carved in stone on the door of the house that our grandparents sold, and it's got three cauldrons and five gold coins. They say the king of France gave the coins to our great-great-grandfather, who lost them in a bet."

"Auntie, you've got it all wrong. You've got no idea what you're talking about. Those coins were a donation from our ancestor, the first Count, to recover the image of Saint John they worship in the town parish."

Though she seldom spoke of it and barely gave it any importance, mother knew much more than Tía Manuelita about our family history.

A week later, Sabina the maid called me aside with an air of mystery.

"Señorita, I got a letter for you. It came in an envelope addressed to me, with another one inside that says, 'For Señorita María Luisa Arroyo.' It must be from your aunt, who wrote down my name in a little notebook when she was here last Sunday."

It was from Jorge.

"I still can't save you from the sadness you're living in, but if I'm able to later, would you agree to marry me? It's the only dignified way for a man to help a woman. If you don't want to, don't be afraid to say so, and I promise to do whatever I can. But in that case, it won't be much."

I didn't get a wink of sleep that night. Me get married? It would mean leaving that house that wasn't mine and never had been, escaping Antonio's attacks and mother's nasty words, and painting with Jorge, who'd go back to being my teacher. And I'd choose my own furniture, paintings, and books, and would read even if it weren't Sunday. And perhaps I'd have a pretty house with a garden by the sea, and Jorge would take me to Galicia…

There was, however, something I didn't want to think about. But who knows? Maybe with him it would be a moot point.

I sent him my response.

"Yes, I do want to marry you. Whenever, however—it doesn't matter. In the meantime, write to me every day and send stamps for me to reply, because otherwise I won't be able to. I'm going to make a sketch of the grape vine twisting in the cold and send it to you."

Everything around me changed. The house was brighter, the blackbirds were announcing the spring, and Sabina sang gaily over her washing. Mother would give me long looks and still wouldn't talk to me, and Antonio had stopped bringing me gifts but hadn't made any new advances, either. And I was living in an excited state of expectation, as if a bottle of perfume had poured into my life and was making me light in the head.

Sabina brought me a letter every day on her way back from shopping, for we'd arranged with the postman not to deliver them to the house.

"What a good and punctual boyfriend you've got," she'd say, philosophizing over the letters. "It's really something, writing every day. Since you can't talk in person, if you didn't write, you couldn't say a thing to each other. But I have to ask, what have you got to talk about every day?"

One morning, Sabina came back scandalized from the square.

"You know what the talk is at the grocery? They were saying Señorito Antonio's filthy rich, has a shop in Madrid, and maintains you and your mother because he's your lover. I thought I was going to burst! Because I of all people know that's a lie."

"What wicked folk," I said, scared because I thought the whole town had turned against us.

And I told Jorge everything in the next day's letter.

"Go figure! All that special treatment finally gave the townspeople something to talk about, and they're lambasting me and saying I'm his mistress."

The reply came two days later and was curt and to the point. The blow had been terrible, but he'd made his decision, and it could be only this: everything between us had ended. A woman whose honor's in doubt has no choice but to accept her fate. He was sorry from the bottom of his heart.

The altar where I'd placed Jorge came crashing down, dragging with it all my faith and hope in a better existence. With my eyes burning and dry and my thoughts in disarray, I lived like an automaton for a week until Tía Manuelita got there on Sunday.

"What in the world did you tell that poor boy? He came over to see me stark raving mad. My dear, you've got no common sense. Why'd you go telling him that?"

"Who was I supposed to tell? He said in every letter not to hide anything from him."

"Nonsense! You can't ever tell men the truth."

"But Jorge, I thought Jorge was different from the others."

"The same, dear, the same! When it comes to their honor—or what they call their honor, which is nothing more than fear of making a fool of themselves—they all say the same nonsense. I'm telling you as someone who's been married twice."

"But Tía, Jorge…"

"Just like the others. Men have to be handled with care. I'll see to setting things straight. You've got no idea what I'm doing for you! And you go spoiling it all over some silly little thing. No more telling stories. Flirt with him, tease him, keep him wanting more. Jorge will be ours, and you'll be married in a year."

198

"But now I don't want to marry him!"

"Ah, so you'd rather put up with the advances of that brute! By the way, not a word to Jorge about whether he kissed you. Watch yourself! I don't need to remind you how happy you'd make your mother and Antonio if you end things with Jorge."

"But they don't know."

"You think they don't know? You've got your head in the clouds! They know it just like you do, and they realize they've lost and are throwing the game. Their bark is worse than their bite! You think your mother didn't tell me?"

Tía Manuelita took Jorge a letter from me, and he answered immediately forgiving me for the headache my childishness had caused him. I never found out what Tía had told him, but from then on I stopped writing to him with the same puerile sincerity.

Carmen and Teresa came with their aunt and uncle in May, and all I wanted was to talk to Carmen. She'd understand me! I could tell her everything!

"Mother, will you let me go next door for a while?"

"Go ahead, go, and if you don't feel like it, don't come back. You can't wait to talk about things you shouldn't."

Sitting and chatting with Carmen on the sofa in her room, I was quick to forget mother's nasty words. My friend was very worried at the moment. Teresita had a boyfriend and wanted to get married as soon as possible, but he was a womanizer and had three years of school left.

"It's madness, Lord, pure madness!"

The news about Jorge was fine by her, but she was scared for me.

"You're so out of touch with the world, and men are so…"

"I'm hoping Jorge won't be like the others. What do you think?"

"It depends what you're talking about. You've already had proof he reacts to certain things just like the rest of them. As for what you're thinking but not saying out loud…"

I found her ideas on the topic most original.

"It disgusts me to think of that cursed night! If it were to happen on a random day in a moment of excitement, so be it! But planned out like that, after months of preparation with the whole family's help, and the Church as a go-between… And after an exhausting day of bustle and friends' double entendres… How disgusting! I just don't know."

Carmen had once had a boyfriend whom she'd liked a lot, but just before the wedding he'd spoken with her parents in private and disappeared for good.

"What happened?"

"I think he had some terrible disease," Carmen replied. "Now I've got another and am determined to get married. He wants to do it right away. Him or another, it doesn't make a difference, so long as I get out of my aunt and uncle's house."

Sometimes we didn't talk. I'd slip my arm around her waist, she'd put hers over my shoulder, and nestled there on the sofa, we'd let hours go by savoring a sweet sensation of abandon, of mutual understanding and heartfelt sincerity.

"It's already twelve," I'd say when the clock struck. "Time to go home. What a pity!"

"Yes, what a pity!"

I'd find mother sewing and waiting for me in the foyer.

"So you're done saying things that you shouldn't?"

And I'd head to my room for my needlepoint in silence.

One morning I got to Carmen's house very nervous.

"I came because Jorge's on his way to town. Tía Manuelita told him he should talk to mother and formalize our relationship."

"I'm so happy for you, dear, so very happy."

"Yes, me too… After all the times I said I'd never get married! I don't know what's going to happen. I'm so scared!"

"Don't be silly! You'll see, nothing will change. Once we get married, we'll look for houses that are close together so we can go and see each other every afternoon. What do you think?"

Yes, yes; of course that was a good idea. But just then I could think of nothing except what was happening between Jorge and mother. Dear Lord, she was going to be a wreck!

But she didn't take it as badly as I anticipated. When I got back home, Jorge had left on the eleven-thirty train.

"Everything's just as you and your Tía Manuelita wanted," said mother. "We'll see how it all works out. Personally, I'm washing my hands of it, though I think it's absurd. Artists were never any good at raising families. But don't get ahead of yourself. All he did was ask permission to visit twice a week and write to you daily. The only way I'll agree to this marriage is if he passes his exams, and that's yet to be seen."

Antonio didn't take it hard either when he came on Sunday. I think he already knew.

"So you're going to get married? Well, dear, good luck. I'll be a witness if you like, so you can see for yourself I don't bear a grudge. I've got a girlfriend myself now, believe it or not, and she's quite a bit better than you. Out with the old, in with the new."

Jorge came on Thursday. Mother didn't leave us alone for an instant but treated him friendly enough. We talked about art and books and theater and all the things I hadn't heard talk of ever since they threw him out of the house. And mother listened, interested in the conversation. Then we went out to the garden, and he pointed out the new shoots of the grape vines, pretty as jewels with glimmers of chiseled gold.

Thank the Lord! I was finally breathing easy after the awful nightmare that had lasted for so many months. Mother started talking to me again, and even though she wasn't very friendly, at least the conversation wasn't forced. Antonio's visits no longer scared me, and I could write and receive letters and listen to interesting conversation. A bright, pleasant path was extending before me long into the distance.

"You've got to start learning how to manage a household," mother would tell me. "Go into the kitchen once in a while. Learn how to cook something. Just think, if you get married—and it's still not for sure—you'll have to keep a humble house and think up all kinds of ways to stretch your money. And then there'll be children to make life more difficult."

The thought of it made my blood run cold. Children! A husband! That horrific first night of which I too was to be a protagonist!

Around that time the whole town was talking about Sol's older sister, Dolorcitas. A rich widower twice her age had asked for her hand in marriage. She didn't love him, but her mother had thrown herself at her feet in tears.

"Daughter, save us. We're drowning in debt!"

Dolorcitas had given in but was starting to look pale, with dark circles under her eyes and a look of pained stupor. Mother was constantly praising her, not without a hint of sarcasm towards me.

"What a good daughter! God will reward her."

Jorge passed his first exam in July and his second one two weeks later. And one morning in August when I was at Carmen's house, Sabina came over with a smile on her face.

"Señorita, your mother said for you to come quickly. Señorito Jorge's here, and his exams are over. And now it's official, you're getting married."

With my heart beating hard, I bid Carmen goodbye and ran back to my house as fast as my legs could carry me. Jorge came out to greet me holding out his hands.

"I got a job, dear. We won! I got a job! I'm hoping they leave me in Madrid, because I got one of the highest rankings. I thought about sending a telegram, but I wanted to break the news in person."

I couldn't speak. Seeing him so pleased, I beamed with happiness.

"What do you think? Tell me, what do you think?" he repeated.

"She's speechless," mother explained. "Her girl friends make her stupid. After you get married, you mustn't let her keep them. She's a passionate soul, and her girl friends always come first over her family."

HONEYMOON

Tía Manuelita was my maid of honor, and I left for the church from her house, dressed as a bride with gauze flounces and a tulle and orange blossom veil.

It's all a shameful memory and still makes me blush after so many years. The cars in a line at the church door; Jorge, his brothers, and the witnesses in frock coats and top hats; me walking down the sidewalk on the arm of Jorge's father between two rows of curious onlookers.

Mother cried and blessed me on my way out of the house, and I kept calm. Deep down inside it seemed like a farce we were acting, and I wanted to play the smallest role possible.

Despite wearing a blazer and derby, Antonio was one of the witnesses. At the meal he took the liberty of telling me some jokes.

"Today you've got to eat more than usual. You won't be getting much sleep!"

It wasn't shame but horror I felt hearing his allusions to something mysterious and terrible I'd have preferred not to think about. Two days earlier I'd been on the brink of calling it all off.

I dreamt that the friendly voice whose thoughts often filled my head while I slept was saying, "Ten years, twenty years will pass, and your desire for him will come to an end, but he'll still seek you out to satisfy his."

That morning I spoke with Tía Manuelita.

"I don't want to get married, Tía. I don't!"

"Have you gone mad? Why not? Did they tell you something about Jorge? Do you think this is all just child's play?"

"No, it's just that..."

"What?"

"Well... I don't like men."

"Good! As long as you like your husband, that's more than enough."

"Not him, either."

"What? Are you really going to tell me you don't like your husband-to-be? Don't come to me with that nonsense! There must be something else. Forget the hearsay, dear. Just look how Jorge gets when he's around you!"

It was true. I'd already noticed, and that was precisely what terrified me most. More than once, I'd seen a look come over his face that made the corners of his mouth twitch. He desired me, and that's why he was marrying me!

"But of course, dear, of course," said Tía Manuelita. "If men didn't desire us women, they'd never get married. All the girls know it and make themselves desirable."

The day of the wedding there was rain, and it was terribly long and boring. We left for Segovia in the evening and got there after dark.

For over a month it was like I'd been living in dreams: the shopping, the scent of fresh cloth filling Tía's house, the perfume of the flowers sent daily by Jorge, and the new life I was about to begin, which was changing everything from my shoes, all brand new, to my hairstyle.

The day after the wedding I woke up tired and sore. So much excitement, such lofty poetry, all for such a poor and vulgar result!

Jorge was still asleep, and I washed and dressed without him hearing me. The most absolute disillusion had emptied me of mind and soul. I leaned out the balcony over the courtyard and contemplated the ground below. Imagine I let myself fall! From four floors up, I'd die from the impact. Just like that, everything over! No more husband or home or children. A real relief! And why not? One jump was all it would take. I studied the large, dirty flagstones with the drain in the middle. Perhaps it was clogged, for the previous day's rain had left a sickening puddle.

I'd fall into that dirty water and die with my mouth and my brow submerged in the squalor. And what would it matter? My body, intact the night before, felt defiled. Dear Lord, to think that I'd loved him!

"María Luisa, where are you?" Jorge was calling.

That first day was followed by others, a month, two, three... And I led the life of a newlywed, that life in which the young wife meekly resigns herself to satisfying the repressed or poorly sated appetites of a man at the peak of his virility.

I thought and thought, at all waking hours. Would things go on like that forever? Did all women live that way? Were all marriages like that? But no woman ever complained! On the contrary, some novels I'd read praised carnal love and the husband's so-called sweet secret. Of course, it was men who wrote novels.

Jorge loved me very much. He loved me with an artist's angst, a child's selfishness, and a man's cordial condescension. But he loved me! He loved me more than anyone before, or so he'd have me think from his constant demonstrations. Then again, my individual existence didn't count for much in our future life.

"When we settle down in Madrid, our house will have a studio. I need a studio to work. How you'll like watching me paint while you sew! Isn't that right, darling?"

"I'd like to paint, too," I ventured to suggest.

"What for? You barely know how... I want something of mine in all the exhibitions. You'll have plenty to brag about when your hubby wins a first place medal. Just wait and see."

It didn't even cross his mind that I could be the one to win the medal.

My husband seemed different from that other Jorge who gave me lessons when I was a girl and talked to me in the town square that distant afternoon. I had to make an effort to unite the two images in my thoughts. On the other hand, he was a lot like father. Lord, how he reminded me of father!

Some nights I'd dream I was going out for a stroll holding hands with father. When I looked him in the face, he'd turn out to be Jorge and father all at once. The confusion would carry over into the day, tinging my relations with Jorge and making them stranger and more absurd, not that I ever told my husband.

"When we move into our house," said Jorge constantly. "When I'm working in my studio... When you see to my clothes and bring me breakfast..."

But I had no desire to have a house, nor to spend the day sewing, nor to serve him breakfast in bed. Those projects sounded to me like a service I'd be forced to perform. Jorge would paint, and I—well, I'd sew and help the maid clean and manage our finances. And to watch Jorge paint would be my sole happiness. It had to be that way! Such was the life of all married women! Society's established order was that and none other.

In November we went back to Madrid, where Jorge had his teaching job and Tía Manuelita had found us a small apartment. What we didn't have was money, so we set up the bedroom and studio with mother's old furniture, gifts from Tía, and some pieces Jorge had his family send from Galicia.

Small as it was, the rest of the flat remained empty save for a cot and a washstand in the maid's room.

I poured all my honest efforts into keeping up with the housework. I planned meals a day in advance, paid the bills, made the beds, and helped with the cleaning. And those chores took all morning long, not leaving a moment to rest, while the afternoon was given over to sewing Jorge's clothes, which had also come from Galicia in a trunk.

Mother visited us from the town and realized right away I was a wreck of a housewife.

"You spend more than you should, and you don't keep an eye on the maid. A liter of oil down the drain in two days. Dear, it can't be!"

Even Tía Manuelita was in complete agreement.

And I thought I was working wonders by waxing the old furniture and sewing patches on Jorge's pants!

His salary lasted till the twentieth of the month, sometimes till the twenty-second, but there were always more days than money. Tía Manuelita lent me enough to get by, but since it had to be returned when Jorge got paid, every month it got harder to make the money last.

That threw me into a constant anguish, and there were times I would try to tell Jorge.

"Look what's left for me to finish the month! And that's after I cut out butter for me and the maid at breakfast!"

"Don't come to me with money problems," he'd answer in a sour mood. "I give you everything I earn, haven't got a dime in my pocket. And by the way, I need you to send for two packs of cigarettes and give me ten pesetas for two tubes of oils."

For he was perpetually in need of tubes of paint or an expensive brush or a canvas stretcher. And it wasn't as though he was painting very much; on the contrary, months went by with him twiddling his thumbs. But whenever he planned a new picture, it inevitably came with a shopping list.

"If only I had the money," he'd constantly whine. "The mountains must be in flower at this time of year."

"It's true! If only we had the money."

But all we had was his meager salary, and half of it went to the rent, the maid, the electricity, professional memberships, and a book subscription. Then came pencils, paints, and canvases, followed by food, only out of necessity.

Some nights I went to bed crying. How difficult it was to be a housewife!

"But of course, dear, of course," said Tía Manuelita. "You just haven't got the knack for it! It's something you learn without thinking. It's every woman's instinct, like raising children."

Books alone made that life bearable. Jorge had gotten his library shipped from Galicia, and we were paying installments for a collection of great works. Reading them took up most of my evening and filled my thoughts for the rest of the day, such that I often forgot to check the time when the maid soaked the garbanzos or came home from shopping.

Jorge would read, too, and had completely stopped painting. He spent the morning at school every third day and stayed home reading the rest of the time.

During one period when mother was staying with Tía Manuelita, she'd come over in the evening and look at us in shock.

"Doesn't your husband have any private commissions? He could be doing something, giving lessons. Since you two are so low on money…"

I found out from her that Antonio had also gotten married. By then he owned the shop and was trying to buy another one.

"He's a real go-getter. His wife can certainly count herself a happy woman. They've got two maids."

I ran into him once, with his red eyes and potbelly, and realized I was happy not to have married him. All the same, he still seemed to be looking out for us.

"Antonio told me," said mother one morning when my husband was out, "that if Jorge would like to make some drawings for the summer fabrics, he's friends with a manufacturer, and you could make some extra money."

Jorge got mad when I told him.

"What do I know about decorative art? I've never designed a fabric, nor do I want to now. You can tell your mother *no*."

"Really, dear, she was only trying to help. And if they pay well…"

"I've got no use for money if it means selling myself out. And neither do you, I don't think."

When I told mother his reply, she paused for a moment and didn't look at me.

"I always thought when a man got married it was his duty to attend to the necessities of his household and accept any paying job that crossed his path. At least, that's what your father always did."

"It's just, he doesn't know a thing about decorative art."

"But being a drawing professor, I'm sure he could buckle down and learn a little something."

"He's a good painter. You know it's true. And naturally, painters have qualms about lowering their art beneath certain standards."

"I'm sure they do. But first he's got to make a living."

"And he's doing that. He's got his salary."

Having kept quiet for months, mother went off like a bomb.

"And what a fine salary it is! It's enough to rent himself a good studio, buy brushes and rubbish he doesn't even use, and smoke his pipe with fine blond tobacco! And to Hell with you, dear!"

"That's where you're wrong, mother. He wants more than anything for me to eat and wear nice clothes."

"And where's the money for that? Tell me, where is it? What he wants is not to know a thing about your hardships, for you to work miracles with a pair of pesetas so as not to spoil his delicate digestion. I knew this would happen! Artists are all alike. That's why I was against this marriage in the first place. And now I want nothing to do with you two. Did you think I didn't know they offered him a lesson and he turned it down? That too would be selling out. Lord help me! Where will we put the saint on his altar? I'm better off staying in the town where I don't see you. Always reading, reading away, as if he had nothing better to do."

"Well, I can't say a thing as far as that's concerned. Let me assure you, I read a lot, too. And if he can't earn a living like other men and has to scrape by on his paltry salary, I'm just as worthless as a wife. I'm a disaster, an absolute disaster."

"I don't doubt it, dear," exclaimed mother with the disdain of a perfect housewife. "I don't doubt it a bit. If you'd married the way I wanted, I'd be living with you, taking care of the house until you learned the ropes. But not under these circumstances. I'm telling you, I'm not coming back to Madrid. Because I pity you, child, and it pains me to see you so skinny and your eyes so sad. They weren't like that before, not even when you played the victim because your mother tried to keep you on the straight and narrow."

Unable to stand her pity, I burst out crying, but mother's voice kept right on grating in my ears.

"Well, there's nothing to do now, dear. My conscience is clear, having always done my duty. The only thing left is for you to grit your teeth and suffer without making a scandal. It's a lost cause when a woman marries badly, and the only honorable and decent thing to do is to keep quiet, try to adapt, and take life fighting tooth and nail… And to pray hard for God to keep you going strong."

"But that's not it! That's not why I'm thin and ill," I protested, wiping my tears. "That's not it at all. I know my duty's to watch over my house and make compromises and bend to my husband's will. I already know it, and I'm not looking or asking for anything else."

"Then why are you so ill and despairing that way?"

"It's just that… I shouldn't have married. I'm useless as a wife."

"Useless? What a thing to say! A woman's only path is marriage."

"Yes, it might be; it might be for other women. But my path it's not, of that I'm most certain."

SINCERITY

There's a woman here who says her name's Sole and she's the mistress's friend," the maid came in saying.

And behind her came a pretty working-class girl, plump, tall, and plain, who embraced me effusively.

"Look how thin you are! And how long it took me to find you! You know I always liked you much more than you did me. So you're a married woman! Me too. My Alfonso's a sergeant, an educated, refined kind of guy. He wanted to come with me, but I wouldn't let him. For all I know, yours could be a bigwig."

"He's a painter," I said.

"A painter? Really, dear! I thought you'd marry above that. Because if you settled for a painter, you could've easily found…"

It took her a while to realize Jorge didn't paint doors or signs on shop entrances.

"Ah, I see. He's the kind who paints pictures. My Alfonso knows this guy who goes around coffee shops selling his paintings, but he doesn't earn much. Yours must make more."

212

She told me she'd searched for months before finding me. In the end, Tía Manuelita had told her I'd gotten married and given her my address.

"That aunt of yours is one elegant woman. She told me all kinds of things about your family. I say, you're people of the highest rank. Of course, that won't *encumber* us from spending time together."

Much to my astonishment, Sole repeated the word four or five times. She must've learned it from her husband, seeing how he was so educated and refined.

The two of them were very happy. They lived in an interior room on Calle de Ave María and had a cheap little maid who washed the dishes and did laundry while Sole embroidered runners for the shelves. Having a maid was a great source of pride for my friend.

"You know how maids are. If you don't keep a constant eye on them... Because my Alfonso's good at heart, but he's got quite a temper, and nothing gets past him."

Then she explained in detail that her Alfonso didn't like soup, and you had to ask just what he wanted. He liked his boots clean and never thought they were shiny enough, and his handkerchiefs had to be pressed with a hint of starch. And God forbid his shirts have wrinkles!

"He's very particular about that. I made him three silk shirts, and you don't know how hard I worked to make sure the collars fit perfectly. I took out each neckband at least ten times. He's a smart dresser, that one!"

The way she said it got on my nerves, as if instead of annoying her, his fussiness gave her an intimate pleasure and pride in serving him.

"If you want to know what I think, he could get his shirts made elsewhere."

"The things you come up with! After all, a woman's only job is to make her man comfortable. Why else would he put bread on the table?"

"Well, I'd like to put it there, too."

Sole looked at me, astonished. What was that supposed to mean? I'd always been so strange! What I needed was a bun in the oven.

213

So? Nothing to report? She was already five months along.

"Yesterday we bought a bonnet, so little I could fit it on my fist. We were almost in tears, the two of us. What a wonderful thing are kids! My Alfonso doesn't know what to do with me now that I'm expecting. Of course, that doesn't *encumber* us from quarrelling once in a while. Even well-oiled gears make friction."

I suspected I was three months *along*, as Sole had put it, but I didn't want to tell her, nor did I like to talk about it.

Several days later, I went to see Carmen, who'd also gotten married while I was away. Mother had *done our duty*, giving her one of the useless gifts from my wedding.

Her husband was one of those men who are hard to put a finger on: no personality, neither tall nor short, fat nor thin, young nor old. Bald, with a long mustache in the fashion of the time, and a mocking sneer on his face.

Carmen had me sit on a fragile sofa in her modern sitting room, and while her husband paced in front of us with his hands behind his back, we chatted about the dirty, uncomfortable inns on our honeymoons, the difficulty of finding a good maid, and the wonderful gift we'd given them.

But the instant Rogelio left the room, Carmen slipped her arm over my shoulder like old times.

"What's the matter with you?" she asked, making me turn and look at her. "Something's wrong. Why are you so thin? Don't you know women get fat after their wedding?"

"Yes, but not me."

"Ah, María Luisa, we've made a big mistake!"

"You too?"

"If you only knew how jealous I am of nuns for sleeping alone all night!"

We spoke at length, lowering our voices so her husband couldn't hear us in the next room over. Poor Carmen! She'd had worse luck than me because Rogelio had plenty of experience in *that* department and would treat her like a woman off the street now and then.

"The things he says and the faces he makes! Expressions right out of a brothel! At times he's in rut for over a month, and even when we don't lie down together, he calls me to his bed in the middle of the night."

But despite her complaints, I saw right away that Carmen didn't feel the intimate desperation I had inside me.

"What we've got to do is adapt," she said, "and try to feel the pleasure everyone's always going on about. And most important of all, they mustn't realize we don't like it. If you could only see Paquita! She's put on weight and walks with a swagger, all rosy and bright. Now she goes around advising all the girls to marry."

Teresita had also gotten married and was living in the house in the town until he finished his studies.

"Now that's what worries me," Carmen confided. "He's already dallying with the mayor's daughter, not two months after the wedding! My poor sister's suffering horribly. If only we did things twice!"

And that's when Carmen let loose her sense of humor.

"How absurd it is not to rehearse things! Just think what a play would be like if the actors didn't know their parts and hadn't practiced what they had to say and do. A disaster, no doubt! They've got to study everything in depth, meet numerous times, even mark the spots on stage where each scene takes place. But in life there aren't any rehearsals. It's no wonder how things turn out!"

She ended up making me laugh, and I got back home in higher spirits than when I went out.

Jorge noticed the change right away.

"What happened for you to be so cheerful?"

"That Carmen, the things she comes up with! She really is funny!"

And I repeated what she'd told me. Naturally, I omitted certain things I would've been ashamed to tell my husband. Jorge didn't laugh, and I saw I'd made a silly mistake.

"You won't go back to that woman's house. You're a child," he said, "and you can't know the damage of such conversations. Did you really think a decent woman talks about rehearsing for marriage?"

"But, dear, it was only a joke!"

"There are things one can't even joke about. And if her husband thinks it's fine and allows her to talk that way, I, on the other hand, do not. I forbid you to stay friends with her... Or rather, do what you want. You're a grown woman. But you'd better watch out for the consequences."

"But she was the only real girl friend I had left," I whimpered.

"I told you, you can keep her, although I thought a wife had enough with her husband's friendship. But if you're of another opinion, do what you want... But not in my house. That woman won't set foot here. My home will always be an honorable household."

I didn't reply, and we both stopped talking. The evening went by in a hostile silence until it was time for bed. At least I'd sleep well that night, with my back to Jorge, seeking the most comfortable position. My chest was still tight when his arm reached around me.

"Darling, dearest! Are you mad? Don't you understand it's all out of love for you? I'm jealous of the air you breathe. If you want, we'll be happy, very happy! Alone in the world, just you and me."

His voice was getting all affectionate, his breathing was speeding up, and there he was, squeezing me tightly. And nothing could stop the sacrifice from taking place: not the child already occupying the space between our bodies, nor my sad resignation, nor the memory of the violent scene.

Days later, Carmen came to see me, but the maid was under orders to always say nobody was home. I heard the disappointment in her voice but couldn't run to meet her.

So all I had left for a friend was Sole. We had nothing in common, and she bored me to death.

"She's a good woman without any sort of sentimental complications," said Jorge. "Very ordinary, as your aunt would say, but truly an honest woman."

Jorge's brothers lived in Galicia and had already come two or three times to Madrid. Both of them were bachelors, slightly older than my husband. José María was the eldest, and he also painted, though he didn't make a living off his art. He never looked beyond the surface of things, and seeing me and Jorge, he confessed to being envious. He was constantly saying he wanted to get married.

The second eldest, Antonio, was tall and slim and bore no resemblance, moral or physical, to the shopkeeper of the same name. My brother-in-law Antonio was a pleasant conversationalist with an overactive imagination. He was extraordinarily observant, to the point he'd sometimes trip up and see things that existed only in his fantasy.

He wasted no time taking me as his confidante, and I learned all about his romances, both those that had failed and those that were still just beginning. He treated me affectionately, peer to peer, and recognized a worth in me that I wasn't used to anyone noticing.

"Why don't you make a go at painting? I'm sure you'd do it better than my brother, without the academic rigidity of those who see art as a science. You're another Madame Lebrun, and you shouldn't sit twiddling your thumbs."

When Jorge wasn't looking, I would show Antonio my sketches and the color studies I made when my husband wasn't home, and he'd always praise them to the skies.

"They're really good, girl! Stupendous, in fact! Why don't you start painting seriously?"

He'd also praise my work as a housewife, and there he was mistaken.

"You keep a charming house. My brother's one lucky guy!"

Hearing those compliments, Jorge said nothing in front of him but protested later on.

"I don't suppose you believe any of that! Because you might yet learn to be a housewife, but never to paint. He talks like that because he's never stuck to a discipline. He's got natural talent, like anyone who hasn't studied and has imagination to spare. But the technique of an art isn't something you learn in a matter of days. It takes years of study and countless tribulations you need not suffer. You women are something else, and your path is another. Home life and motherhood fill the prime of your life, and there's no time for slow and painstaking studies that would distract you from the true callings of your feminine nature. And most important, it's enough for me to paint in our household."

I said some of that to Antonio, making him laugh.

"My brother is tremendous! The most feminist, tolerant, and revolutionary of men! We'll see him with a potbelly, joining the Conservatives!"

Jorge and I went to the Prado a couple of times, after which I had no desire to return. He'd stand in front of a painting for hours, making me marvel over the confident brush strokes, the blended colors, the harmony of the lines. But the second I paused in front of something he didn't like, he'd get angry and rush me along.

"Don't tell me you like actually like that! It's rubbish! They ought to burn it."

"To tell you the truth, I did like it," I once took the risk of replying.

"Well, that proves you don't know a thing about painting. Nothing! And it's you who wants to paint? Honestly!"

We didn't like the same literature, either. Sometimes we'd agree on a work's observational skill, or the clarity, precision, and beauty of the language, but almost never on our like or dislike of the main characters, particularly when it came to women. According to my husband, all female characters who weren't docile, submissive, and sweet in the extreme had sprung from their author's head without a life of their own.

"In any case, if you like her, I needn't say a thing," he'd say, getting all serious and aggressive. "But in real life, if I met a woman with such a strong, masculine personality, I certainly wouldn't marry her."

And I felt closer to that kind of woman than to the others!

One afternoon, Tía Manuelita came to take me to the movies.

"Let's go, dear. You'll start to rot if you stay shut up here with that brute. We're going to see a lovely picture about the life of Our Lord!"

Real or fake, the landscapes of Bethany, the iris-lined roads of Nazareth, the impassioned figure of Mary Magdalene, and most of all the solemn music of the orchestra filling the theater moved me so much, I couldn't wait to get home and tell my husband.

"You can't imagine anything more beautiful! I've come back brimming with poetry. We've got to go back and see it together."

"I don't have to see a thing, nor have I interest in any such nonsense! You'll end up going to mass and confession."

"Really, dear, what's religion got to do with a work of art?"

"I told you, I want nothing to do with it, and you can keep your thoughts to yourself. I don't give a damn! I'm starting to observe we never agree about art or anything else. Get out of here!"

I answered back, angry at his injustice, and Jorge, nervous and overly literary, made a terrible scene with lines out of a play.

"You and I made a huge mistake! You should've married the shopkeeper, who suited you. Ours is an immense misfortune! We'll live the rest of our lives with the cadaver of our love coming between us!"

Then came a tearful reconciliation culminating in an excessively vehement and passionate embrace…

No, what was going to come tragically between us was not the cadaver of our love, but rather that of my sincerity, my naïve sincerity that was dying of a slow consumption.

I was dead set against causing another scene like that one, which had left me exhausted, sad, and definitively disillusioned. I'd adopt a literary role of the kind Jorge liked and play it with the skill of a leading actress. That pastime filled many years of my life, so many—alas—I came to forget who I was.

219

And since Jorge tended to forget things fast and live on the emotions of the present as if they'd never change, not a month had gone by when he declared to his brothers, "María Luisa and I think the same about everything."

"How boring," mocked Antonio.

"What do you know?"

In those days, a new element came into our life. In preparation for an exhibition, Jorge brought Joaquinito to the house, a young painter, slender and lithe, blond-haired and smooth-skinned, who was my friend before long because we had the same tastes and pastimes.

"He's the only girl friend I've got left," I joked with Tía Manuelita. "He knows much more than me about fashion, and he advises me about how to alter my dresses, and he knows how to set the table, and what flowers are in style, and how to arrange them in vases... And you should hear him recite! You'd really like it."

"Tread lightly," warned Tía. "Friendship between a man and a woman is always a path of thorns."

I had to laugh. Joaquinito wasn't a man; at least, I'd never thought so.

What's strangest is that one time he told me, "María Luisa, darling, you've got no idea how I love you! On the outside you look like a woman, so sweet and feminine, but what do you know? I've discovered you aren't one."

"Well, then, what am I?"

"I really couldn't say! What I do know is that you and I have something in common, and you'll never have a girl friend who understands you like I do, nor I a pal as dear to me as you. But don't tell Jorge. He's too much of a man."

"It's true!"

Didn't I know it, much to my misfortune.

A week after that conversation, Jorge sat me down.

"I just got done ordering the maid to tell Joaquinito next time he comes that you went to stay with your mother for a while. He's not too fond of me, so I hope he doesn't come back."

"But what were you thinking?"

"I heard that your dear Joaquinito is an invert. A filthy pig!"

"What's an invert? I don't know."

"Nor do you need to. That's the end of it. There'll be no more talk of any such thing in this household. From now on, it looks like we'll have to close the door on the rest of the world. Isn't it true, dear, we're better off alone?"

"Yes, you're right. Whatever you want."

And my lonely soul shed bitter tears on the garden I was sowing inside me.

MATERNITY

Two weeks before I gave birth, mother moved in with her wooden bed, mirrored wardrobe, seven conditions, and rigid sense of duty.

For two years she'd made my life unbearable trying to coax me into what she judged my happiness. Now she was putting that same tenacity into sparing me the slightest worry, anything that could endanger my health or that of my future child. For that was her motherly duty: to spend sleepless nights caring for me to the point of exhaustion.

Then came the terrible trial, frightful and superhuman, painful beyond description, and mother's hands, soft and cool, parted my bangs from my sweaty brow, helped me change position, steadied my jerking hips, freshened my pillow, and greeted the bloody, viscous infant that was writhing and squealing like a wild animal.

"It's a boy, it's a boy," I heard the doctor say, wrapping it in a sheet and depositing it in the cradle as if it were nothing important.

It was I who required attention and was bleeding to death; I who, exhausted of the agony of labor, wished only to let myself go in that gentle release from life.

Jorge hadn't left my side, either, not since the start of the birth pangs, but he was worried sick over two picture frames that were a little longer than what he'd ordered. He'd brought them into the bedroom between contractions and was measuring them right in front of me.

"The man's lost his mind," muttered mother, angry. "What do you care about frames at a time like this?"

She was right. The frames were the least of my concerns, but I looked at them and agreed they were bigger than they should've been. I was so used to feigning other people's emotions!

When the doctor had deemed I was out of danger and had tucked me in a clean, fresh bed, he turned his attention to the boy, whose bawling was sounding more and more urgent.

"But it's a girl," I heard him say.

"Well, I'll be!" said mother. "If we haven't got ourselves another María Luisa! It was the same with her, and nobody knows the trouble she's given me."

I got scared when they brought her to my bed. She had a tiny red face, wrinkles on her brow going half-way up her head, cloudy eyes, and hands like claws.

"Mother, come closer. Be honest, did I have a freak?"

"Are you kidding? She's a precious little girl, and very pretty. Isn't that right, doctor?"

"Yes, ma'am, indeed she is. She's a fine specimen, the largest baby I've delivered this year to date."

"But she looks like a monkey," I protested, amazed at what they were saying.

The doctor gave a hearty laugh while washing his hands.

"Of course she does. You've never seen a newborn, and the society columns are always saying 'Countess So-and-So had a lovely little girl.' So you thought... But all babies are born with old-people faces, sometimes with those of old drunkards. An infant is a sketch for a human being, and as in old age, its lines are blurry."

223

Tía Manuelita and José María would be the godparents, and the baby's name would be María José. Mother disagreed. Why didn't we name her María Josefa?

"Because Saint Joseph, to whom you're so devoted, was called José and not Josefa. Josefa's a vulgar adaptation."

That was enough to convince her immediately.

As for Tía Manuelita, she thought the masculine and feminine mix gave the name a princely ring to it.

I went around awestruck for the first few days. I couldn't understand how that red-faced monkey that clung to me howling had anything to do with me.

"But don't you love her?" asked mother, dumbfounded.

"No." Then, in jest, "Don't you see? I've barely met her yet."

Mother was shocked just listening to me.

"You're destined to be a strange creature! Children are to be loved from the moment they start moving in the womb. They're flesh of your flesh, blood of your blood!"

Despite what she said, the instinct all women carry in their entrails was slow to reach me. But when it finally awoke, everything was a frenzy, an outburst, a sort of sheer madness. Nothing else mattered to me but my little girl. My darling blonde, pale skin and golden eyes, who sunk her tender little nails into my swollen breast. My daughter! My daughter! My daughter!

"Just like you, exaggerating as always," said mother. "Remember, a baby's a fragile life, and you could end up losing her. You've got to be reasonable, woman!"

I nursed her and dressed her and bathed her, slept with her in the big bed, and took her for walks in the Retiro in her carriage. I bought all the books about childrearing I saw in shop windows, and within a few months I knew all about the painstaking care and attention that had to be lavished on a child beset by terrible dangers and fatal diseases.

A month before María José was born, Sole too had delivered a baby boy, fat and red as a tomato. She was already feeding him garlic soup and letting him suck on a strap, and she barely ever bathed him.

"Woman, don't do that. Just watch, he'll go and get sick on you. You'll see, I'll give you a book."

"No, no; no books for me. Mother gave him a spoonful of vintage wine to strengthen his stomach the day he was born, and he can eat whatever he wants. I don't know why you people believe everything you read in books. Half of it's hogwash."

Sole was the only friend I had left, and motherhood was drawing us closer. I'd visit her and her parents almost every day, on the way home from the park or on cloudy winter evenings, and we'd sit around a table with an oilcloth.

They were working-class folk, and at first they thought highly of me and appreciated my friendship with their daughter. But later on, when thanks to our conversations they realized I was just as poor as them, had no other friends, and relied on them for my social life, they tried to give me advice and find fault with me and Jorge.

Why didn't my husband go out with me and the baby? He didn't do anything else in the evening, and it was precious to see a married couple out and about together! So much reading couldn't lead to any good. What Jorge had to do was find another job to boost his income. They knew of a milkman who was going to open a shop and wanted to decorate the walls with cows and meadows. If I wanted, they'd tell him about my husband.

Sole and her parents would also get visits from other friends: doormen, maids, a soldier, a leather worker's wife given to cursing for no rhyme or reason.

"I don't see what you like about spending time with those people," said Tía Manuelita. "I don't understand it."

225

"I do it for the baby, since Sole and I are both nursing... Besides, Tía, I get bored at home. I can't even read because the girl won't let me. I'm sociable, you know. I like to talk and be around people."

"That's well and good, but you should stick with your own, with people like yourself, cultured people."

"But Jorge keeps all to himself."

"He's an ogre," grunted Tía. "If only I'd known!"

José María came to Madrid for his goddaughter's first birthday. How lovely he found her! Blonde and chubby, with skin smooth and pink as a rose petal. She was already walking and would call to us and hold out her little arms to her uncle.

"Did you know I'm getting married?" my brother-in-law asked. "I'm getting married this coming month."

He'd brought along a portrait of his betrothed to show us. She had irregular features but was attractive on the whole, especially for her sweet, sensible, homely look.

"You're right!" said José María. "She's just like you said, and you're both the same age. A little young for me, but charming. I think you'll like each other."

Having written to my future sister-in-law, she answered me in Sacred Heart handwriting and polite turns of phrase that imposed a tone of restraint on our nascent friendship, a far cry from my letter's enthusiasm. She too was looking forward to meeting me. She hoped to find in me a true sister and mentor, since two years had gone by since I'd gotten married.

Already two whole years!

After terrible arguments and dramatic scenes from which he recovered instantly and I emerged in pieces, Jorge and I had found the least painful arrangement. Or rather, I'd been the one to discover it. It involved me accepting all his opinions, no questions asked, praising him as an artist, condemning human frailties, and not so much as thinking the same thoughts as women who didn't fit the mold he deemed proper. And talking and talking about it all for hours… Poor Teresita back in the town! Rumor had it she was cheating on her husband. Wasn't it awful? She should've knuckled down, tended to her home and her children. So he was a philanderer and a deadbeat? So he'd spent her very last penny? True, but her duty was to go down fighting, fending for hearth and home. Then what an admirable example she'd make! What a marvelous role model! Motherhood, oh, motherhood! The love of one's parents, the respect of one's sons, and the sweetness of daughters, beyond all description!

Mother and Jorge were on the same page when it came to all of that. Jorge, because his masculine instinct led him to praise feminine qualities that could be to his benefit; mother, because she read too many serialized novels written with that same instinct. But I read more than she did and chose better literature, and thus I could talk more eloquently and find just the right words to touch Jorge's soul and bring tears to his eyes.

"How well we understand each other," my husband would say after one of those long conversations in which I expanded on his ideas, keeping my personal convictions to myself.

What I still found insufferable was my wifely duty. I'd make excuses to get out of it. Today I had a headache, tomorrow I had to get up early, yesterday I was so exhausted! But once in a while, he'd seek my caresses, always at the least convenient moment, when I was worried over my daughter's cough when she caught cold or was doing the math to make it through the month on my last five duros.

The morning after, I'd scrub my hands and face before setting foot near the baby's cradle. How horrible! But how could it be? How could humanity keep behaving so filthily? It was an unnatural act! And nobody realized it but me. By some special favor or some inexplicable disgrace, I'd been granted an intellect that saw clearly, never lost its wits, never let passion cloud its judgement—and that always saw love at its most absurd and repugnant. I'd always been horrified of beings who lacked an arm or a leg. The missing limb's stump, swinging awkwardly back and forth, was a source of fear. And nature had endowed the male of the species with just such a thing to keep his line going.

I would clutch my temples, afraid I was going insane, and look at myself in the mirror, certain my thoughts showed on my face. But no, I got paler and thinner by the day, but I was a woman like the others, even more of a woman than them, for the feminine attributes of resignation, affectation, deceit, sweetness, and docility were stronger in me than in other women.

Jorge's brother Antonio would look at me, often disturbingly curious.

"What's on your mind, María Luisa? You're so strange! You've got a garden inside you, all your own. I'd like to know what flowers grow in your garden."

It wasn't easy. Even I didn't know! Back then I had no way of putting my feelings into words. But I was more honest with Antonio than with Jorge because he was more tolerant and understanding, and we'd chat for hours while my husband was at school.

José María was already married, and his wife was in recovery, having fallen gravely ill just days after the wedding. They were coming to Madrid on a belated honeymoon.

Consuelo was prettier and more charming in person than in her portrait. I went with Jorge to the station and was immediately taken with her. What a lovely little sister-in-law!

They were staying in a hotel on the Puerta del Sol, and the next day I paid them a visit with María José, who was two years old and growing quickly. Her hair was so blond and her skin so tan, the pure gold glow of her bangs on her brow was all that set them apart.

Consuelo opened the door of their room, barely dressed in a night gown that clung to her slim waist and long legs and nearly revealed a porcelain white shoulder with blue veins. She threw her arms around me, speaking in her sweet Galician accent.

"Oh, what a darling, golden like a loaf of fresh baked bread! María José, pretty one!"

And caressing my daughter, she sat on a sofa and made a spot for me.

"What did you expect? We spend our days under the sun in the Retiro. Are you here for long? Where's José María?"

My brother-in-law had to go out most mornings, and I promised not to miss a day keeping Consuelo company, going shopping, and taking her to my dressmaker. At first I went with María José, who babbled in a corner playing with toys her aunt and uncle had bought her. But when we planned to go out, I'd drop her off for Tía Manuelita to take her for a walk.

It was the beginning of June, and the streets of the center smelled of roses and apricots, with their tall apartment blocks flooded in morning light that made them look warm and inviting. Consuelo and I would go around arm in arm, youthful and happy, pausing at shop windows, chatting and laughing like two carefree girls.

"Who'd ever guess you have a daughter?" she'd say. "We're just like girls on the way home from school."

I'd grow sad when it was time for us to separate.

"I guess it's goodbye till tomorrow."

"You could come evenings," she answered one day. "Sometimes we don't go out."

So I started going again in the evening after leaving my daughter in the Retiro with the maid. José María would take us out to supper or for a drive to Moncloa.

"Why doesn't your husband come? He's become quite the hermit!"

Jorge always refused the invitation. He'd planned to start working that very instant.

Antonio came to Madrid to spend a few days and joined us on our outings. He had a girlfriend and needed my advice. To help me out, he described her down to the smallest detail, with overblown praise that made us both laugh.

"You're very fond of Antonio, aren't you?" asked Consuelo one morning.

"Yes, we hit it off. He always tells me what's going on with him."

"Well, you two are wrong to act like that. José María's worried your friendship has gotten too close. He says he finds you more talkative and even more natural with Antonio than with your own husband."

"It's certainly possible."

How well José María had observed me!

"But don't you see? That can't be. It mustn't! One day you'll wake up thinking you'd have preferred to marry Antonio!"

"Believe me, I already have, but the very thought of it appalled me! No, as a brother I think he's delightful, and I wish he were always here with me, but as a husband—nobody!"

"Besides Jorge, of course."

"No, not even Jorge. Nobody."

Consuelo didn't understand that. She was very happy to have gotten married.

"Really, dear," she laughed at an indiscreet question. "I won't say it's all milk and honey, but it's not bad!"

"Aha! And the morning after? Then what do you think?"

Consuelo looked at me in surprise.

"The morning after? Nothing, really. José María treats me nicer and laughs at the sight of me. It makes me blush, and I end up laughing, too."

"How strange!"

Consuelo was so sensible, sweet, and homely, it was if she and I came from different races. As a girl she loved dolls, and now she kept one with her wherever she went. One time she showed it to me.

"It's not like I'd die without seeing her, but José María thinks it's funny to find her in the closet."

Consuelo had delicate hands with long, tapered fingers. On one hand she wore her wedding ring and on the other a platinum band with an emerald. I'd take her hands in mine and toy with the green gemstone. Her eyes were long and almond-shaped and mildly slanted. But best of all was the perfect oval of her face, which gave her a calm composure all her own.

She'd gone to a boarding school run by nuns and would describe the place in delightful detail: the obsessions of Sister Loreto and the Andalusian wit of Sister Viviana, the mortifications of Sister Estanislao and the harmless pranks of Leoncio, the errand boy. Listening to her talk, I'd forget it was time to pick up my daughter from the park.

Later I wound up going straight home.

"Don't wait for me once it gets dark out," I instructed the maid. "And if I'm not back by eight, tuck her in bed and have her drink a glass of milk and go to sleep."

Jorge didn't say a word to me, nor did I notice him stomping around the studio.

One afternoon, I went to see Consuelo like always after lunch but realized at the hotel entrance they probably hadn't finished eating. It was half past two. Too early! My brother-in-law had been seeming grouchy those days. Maybe his business was going badly. I waited till three in a doorway across the street without taking my eyes off their balconies. Consuelo lifted a curtain to scan the ground below. She was expecting me!

I crossed the street running and entered the lobby.

"Are you going to the Medinas' room?" asked the doorman, stopping me.

"Yes."

"Well, they're not in… They went out for lunch and won't be back until tonight."

"I know for a fact they're in their room now."

"I'm telling you, ma'am, the Medinas went out and haven't come back yet."

"Well, I'm telling you, sir, they're here!"

"I don't know if they're here or not," replied the doorman, exasperated, "but I do know they told me to say they went out. Aren't you Señorita María Luisa? Yes? Then the lady and gentleman are out!"

When I finally got the message, I went away dying of shame and sorrow. I walked down Calle de Alcalá as far as Recoletos. Tears were streaming down my face, and people were turning to look at me.

I ducked into the Church of San Pascual and, sitting in the shadow of a confessional, cried till my eyes were tired and dry. I looked at the time. Already five o'clock! I'd stop by Tía Manuelita's and tell her what had happened, assuming she hadn't gone out.

She opened the door in person.

"I was just about to stop by for a chat, but since you're never in… Anyway, I've got to talk to you. You've been crying, have you?"

"Yes, something terrible just happened."

"With Jorge?"

"No, something else."

"All right, you can tell me about it later. Right now we've got to talk about José María and his wife."

"Why? What happened?"

"What happened is you're always there, and they're practically newlyweds, and inseparable, to boot… And you've worked your way between them and won't leave them alone. They can't go anywhere without you tagging along. You turn up when they least expect it. Your brother-in-law told me so this morning on the street. Consuelo's more patient than he is. You know how men are! What I can't understand is how you go out at nine in the morning, go home for lunch, then go back out till ten at night with your mouth still full of food. You who love your daughter and are always so careful not to upset Jorge! Doesn't your husband say anything? Really, dear, the things you do!"

I felt so ashamed, I couldn't say a word. All of a sudden, I realized what my life had been like over the previous month.

"I think I've gone mad," I finally stammered. "I don't know what's come over me. Tía, I'm afraid I'm losing my head. I must have an illness of the brain. I've suffered so much!"

"Don't say that, dear, you're scaring me. If you want, we'll go and see a doctor."

"I won't see my in-laws ever again!"

And the resolution made me break into desperate tears.

"Now, now, child. Don't be like that. Why would you never see them again? They're your husband's kin. Of course you're going to visit them from time to time, but only once in a while."

María José wasn't in bed when I got home, and she met me with shouts of joy.

"Mama, mamita!"

I bathed her and fed her and tucked her in bed, and she fell asleep with her tiny hand in mine.

"Daughter, dearest, forgive me! Never again will I leave you alone!"

SUMMERS

All my daughter's childhood appears to me now as a series of summers. The summer in the town in La Mancha, bathing my girl in a sunlit tub under the branches of the fig trees, singing her to sleep at the hour of the siesta, swaying us back and forth in the wicker rocker. We never left the house, where the newly scrubbed floors were always shining and the air smelled of a cool clay jug.

Albertina came to see us with her sister Caridad, a serious, pensive girl who already had a boyfriend and sang with a sweet, tuneful voice that delighted María José.

And Sol came one afternoon with her mother. She'd grown very thin, and her eyes, made soulful by her illness, looked around sadly. Her sweetheart had married another woman, and Sol was dying.

"Don't say that, dear. You'll get better soon. These things pass, and later on…"

"No, I know I'll never get over him. He's the only one who ever loved me. Who else would, with me being lame and ill? Who's wicked is his wife, who knew full well…"

Talking to mother, Sol's mother was crying as we went out to the garden.

"She's not eating. She's always been frail, but we'd managed to strengthen her up with all our sacrifices, even when we couldn't bear it, when my daughters had to give up dessert for a week to buy her a tonic. And now that her sister, my poor Dolorcitas, gives us everything we need thanks to the generosity of Don Sebastián—now she refuses to take it! That scoundrel of a boyfriend killed my girl!"

That very winter the poor woman could say it with absolute certainty. Sol died of tuberculosis of the stomach, and with the absurd pride of the wretched, she claimed to be dying very happy.

The following summers we stayed in Madrid under the Retiro's trees. The maid would bring us lunch at noon, and we wouldn't go home until dusk. We'd go here and there in search of a cool, shady spot not far from a gate. One morning I heard someone calling me in the bench-lined square where we were sitting.

"María Luisa! Is that really you?"

Paquita! Paquita, fat and round, with earrings and bracelets and rings on her fingers and a little boy ugly as a toad. She spent the day there and could assure me it was the best spot in the park. Besides, a little while later a bunch of her lady friends were coming. Nobody but her ever stayed for lunch, but they'd be back after eating for sure.

"They get back all hot, though. Go figure! As for me, I don't budge an inch until René comes to pick me up at seven in the evening."

René was her husband, the Frenchman, whom she greeted smiling lewdly.

"He's a naughty boy," she whispered in my ear. "What with the things he knows! I'm telling you, I have it good, really good! He's getting skinny as a beanpole, while I... Well, you can see for yourself, he's good for me."

The two of them genuinely disgusted me.

One of Paquita's neighbors would come at eleven with two pretty little girls. They were much better behaved than my María José, so they never did get to be friends. Their mother was in mourning over her husband's death two years earlier. All she talked about was the month she spent in Paris with her dearly departed, as she always called the father of her girls.

One day my daughter, who told Jorge everything, gave him a surprise.

"You know Cachita and Marité? Their father was a dead man!"

There was also a blonde, fair-skinned and rosy-cheeked, the wife of a doctor. She told me she had a baby every year and didn't try to get out of it so as not to ruin her health. Besides, why else had she gotten married? She sent her kids to be nursed in a town and didn't bring them back until they turned five years old. Then she entrusted them to her mother, a strict old woman who kept them on perfect behavior and lived in Ciudad Lineal.

"At seven on the dot she sits them on chamber pots, and it's no breakfast for them until they do their duty. She raises them just like soldiers."

Apparently, the blonde assumed the same system was used in the barracks.

She'd come with a girl who was blond like her and had curls. The girl was so pretty, her mother hadn't mustered the strength to send her away.

"Everyone compliments us on the street!"

Another woman, a squat brunette, also had a baby every year, but lost them after five or six months because they inherited their father's illness. The only ones left were the lame eldest boy and a three-year-old girl who was mentally retarded. Just then she was overdue on another.

María José would play with four kids under the care of a French governess. Her name was Jeanette, she was pretty and *chic*, and she always addressed the children in French. She was the only one there whose company I enjoyed.

She only came in the afternoon, and it wasn't often I got to sit beside her, not that I didn't try. Every chance I got, I'd stand up and sit down again in a different spot.

She told me she'd lost her mother two years earlier under mysterious circumstances. She suspected her father had murdered her with the help of another woman. That's why she came to Spain and wanted nothing to do with her family. Her employers were very demanding and took advantage of her sorrow and solitude to exploit her. Besides teaching the children their lessons and taking them out, she dressed them, bathed them, and stayed up all night taking care of them when they were sick. And all she got in return was a pittance, never permission to go out alone!

Some afternoons, the parents came to the Retiro and stopped by the square to see their kids. The mother was a tall, fussy Cuban woman. She was so very delicate, she couldn't bend down to kiss the little ones, who had to be lifted to her lips. They'd always leave without so much as looking at Jeanette.

I hated them with all my might, the fools. To have a delightful, unlucky girl in their house and not take care of her! If only I could've hired her! But who knew? Jorge was talking about sending one of his paintings to the autumn exhibition.

"Hang on as long as you can there," I told her one day. "Maybe next year I'll be in a position to offer you a different situation."

When all the women went home at seven, my daughter and I accompanied Jeanette to the entrance of the opulent house where she lived on Calle Velázquez.

Mornings in the Retiro were uneventful and boring. Paquita would expound at length on the difference between a wife and a mistress.

"Come his wife's birthday, a husband gives her a dresser or dinnerware or a piece of fabric to make sheets. But come his mistress's name

237

day, and does he think about things for the house? No, of course not. The most expensive ring, the most diamond-studded bracelet."

"That must be if he's rich," I observed.

"No, it's just that men make money grow on trees when they fall for a woman. That's exactly what a woman must know how to do: make them lose their head."

Paquita was downright detestable!

After lunch, she'd invariably nod off, giving terrible jerks that nearly toppled her off the bench. María José and I would stroll along the promenades that branched out from the square, not wandering far, and she'd ask me a thousand clever questions.

"If the lion gets out, will he eat Paquita whole? He'd better watch out if he does. Her rings will stick in his throat. She's got a pointy one!"

The sun was drawing its arabesques on the sand, streaming through the leaves of the trees, and the thick air smelled of myrtles in the heat and a distinctly pagan perfume. Jeanette was approaching along the path that ended in the Paseo de Coches, and María José ran to meet the kids, her great friends. And I felt happy in the balmy and fragrant siesta.

Some days they came so late, all those odious women got there before them and started into one of their stupid conversations, slow and humorless like the thoughts in their heads.

"Men are so selfish... Cod was more expensive today than yesterday... The doorman didn't bring the newspaper up until eleven. By then the whole family could've read it... My husband's sister wrote from San Sebastián. Luck seldom goes to those who deserve it. You wouldn't believe how ugly she is!"

There was Jeanette, at long last. She couldn't come earlier because the mistress had ordered her to clean four pairs of sandals for the children, even though she'd cleaned them that morning, as usual. Now she had to sew an entire bag of socks.

Bent over her work, she'd sew all afternoon without looking up. She never had time to read! She'd lend me books, and later we'd comment on them with real enthusiasm, to the surprise of the other women.

"But none of that's true! What a pair of crackpots," Paquita would say.

One afternoon, Jeanette was fidgeting about nervously on the bench. She was thirsty, she said, and if I stayed to look after the children, she'd go around the corner to the Fuente de la Salud, which was known for its excellent water. And she was off. María José and the four kids were running themselves silly playing chase and didn't notice the governess's departure.

Minding the children and watching the path down which Jeanette had disappeared and would soon return, I overheard the women's conversations. The widow of the dearly departed was talking about her maid, an old woman who sometimes accompanied her to the park.

"She was our maid when my parents were alive, and when I got married she came to live with me. I'd be helpless if it weren't for her. She's from Burgos."

"Burgos makes excellent maids, as does the Alcarria," said Paquita.

The lame boy's mother was talking to a cousin of hers who'd brought a pair of twins in a baby carriage.

"Times are tight. They only give my husband eight duros for keeping the books for the newspaper, and with that we go to the theater twice a month. If only we didn't have so many kids! Every year, a baptism and a burial."

"You two are to blame, and don't act so shocked. That's right, the two of you. There's a reason chastity belts have locks. Take a look at me: the twins after four years of marriage and that was the end of it. We won't have any more."

Then she whispered in her ear.

"Enough! For heaven's sake," said the brunette. "My husband would blush to buy such a thing!"

"Just like a man! Embarrassed about some things and not about others."

I stopped listening to look down the path. No sign of Jeanette! What was taking her so long?

"María José! Don't go any farther."

My daughter was just like me when I was her age. I'd been just as wild and daring. They'd done a fine job clipping my wings. Daughter dearest, I'd never clip yours, not ever! Wings, wings to fly, to look down from above like a bird on the path I'd failed to discover, but that you, child of mine, will still find for yourself!

It was getting dark out, and Jeanette hadn't come back. What was taking her so long?

The blonde and her husband were saying goodbye after he came to pick her up.

"See you tomorrow. Tonight we're staying in. We've seen almost all there is to see here. Madrid's quite the ghost town in the summer!"

Paquita was also departing, as was the brunette with the sickly kids and her cousin.

"I don't feel well today," she was saying.

"What's wrong?"

"I've been past due since the tenth of the month."

"María José! Don't go any farther. It's getting dark out."

"Where's *mademoiselle*?" asked one of the kids.

She couldn't possibly still be at the fountain!

Little by little, everyone was clearing out, and the children made their way to the empty benches, mildly afraid of the dark. María José was the only one bold enough to keep running in the woods.

"Scaredy cats, scaredy cats! Bet you don't dare run over there where it's dark!"

And she ran down a path under the leafy trees until her little white dress disappeared from my sight.

"Jeanette's taking a long time," I worried out loud. "She left over an hour ago."

"Why don't we look for her?" the eldest boy proposed.

"All right. She said she was going to the Fuente de la Salud."

And what if we didn't find her?

"Hurry up! Let's go," insisted the children.

"Yes, but what about María José?"

She was already approaching, running at full speed, as if she were being chased. She took refuge with me, looking back over her shoulder.

"What happened? Tell me, what was it?"

And I made her lift her little face to look into her eyes.

Woe unto me! I knew that terror, a mixture of shock and inexplicable anguish!

"Tell me! What was it?"

"A man, there was a man who…"

"What?"

"Who was naked… Or not naked, but…"

I took her in my arms and kissed her on those eyes that had seen something horrible, on that innocent brow that still didn't understand.

"Daughter of my heart! Come on, let's get out of here. It's too late to be out among such dense trees. Let's find Jeanette."

The kids brought along their hoops and their ball, Jeanette's sewing bag, and my basket with the book and the leftover snacks. Meanwhile, María José was clinging to my neck. They all wanted to know what had happened to her.

"Was the man you saw a thief?"

"He must've been the Bogeyman. Tata María says the Bogeyman sells human fat."

"Leave her alone, and don't talk about that! Can't you see she's afraid?"

We were finally emerging from the dark paths onto the broad avenues leading to the gates. There was still some light, and the last lingering couples were walking briskly towards the park exit. Some kids and a woman were filling their glasses at the fountain. And Jeanette?

"There she is," pointed María José, still clutching my neck, "at the little table by the stand."

And there she was, at the refreshment stand, with a man who had her practically entwined in his arms.

"Look! Jeanette's got a boyfriend, and he's hugging her," said one of the children, causing me an almost physical pain.

Maybe she heard us; she definitely saw us. Hastily waving her companion goodbye, she came in our direction.

"Oh, *madame*, forgive me. I'll explain everything *demain*… He told me to meet him here, and I couldn't tell you the truth, because… *Au revoir, madame*… And thank you, thank you."

And she left almost running with the kids in tow.

We continued slowly on our way. María José had nestled her head onto my shoulder, and I felt profoundly unlucky. What a disgusting life! The man on the dark path, Jeanette's boyfriend; humanity, oh so gross! And Jeanette had seemed like such a good girl.

"You're crying, mamita. I won't leave you ever again!"

"There, there, dear."

"We won't say a word to father."

"No, dear, not a word. Heavens me, what a pity!"

"Why is it a pity, mamita?"

Jeanette didn't show up to the square the next day. I couldn't stop checking the time. Five thirty… Six… She wouldn't come now! We went to look for her across the street from her building and walked back and forth, eyeing the entrance.

"Why did we leave the park?" my daughter was asking.

"Because your friends weren't there. Who were you going to play with?"

242

"But surely they went. They must be there now, mamita. Shouldn't we go back?"

We ran back to the park. Not a trace of them! They didn't come that day or the next or any day afterwards. What had happened?

"They must've been hit by a car," snarled Paquita. "Or maybe they fell in the pond. You sure are worked up over that blasted little French girl! It's as if you'd fallen in love with her!"

The women all laughed at that one.

On the way home, we went into the building on Calle de Velázquez.

"Is Mademoiselle Jeanette in? The governess who used to take four kids to the Retiro?"

"Yes, I know the one," said the doorman, "but she's not here anymore."

"Did she leave for good?"

"I couldn't say if she left or they kicked her out, because I don't stick my nose in the residents' business… Anyway, she's gone. Now the kids go out with Tata María, an old woman who used to be a nanny."

I sat down on a street bench, my legs giving out from under me. I couldn't think, couldn't focus on a thing. So there was no more Jeanette! Never again would we cross paths. Why must the world be so vast?

My daughter and I didn't go back to the square but finished out the summer at the other end of the Retiro. We had long talks, just the two of us. I taught her poems, and she learned to read from a book of ballads. When nobody could hear us, we'd sing the Ballad of Delgadina, and we were back to being happy before autumn.

The following summer we went to the mountains, where Tía Manuelita had rented a house for us. But that winter my daughter had measles, and mother gave me a thousand pesetas to take her to the sea the summer after.

I hadn't been back to the beach since I went with mother. María José was holding my hand the first time she saw the ocean. She looked at it speechless, and I didn't ask any questions.

"How it smells!" she said, taking her fill of the horizon. "Why do they put those black ribbons on the sand?"

"That's seaweed. The ocean washes it ashore. There in the distance, where the sea meets the sky, the water's very deep, and the seaweed grows in thickets where the fish swim. There are fish big as elephants and small as flies, and at the ocean floor, amidst stands of the stuff, there are ships that sank long ago with lost treasures, never to be found, and fish that are blind or that glow in the dark, and coral reefs, and sea snakes."

My daughter gazed at the sea with her golden eyes and saw it just as I had, mysterious and unsettling, terrible and candid like a great deity who was holding out its crystalline hands in her direction. She asked me to take off her shoes, then dipped her feet in the water, laughing and happy.

I didn't buy her a bathing suit until she asked my permission to swim in the sea. From then on she'd wear her light blue suit from dawn until dusk. She didn't meet girls to her liking there, either, but she did meet two rowdy little boys. They got together to make sand castles and boats that the waves washed away at high tide. As for me, I stayed away from the groups of wives who sat making sweaters and criticizing the women walking on the beach.

I didn't even feel like reading. I had books all winter long. For now I'd feast my eyes on navy blues and emerald greens and drops of light dancing on the foam of the waves.

"Are you María José's mother?" asked a voice beside me.

"Yes, *señorita*, and you must be Mary, the aunt of the boys who play with my daughter."

And so we began a summer friendship not even worthy to be called that. Mary was twenty years old, a vulgar little girl whose empty little head couldn't produce one original thought. A single detail made her attractive and likeable in the extreme. It was her lips—plump, smooth and fresh, and red as two cherries. But I realized right away the comparison was inexact. She had lips like two chocolates, so sweet and tasty they must've been.

Holy Mary, mother of God! What nonsense I came up with!

"Come along, María José. It's time to eat lunch."

My daughter, slender and lithe, with classical lines like Diana the Huntress, came over and took me by the hand.

We'd eat just the two of us at a little table in the vast dining room with mirrors and potted plants. My girl would eat very little, just like me at her age, and I had to whet her appetite.

"Would you rather have ham than roast? You can have flan instead of ice cream."

She was already eight years old, restless and rebellious at play, but quiet and thoughtful in moments of calm. She was just like I'd been, and I was raising and pampering her the way I wanted to be raised in my childhood.

Jorge had stayed behind in Madrid and would write to us twice a week. María José would always add a scribble at the end of my letters.

It was the end of August when my husband announced he was coming for us. My happy summer chastity was drawing to an end!

"Daughter of my heart! What will you do when you grow up? We'll put our heads together so you don't start down the wrong path. Isn't that right, dear?"

It was already September! The first... The second... The fifth was coming! I felt irritable and nervous, and my happiness had clouded over.

My husband hugged me nervously at the station, and later the three of us dined at our little table. María José was beaming. That night she'd sleep in a cot beside the big bed that we had been sharing before.

In the middle of the night, I saw Mary's plump lips in the darkness like a nightmare... What a stupid dream! I might as well have been seeing the lifeguard's feet! And all because the desires of the flesh were making me feverish, attacking my brain. No, there was no doubt about it.

The following day, I knew for a fact I was mad. It was a queer madness, one I'd never heard of, but madness through and through. The moment I set foot in Madrid, I'd go and see a doctor with Tía Manuelita and would tell him everything, absolutely everything.

We stayed a week longer and went home before the fifteenth. Classes were starting, and Jorge had to give exams to those who had failed back in June.

We found mother at our house with Sabina, the two of them having settled in three days earlier.

"Well," mother explained, "they sent news Tía Manuelita was in very bad shape, and I came on the very first train."

"What?" I began, immediately worried.

"In any case, there wasn't any need for it. The maid found her dead when she went to serve her breakfast. She said she was already cold, so she must've died early in the night. Of course, they didn't want to tell me the truth by telegram."

So there was no more Tía Manuelita! She'd departed in silence, not bothering a soul, with elegant discretion, as she would've thought.

She'd been living on a pension and several thousand pesetas in government bonds, which she left to my daughter in her will.

Mother no longer had any desire to go back to her house.

"I'll stay here and live with you two. I'm too old to go back and forth from the town. We'll move into a bigger house and all be better off for it."

MY MOTHER

At the new house, Jorge made his studio in a sitting room with two large balconies, and mother arranged the office and a spacious, bright bedroom for herself. María José and I slept in an interior room that opened onto a patio but that I preferred over all the others for its soft northern light.

Sabina cooked, and my maid cleaned the bedrooms and took my daughter on walks when I had to stay with mother, who was aging rapidly and couldn't handle María José's noisy games.

"That girl's a natural disaster! What are you thinking, letting her bounce the ball in the hallway? Good grief, if she keeps up that racket, I'll go insane!"

She also complained about the girl not going to school.

"But she doesn't know a thing! You were already learning fractions at her age, and doing needlepoint, even if it was bad."

"But she draws very well, much better than I did. Didn't you see her sketchbook? And she knows lots of poems, too. Come here, María José. Recite 'Triumphal March' for your grandma."

But she whose recitations were simple and harmonious when we were alone would always refuse to recite for anyone but me and Jorge.

"Fine, leave her alone," mother would say. "Some use poetry will be when she grows up! I don't know why you don't send her to school. What's she doing at home making trouble all day?"

I was staunchly opposed to separating from my daughter, but in the early days of winter mother fell gravely ill, and I couldn't budge from her side. Forced to keep quiet from morning to night, María José was having a hard time of it.

One day Antonio came with his wife to see mother. By that time our former shopkeeper had three stores of his own, and his wife was tall and pompous and talked to us condescendingly. She knew of a magnificent school. Naturally, it was expensive, and not just anyone could part with that kind of money, but if she had a daughter, she wouldn't send her anywhere else.

Mother didn't seem to take any pleasure from their visit and even got slightly red in the face just talking about them. What a pair of dimwits! The three stores had gone to Antonio's head, and now he thought he was a bigwig. Poor thing! He was even more ignorant and ordinary giving himself airs than when he didn't have a penny.

"Did you hear him? He said he bought land in the *outerskirts*. As for the school for María José, find out if it's as good as that woman made it out to be, and take your daughter along."

"But mother, she said it was very expensive."

"So be it. I'm footing the bill."

A week later, María José was already attending the school. She spent all morning and part of the afternoon there, to my chagrin and her even greater dismay. I thought she'd like having girl friends to play with, but that wasn't the case, and she always came home sad.

"They're a bunch of fools and tattle-tales. I don't want to go to school, mamita."

But the decision had been made, and there was no turning back.

What's more, we decided she would stay there instead of coming home for lunch. It was such a long way from our house to the school, the maid was wasting time going back and forth.

On school days I got up before María José to help her take a bath, accompany her at breakfast, and hear her say her lessons before putting the books in her satchel. Then I stood at the door waving when she left with Sabina, who took along her basket for the shopping. And just for good measure, I leaned out the balcony and watched them disappear at the end of the street.

"You can't raise a child any worse than you are," said mother at first. "You told me once you were on the wrong path, that you weren't born for marriage. Well, dear, you weren't born for motherhood, either. You're spoiling her, making her think that she's the most important thing in your life and that the entire household's subject to her whim. It's the best way to make her completely self-centered. If only she were a boy! But she's a girl, and her life will be like any other woman's, a constant sacrifice."

"My daughter won't get married."

"Sure, just like you."

I didn't tell mother what I thought about that and tried to avoid arguments.

She didn't argue with Jorge, either, and always took his side on everything, even if it meant contradicting me on matters I knew they disagreed about.

In the afternoon, I'd stroll through the Retiro with mother on my arm, and we wouldn't go home until supper. I'd rush us back thinking that María José was already waiting for us.

"Woman, not so fast. Let her wait a while, let her get used to it. A woman's life is waiting, always waiting."

"I don't want her to be alone with the maids. You don't know how they made me suffer. That Casiana…"

Mother would listen in astonishment.

"That's true? You're not exaggerating? But why didn't you say anything back then?"

"You wouldn't have believed it. At least, you wouldn't have wanted to believe it. Nobody ever gives kids any credit. Besides, everything seems fated in childhood. Things are what they are and not any other way. I thought all maids were alike and preferred Casiana over a stranger. She'd take me to her bed when I was afraid and feed me in the kitchen when I was in trouble."

"That's because we told her to. You couldn't have gone back to school on an empty stomach! But we weren't going to call you back to the table after punishing you!"

At twenty-six years of age, as a wife and a mother, I had enough authority to argue with mother almost as equals. And little by little, my mother was discovering me, and I was discovering my mother.

Under her severe exterior and unbending sense of duty was an immense affection for us all. I remembered her always dressing modestly, making do without things that any other woman would've considered essential, saving the funds for us to lead a tranquil life, cent by painstaking cent. And everything was so expensive: the doctor when we got sick; a good tailor for my father and brothers, though she went to the cheapest dressmaker; the bill that came due for the shop just when times were tight.

And incapable of showing the least affection when anyone else was looking, she'd watch over María José in her sleep and lovingly kiss her a thousand times over after checking to be sure none of us was watching.

Now I recalled having seen her in dreams in my childhood, having felt on my brow the warm kisses she withheld during the day.

She didn't let me criticize Jorge in the slightest.

"He's your husband, the father of your daughter. It's your duty to bear him through thick and thin. You and he are a single person."

Mother lasted for less than a year. A consumptive disease made quick work of her, and her strength and surly composure came crashing down into a weakness that forced her to rely on a cane for every step. In their place surfaced all the softness she'd hidden like a sin in the course of her life.

"María Luisa, want to read out loud?"

"Yes, mother."

"I'd rather listen to you than go out for a walk. Read, and even if you think I'm asleep, keep reading. Let me hear your voice, now that I can barely see you!"

Her poor eyes lost their shine in just a few months, and her speech grew awkward and weak.

Months of not leaving her side, day or night, left me pale and thin.

"If you keep this up for much longer," warned the doctor who visited mother, "you'll be the first one to bite the dust. Make it your duty to go out for a walk an hour a day."

Jorge too was insistent, and I decided to pick up María José from school every day while Sabina stayed behind with mother.

In the end, I was happy to go out, and I'd make the trip the high point of my day. I'd take my time getting ready and amble down the longest route with a joyous sense of freedom.

And when I glimpsed the high garden walls surrounding the school, my heart would clench. My daughter was a prisoner there all day long, held against her will! Because the school, the school lunches, her classmates and their games—all of it sat with her badly.

She'd come running out to meet me and jump up for a hug, showering me in kisses. Then she'd take me by the arm, and we'd talk about the same things as always.

"They make a white flour soup that really disgusts me… A girl told me I'm going to Hell for not attending mass. But there isn't a Hell, is there mother? When are you going to let me stay home with you?"

"When your grandma gets better."

Sometimes another woman with a smaller girl would come up beside me and offer the girl as a role model.

"My Rosarito cries on Sundays because she doesn't like to stay home. All the girls are so happy to come to this school."

All except mine! My daughter María José was only happy by my side. Only with me did she feel understood.

One afternoon, I got home to find my poor mother in her armchair, as always, only the expression of her blurred eyes and twisted mouth was more comatose than ever.

"Mother," she whispered, "mother… Kiss me… Kiss me, mother."

I thought I'd heard wrong, but no, mother had retraced her life in an hour and was back in her infancy. Our roles had switched irreversibly, and she was a poor, weak, infantile being who was clamoring for a kiss with stubborn affection.

I sent away María José to spare her the gut-wrenching spectacle, then kissed mother and cried. My mother had died on me!

But no, she lived four months longer, no longer herself or anything resembling her. Profoundly moved, Jorge lived isolated and silent, confining himself to his studio. Sometimes he'd go for a walk with María José; other times he'd paint something. That was around the time he sold those two paintings that made the newspapers.

One morning after a sleepless night, I was watching the sun come up through the balcony windows when I saw mother struggling to breathe, nostrils flared and eyes sunken.

I sat her up on a pile of pillows and called for the maid.

"Send for a doctor, but don't wake anyone. Tell him to come right away, that mother's in very bad shape."

In the meantime, I kept my fingers on mother's pulse and she opened her eyes.

"Daughter, my daughter," she said, recognizing me for the first time in a long while. "Don't go, don't leave me alone."

"No, mother, no. I'm always here with you."

When the doctor arrived, she'd closed her eyes again and was breathing tranquilly.

"She's dying," he said, after a moment observing her. "It's a matter of minutes."

The maid thought it obligatory to burst into a fit of tears.

"Quiet, woman! I'll have nobody else finding out, nobody else waking up in this house! I want to spend these last few moments with my mother in peace."

I made her leave the room and bolted the door, then opened the balcony and returned to mother's side. The doctor was examining her attentively.

We sat there watching her, maybe for five minutes, maybe for half an hour, when suddenly she opened her deep, black eyes and looked—looked beyond the street, beyond the rooftops outside the window, beyond the clouds tinted pink by the rising sun.

"She's dead now," said the doctor, "and she's looking into infinity."

Only then did I fall to my knees crying. All my youth was ending with her, with she who never knew what to make of me, nor I of her. We were separated by many years and our own different natures but united by the mysterious cord that never breaks between the spirit of a mother and her children.

A month later, we sought out a house in the country and moved. It bordered on the walls of the Pardo, far from Madrid, which forced Jorge to go to school on a bus that would stop at our door every morning and come back the same way at lunchtime. Between mother's modest savings and the inheritance from Tía Manuelita, we became a well-to-do bourgeois couple, free of financial worries.

We even considered buying the house, which wasn't very nice but was surrounded by a garden with holm oaks, high-reaching poplars, and an immense elm that filled with birds at dusk.

The studio was set up in a windowed turret, while María José's room overlooked the Pardo forest and Jorge's and my room opened onto the garden. From the mirador I'd gaze at the sky, somber like the background out of a Velázquez, and through who knows what association of ideas, I'd think of my mother.

Believing the country would give me the balance I'd always been lacking, I made the earnest decision to adapt myself to life, to the double life that everyone leads, and to slip at long last into the human stream and the gentle peace of domestic bliss.

SUMMER'/ END

"María José, dear, look out the window. The swallows are back. Do you hear them?"

Pirrrrrrr......... Pirrrrrrr......... Pirrrrrrr.........

"Look how they draw a straight line in the sky, complete with a comma at the end. Look how they plunge!"

"I can't hear you, mother. What are you saying? Over all those birds' screeching, I can't understand you."

"Come down to the garden, dear. It's a lovely morning."

María José came running down, her delicate frame robed in her dressing gown. She put it on when she got out of bed and didn't take it off until after her bath. She'd grown so much, it only went down to her knees, leaving her legs exposed, long and too skinny.

"What were you saying, mother? That the swallows are back? I heard them bright and early, before you got up. They were screeching so much and at such a high pitch, they must've poked holes in the sky. It's like they put our house in parentheses."

My daughter and her imagination, always outdoing me! Eleven years, too sacred for words!

"We've finally got something to do today," I said. "We're going to make nests out of wooden boxes and hang them in the attic. They say happiness enters the house where swallows make their nest."

Because my little girl, who'd always been fit as a fiddle, had been running a fever in the afternoon, and I didn't want her to study or do anything but play and laugh.

"But mamita, it's nothing. The doctor says I'm in a growth spurt. You're going to have a daughter like a tower!"

Jorge, who adored María José, bought an enormous cage for doves because she wanted to keep them. She'd fallen for the myth of their sweetness, fidelity, and lack of gall.

And she and I spent entire days in the shade of the elm, sitting and watching them.

"There they are quarrelling! Didn't you say they're all married couples? Look, the tufted female's cheating on her husband with the pot-bellied male, and the husband sees them and doesn't care."

My daughter had glimpsed the secret of reproduction in animals, and I didn't deny it. That discovery, made in that way, chastely and free of malice, was better than a dirty secret whispered in the ear by another girl.

"Yes, but for his part the poor tufted male will cheat on his wife with the pot-bellied female, and he'll make a good father to the babies, without going to the trouble to find out whose children they are," I said, giving María José an immoral lesson. "Marriage among doves is a happy bond between two who come together to nurture the little ones."

We also had hens, and in the spring a broody hen had hatched fifteen baby chicks. They were already tall on their long, gawky legs, and they ran madly after their mother, with wings short as hands tucked in pockets.

On cool spring mornings, my daughter and I would meet in the garden, for she too was an early riser, eager to embark on the marvelous adventure of each new day.

Together we'd open the henhouse door and watch them exit, one by one. They'd hop on two feet at a time from the door to the ground and take several hesitant steps, blinded by the light. Then it was off to scatter kernels of wheat on the patio, which the hens would storm in a frenzy, pecking and pecking against the flagstones with the blows of a violent hailstorm.

Once in a while, a hen would lift her head with the red bonnet of her crest swaying side to side, listening first with one ear, then with the other.

María José filled her notebook with sweet sketches of hens, and doves puffing their chests, and swallow silhouettes, and bats flitting blindly through the garden before sunset.

But her favorite model was Catalina, a tabby cat with stripes like a tiger, intelligent and loving. In the month of April, she'd given birth to four little kittens who lived for days in a basket in María José's room.

"Those cats must have the place all fouled up," said Jorge, unaware that mother cats clean anything that might stain their children's skin with the stiff-bristled brush of their tongue.

But Catalina, so sweet and affectionate with us and her little ones, was a savage fiend on nights when the moon was out. Like the man who turned into a wolf after sunset, she turned into a tiger that plundered the henhouse and stole the chicks from their mother.

María José caught her one morning sinking her ferocious fangs in the innards of a poor little chick whose heart was still beating. One by one, she was eating them all.

And it made no difference that her bowl was always full of garbanzos and chunks of beef and bacon. After dark, Catalina scented hot blood like a wild beast.

Jorge made it out to be a tragedy.

257

"I knew this would happen! That's life in the country for you. What were you expecting? Animals eat one another. That's why I didn't want to leave Madrid. Civilized beings have no choice but to live in urban apartments, the bigger the city, the better. That cat will eat all your chickens, rabbits, and ducks, and then she'll be eaten by a fox or a marten. Watch and see. I don't want to see hide nor hair of your critters."

That wasn't true, for he too spent hours watching the cages, the pen, and the hutches. But the second he got angry over anything at all, he inevitably blamed his daughter and me.

Sabina had gotten married and was living in Puente de Vallecas, and it was she who took Catalina away, promising to look after her and love her.

"My husband's so good, he'd rather us go hungry than the cat!"

Shut up in her room, María José refused to see Catalina off.

"No, no; I feel sorry for her. For heaven's sake, I hope she's being careful with her! Are you sure she won't suffocate in the basket? Did you see if she could breathe okay?"

Later, the three us of were sad but didn't say a thing, having made an agreement not to speak again about the cat.

In the pond we had three ducks who slept in a hut next to the henhouse. In the morning when we opened the door, they'd emerge one at a time and march single file, waddling back and forth, swaying terribly, glum as if they were heading to the office. Reaching the pond, they would let themselves glide over the water and float there peacefully, submerging their bellies to the same depth every day. Sometimes they'd search for worms on the bottom, and for a moment the keel of their tail would rise straight up out of the water, their carrot-colored feet kicking in the air.

Every week, Tío Candelario brought us a cart-load of grass for the ducks and the rabbits. Delivered by the armful, his clover made Perico the Donkey turn to look with a little boy's eager anticipation.

María José would pet him on the face and save him sugar cubes that he'd take with his lips in order to keep from biting her.

"Gee up, let's move," Tío Candelario was always shouting for no reason.

Perico would never go faster, and sometimes his thoughts were so distracting, they'd force him to come to a sudden halt. Then Tío Candelario would fly into a rage and direct the most terrible insults at him and his family. Perhaps that's why Perico stopped again an hour later, reflecting at length on his mother's honor.

In the evening, at dusk, hundreds of birds came to roost in the leafy elm. They all wanted a place on the branches near the trunk, and those who were lucky enough to get one had to defend their bed with their beak, furiously flapping and chirping while the others answered rudely, with shrieks so shrill you couldn't hear yourself think in the garden for an hour.

That was the time when the flocks came in from the fields, and María José and I would go out to the road to see the sheep crossing, jumping the ditch with their stubby legs, which crackled like reeds and raised a cloud of dust.

One night my daughter called to me after getting in bed.

"Mother, do you hear that? Catalina's meowing in the garden. She's out there!"

We couldn't believe it. We switched on the light between the door and the entry gate and saw a miserable cat, all skin and bones, who was whining pitifully against a stone step.

"I don't think it's her. But yes, yes it is! And look what a horrible mess!"

Catalina was afraid of us. She knew our selfishness, indifference, and lack of understanding had banished her from a house that was just as much hers as it was ours.

Even more hers, in fact, because she knew all its nooks and crannies, all the cobwebs in the basement and hiding places in the woodshed; all the little secrets we'd never know.

"Here, kitty, kitty... Poor little thing. Poor Catalina!"

Jorge went down to the garden and carried her back in his hands. She was caked in mud, fur matted to her legs, bleeding out one ear, eyes bulging in terror.

She hadn't touched food or water for a week! Who could know the dangers she'd braved coming from Puente de Vallecas to the Pardo walls? So many hours, trembling in fear over a barking dog! So many anguished hours, hidden in the brush, fleeing from stone-throwing boys! Days and days without eating, no water to drink save the mud puddles from the last time it rained. She couldn't tell us her pain and suffering, but they were written in the scratches on her skin and the fear in her eyes.

Catalina lapped up her milk, still suspicious, not understanding how we could greet her so kindly after kicking her out. She slept in the basket near my daughter's bed, and the following day we sold the whole henhouse half-price to Tío Candelario, who hauled it away in his cart pulled by Perico.

"Mother, did the hens have their legs tied? They didn't tie them too tight, did they? They'll swell if they don't undo them soon. Poor things! They must've been just as sad to leave home!"

Irritable as always, Jorge got mad.

"Not another word about the hens! I didn't sleep all night worrying about them and the cat. It's awful, this constant anguish over all the animals! I told you, civilized people can only live in skyscrapers, and civilization is the polar opposite of nature."

Some little birds had made their nests in the stand of poplars leaning over the Pardo walls in the corner of the yard. One day we heard them screeching in despair. A big black bird was flying off with a baby in its beak, and the parents were calling for help at the top of their lungs.

By then María José had a fever all day long, and she saw it from the canvas chair where she passed the time resting in the shade of the trees. She almost fainted from the shock of it.

"It was awful, mother, simply awful! The poor little birds were screeching in a frenzy. They threw themselves at his head and his eyes, but the raven—it must've been a raven—took their baby away. And he'll be back for more. Wait and see, he'll be back for more."

We had to change my girl's place in the shade so she wouldn't witness the black bird emptying all the nests.

And the summer wore on, silencing the beasts of the field. No more birds raising babies, no more swallows playing chase, no more crickets chirping. The swallows, they go away so soon! A single cicada sang faintly in the day's hottest hour.

Sometimes I'd feel a sense of anguish. The house and its walls were a prison where I was dying of boredom. And that same strange disquiet would take hold of me once more, the lack of understanding and frustration with my being upon which my whole life was built.

"Tomorrow I'm going out shopping," I'd say at times like that. "I'm going to Madrid to buy some things I need."

In truth, I didn't need to buy a thing, but I longed to calm my anguish walking down the streets, pausing at shop windows, sipping a cool drink, feigning a liberty I didn't have, and going where I wished without Jorge's questioning eyes or my daughter's sad looks always following me.

Freedom, sweet freedom! To be like the breeze, coming and going with no questions asked. Lucky modern girls! I saw them alone on the street, satchel in arm, on the way to the university or the academy or the school. Why had I come into the world ten years before my time?

I'd always get home late, having missed the first bus.

"The girl was nervous and refused to eat without you," Jorge would say.

And I'd take that as a reproach and answer in a rage.

"Well, you and the girl ought to know that I too have the right to get out of this prison, and sometimes I need a change of scenery. I'm suffocating here. I can't take it anymore!"

One day when I was talking like that, I saw María José's chin quiver and big, silent tears roll from her eyes. Daughter of mine, what rivers of tears I've spilled over the pain that I caused you!

The inclement wind of September filled the Pardo oaks with its whispers. The family of trees who lived in our garden walls gestured energetically, like a family of blind folk checking they were all there. "Are you there? Are you there?" they said, touching their branches. Sometimes they gestured too violently, as if they were angry. But no, though they belonged to different species and had come from different places, they never fought and always agreed. Not a single discordant note. They would bend as one in the wind and rustle their leaves in perfect harmony, always in the key of F-sharp. What great maestros of domestic perfection!

María José could no longer go down to the garden. She'd spend the day in bed, opposite the open window overlooking the Pardo forest. A ray of sunshine would pay her a visit in the late afternoon, falling directly on a painting of two bunnies she'd made in watercolors. Later it wrested colorful sparks of light from the nickel-plated bed, then finally glided up the quilt to my daughter's hands.

"Look, mother, look how transparent they are. I can see the bones through the flesh."

* * *

The summer went away taking all I had with it, the yellow leaves of the poplars and my daughter María José.

One afternoon, the ray of sunshine couldn't find her hands, covered with flowers, but lit up her aquiline nose and her golden eyes that had seen their last. Jorge's cries rang through the house like heart-wrenching howls.

No, no; let no one mourn my daughter, she who was mine alone. Nobody but me has the right to mourn her, she who sprang miraculously from my womb. And, alas, I mourn her not because I loved her so much, but because there were times I didn't love her enough. Daughter! Daughter! My daughter!

PART III: AUTUMN

HOUSEHOLDS

t was getting light out, and Jorge and I were standing on deck, watching the burning red sun rise out of the silver water, thick with oil.

For the first time in two long, bitter years, my heart clenched with a new sadness, not my habitual sorrow, but rather the mystical emotion of beauty, no less piercing and painful, but lacking the agonizing grief of irreparable loss.

After three days doing a devilish dance, the ship was slowly entering the port—solemn, sensible, and serious, as if it had never misbehaved. It was aware that hundreds of eyes were watching it from the dock.

Perhaps José María and Consuelo were there, having called us to their side after ten years without seeing them. Jorge thought he recognized them in every group.

"That's them over there. Here, take the binoculars…Them, the ones by the little stall… No, dear, you're looking in the wrong direction. Next to the lighthouse on the point. There's a boy dressed in white; he must be Juanito."

The ship was going so slowly, it was barely advancing. Everyone on board stood on deck contemplating the city, whose towers shone red in the sun of that mild fall morning.

Long before the ship came to dock, we spotted José María opposite the group where we thought we'd seen him. At his side, a fat woman was smiling at us and a nurse with a white apron was holding up a little boy with curly blond hair. They were surrounded by other people who were also smiling as if they were expecting us, though Jorge and I didn't know them.

The tall gentleman was the schoolmaster, accompanied by his wife and small daughter; the short, fat man, the literature professor, his two sisters in tow. There was also a priest who taught Latin and a dark, skinny chap with a mulatta-looking wife.

Jorge got teary eyed embracing his brother, as did I feeling Consuelo squeeze me to her copious bosom. We had the look of beings who'd suffered a lot, and my frail frame and black dress wiped the smile off everyone's face. They greeted us without excess words and helped us load our luggage into the car that was waiting.

José María had a big house surrounded by a garden in the highest part of the town. Four rowdy little kids ran out to meet us.

"Don't annoy your aunt and uncle; they've had a tiring trip. Shoo, shoo! One kiss and you're off to play without making a racket."

"That's okay," said Jorge, "let them stay so we can meet them."

The eldest was Juan: nine years old, pale skin, blond hair, blue eyes. The clear, serene eyes of the Renaissance poet, just like María José's! The second eldest was Lucila: seven years old, brown skin, jet black curls. Then Titina, four, and Jorgito, two. The youngest was Antoñete, just eight months old and still with a wet nurse. He'd already made friends with us in the car.

With its porch and its interior patio full of palm trees, the happy house smelled like a hatchery with newborn chicks, like wet wool blankets and urine and sour milk.

"Antonín's always throwing up," apologized my sister-in-law. "The nurse's milk is too thick, and in these tropics…"

Consuelo! Who'd have recognized her in that matron who waddled when she walked? She'd lost everything: her youthful grace, her classical lines, even the sweet Galician accent that annoyed José María. Her oval face had grown too round but still showed traces of her calm and composure.

I noticed early on that her husband was easy to anger and would often sit her down and lecture her.

"Haven't the kids eaten breakfast yet? Consuelo! What are you thinking? Must I do everything myself?"

"No, no; they're about to eat. It's still early, dear, and since they don't have school until nine…"

"My office isn't clean. Consuelo! I told you, I need it clean first thing in the morning. You don't know how to run a household, Consuelo!"

That day I saw tears in my sister-in-law's eyes, and in our time staying with them I witnessed several violent scenes over trivial matters in which José María reproached his wife with the harshest of words.

According to him, a mother and wife must be the first to rise and the last to turn in at night, must be firm and just with the servants, must educate each of her children according to their temperament, must be constantly vigilant for torn seams and missing buttons, must be even-tempered, happy, and tirelessly energetic… And must experience art and beauty at the same time as her husband, the two of them vibrating in unison…

"And what else?" I asked one day, fed up with his preaching. "You read all that in *The Perfect Wife*, and now it's out-of-date! Have you ever come across a book about the duties of a father and husband?"

I understood he hadn't liked my interruption one bit, and from then on he always mistrusted me.

After a week we moved into our own place, a furnished apartment in the center of town. It was tasteless and pretentious but cheerful and comfortable enough. Consuelo sent me a maid, an island girl who went barefoot around the house and did everything slowly and silently.

Slipping us a list of names and addresses, José María warned us we had to send calling cards to certain people or risk offending them most gravely. But Jorge declared he wouldn't make visits even if his life depended on it. The most we could require of him was to invite over his school colleagues.

And so it was decided that I'd be the one to receive visitors, informing Jorge only as the circumstances warranted, and that my sister-in-law would accompany me on visits.

The day after sending the cards, a deluge of well-heeled strangers starting show up at our doorstep, always saying the very same things.

"So, do you like the island? How's the weather treating you? It's a major boon to the health! Do you have any kids? There's still time; you're still young. You could use a pair of little ones."

When Consuelo thought the time was right, we started returning the visits. The majority of our hosts had small children, and their houses smelled of diapers, wet wool blankets, and sour milk.

The schoolmaster and his English wife were quite old, but their eldest daughter lived in their house and had a husband and a six-month-old infant. The Englishwoman received us on a windowed terrace overlooking a garden that smelled of geraniums. She told us her daughter was in bed with aches and pains; their maid had quit her post, forcing them to do all the housework.

From there we visited the math teacher and his mulatta wife, whose two scrawny boys had just stolen their mother's scissors. After showing us into a high-ceilinged room with a window near the top like a prison cell, she set about chasing the boys around the table. They hid behind chairs and made the most amusing escapes.

"Brats, idiots, imbeciles!" shrieked the mulatta, furious.

Tired of running around the room in circles, the boys dashed out onto the porch with their mother on their heels. Later we saw them in the garden, the mulatta still in hot pursuit. In a fit of desperation, she grabbed a flowerpot and hurled it in their direction. The younger boy fell to the ground like grasshopper, and his mother let out a terrified shout.

Consuelo and I had gone out to the porch and saw the math teacher rush past us without a glance and go straight for his wife like a wild beast.

"Brute, savage, animal!"

That's all he said that was fit for print. The rest was so foul, Consuelo and I looked at each other scratching our heads.

We went back to the room with the high window, and a little while later the mulatta joined us, confused and embarrassed and wiping her tears as they streamed from her eyes.

"They've got no respect for me, seeing as Don Joaquín insults me so much!"

Don Joaquín was her husband.

"That's what I get for being a poor country girl. Just a poor little thing! It's to be expected, seeing as Don Joaquín is a gentleman and all. Poor little me!"

Consuelo and I comforted her as best we could and left right away on the excuse we still had to make two more visits and get home in time for supper.

The Latin teacher was out when we stopped by, and his two sisters received us in their bedroom because he locked the other doors before leaving.

We sat on the beds while the sisters caught us up on all the town gossip. Had we been to the schoolmaster's house? We had? And they hadn't said anything? Well, they were having a terrible time of it because the maid was pregnant, no longer a maiden. And she was the third one to leave the house in that condition!

"It's because Conchita refuses herself," said the eldest sister. "You know what I mean? I may be single, but I know a thing or two. She won't let her husband near her, and he's got to do something to let off steam."

Then they talked about some families I hadn't met and finally got around to the mulatta.

"She's a savage beast," assured one of the sisters. "He hired her as a cook when he came to the island, and she stuck around for the whole kit and caboodle. And they're married now, as if there were no young ladies here who could've made him happy!"

Out on the street, Consuelo told me they called the younger sister a bluestocking because she wanted to study and was rather clever. But her brother had strictly prohibited it and banned her from reading so much as a newspaper. That's why he locked the rooms when he went out—to safeguard his books from her curiosity.

Doctor Álvarez, one of the city's leading figures, greeted us in the company of six of his twelve children. The eldest girl played the piano while the second eldest regaled us with her lovely voice, singing some songs of the island. The singer was married, and she and her mother were due to give birth on the same day. I thought that was highly un-usual, but the older woman informed me it was a family tradition and that she'd nursed one of her sisters.

They were a large, loving family. There were ninety-five people around the table at Christmas, between siblings, parents, children, nieces, and nephews.

"Yes, they're loving all right; too loving," my sister-in-law explained. "People say the doctor had a kid with his mother-in-law and his wife's pregnant with her cousin's child."

We also visited a man who was the island's most important poet. His wife was blind, and though he wasn't old, he had bloodshot eyes and trembling hands.

A pretty young maid in a bonnet and silk apron served us tea in a sitting room done up in tropical décor. I observed that the poet was eyeing her too closely.

"He suffers from satyriasis," said Consuelo.

"What? What's that?"

"Some sort of erotic delirium, very inconvenient for the women who live with him. Even the poor blind woman needs a broom to fend him off once in a while."

In general, if there were young children around, Consuelo and the lady of the house launched into a technical discussion of feeding, the effects of the heat, how much bedding to put in a crib, how to fasten baby outfits and warm baby bottles.

Meanwhile, I'd look around at the ugly rooms, whose only personal touches were utterly tasteless: garish prints on the walls, vases of dusty artificial flowers on the side table or piano, door mats decorated with a lion looking something like a cross between a house cat and a water dog. That would go on until the lady of the house noticed me looking.

"We're boring your sister-in-law," she'd say. "Naturally! Since she doesn't have kids, these things don't interest her. You've never had children?"

And before I could make the painful effort to answer, Consuelo would come rushing to my aid.

"Yes, she has. She had a daughter who died when she was eleven. It's better not to speak of that."

"That's right! I heard as much, but with this head of mine… You know, you can still have others. You and your husband are young. When you least expect it, you'll wake up with morning sickness and have a little angel."

And the blood would rise to my cheeks like when I was twenty. How could people say such things without even blushing?

Since the death of my daughter, Jorge had respected my pain, which cloaked me like a blanket of ice frosting over all my desires. But one night after arriving on the island, I found myself back in his arms, not knowing how I'd gotten there. The morning after I felt that same old delirium verging on madness.

273

Was that possible having witnessed the terror of death together? Why was I reliving that nightmare? Would that shameful life never end? And all women simply gave in to it. All of them! Even Consuelo, who after a long, exhausting day of housework, would fumble down the hall to her husband's bedroom while everyone else was sound asleep.

"Don't go," I'd tell her. "It's an insult to require a mother of five to keep on playing the lover. Don't go!"

"But it's my peace in life," answered Consuelo calmly. "I only refused once, and he didn't talk to me for a week. The next day he's nicer and yells at me less."

"Yells at you? But what gives him the right to yell at you?"

José María made me mad with his air of self-importance and lectures to his wife. Still, he was more sociable than Jorge.

At his place I met a family of fat, rheumatic gluttons who spent all year pinching pennies to host two annual banquets.

"I managed to get you invited," said my brother-in-law. "It's a real show, and Jorge's got to be there."

He went to great efforts to convince his brother, and the night of the banquet over fifty of us took our seats around a table that could barely fit half that number. The house belonged to three brothers married to three sisters. They all lived under one roof with their fourteen little kids, seven of whom were already in bed. The other seven were sticking out their hands towards butter rolls, appetizers, and prawn pyramids.

Like all the household's banquets, that one was famous on the island and outdid everything I'd been told to expect. Partridges with truffles, artichokes with ham, meadow larks in suckling pigs, sea bream in vinaigrette, turkey and gelatin… There was no getting past the third course! The parade of delicacies began at seven in the evening and kept on coming at ten. By then I was sick to my stomach. I looked around the table. None of the other diners could have been my friend.

Flushed and annoyed, I signaled to Jorge that I wanted to excuse myself.

"Are you getting sick? You must not be able to eat any more. María Luisa has a sensitive stomach, and it's not good for her to eat a heavy dinner."

He was talking to one of the women of the house, who expressed her regrets as if a terrible misfortune had befallen me.

At the other end of the table, a young man stood up at the same time as I did.

I made friends with her in a sitting room that opened onto the garden in that warm, starry, jasmine-scented night. For she was no man, but a woman in a tailored suit and man's tie, her short hair slicked down on her head.

"Fermina Monroy," she said, sticking out a hand. "Thirty-five years old, single, born on the island. And you must be María Luisa… María Luisa Medina, is it? I don't know your surname."

"Arroyo."

"Arroyo, then. I was really hoping to talk to you. To be honest, the only reason I'm here tonight is to see you."

She kept going despite my astonishment.

"I spotted you the day you got off the boat. You were wearing that same black suit, with a shirt of felt and gray silk. Among all those other women primped up like parrots, it was obvious, what you were… Forgive me if I'm bothering you! I told myself then, you've got yourself another girl friend."

"I've been wearing black for years."

"It's not the color but the cut. Did you have a tailor make it?"

"Yes, my husband's."

"Well, he's very good. The tailors around here don't know how to make women's jackets, to say nothing of skirts. They're fools, just like the shirt makers! You ask for a shirt, and they make you some lousy blouse. Good thing there are mail order services from London!"

Her striped silk shirt had a small embroidered crest and fit snugly over her chest's slight curves.

A maid brought us a tray of fruits, cakes, and ice cream.

"The banquet goes on," laughed Fermina. "You could hide in the farthest corner of the garden, and they'd still hunt you down with a tray!"

"Nobody's at risk of dying of malnourishment here."

"But of indigestion, on the other hand... Two kids already died of it. And they purge them and practically starve them for two days before every banquet!"

She took out a cigarette case.

"Do you smoke?"

"No."

"That's where you go wrong. To know all life's pleasures, you've got to know its vices... Tell me, what kind of life do you lead here?"

"I don't think it is a life."

I sounded so pathetic, Fermina started laughing again.

"I play the housewife and see to our second-hand furniture."

"What?"

"Yes, we rented it furnished... And I read my brother-in-law's books, because ours are in storage in Madrid, and visit Consuelo in the afternoons. She and I inevitably visit all the local dignitaries and smell all the diapers and baby vomit in the city. Good God, the kids this place produces!"

Fermina stopped smoking to laugh again.

"Aren't you funny! I knew you would be. But make no mistake, they're no more fertile here than any other place. Women our age are in full production... Yes, you're funny all right!"

She tipped her head back and exhaled a mouthful of smoke while gazing up at the ceiling.

"And you're an artist, too, I'd swear to it."

"No, not an artist! I paint a little, not very much. Jorge doesn't like me to."

We fell silent for a moment as if both of us were thinking the same thing and didn't want to say it.

"What a disaster," she finally said. "A real disaster. A woman of our kind getting married!"

Why did she keep comparing me to her? Besides our clothes, I couldn't understand what we had in common. Maybe she painted.

"And you, do you paint?"

"No, I write. Didn't they tell you? No, they didn't say a word. The men want to get rid of me, as do some of the women. I'm a correspondent for some newspapers in America and a writer for one of the papers here. I sign as Fermín Monroy. It's been that way since I started, and not because I like to be a man… I just published a book of poetry; I'll give you a copy. And you've got to come and see my place. You'll meet another girl who paints. We get together every Monday," she said, handing me her card.

The men were starting to get up from the table and come into the house, and I assumed the banquet was over.

"They'll be back at it within the hour," Fermina corrected me. "There'll be glazed ham at midnight, and turkey with truffles, and jello, and cognac. Cakes and pies and brandy at two, then at four and at six. The feast lasts all night long. Last time two gentlemen fell flat on the ground, completely stuffed, and the others had to make them vomit some of what they'd eaten. Otherwise they would've died, what with their stomachs crushing their other organs. They're all perfect beasts!"

I peered curiously at the men coming into the room, their faces flushed, their eyes shining bright, a giddy look on their face. All of them were honorable people, upstanding folk who had no qualms whatsoever displaying their gluttony.

"So you're a romantic," said Fermina, hearing my observations. "All these gentlemen are genuine pigs at the table, not to mention in bed. Of course, they tend to make do with their fat old wives, and the Holy Mother Church gives them its blessing!"

Later we talked about her house and her mother, her translations and her exploitative editor.

"I work like a galley slave ten hours a day, but I'd rather work six hours overtime than live like those women. I'm not criticizing them, of course; they're happy like that, but I'd rather jump off a cliff."

"I'd be happy with your independence, too, I think. Between that and painting I'd lead a full life. These days I haven't got the time, between seeing to the housework, cleaning shoes, and sewing clothes. One maid is all we've got! I used to draw a bit, but ever since my little girl died… The sea is a different color here than on the coasts of the mainland. Oh, how I'd like to paint the waves breaking on the levee!"

"Then get painting. Don't you see? Your life's slipping by, and later you'll have regrets. There's nothing more painful than a wasted year of life! How old are you? Thirty-two? You're still young!"

"That's what they all say. The women I visit all insist I need a kid!"

"Yes, a child of the imagination, your very own creation, but not of the flesh. We'll talk about it more if you come over. Will you?"

Just then Jorge came looking for me.

"It's already midnight. Let's go, I've got to get up early tomorrow."

"Get painting," repeated Fermina, holding out her hand.

"What does that woman know about you?" asked Jorge on the street under the faint light of the lampposts. "Why did she tell you to paint? What did you two talk about?"

The next day Consuelo called me aside.

"You sure did talk a lot to Fermina Monroy last night. I'm warning you, she's got a bad reputation, and in small cities like this one, a married woman must choose her friends wisely."

MY WORK

At Fermina's house I met Lolín, a pretty young painter who smoked one cigarette after another and looked carefree and impish as could be.

"Not at all," warned Fermina. "She's a miserable girl, all heart, who a year ago made the silly mistake of marrying a wreck of a man."

We met twice a week in Fermina's sitting room, where I discovered a taste for English cigarettes, Beethoven, and Fermina's unparalleled Puerto Rican coffee.

Sometimes we read bits of the latest interesting novel published in Madrid, with all the regulars chipping in to have it sent from the bookstore on the square. Other times we discussed amusing events, and we always listened to records and never criticized a soul.

"The people we know are too vulgar for us to discuss them," said Fermina. "It's enough of a drag to have to be around them."

Rafita stopped by most Mondays. He was the director of the newspaper where Fermina worked, a small, chubby man with a whiny voice and a penchant for reciting poetry. Whenever he tripped up in the middle of a performance, which happened more often than not, he crumpled into an armchair sobbing and we had to comfort him. With him came a gray-haired man, a great poet who'd had to devote himself to shipping bananas to England in order to support and educate his forty-five kids by tenants on his estates.

We never talked about our private life or family and were all strangers to a large extent, but we bared the best of our soul to one another, the meetings were cordial, and we bonded over art like travelers who come from far and wide to admire the same landscape together.

I tried to hide those visits from Jorge's inevitable disapproval, but Consuelo must've known and José María must've said something to my husband.

"Do you know about that woman's reputation?" asked Jorge. "If not, you can ask around. She's the talk of the town. Of course, if you already know and still want to be friends with her, I won't say a thing. I've never stuck my nose in your business, but I can certainly form my own opinion!"

"But what exactly do they say about Fermina?" I asked Consuelo.

"Well, I can't swear to it, but they say she falls in love with women and has had several girlfriends, and they've used her to criticize two or three other women."

"How can that be?"

"Who knows? Hysteria… The stuff of single women…"

"But I don't understand."

"Me neither, but what did you expect? There are many things we don't understand, and that doesn't make them any less real. She's just like that Rafita. They say he's an invert, too."

It was two or three days before Jorge resumed talking to me, and he was still keeping quiet when it was time for me to go and see Fermina. After lunch I sat by the balcony reading a novel. I wouldn't go! That small pleasure had come to an end after just two months giving me a semblance of happiness. Jorge was pacing the dining room, his hands behind his back.

"You're not going out?"

"No, I'm not."

Our relationship had changed a great deal, with two years of deep desperation having eased my self-discipline. Sometimes I'd contradict him on the very same points I'd been conceding for years. My husband would look at me dumbfounded and either purse his lips or shout in exasperation.

"So now we don't agree?"

"We never have, not on this," I would answer, keeping my composure.

"But you, you said..."

"I said so then, but it wasn't true."

"Then you were lying to me or lying to yourself."

"To both of us."

I felt a dull anger against him for obscure offenses and bitter disappointments I could never quite put into words. But seeing him sad and defeated over what I'd said and our long periods of abstinence, I would inevitably pity him. I'd watch him coming and going, silent and crestfallen, and would try to be loving and tender, show him attention and care, never contradict him. Poor thing! I was incapable of causing that weak, will-less being the slightest unhappiness.

But that would only last a few days, because Jorge's extraordinary capacity for adapting to new situations and forgetting the past made him authoritarian, domineering, and tyrannical.

Until finally he'd manage to make me mad and my temper loomed up again to put him back in his place.

"This constant back and forth is wearing me thin," I told Consuelo. But she barely listened, always so absorbed in her housework under her husband's watchful gaze.

What most exasperated Jorge were my drawings. Just looking at them changed the expression on his face and put up a wall of disdain between us.

"Look, I wanted to show you. I made a sketch of the pier."

"It's not bad," he'd say, taking it with a forced smile, somewhere between scornful and mocking. "There's not much technical skill, not much at all."

And he wouldn't say another word. Still, he kept a file in his closet with the first drawings I'd done as a girl under his direction.

Lolín had her studio in the attic of her house, where she'd installed a whole wall of windows. It was a small room, tastefully decorated, cheerful and inviting. By then we were meeting there instead of at Fermina's. I hadn't gone back to her house on the excuse it was too far away.

I found in Fermina a strong, serene attraction, but she never said anything around me to make me think what my sister-in-law said was true. Sometimes she and Rafita laughed over things I knew nothing about and whose humor I seldom understood.

One day I ran into Lolín and we talked about painting.

"The shop on Calle Real sent me these hand fans to paint. They're samples. Later they'll put in an order for the ones they like best. Do you want to paint them? It would be doing me a favor. Right now I'm busy with a portrait of the Count's daughter. And you could make a few pesetas."

I painted them in hiding from Jorge, taking them out after he went to school and putting them away before he got back. I could still see those last months I'd spent at my daughter's sickbed, overlooking the Pardo walls.

Lolín, who was good and loyal, was thrilled when I took the freshly painted fans to her studio.

"They're lovely! Aren't you talented!"

"But I don't know a thing! I've never made anything like them."

Her favorite was the one with swallows playing chase against the clear blue sky of May, the first diving down with its velvet wings to the fan's wide ribbing, the last flying off the edge of its leaf like an inverted circumflex accent. She also liked the fall design, with the crowns of the trees bending to the gusts of a storm in a single harmonious bow of shared resignation. Its ribbing was scattered with yellow leaves that had fallen from the sapless branches.

And by some strange coincidence, the shop owner also liked those two best and ordered three dozen of each of them.

"What good luck!" said Lolín, who'd gone with me to the shop. "What excellent luck! It's the best thing that can happen to an artist, for your work to be popular without being tacky. You'll make a fortune!"

I was happy and worried. How and where was I going to work so much?

Jorge had rented a studio in our building and would work all afternoon on a large canvas he was planning to submit to the National Exhibition. It was the one thing we talked about.

"I think it's my best work yet, don't you? The colors are perfect, and there's air between the figures... Damn! There's the neighbor lady singing again. So much for painting today! Later she'll start her sewing machine, and my mind will go completely blank... There's nothing more worthy of respect than an artist's work! But people today are in a savage state... You know those tubes of oils I ordered? They still haven't brought them... You need to sew a thicker curtain for me, one that will filter the light better... Did you contact the carpenter about making me a taller stool? Without what I need I can't work!"

José María dropped by the studio every evening to see how his work was going.

"It's magnificent," he'd marvel. "You're guaranteed a medal."

"I know, but I'm going for first place!"

My work was coming along, too. I'd paint in the bathroom, sometimes sitting on the floor, using Jorge's discarded paint tubes. Afterwards the fans dried in Lolín's studio.

What a great day when I could finally submit them and pocket the first of my very own income!

"Girl, you're a success," announced Lolín the following day. "Two shop windows full of your fans. Every woman who fancies herself elegant will have to buy one. You should tell your husband; he's got no choice but to be happy. You'll see."

I met Jorge at school when classes were getting out.

"I just went shopping, and I want you to go back with me and buy me a fan."

"A fan? What do I know about fans?"

"Yes, dear, they're painted."

"I'm sure they're tremendously tacky. Come on, leave me alone; I want to get to work right away."

"But we have to pass the shop either way. It's just a little detour, five extra minutes."

Jorge paused at the shop window, looking attentively.

"They're good, really good! See what I always told you? Whoever painted them has a sense of color, a good imagination. Real talent, if I may say so myself! Nothing here is static, no sir! A fan is all about air, and the painter knows it. The air in the wings of the swallows, the wind whipping the trees in the fall."

I listened to him with my mouth hanging open. Truth be told, I hadn't thought of that while I was painting them.

"Besides," continued Jorge, "the painter is greater than his work. He's a master technician of the art. This little project was child's play for him. I'd like to meet him. They must have brought them from abroad, because nobody here can paint like this."

"It was me," I said, but he was too absorbed in the fans to hear me.

"It was me who painted them," I repeated. "I did."

"You!"

"Yes, me. They put in an order with Lolín, and she passed it along to me."

"Well, that's great," said Jorge, much less enthusiastically. "They're very good… I suppose you got paid for them."

"Yes, of course. Just yesterday I came to get paid. I've been wanting to tell you. Now I'm going to buy myself a canvas and brushes."

"I don't know what for," said Jorge, gruffly. "Surely you don't expect to get commissions like this one every day!"

We went home in silence and didn't say another word on the matter, but when José María and Consuelo came over that evening, Jorge mentioned it in passing.

"And they're good, very good," he said, not giving details but nonetheless doing my work justice. "I don't know if it was a coincidence or if María Luisa's destined to be the heiress to the art of the hand fan… But they're good."

My in-laws ran off to see them and came back brimming with compliments.

"You sure did keep it quiet," said Consuelo.

From that day on, Jorge kept his studio locked and was always complaining he was running out of paint or his brushes were going bad.

"I don't know who's been meddling in my things, but the second they're gone or ruined, I'm slashing my canvas with a knife and never picking up another brush!"

By that time, a new happiness had started to flow from my soul, a calm, quiet joy, entirely my own, so firm my husband's harsh words bounced off it without leaving a dent.

Fermina had gone to America with her mother, and I only saw Lolín twice a week so as not to annoy Jorge going out every day.

His painting was packed with the utmost care, with all of us lending a hand. Meanwhile, my husband paced back and forth, nervous and overexcited. The days it was on the boat, he couldn't sleep and was constantly wondering if they'd put something on top of it, if the packaging would ruin the colors, if they'd break the box unloading it.

I invited Lolín over to see the painting.

"You can be sure of the prize," she predicted. "It's got all the requisite academic stuffiness. Fame and fortune will come knocking at your door hand in hand."

And so it came to pass. People were talking about Jorge for over a month, and we ordered a boatload of magazines and newspapers from the mainland. My husband got his picture taken in three different poses to send to all the Spanish publishers and even some foreign ones. All the island's dignitaries came to say congratulations, and several thousand pesetas flowed into our coffers. All the while, Jorge was beaming.

As for me, I got another order for fans, which I painted in the attic so as not to cloud Jorge's happiness. They paid me twice what I made on the first order. This time, remembering what my husband had said about the dynamism that should preside over the art of fan-making, I painted a colony of seagulls skimming the waves and the desert wind blowing its golden sand and wild ducks over the island.

Jorge found out and might've even stopped by the store, but he didn't tell me about it.

By then he was resting and had shut up his studio for good. He was letting his paints dry in their tubes, and I didn't dare even ask for them.

Lolín was starting work on a painting for the Autumn Salon.

"Why don't you do one, too, and we'll submit them together?"

"Me? I'm afraid I'll make a mess of it."

"If it doesn't work out, then you put it aside and nobody's any the wiser. We scrape the canvas, and the only thing lost is some paint."

A little blond boy with wide, surprised eyes posed for a week for my painting, and I had to admit, two sessions were enough for me to block in the figure, and I could keep painting from memory after seven days. Even in dreams I'd see his bright young eyes and his chubby hands cutting out a paper horse.

But the only place I could work was in Lolín's studio. How could I take the canvas home?

"Go on, tell your husband. I think you're worrying too much. Once he sees your work, he'll realize he's got no right to keep you away from it. You'll see, he'll like it. And he could even lend a hand, though I don't recommend it. The spontaneity, lightness, and grace of your brush are just what set you apart from Jorge's rigid standards."

I was right, though. The day I told him I was painting a picture for the Autumn Salon, he erupted in protest.

"So now you're making paintings, too? This is madness, pure madness! Now they'll say you're responsible for my work. It's just what I need to give up painting once and for all. I know what's in store for me, with so many people jealous of my success."

I gave up working on the portrait and asked Lolín to finish it if she wanted.

"I'm no good for that kind of work. It's slow going, and I get bored, but I thought of something that suits me better. Painting tapestries will be faster and more entertaining. I'm going to give one to Consuelo for her birthday."

So I bought some fabric and nailed it on the foyer door behind a drape, hidden where Jorge would never see it. I primed it in Prussian blue and painted a street in an old city with a figure of Christ in the foreground. From high on a wall, an oil lamp's flickering light was dimly illuminating a masked horseman as he disappeared around a corner…

Such was my success that commissions came raining down on me from my in-laws' friends. But summer was coming, Jorge wouldn't leave the house, and I couldn't work when he was around. I filled just one order, getting up at the crack of dawn to go to the studio and come back before Jorge woke up.

One day he heard me talking to Consuelo.

"You look awful," she said.

"Yes, I haven't been getting much sleep. I get up so early to get to my work."

"To your work," Jorge scoffed. "You women are idiots. *Your* work! And what work might that be? You're starting to sound terribly pedantic. I'm only warning you so you don't make a fool of yourself; otherwise, I don't give a damn."

It scandalized Consuelo that we never went on visits anymore.

"You're falling out with everyone! They come to see you, and most of the time you're out, and you never go and see anyone."

"I realized those visits bore me to death. Besides, do you think it's really possible to live life going from house to house talking nonsense?"

"Apparently I bore you, too," she said, hurt, "because you don't come over like before."

"Because I go to Lolín's studio. You saw, she got me into making fans."

"I know, but I don't understand why you're so keen to work when there's no need for it. Lolín's another matter. She married a good-for-nothing and has to support him. But Jorge earns a living, and you two have some money in savings."

It was hard to explain to Consuelo that my work was the one thing starting to make my life interesting. Not even I had formulated that thought until one day when Jorge was talking at the table.

"So," he said, after days of reproachful silence, "do you plan to keep *working* your whole life?"

"Yes, of course! Until now I've been living with no sense of direction, no compass, no dreams, as if I were empty. Now I see everything differently. I've been carrying something in my head and my heart, and now I feel it growing like a child. And this time it can't go and die on me."

My quasi-dramatic tone left Jorge impressed.

"I thought," he trailed off. "I always thought a man's dreams and successes were enough to satisfy his wife. If I was wrong…"

"Perhaps they are for other women, but not for me."

I tried to say it humbly, as if I were confessing a personal failure.

"Not for me," I repeated. "But I've always asked you to help and correct me."

That got on his nerves.

"That's exactly what I mean! You know what an enormous effort it is for me to pick up my brushes and paint my works. And now on top of that I have to fix your mistakes."

"No, I'm no longer asking anything of you."

All the same, my husband and I had several cordial days after that conversation. Once I showed him some sketches for tapestries, which he corrected here and there with very good sense. He really was talented! And we talked about what I'd gotten paid and Lolín's studio and the profits off her portraits.

"Your friend's not very good. She knows how to draw and flatters the ladies who sit for her. That's the key to her success."

But since Jorge had to strain to keep up that attitude, he was quick to relapse into his interior monologue, silent and hostile. Whole days would go by without him saying a word to me, and once I found him trying to sew a button he'd lost.

"Stop that, dear. I've always sewed them for you! Why should now be any different?"

I did my best to always be nice and to attend to his every need, and I kept on hiding in order to paint. But when I finished a piece, I didn't dare submit it until he gave his blessing.

Just then Rafita had started commissioning cartoons for his newspaper, and I found I had a certain ingenuity and wit very well suited to that sort of work.

"What do you think?" I asked Jorge, timidly showing him my work. "Is it acceptable?"

He answered without even looking at me.

"One should never take a commission without being certain of its success."

The times he did finally look at the drawing, he'd correct it with skill and great care.

"Here, it's ready to go."

But one day when he was organizing his closet, I went into his office with a header I'd been commissioned to make for a story.

"You've got no use for me," he frowned, waving it away. "If you can't do it yourself, that's your problem."

His own words were working him up.

"Leave me in peace with your work! And take this away while you're at it!"

He held out the folder of my childhood drawings.

"Take it! I've got no reason to save them for you, nor do they interest me any longer!"

And with that he threw them at my feet.

REVELATION

In those days Lolín was acting very nervous. Her husband was unbearable and wouldn't leave her alone. If only he had something to keep him busy.

"He's like a cat in heat," she'd repeat, never providing any further explanations to my questions.

Sometimes he'd come by the studio, always eating candies and rubbing his hands as if he were very cold. He was young but bald, and pale and soft as a sick man. And maybe he was sick…

"Can't you take your candies somewhere else?" said his wife.

And off he went, silently and never protesting.

"You can't complain he's not obedient; I've never seen a more docile man."

"Sure," scoffed Lolín. "Now he'll go and pinch the maid, the swine. None of our maids lasts more than a month. Stupid girls, I don't understand why they don't go along with him. We'd all live in such perfect harmony. All the floozies around here, and it's no use; all we get at my house are the goody two-shoes."

I laughed at the things she came up with, assuming she was stretching the truth. She'd never talked that way before; on the contrary, I thought she was deeply in love with her husband. We never talked about love, and though she must've suspected the ups and downs of my tepid relationship with Jorge, she didn't ask questions. Matters of the heart had no place in our friendship.

One day she told me about Rosita Aguilar, a reciter of poetry.

"I don't know who she is."

"You don't? Well, she did get famous very quickly. She was born here because her father was a lieutenant colonel garrisoned on the island and her family never left when he retired. They lived here till last year when the father died. That's when Rosita, who recited at all the charity balls, turned her hobby into her livelihood. Now she's enormously successful giving recitals. She's stopping here on her way to America. Haven't you seen the posters announcing a party in her honor at the Teatro Principal?"

Yes, now I remembered seeing them and reading a notice at the foot of her portrait in Rafita's newspaper just that morning. I could even repeat the reporter's words from memory: "The lovely Canary Islander who, separated from us under sad circumstances, will be our guest for several days."

But nobody knew her better than Lolín did, nor were they awaiting her so impatiently.

"You heard. They think she's coming on the Ciudad de Cádiz, but she's really coming tomorrow on the Cap-Polonio. Just today I got this telegram. Rosita can't stand a big show, and people here have such bad taste, they're liable to greet her with music. We'll go to the dock together. Want to?"

Yes, yes; I'd like that. I was interested in meeting her.

The next day I took tea with Lolín at her studio, and later we went to Hotel Quisisana and picked out an airy, luxurious room that she ordered be filled with armfuls of flowering broom plant. At the hotel they brought us word the ship was coming into port.

"It won't dock until nightfall because of low tide."

We went down to the dock in the hotel car and got there just when the ship's great bulk was inching towards the end of the levee. I felt Lolín's arm in mine while we walked around waiting for the passengers to disembark. The crowd was thronging around us, straining to recognize the people on deck. Nervous, my friend drifted away from me, and I took a moment to study her. She was wearing a tailored jacket and white silk shirt and didn't have a hat over her boyish curls.

Without warning she came back up to me.

"I'm interested to know what you think of her. You've got good taste. She's lovely! And interesting, above all. On the stage she's fearless, like some classical heroine. Let me know what you think."

"Really, dear, what am I supposed to say?"

"You know… Don't come to me acting all innocent. You can't fool me!"

I don't know what, but something in her voice and her eyes gave me a glimpse of something unexpected, something totally unknown to me before then.

The ship's lights came on, and the passengers started disembarking. The crowd came between me and Lolín and sent me into a momentary panic. Scanning the scene, I saw her coming towards me with a pretty girl on her arm.

She too was hatless, with curly hair, a light travel coat, and a white silk kerchief tied at her neck like a scarf. Her red lips were smiling to show off her perfect white teeth. All I saw was that and her marvelous black eyes.

"María Luisa Arroyo, painter; Rosita Aguilar, reciter and poet, art made woman," said Lolín.

I got a vigorous handshake and helped carry her luggage to the bell-hop. Two Englishmen were already waiting in the car, and Rosita sat beside them opposite me and Lolín.

Only then could I contemplate her unsettling beauty in the gentle twilight. She was around thirty, I guessed, and extraordinarily attractive. I wasn't in the habit of underestimating feminine beauty, so her large mouth and wide nostrils, far from being defects, seemed to me to be her greatest charms. I only stopped looking at her when I felt a sharp pain in my arm, a pinch from Lolín!

I saw she was frowning and serious, her face so tough she looked like a different woman.

"Do you like her?"

"Very much, she's very pretty," I said, talking under the noise of the car.

"She's my friend, got it?" whispered Lolín in my ear. "I already told you. I regret that you came, but since the damage is done, you ought to know I'll fight for her tooth and nail. It's best this end here and now!"

Her voice was hoarse; her eyes, threatening. I didn't know how to answer. Rosita was studying me, and I looked away from her. Gazing out the window, I saw that we were crossing the Plaza de Weyler. I had to get out.

I bid them goodbye and hopped to the ground, then plunged into the labyrinth of dark streets, walking at random and trying to avoid my way back home.

Good God! What had happened? What had I done to be ousted like that from Lolín's tranquil friendship? All the same, my heart was pounding in my chest like a victory bell. So Lolín and Rosita… What Consuelo had told me about hysterical aberrations… Something luminous and sweet I'd been waiting for all my life was flooding my thoughts.

Lolín was an intelligent, hard-working woman. My husband complained that I dressed like she did… A normal man's repulsion, no doubt.

"That butch," he'd say whenever he spoke of her.

But no, Lolín wasn't a butch. At most she was somewhat boyish, like an awkward adolescent whose voice hadn't changed, with smooth skin and a womanly throat.

I liked walking, walking in the shadowy streets, getting lost in their twists and turns, just as I was losing myself in the maze of my thoughts, once thrown off balance by the revelation of men's brutal love, and shaken up now by a new revelation.

I got home late, complained of a headache, and went to bed without eating dinner. There was something new on my brow and in my eyes that nobody but me was to decipher.

I slept badly and didn't dare go to the studio the next day or the following. I worked all morning while Jorge was at school and sewed and read in the afternoon. Later in the evening I went down to the dock. There, at the end of the porticos, was a rocky outcrop where I liked to sit and smoke a cigarette. I couldn't do that at home because my husband considered it sinful.

On Saturday I arrived later than usual to my meeting with the sea. I could no longer see it and barely knew it was there from the slow and heavy blows of the waves against the rocks. My cigarette must've been a dot of light in the darkness. I heard footsteps and got to my feet.

"Is that you, María Luisa?" asked a shadow coming to a halt.

"Yes, Rosita."

I recognized her from the ivory of her teeth gleaming in the darkness.

"Am I bothering you, dear?"

"On the contrary! I was thinking about you."

That wasn't true and came out on its own.

295

"Really? Me too, I've been thinking about you every day lately. Why haven't you come for a visit?"

I didn't know what to say and said nothing.

"Tomorrow is the party they're throwing in my honor. I'll recite something, and I wanted to see you before then. You've got no idea how hard it was to find out where you live! Your maid said you come to the dock every evening. I'd already lost hope of finding you when I glimpsed the light of your cigarette, and like Tom Thumb in the forest, I came up to you fearing I'd find the ogre in your place."

"Which would've been only natural, since women don't generally smoke!"

"But I knew you did."

"How?"

"Dear, some things one just knows... Your outfit, a certain air about you... A look in your eye..."

"Really? Please explain."

Rosita laughed like women always do when they don't want to answer.

"And Lolín?" I asked.

"What do I know? We fought the day after I got here, and I haven't seen her since. But I do know she's spying on me and stops by the hotel grounds every day. Really, it's ridiculous! We haven't seen each other for over a year, not since she got married, of course. Now that was a stab in the back! She must've already told you."

Being loyal, I should've said no, Lolín had never told me any secrets. But I was feeling treacherous.

"Yes," I nodded, "I know."

"Then you know I was completely in the right. Five years we were together, five whole years! I rescued her from the clutches of the American consul's daughter, a whore if there ever was one, and helped her whenever I could. I was mad about her! And that's how she went and repaid me, turning around and marrying that good-for-nothing, who was my boyfriend to keep up appearances."

"But before he'd been her boyfriend."

"Did she tell you that? I assure you he wasn't. It was she who suggested I accept his advances so people wouldn't gossip about us. I went out with him every evening until a month before their wedding. I'm telling you, I've never understood it."

But I did, I understood. Lolín had married him out of jealousy for Rosita. That way he wouldn't marry her. But I was careful to keep my mouth shut.

"And now she comes to me for explanations! Do you think she has the right? Now that would be something! Anyway, it's all over. Now I'm a free woman. I signed a year-long contract to perform in America. If you want to come…"

"Me?" I said, feeling a dryness in my mouth. "Me? Don't you know I'm a married woman?"

"Bah! In name only."

"Yes, but I've got a home, and I'm tied down here."

"Poor María Luisa! What silly decisions young people make, isn't that so? I alone have been level-headed enough to stay off a path that isn't my own."

She talked to me at length about her life in Madrid with her mother, about her hopes for America. She'd come back with a few thousand duros to rest for a while and buy her mother a cottage with a garden on the Mediterranean. She'd like that since she was from Murcia.

"It's chilly," she said, suddenly getting up, "and we shouldn't be out at night by the sea. Shall we?"

"Sure, I don't care," I replied, suddenly feeling infinitely miserable. "Here or there, nothing matters to me."

"Thank you very much, dear!"

"What I meant," I said, trying to correct my blunder, "was that… Since you're here temporarily… If you were to stay, then I… Every day I come here because nothing interests me anywhere else."

"It's worse with sugar coating," teased Rosita. "Don't try to take it back, because there's no fix now. Let's go."

We walked side by side in the darkness. I knew the places where the cargo was piled and guided her gently with her arm in my hand. It disturbed me to feel the smooth silk of her skin through the fabric of her dress. We walked in silence. I would've liked to find something to say, but nothing occurred to me. We could already see the plaza's electric arc lights nearby.

Rosita took me by the arm, sending a jolt right through me.

"What's wrong? Am I annoying you?"

"On the contrary! I'm cold, is all."

And we kept walking, arm in arm, hurrying as we reached the end of the dock.

"Ah, silly me! I almost forgot to give you the ticket for tomorrow. That was my whole reason for coming."

She opened her bag, shuffled through some papers, and found an envelope with the ticket. We were standing under the last portico, and the light of the plaza's lampposts reached us dimly. There was a gleam in her eyes and on her moist lips. We looked at each other in silence.

"I'll be gone after tomorrow," she said slowly. "Will you regret it?"

"Look at me," I sighed, "I'm all alone." I said it with the same conviction as if we'd been friends for many long years. "I don't see Lolín anymore."

"She's jealous," purred Rosita. "She's made some real scenes since I got here! As if I had anything to do with her!"

"Jealous of you?" I asked.

"And of you, sweetheart… Don't act so surprised."

I covered my eyes with my hands. For the first time in my life, I found myself in a situation the whole world would consider absurd and that for me was awkward and shameful. I didn't know what to say.

Standing in front of me, Rosita must've seen my surprise.

"You're too sensitive, child!"

Then her hands took mine from my eyes, and she came so close, I could feel her breath in my face. Throwing her arms around my neck, she pressed our mouths together, and I felt the moist pulp of her fleshy lips into which mine were sinking. And the whole world ceased to exist.

Suddenly my support gave way, and I heard Rosita's footsteps as she ran into the distance. I tried to follow her, but my legs were jelly, and I had to sit down on a crate of oranges. All the sweetness of its fruit had poured into my heart, and tears were streaming down my face.

I had to pull myself together. It must've been late, and they'd be worried at home.

I rose and walked slowly out of the dark. In the plaza I stood up straight, trying to regain my composure and my calm, swift step. I crossed under the lampposts, skirted the gardens of San Francisco, and was about to turn up a dark street when I saw a shadow step out from a wall. And all at once, a slap in the face and a dirty word buffeted my human dignity. The slap was the strongest I'd ever endured; the word, one I'd heard but never understood.

And both of them came from Lolín!

FLORINDA

Summer had come, and the city was a steam bath, sapping us all of our energy. Consuelo had gone on vacation in the country with her kids, and we rented an estate on the mountainside not far from them.

I was no longer painting, and Jorge didn't leave the house and was always hovering around me, anxious and ill-tempered. I would sew, read old books out of closets, and sometimes recall my music lessons on the decrepit piano in the hall. Its notes sounded guttural and distant like voices from other eras. I'd found some old waltzes and romantic serenades in a music cabinet and would practice them in the long, empty hours to avoid hearing the constant hissing of the Monk's Peppers, whipped day and night by the wind from the sea.

Consuelo came over some evenings with the kids.

"Aren't you painting anymore?"

"That's all I'd need not to pick up a brush all summer long," answered Jorge, gruffly.

"Florinda's here," announced Consuelo one day, "and we must go together and see her. She's one of the richest, most notable people on the island. A single woman, the descendent of the last Guanche princess. She's sure to intrigue you, and in any case, her friendship will do you better than those girl friends you liked so much this past winter. By the way, what ever happened to your friend Lolín?"

"I don't know, I haven't seen her. We argued."

"Thank goodness. I didn't want to say anything lest you say I'm always in your business, but don't think her friendship did you any favors, either. She's just like Fermina. At least she got married, but she's crazy all the same, and worst of all, she acts like she doesn't give a damn what people think. No, she's no proper woman."

"Well, dear, what did you expect? It just so happens I've always taken an interest in improper people."

"Yes, it's a shame, but you'll see, Florinda will intrigue you, even if she is an honorable woman. She spends most of the time at her house in England and four or five months of the year here, at her estate in La Orotava. At the moment she's still in Santa Cruz at her uncle's house, and we'll take the opportunity to pay her a visit. Because La Orotava is far away, and without a car... When do you want us to go?"

"Tomorrow."

"No, not tomorrow. My order hasn't come from the dressmaker."

"Well, you were the one who asked me when I wanted to go... You ought to know I'm free and that unfinished dresses have absolutely no influence on my decisions."

"Look, that's something else I wanted to talk about. Around here there's a certain prejudice against women who dress the way you do. They won't say a thing about you because you're married, but it wouldn't hurt to have a fancy blouse made."

"So they talk about that, too, do they? Who knew these small provinces were so delightful?"

"Yes, but they've got other advantages. You'd have never received so many commissions in Madrid or made a name for yourself in less than year. I mean it," she added, seeing my contempt, "word gets around, and Rafita published your portrait."

A few days later we took a tram down to the city and reached Florinda's uncle's house on a wide avenue. It was practically a palace, with a spacious courtyard full of palm trees and a fountain.

A white-clad maid showed us into his lordship's upstairs chambers and left us in some kind of vast mirador with blinds on all sides. Consuelo made me look at a glass display case mounted on the wall.

"Those are all souvenirs Florinda brought back from her trips. She's done a lot of traveling! Every year, she sets aside quite some time for visiting strange places."

She was interrupted by two pure-bred dogs with ferocious red mouths and drooping jowls who sniffed us and laid down on the tile mosaics, splaying their legs to feel the cool all over. The floor was shining like a mirror.

Almost immediately, Florinda appeared and embraced Consuelo.

"Is this your sister-in-law? I hear she's a fine painter."

She was staring at me with her long almond eyes, slightly slanted.

She looked like a woman in the prime of her life, but I'd be incapable of estimating her age. Her hair was so black it looked blue, and she wore it parted in two, with buns over her ears. Very high cheekbones, broad and prominent; a large mouth with thick, sensual lips; perfect teeth; pale olive skin, even in tone without any makeup. Like Consuelo said, she was a pure-bred Guanche.

"Come closer," she said in the island women's sweet accent, making room for me beside her on the wicker sofa. "I wanted to meet you. So you're from Madrid? I don't know what it is about you *madrileñas*, but you bear the charm of your city. The friendliest city on earth!"

She asked Consuelo about the kids, inquiring at length about their health and the schools where they sent the eldest. Then Consuelo asked her about people I didn't know who were traveling.

"Jacinto's in Stockholm. This summer he wanted to see the midnight sun. And my sister María's in Athens to see Isadora Duncan dance. I'd have gone with her, but after almost a year away from the Canaries, I started hearing the call of the land. I traveled a little in the spring and brought back some interesting finds. I'll show you after tea."

The tea arrived on a trolley pushed by an English maid. Lemon wedges and ice cubes were floating in the crystal kettle.

"Iced tea," explained Florinda. "This time of year, it's impossible to drink it hot."

She served it with English distinction mingled with something vaguely oriental, rhythmic and slow like a ritual.

Then she showed us some porcelain and Romanian lace, a Bohemian crystal goblet the maid brought in a case, and a transparent band with gilded Arabic script.

"A sura from the Koran," I exclaimed, recalling that Tía Manuelita had one just like it.

"Yes, on gazelle skin. I bought it in Turkey," said Florinda, eyeing me curiously. "If you like these things, I can show you some other interesting pieces still in my luggage and others at my house in La Orotava."

We talked about archaeological discoveries. I remembered some Roman coins I'd found in the garden in La Mancha, and she told me about a tiny idol unearthed on one of her estates near a prehistoric burial ground. Florinda got starry-eyed just talking about it.

Slightly bored, Consuelo rose to examine one of the figures in the display case.

"Come over alone tomorrow, and we'll talk," said Florinda, lowering her voice. "Until tomorrow?"

I managed to go out the following day on the pretext I was shopping in the city. That left Jorge grumpy and bored.

"Why don't you start another painting?" I suggested.

"Because I don't want to. Now that you paint, there's no need for another painter in this household."

"That's not true! I'm not painting now."

"But you'll get back to it. In any case, I'm through with work."

The day after that, I had to invent another excuse to go out because Florinda insisted I take tea with her. She was extremely cultured, perhaps to a fault. She spoke five languages, read Latin and Sanskrit, made paintings and poems. Her dresses were custom-made in Paris, and her undergarments must've been expensive, for a rustle of silk accompanied all her movements.

"María Luisa, how was I to know I'd meet a fine pearl like you here?" she asked, addressing me as a friend two days after we met. "This place is a social wasteland!"

Her only flaw was to be so absorbing. She wanted me to visit her every afternoon, and she sent me letters every morning. And the moment I missed two days, she'd show up on my doorstep. Her car would pull up silently to the door, and she'd enter without knocking and look for me among the Monk's Peppers where I was reading in the shade. I never heard her approach until her hands were over my eyes.

"Guess who? I bet you can't guess!"

"Florinda!"

"The very one who's furious with you for not going to see her. You, sir," she turned to Jorge, "are a terrible tyrant. Why don't you let your dear little wife leave the house? Don't you know she's made to shine in society?"

"She can shine all she wants," Jorge would answer. "As for me, I can't stand people, and it gets worse every day."

"Insufferable savage indian," griped Jorge when it was just the two of us. "We really hit the jackpot with your and Consuelo's visit!"

"But I enjoy spending time with her," I ventured to reply.

"Well, don't let me stop you. You can visit her whenever you like!"

The summer ended without Florinda deciding to leave for La Orotova despite the terrible heat in Santa Cruz. Classes had started, and we were still in the house on the mountain. Day after day, Jorge would go down the road to catch the tram, and he was talking about us spending the winter in the country.

Autumn is sweet and mild on the island, but the afternoons get shorter, the wind whistles stronger, and a gentle sadness descends over the fields exhausted by the summer heat. Consuelo and the kids were back in the city, and I hadn't left the house for a week. I opened the windows and was at the piano playing the deep, somber chords of the Basque Serenade, when an eager pair of lips alighted on my neck.

It was Florinda, pale and slightly agitated.

"It's me. Why aren't you visiting? A whole week of you leaving me alone in the afternoons. I decided not to come, not to complain, but alas, I couldn't help it. Don't you know you're the only reason I haven't left for La Orotava?"

Her eyes were brimming with tears.

"Really, dear," I said, startled to see her like that. "Don't take it the wrong way! I had to help my sister-in-law pack her suitcases, and Rafita wrote saying he needed a cartoon on short order, of the dance with the Japanese sailors. Until just now I was working on it."

Little by little, Florinda calmed down, and we chatted about the new school year, the upcoming parties at the club, the new schoolmaster, and the banquet to be held for his predecessor.

"When is it?"

"The day after tomorrow."

"So does that mean you'll be alone for the day?" asked Florinda.

"Yes. Consuelo will insist I go to her house, but I don't want to. Right after lunch, I'll pay you a visit. Would you like that?"

"No, I'd like something much better. I'll pick you up at eleven in the car, and we'll spend the day in La Orotava. You'll see the estate and the house. We'll eat lunch and swim on my private beach, and I'll bring you back after supper. What do you say to that, my girl?"

"I say, it sounds like a plan! As long as Jorge doesn't object. I'm sure he won't say *no*, but sometimes a frown means more to me than an order. I won't tell him till tomorrow."

From that moment on, Florinda spoke only of the estate, where she'd been born in an old house that was later knocked down by a cyclone. All her siblings had inherited a similar estate from their parents, but hers was the prettiest and richest in traditions. It was still home to the tree under which one of her Guanche ancestors meted out justice to all the island.

"Eight o'clock," she said, giving a jolt. "My uncle must be waiting at the table. So long, Marilú. Till the day after tomorrow. What day is that?"

"October twentieth."

"I'll have it engraved in gold."

I too was anxious for the appointed day. Jorge was going to the banquet, and I woke up bright and early to see that his shirt was well ironed and his pants well creased. Gold cufflinks, blue tie, pressed jacket, shiny shoes—I saw to all of it.

But as always, my efforts were in vain. At the last minute, he found that his hat was too old, his kerchiefs too tattered, the heels of his shoes too worn. With that, he let himself fall into his chair in despair. He complained that he was a miserable wretch, that he couldn't set foot around well-dressed folks and wasn't going to the banquet.

"I'd rather stay in. They're all a bunch of idiots who'd be better off at home, not meeting to eat like donkeys at a trough. Imbeciles!"

After undressing and redressing, cursing the world in general and the other teachers in particular, he finally wound up going, leaving me nervous, exhausted, and sad. Eleven o'clock! I had just enough time to get dressed before Florinda came.

I was knotting my wrinkle-free tie at the neck of my button-down blouse when I heard the car horn at the door.

In a cretonne dress and a Pamela hat decorated with cornflowers, Florinda looked almost like a girl.

"My dear, always so formal," she said, seeing me climb into the car.

"I haven't got dresses like yours."

"Nor do I want you to dress any other way!"

The green of the landscape passed before our eyes, strange and volcanic, and we barely spoke. Florinda had taken one of my hands and would occasionally comment on what we were seeing. Those caves, still inhabited, were once the dwellings of the island's first settlers... Sometimes there was a fever-inducing lake in that floodplain... And in those clearings was a Guanche cemetery... Reaching a high place, she ordered the driver to stop.

"La Orotava! Look down there. There are the botanical gardens, and there are the banana plantations and the sea," she pointed. "When they came to the island and reached this place, my ancestors the Egyptians kissed the earth and praised the Lord Creator. I believe an Englishman later did the same. But not us, because the driver would burst out laughing."

The sea was shimmering like liquid silver caught in the coast's emerald embrace. Little by little, the car wound its way closer on the zigzagging road lined with gardens and trees that always stayed green.

"See that wall with the iron gate? That's my estate."

But before I could look, it had slipped out of sight, reappearing and disappearing with every switchback.

We were greeted by a dozen servants standing in a line, their skin the color of earth and just as parched and cracked. They were intoning a chant I couldn't understand apart from the words, "Your ladyship, your ladyship."

"Are you her ladyship?"

"I am," replied Florinda. "We're still in the eighteenth century in these parts. They're good, honorable folk with the souls of serfs, no thanks to the Spaniards, who treated them like slaves. In any case, you're not to blame."

The banana plantation had big open spaces with Australian grass like a plush, elastic carpet. The house was a wooden indian bungalow brought from the United States and assembled on a stone foundation. With its white painted walls and its bright green shutters, it was pretty and neat as can be. And what was that perfume?

Inside, the house was a bit like a boat, with everything perfectly laid out: the dining room with its linoleum floor, the spacious hearth between shelves of exquisitely bound books, the lacquered furniture and large table, the apple-green bathroom, whose stained-glassed windows simulated the sea floor with its fish and its coral. As for the bedrooms, I counted eighteen of them!

"I always have guests," explained Florinda. "Last year I was at a castle in Scotland before coming back here with five friends."

But what was that perfume all around the house?

In her bedroom, which Florinda showed me last, it grew so intense that I had to ask.

"Look," she gestured, opening a window at the back of the house, "this heliotrope climbed all the way up here. They tend to be small in Europe, but here they cover half the house. And they flower all year long…"

Everything in Florinda's room was wicker, even the wide, low bed. There were oval mirrors, white and purple easy chairs, a bathroom, and a separate dressing room.

"See how frivolous and fragile everything looks? I miss it when I'm at my house in London."

She left me in the hall smoking a cigarette while she spoke with her servants at the door of the house. They all had voices like birds and talked quickly and understood one another barely pronouncing their words. Shortly after they left, a small boy brought me tennis shoes and a racquet.

"We'll play badminton while they're making lunch," said Florinda. "Oh, how I love a Guanche lunch!"

I took off my jacket, and we played on the Australian grass until Florinda begged for a reprieve.

"I'm getting exhausted," she groaned, letting herself collapse on the grass. "Getting old is awful!"

For lunch we ate squash and pea soup, salted fish with black potatoes, and ham with bananas. But bananas like the essence of all bananas known to man: small, golden, fragrant, and exceptionally sweet.

"Nobody but me grows this variety. They're named after the Prince of Wales and have been grown for him on my estate for the past two centuries."

Nana María, an old Guanche woman with a tiny hat and veiny hands, served us coffee in Florinda's bedroom, and while I finished drinking, Florinda disappeared into her dressing room and came back wrapped in a white robe. She'd let down her hair, and the black braids of her buns were hanging on either side of her face. The old woman left after kissing her hands.

"Get comfortable," instructed my friend. "At five we'll go swimming, and we've got to wear bathing suits down to the beach. You'll find robes to your liking in the dressing room."

I resisted a little, but she insisted and I finally gave in. Picking out a striped robe, I took off my clothes and hung them next to Florinda's, which were lovely and smelled slightly of cinnamon.

"I'm ready, but look what a sight I am," I said, returning to the bedroom where Florinda had lain down in bed. "One of your brothers must've left this here."

"No," she replied, "it belonged to the nephew of an eighty-year-old English lady I had as a guest last year. He was twelve years old and much taller than you. Yes, indeed! You, my girl, are of petite Latin stock. Sit on the bed, and pardon me for lying down. It's an old habit that I can't give up."

Florinda was prettier from above than face to face. Her eyes were more slanted, her cheekbones higher, her mouth cooler and fresher. The heliotrope's disturbing perfume, the opium of the Egyptian cigarette, and the green semi-darkness led us to speak in confidence.

Had Florinda ever had a boyfriend? No, she'd never felt like it. Men's first thought was for her fortune, and she was very independent, very accustomed to always doing as she wished. Besides, she hadn't fallen in love!

"And you? Have you had any flings?"

"Never! I… I'm terribly unlucky… I don't feel the desires of the flesh, and never have."

"Not for anyone?"

I rested my head on her pillow and studied her up close. Her lips were so full, her cheeks so broad! And what a shine in her eyes! I felt flustered and lowered my gaze.

"Don't play dumb. Are you sure? You've never felt love? Not ever?"

"You're an Egyptian," I said without answering. "What a strange creature you are! Your skin is pale like an indian's."

"But tell me," she prodded. "Haven't you ever fallen in love?"

My temples were pounding violently, and my voice came out hoarse. "Yes, I have… With you… With you, beautiful!"

···

When I waved her goodbye at the door of my house, I could've glossed the poet king saying, "Behold, thou art fair, my love!" But instead, I kept my mouth shut.

THE NAUTICAL CLUB BALL

The second the ball was announced, the local ladies could talk of nothing else. Even Consuelo was flipping through fashion designs and asking my advice about how to make an evening gown out of her wedding dress, which she'd dyed black.

"I've got no idea. You know that by now."

"Yes, you do. You painters know more about fabrics than anybody else."

I managed to draw her a pretty design that would be easy to follow. She took it to the dressmaker, all excited, and even said it was a great success and that several ladies had asked permission to copy it.

"What about you?" my sister-in-law asked nervously. "Aren't you going to have a dress made? There are just two weeks left, and no dressmaker would commit to making one on shorter notice."

"I'll go like this."

"What? You'd go to a ball in a suit jacket?"

To be honest, I had no interest in going to the ball. Over four months had passed since Florinda left for England, time enough for me to grow sad and isolated from the outside world.

Over the winter, while she was still on the island, it was as if I were living in a dream, docilely playing along with Consuelo's rules for life, visiting the teachers' wives, taking tea at the home of some recent English acquaintances, drawing cartoons for the newspaper... And looking forward to Wednesdays, when Florinda's car came to take me to La Orotava.

"See?" said Consuelo. "See how none of us objects to that friendship? Florinda's an honorable woman, although I don't know how you can stand her antiquities and intellectual snobbery. She's too refined for me! This Wednesday I'll go and see her with you. It'll make the visit less boring."

That only happened once because that day Florinda sat her down for a lecture on the islands' probable origin: pieces of Atlantis that had sunk to the bottom of the sea. And she insisted on reading us all the evidence she'd collected. Right after tea, Consuelo said she had to go home because Antoñete had a cough and she was afraid it was tonsillitis.

"Dear, I'm so sorry! You can't leave now because the driver has off until eight and who knows where he is. Have fun with Milor while we play badminton."

Consuelo stayed with the dog, and we took the racquets and birdies to the meadow.

"What made you think to bring her here, Marilú?"

"It was her idea. You know I would never..."

"Yes, I know. Well, the afternoon will be only half boring."

We played for a while, then went down to sit on the rocks, still warm under the bright winter sun of the Canaries. Florinda nestled her head on my shoulder, I stretched an arm around her waist, and we contemplated the sea in silence, full of peace and awash with emotion, happy to feel so close that our hearts were beating as one and we didn't need to talk to know what the other was thinking.

Back at the house we found Consuelo pacing out front, bored out of her mind. My sister-in-law refused to ever go back there.

"If it were just a short trip, fine; but to be stuck there all afternoon, like it or not... And you two run around and play because you're in good shape, but I get tired out..."

Some mornings Florinda would show up at our house to spend the day with us. Jorge would frown before giving in.

After lunch we'd go shopping and inevitably wind up at the Nautical Club, where we'd contemplate the port from the terrace and take tea watching the boats come and go.

"I'll be leaving soon," announced Florinda one afternoon.

"What?"

"Yes, my brothers are already waiting for me in London. We always spend the month of March together, the month when my parents died. A decade apart, but in the same month. I can't miss this year."

"But what does that mean? It's February twentieth."

"Yes, I leave on Friday."

"But you didn't say a thing!"

"What would've been the point? It's bad enough I've been suffering since I set the date. I've spared you days of worry. I had no choice," she sighed. "Besides, it's in our interest to spend some time apart. People are starting to see us together all the time, and they've never gossiped about me on the island. There'll be talk if I don't go now like I always do, and we must keep up appearances!"

"Will you come back soon?"

"You can count on it. No trips this year, I'll be back right after March. Ah, and you won't see me off at the dock, nor will we see each other again after Wednesday. You understand, don't you? Then don't give me that tragic face!"

We said goodbye the following Wednesday. Florinda cried in my embrace, nestling her head in my chest. She'd write to me with every post, and I was to do the same, but discreetly, because a letter can go astray.

Back at home, I found myself with Jorge. I'd forgotten all about him since autumn. I don't know if he'd been watching me or what kind of mood he was in while I lived by his side like a sleepwalker. But right then I was surprised to run into him. What was he still doing there? Why did he ask about my comings and goings? What was he in my life?

I got angry the first day Consuelo came over to take me on a visit. Those visits were torture, and if I'd gone along with them before, it was only because... Well, why not? But I was no longer willing to continue that life.

Jorge looked at me, astonished.

"The look on your face has gotten so tough. Really, you're not very feminine."

Florinda's first letter arrived. It was short. All she did was describe her trip and sign affectionately. I wrote back, desperate. The city was unbearably sad, and spring was awful with no new buds, no new leaves on the trees that never lost them, no strawberries and asparagus from Aranjuez. Like the seasons, the days were all the same, and I couldn't live without her!

Her reply came in the next post. She begged me to remember our last conversation; she was doing everything she could. I knew how much she loved her island, how she carried it in her heart. That's why she'd come back as soon as possible.

It wasn't true. She wrote to me from Paris, then from Rome, Venice, Naples... There was no use responding; by the time her letters reached me, she'd already moved on, and she didn't stay anywhere for long.

Jorge wasn't painting and hadn't set foot in his studio for ages. He lurked silently around the house as if he were trying to catch my attention. One night after we'd gone to bed, I heard him get up and feel for my bed in the darkness.

"Where are you going?" I sat up. "Leave me alone. Leave me alone, I said!"

He went back to his bed without insisting, but from the next day on he was more irritable and sarcastic with me, especially around other people. There were times he got truly furious. At the drop of a hat, he'd be throwing and breaking things.

One time he was rude to a family of visitors, and they spread the word he was off his rocker.

And the months passed, no sign of Florinda!

The club was to host its end-of-season ball, and all the island's painters were decorating the walls in the dining room and ballroom. I too was called to help decorate the powder room, and I painted thousands of confetti on the two white walls on either side of the big mirror. On one side I made a woman in a hoop skirt with a black lace veil over her pink dress. She was busy flirting, uncovering her marvelously beautiful face. On the opposite wall, a romantic gentleman was falling to his knees with his hat in his hand while watching her.

Jorge refused to go and see it, but lots of people congratulated me, and Rafita's newspaper published a detailed description of the decorations that heaped me with praise. I was satisfied; I knew my work wasn't bad, but also that it could be better.

According to Consuelo, that's why I couldn't miss the ball. They'd paid me well and given me a magnificent bouquet of flowers. My absence would be an insult to the board.

I went in my black silk dress, austere and unadorned, with a Manila shawl on my arm as was customary at such balls. Elated to take me with them, Consuelo and José María spun like tops on the dance floor. But no dancing for me! I stayed in a corner hearing one of the military governor's daughters talking nonsense, my back to the dancing because it made me dizzy.

"I don't like to dance, either," said the girl, who was so ugly it wouldn't have made a difference anyway. "Never have. It's a shame you get sick from watching, because some of the dresses are worth a peek. Those Englishwomen will wear anything! There goes the eldest Hernández girl in white with ivory lace, and Doctor Juliá's daughter in pale blue, which doesn't suit her dark complexion. You know what they say about blue on dark-skinned women... And look, Paquita Gutiérrez is wearing the same apple-green gauze as last year. I don't understand why she doesn't dye it! If you're going to reuse a dress, at least take the time to dye it. Who really looks good is Florinda, always wearing the latest designs! I heard she was traveling."

"Florinda?" I interrupted, turning to look... And there she was.

Yes, it was Florinda! She was dancing with a tall, clumsy foreigner.

"And Araminta's in yellow," the ugly girl continued. "They say she's getting married to the Bethancourt boy. I don't believe it, because he's oozing money and she's barely got a penny. She's pretty, all right, being so young and all, but the second she gets married and gets fat like her mother..."

I finally gave up listening. That odious girl was driving me mad with her predictions! Without knowing how, I found myself on the terrace, gazing into the darkness of the horizon. I was facing the sea and could hear but not see it. How sad! Florinda had come back without even telling me. Florinda! That amber-skinned Guanche from La Orotava had nothing to do with the woman who was dancing with the Englishman.

The music ceased, and several couples came out to the terrace. I tried to slip past them and go back into the ballroom unhindered, but José María and Consuelo were at the door looking all over for me.

"Where were you hiding, dear? We were beginning to think you'd gone home alone. Have you seen Florinda?" asked Consuelo. "She was happy to hear that you came. She introduced us to her fiancé. She's getting married!"

316

"I don't believe it," I exclaimed, not knowing what I was saying.

"I don't know why not. She told us so herself! She's to be wed immediately. He and his family came to get to know the island, then they're heading back to London to get married. He's filthy rich! But she didn't say so, only Margot."

"Who's Margot?"

"A close friend of Florinda's who's been traveling. You don't know her because she's been gone for over two years. It's a night for encounters. Why, we've run into all kinds of people we haven't seen in ages!"

The music started up again, and everyone rushed to the ballroom. They danced and danced! Even the ugly girl crossed in front of me dancing with an autumnal gentleman. That ball would never end. There went Florinda in the arms of her Englishman! I tried to approach them and to catch her attention.

"Aren't you going to say something, Marilú?" She pulled her partner aside and introduced me as María Luisa. I didn't understand the clumsy man's outlandish name.

"When did you get here?"

"This morning… What's the matter with you? I thought you'd be thrilled to see me. I didn't want to say anything to give you a surprise."

"Well, you certainly did. Does the gentleman speak Spanish?"

"Not a word, dear."

"In that case, you owe me an explanation."

Feeling me grab her by the arm, Florinda jerked away.

"Oh, my! What's gotten into you?" She glanced at the Englishman. "He doesn't speak Spanish, but body language is the same all over. We'll talk soon."

"No, now."

"Wait, I'll leave him with some friends. Have some patience, dear."

I followed her fearing she'd get lost in the crowd and finally managed to get her into a dark corner of the terrace, but not before meeting my in-laws at the ballroom door.

"Florinda, tell María Luisa you're getting married," said Consuelo. "She refuses to believe it!"

"Understandably," she replied without a flinch. "A week ago, I wouldn't have believed it myself. Fate works in mysterious ways."

"Let's go, and you'll tell me!" My voice was so changed, I could barely believe it was me talking. "Come on."

We reached the balustrade not saying a word.

"Well, now you know, dear," started Florinda, the two of us leaning on the railing. "I didn't want to tell you like this, but now you know."

"Yes, well… Do you love him very much?"

"Yes, like a schoolgirl."

"And your theories about men's self-interest?"

"This time they were wrong, because he's ten times richer than me."

"So you've stopped loving me."

"Who told you that? On the contrary, since the moment I saw you tonight, I think I love you even more."

"Look, you don't have to lie anymore. You don't love me; now you love him. That's the end of it."

"Jesus, Mary, and Joseph! I love you both! What's one thing got to do with the other? He'll be my husband, and you, my friend."

"But I wasn't your friend. I was more than that."

"The stuff of single women, dear! Why go back to that?"

"I'm not a single woman," I said, lowering my voice out of anger and pain. "I have a husband, but I liked you better, back when you loved me."

"Now don't go getting angry. Your case, I've never understood it. You're very abnormal, Marilú. I, on the other hand, am a primitive woman from a primitive race, free of decadent complications. But why say more? I'll send you the car on Wednesday, and you'll come and take tea with us and meet my future sister-in-law. She speaks French."

"I don't want to see you again," I said, spinning to face the stormy black horizon without a single star. And I heard Florinda's footsteps receding into the distance.

At one fell swoop I was alone again, face to face with my aimless life, lost on a strange path that I had to walk holding hands with Jorge. Jorge, always nervous and irritable, stifling my personality and seeking my caresses whenever he needed them, even when he was mad at me; seeking me like a man seeks a woman for pay.

"What a miserable life," I bawled, as on some long-past day with Tía Manuelita. But this time I had nobody to hear my grievances. I was alone, completely alone! And I cried heart-rending sobs over the balustrade. I'd been the plaything of a depraved old maid! What an embarrassment! What a disgrace! Lord in Heaven, if only I were a believer and could throw myself at the feet of a confessor and water the ground with my tears. My God, what had happened?

I tried to calm down. Nobody would ever find out. I would leave that place, return to the mainland, to Madrid, where life is sober, the climate harsh, and the plains of Castile ascetic and chaste, just like I'd always been. Me, a patch of Castilian earth strewn on the luxuriant volcanic soil of that African island!

Jorge was still up when I got home.

"Did you enjoy yourself?"

"No, I was bored to death. Not my cup of tea. Besides, I don't feel well... This climate is sapping me, and I'm liable to die if I stay here."

"But I thought you were happy with *your work* and all your friends."

"I was at first, but now I can't go on like this."

"As far as I'm concerned, we leave tomorrow," said Jorge, delighted to see how easily I was renouncing everything he detested. "All the better if you don't regret giving up the newspaper and that idiot Rafita, your teas on the terrace and your friends. In Madrid we'll go back to our old life. A humble home with a studio for me to paint. I could even embark on a new life of work and put on a show in the next couple of years. Because people there forget you in an instant. It wouldn't be bad for me to put on a show! And I'm going to take up making portraits—artistic ones, naturally."

He talked on and on, envisioning the life he had in store for himself and for me. He would paint, but only him. He didn't say so, of course, but the implication was clear in his words. And I would watch him paint, endure his bad moods, tidy the studio, and cheer him on when he threw down his brushes in moments of helplessness. And my praise would be just, since I knew the trade... Him! Him! Him! It was always about him, and me an extension of him, no ideals but his, no aspirations but his, no joys but the few his melancholy character allowed him. I was to cry when he wanted, to make dramatic scenes—in short, to return to the first years of our marriage.

I listened without protesting. The important thing was to get out of there.

We were up until dawn planning our trip. He'd ask a colleague to go in with him for a transfer. Even in Madrid, it wouldn't be hard to find one, as the salary was higher on the island. I'd go ahead of him to look for a place to live and to prepare it in time for winter. The best time to find unrented rooms is at the end of summer. By September the worst of the heat has passed, and people are still on vacation.

The next day we informed José María and Consuelo of our decision, leaving them astonished and offended.

"But María Luisa," my sister-in-law sobbed, "you were so very happy here!"

AUTUMN

That autumn outdid all the other splendid, golden autumns I'd known in Madrid, where the season is always magnificent.

After the first frenzied days of finding somewhere to live—moving furniture, arranging books, organizing closets, cleaning house—came a period of calm with no pressing chores, when I savored the joys of a tidy home, welcoming, comfortable, and quiet.

Only two things were worrying me: my work, which I wanted to have underway when Jorge arrived, and in support of which Rafita had sent a letter of introduction, still unanswered, to the director of a magazine; and my rather broken down health, with its odd irregularities, dizzy spells, and lack of appetite.

Our usual doctor had died, and I didn't know any others, so I visited a practice having only seen the doctor's name on a metal plate on the door of his house nearby mine.

The doctor turned out to be a middle-aged man with inquisitive eyes.

"Maybe you're pregnant," he said, after examining me at length and asking about my family history and medical record.

"But I can't be!"

"Why not? You're still a young woman. Thirty-five? I mean, that would be the most natural thing."

"Impossible!"

"Why?"

"Well," I began, only to be interrupted.

"Don't be afraid to explain. You're here for a diagnosis and a cure, and I've got to assemble as many facts as possible in order to carry out my duty. Tell me, how can you be sure you're not pregnant? Are you separated from your husband?"

"Yes, sir, for the past two months."

"That's nothing, though."

"But it's been over a year since…"

"Is your husband ill?"

"No, sir."

"Did you have a falling-out?"

"No, it's just that… I can't… I can't bring myself to… And it gets harder and harder. It feels like an unnatural act."

"Aha!" he said.

"I've been married for eighteen years, but I can't get used to it. I can't! Sometimes I think I'm insane."

"Aha!" he repeated.

"Because I see how all women go along with it, even like it. But not me. I do everything I can to bring myself to reason. I tell myself it's a law of nature, that it's sacred in every religion, that we were all born of it. But then the time comes, and back comes my dread."

"You told me you had children."

"Yes, that was the one thing I could find to justify it. Because otherwise… The morning after is even worse. I feel violated and am convinced people can read it on my face, and I hate him with the same horror as if he'd raped me."

"I see!"

"And he's not cruel, no sir. I don't know how to explain it. On the contrary, he's a sensitive man and would like for me to be more feminine."

"Is that so?"

"He tries to make me feel pleasure, and sometimes he's completely successful… You understand! But the morning after, how horrible! I can't live with it! I look at women's faces trying to discover the same horror of the male, but no, it's just me!"

"Hmm… Tell me," he said when I least expected it, "have you ever had sexual intercourse with a woman?"

"Yes, sir."

"Aha!"

"But I regret it. I know it's wrong, that it's beneath me. It won't happen again."

"I see. And are you an artist?"

"A painter."

"Good, very good," he said, with a satisfied look, as if he were going to commission a picture. "Your fear of men's masculinity dates from your earliest girlhood."

"Yes, sir."

"Very good. And you played like a boy, your family called you a tomboy, you despised feminine frills. But there were swings between femininity and a violent mannishness. A pronounced timidity, periods of absolute chastity coinciding with more intense artistic work. Mysticism."

"Yes, very much so!"

"Very good. Ovulatory dysfunction, irregular periods, dull pains."

"All that."

"Stand up... Now turn. Strong back muscles... Yes, all the symptoms... Well, what you've got is outside of my area of expertise. You ought to see a psychiatrist; I'll give you a referral. I can recommend a good one who won't cost you a fortune. In the meantime, get rid of your men's suits, don't paint so much, and see to the housework. With the desire for perfection I see in your eyes, you'll overcome the imbalance of your nature... And you'll try to please your husband without causing yourself too much trouble."

He was smiling and writing the referral.

"Your case is more common than you'd think, especially when it comes to artists. I'd almost say an artist isn't complete if he isn't...."

Out on the street, I read the referral, which he'd sealed in an envelope against all common courtesy.

"A typical case of inversion of the instinct in an honorable person, just what we were talking about the other day. I believe it will interest you."

In other words, he was sending me to the psychiatrist like a guinea pig to a laboratory. No thank you! I wouldn't go. I slipped the referral in my pocket and thought over his advice. No more men's suits, care for the house, please my husband... A desire for perfection... Yes, that was true. Since the cure was within me, I'd apply it faithfully. Jorge was the one thing I had in the world. Now, after my shameful experience of feminine love, I felt chaster than ever, my sensuality severed, my appetites extinguished, sexless as a being on the verge of divinity.

I got home to find a telegram from Jorge: "Arrive Madrid Saturday 9 p.m. Hugs."

My husband was coming! The peace of my days and the chastity of my nights were about to end. Surely now, after so much time apart... I needed to come up with a plan. I got into bed but couldn't sleep for all my tossing and turning. I'd uncover the sitting room furniture, have the big easel moved into a corner of the studio, and unpack the living room rug. Most importantly, I'd visit the magazine and ask for a reply

324

to Rafita's letter, just to be sure I'd have work. I didn't plan on obeying the doctor on that count; on the contrary, my art would have to compensate for everything else.

The next afternoon, I stopped at the magazine office and insisted my business card be given to the director. I waited in a dingy reception area with the faded, smoke-stained walls common to all editorial headquarters. And I waited so long, I thought they'd forgotten me. But no, an office boy brought me a letter, and I went out to the street.

It was already dark out, and I read the laconic reply under the light of a lamppost. The director was familiar with my work in the newspaper from the island, and despite his interest, at the moment he had nothing to offer me. The magazine had a full slate of writers and contributors. He'd keep me in mind if he needed an illustrator. In other words, a polite rejection.

I had no place to work! Madrid's not the province, and it's harder to get a foot in the door... I was back to being the housewife Jorge wanted.

On my way past a church, a waft of incense heightened my growing disillusion. I slipped inside and saw the altar flooded in light, the pews full of people, and a preacher in the pulpit. I found a spot beside a confessional and sat down to listen.

The priest was waxing eloquent about the perfection of adapting to destiny. Back in the bright years of youth, we saw the infinite paths to eternal life stretching before us and went down the one that was to always be our own, freely or forced by our circumstances. Only if the path was dishonorable did we have to turn back. But if the chosen path was pure and upright, we were to pursue it fervently, passionately, like a divine task God had put in our hands.

Then he spoke of the perfect priest, the perfect nun, the perfect family man, the perfect mother and companion to her husband.

Out on the street, I remembered only the first words I'd heard in the church: "If the chosen path was pure and upright..." That was my case, for marriage was a sacrament. Everything else was the absurd imagination of an abnormal brain like my own.

One more day and Jorge would be there! The months of separation had imbued my memories with a poetic distance, and I was resigned in advance to accepting all my wifely duties. I took a moral pride in feeling strong enough to combat the imbalance of my nature.

The next day I'd buy a silk blouse, put on some earrings, and be a woman! And I was happy to be one, with my house so neat and tidy. All that talk about a happy home revolved around me, and a wave of my hand was all it would take to change the whole place, for I was the queen of that small state.

The following day the house took on a festive appearance: flowers in every room, lace sheets on the twin beds, magazines on the sitting room coffee table, the book of the month on the nightstand, pastries, cake, and sherry.

I stayed home in the afternoon to be more rested and started getting ready two hours before leaving for the station. I brushed my wavy hair to make it shine gold and polished my nails till they glimmered. I was debuting stockings, shoes, and a fancy blouse that I'd bought just that morning. I'd carry my mid-season coat on my arm because the October night felt almost like summer.

On the platform at the station, I was surrounded by people milling about and waiting like me for the train from Andalusia. A tall blond lady in mourning who looked like a foreigner kept on crossing paths with me.

The whistle sounded in the distance, then closer. Then the lights were approaching, and the train came clattering into the station, all out of breath. Jorge was leaning out the window of one of the final carriages.

Making my way through the crowd that had rushed to the edge of the platform, I watched him help a white-bearded man get down from the car with a boy. The blond lady from before was hugging them and crying.

Jorge kissed me quickly and turned to the group beside us.

"My wife," he introduced me. "My teacher, Maestro Galiano, and his grandson and daughter, Julieta."

We shook hands and parted at once in the bustle of suitcases, porters, and cars.

Jorge gave me a pleased look in the taxi.

"Darling, you look lovely. You've put on weight… My teacher just got here from Italy… But really, you look lovely! And what a surprise! I didn't expect to see you at the station."

"Who was that foreign lady?"

"Julieta? She's not foreign. Her mother was Italian, and that's where she got her looks. I told you, she's the maestro's eldest daughter. She's divorced, and the little boy's her nephew. His mother just died in Italy, a real tragedy. Sometime I'll tell you about it… We'll go and see them one of these days. The maestro was really happy to see me. Before they lived in Málaga, not Madrid… And his daughter writes poems, the kind people write now and nobody understands… But really, dear, you look lovely! I think we're going back to the good times, don't you? In Madrid we'll be closer than on that blasted island, where we each went about our own business."

Jorge had reached his arm around my back and was nervously pressing me against him. I did what I could to act affectionate and rested my head on his shoulder, for that was an essential part of the plan I'd traced out for myself.

"Did you miss me?"

"A lot."

"But it didn't seem like it in your letters. You sounded so happy, as if you didn't need me in the slightest. I started thinking I'd be doing you a favor if I never came back."

"Nonsense! Just wait and see what a lovely little place I prepared for us. The maids are tidy and capable and delighted to work for such a small household. Are you hungry? I had them make a dinner entirely to your liking, and you'll find the bath already drawn."

Jorge studied me carefully, looking more enthusiastic by the minute. How happy I'd have been with his brotherly love! But that was unthinkable. I was his wife, and Lord, we'd be just as happy married! I loved him, was delighted to see him, desired his happiness whatever the price. For what did I care what it took to make him happy?

Back at home, he took a bath while I unpacked his clothes, laying out his pajamas and placing his slippers at the bathroom door.

There were flowers at the dinner table, and we were served by a little maid all dressed in black. Jorge signaled for me to send her for something in the kitchen so he could kiss me lovingly on the hand, just as he did when we were newlyweds.

"María Luisa! These past few months apart were time well spent; instead of separating us, they've brought us closer together. Isn't that right, darling?"

"Quite right."

I wanted to give him a thorough tour of the house, explain why his dresser wasn't in his bedroom, why Dante's bust was on the table, not the desk. But he wouldn't hear a word of it.

"I'm exhausted, dear, let's save it for tomorrow. It's time to sleep."

And he lay down in bed.

"Aren't you coming?"

I paid the cook and undressed slowly in the bathroom, then braided my hair and slipped on a nightgown. Jorge was waiting in the bedroom with the light on.

"Tonight you'll sleep in my bed."

His voice was tender, his eyes glowing bright, and I knew the expression on his face!

328

I turned off the light, shut my eyes tight, and fell into his arms as if I were jumping off a cliff.

I woke up the next day in my own bed, having gone there at dawn without Jorge hearing. I woke up crying and trembling, head heavy and thoughts astray. I rubbed my temples. That wasn't for me! No, sir! If the whole world accepted it, if that was a normal life, then I was insane through no fault of my own. Lord in Heaven, what was to become of me?

Trying not to make a sound, I got up, took a bath, helped tidy the house, organized the meals, and took Jorge breakfast in bed.

"No, not here. I want to eat with you in the dining room."

That's when he went around the house, leaving nothing untouched in his wake.

"I don't like the coffee table in the middle of the room. You know I get nervous with clutter in the way... Dante is better off where he's always been, and I need my dresser in my bedroom... And that sitting room you're so proud of is useless. On the other hand, I need an office."

"But the house is rather small, and we need a room to sit and host guests," I said timidly, afraid of upsetting him.

"I don't suppose you'll devote yourself to visits now, will you? The office will be just fine for sitting and hosting, at least for the people I need to host. Before you barely saw anyone in Madrid, and I expect we'll continue the same way now."

He frowned seeing my easel in the corner of my closet, folded and propped against the wall.

"You plan to keep painting?"

"Yes, here at the window. There's enough light."

"In that case, have my bed moved somewhere else. I don't want paints in my bedroom."

"But dear!"

329

"No buts," he answered sarcastically.

Later he saw some portraits on my sewing box.

"Who's that?"

"A movie star. She's lovely, isn't she?"

"Oh, she's lovely! Just the thing to decorate a married woman's sewing box… And isn't that Fermina?"

"Yes, she gave me her portrait when she left for America."

"Well, she should've kept it. I imagine you'll destroy it."

"Why would I do that? I liked her. She was always kind and good to me."

"She was shameless, more or less like the actress you like so much."

"I had no idea, and I don't believe it."

"You'd better believe it, and even if she wasn't, her reputation was bad enough. A decent woman shouldn't have portraits like that on her table. The actress I can live with, though it's really not right, but the other one…"

"But I… I…"

"You what? I don't know about you, but I won't have that wench in my household!"

And he snatched the portrait and violently tore it into pieces.

I had enough self-control to keep quiet, but Jorge, furious over his outburst, stormed back to bed vowing not to get up again. As always, he was mad at himself for losing his temper.

"I've got nothing left to live for, don't plan to paint or go to school. All I want is to burst into pieces once and for all."

I ate lunch alone, then served him in bed. He was in one of his brooding tantrums: face to the wall, pretending to be asleep. I'd almost forgotten he had them. It took all my patience and self-discipline to convince him to sit up and drink some soup at four in the afternoon.

I talked to him naturally, like nothing had happened and there were no hard feelings, and he ended up happy and talking non-stop.

"Tomorrow we'll visit the maestro, and you'll see how good he is. I've barely met Julieta because she was already married and living in France when I was painting with her father. She's older than you… Want to go tomorrow?"

"As you wish."

"I plan to start painting immediately. I brought a sketch with me, and I'd like to put on a show next winter. People here have already forgotten me; it's been forever since they last heard my name, and that's a terrible thing for an artist. In Madrid you've got to build your reputation day by day… The studio has northern light, doesn't it? It's the only light I can paint in."

All evening he didn't stop talking about his hopes and dreams, about his painting for the National Exhibition and his other projects, about his maestro's compliments on the train. It wasn't as if he believed them—such praise is always over-blown—but it was nice knowing a man like Maestro Galiano recognized his worth. As for my work, my dreams, what I might achieve—not a word.

Tired and sad, I ate dinner at his nightstand and went straight to bed. It was the one time of day I could retire into myself and reflect, cry if I wanted, let out the tightness in my chest, gather together all the scattered reasons why I had to accept my destiny and be stronger the next day, braver and longer-suffering.

I was drifting off to sleep when I heard Jorge's voice.

"Darling, sweetie… You still mad at me? Won't you lie beside me for a while?"

HIDDEN PATH

Three more years came crashing down on our tortured lives. Jorge, whose apathy had worsened, was no longer painting. For my part, I went behind his back to get some small commissions from magazines. Seeing them in print plunged Jorge into days of silent fury.

My husband's brothers remained far from Madrid, and Maestro Galiano and his daughter Julieta were practically our only friends. Julieta had made friends with me to the extent her natural reserve and aloof personality would allow of friendship.

Several years older than me, she was sweet and kind, but her soft voice and delicate manners masked a cold, hard interior, brilliant and gleaming as a rock crystal. Despite us being on friendly terms, she never said a word about her divorce or anything else about her past. Her conversation was clever and captivating and flowed from her powerful intellect like an infinite wellspring of original ideas.

She and her father had inherited a villa on the Italian coast, and they planned to pack up and go live there for good. Later we were invited to spend a month with them at the end of the summer heat.

Villa Rosina was a large, cypress-filled estate with a two-story house in the middle—cozy, spacious, cheerful, clean, and full of local color. The staircase ran up an outside wall, belying the house's comfort.

We enjoyed absolute liberty there. The maestro had his rooms in the studio and barely left them, Julieta lived in the back of the house, and we had the whole first floor to ourselves. The boy and his nanny spent the day in a pavilion on the far side of the garden.

Julieta and I were both early risers, and we met at the pergola to eat breakfast under the arch formed by the cypresses, fragrant and green, over a bed of old stones with patches of grass.

Julieta usually made me look at some flowering plant or newly-mailed book, but one morning we talked about marriage—about marriage in general as a crime against love and my marriage in particular.

She agreed that I shouldn't have married, that artists shouldn't marry. But the lesson comes too late, when the damage is done.

"Perhaps the artist is the third sex," I said, only half-joking. "When I found out queen ants don't work and female workers are sterile, it was like a new world opened up to me. I think with humans, it's artists who shouldn't reproduce, who don't have the duty to pass on the torch to a new living thing."

"Yes, something like that," replied Julieta. "Michelangelo, Raphael, Leonardo da Vinci: none of the greats ever married. Because the artist's mind and soul combine the two sexes in a strange hermaphroditism capable of creation. Children of the flesh and children of the spirit can't be created with one sex alone. It's an eternal truth, even if men just found out recently… So many miserable beings, insulted and humiliated over an inversion of the instinct beyond their control! For sometimes an artist's opposite sex takes revenge by making him an invert. Alas, there's no denying pleasure, nor replacing physical love with all the platonic love in the world. Anyway, this conversation could take us too far."

Julieta rose to take her daily walk through the cypress grove. That early in the morning, the trees were emitting a pagan perfume mixed with the cool, salty smell of the sea.

We strolled down the sandy paths, and Julieta bent down every so often to pick a strawberry, straighten a stem, or pull up a stray blade of grass. Meanwhile, I pondered the things I'd just heard, not wanting to end a conversation I saw as giving me a dignified place in an unsympathetic world.

"My mother used to say I was a constant failure, and she was right," I went on. "I failed as a woman and a wife; I failed at motherhood and art."

"That's yet to be seen," replied Julieta. "In your personal life you took the wrong paths, or perhaps you were forced to take them. But in art you've struck out on your own at an age when you know what you want. Take the path that's been hidden till now, and step with solid footing. Brush aside the obstacles holding you back, and if you can unite your personal and artistic lives as one, you'll find that you never fail."

Up until then, Julieta and I had never discussed anything out of the ordinary, but those words convinced me to keep on telling secrets, certain she knew more about me than I'd realized.

"I never told you, but one time I went to a doctor, and talking about my physical and mental imbalances, he gave me a diagnosis. Not to my face, though. I read it in a referral to another physician."

"And it said…"

"A curious case of inversion of the instinct, just what we were talking about the other day."

"I see," was her only response.

"He told me it was common for artists, even that they're incomplete if they aren't…"

"Very good, he was abreast of what other doctors have said."

"I've always been a sorry case. What wouldn't have mattered to a single woman turned into my life's tragedy. Sometimes I'd go along with it, thinking it was practically a law of God. Other times I considered myself prostituted, doing it for the peace of my household—no desire, no love, like women who sell themselves for pay. I'd have fits of near madness. And so, ten years passed, fifteen, twenty… Refusing myself, postponing, but consenting in the end… And poor Jorge, not comprehending, not knowing. A nervous wreck from prolonged periods of abstinence, sometimes for years, suspecting only that I didn't love him."

That made her angry.

"And you said nothing! Why not? What were you protecting, squandering a life that could've been fertile for art and playing the perfect little housewife? You're making me mad! In the end, it's all a matter of cowardice, indignity, routine, fear of life."

"And pity for Jorge," I added, feeling the sting of her words. "He couldn't understand, saw only my lack of affection, was sick because of me."

"And who takes pity on you? Tell me, who? You too are sick, of solitude and mistakes, of adapting to a milieu that wasn't your own and never has been despite your best efforts… And also despite your lack of understanding… Sick for want of a feminine companion, of a feminine soul and body, of a woman to complete you and give you the pleasure necessary for life and for art. Forgive me dear, but this is the moment of truth."

Not wanting to admit I knew such companionship, I kept quiet, slightly ashamed.

"Aren't you deserving of pity? More than him, one hundred times more, because your whole life's been a struggle for something you lack even now, in the autumn of your existence. Thirty-eight years! A failed life! I, for one, pity you. Poor darling," she said, slipping an arm over my shoulder. "Poor, poor dear! But I'll be the only one, and only cowards want to be pitied. You've still got time. Be honest with him for once, or don't, but act according to your nature. Pardon the metaphor, but anything would be better than to stay in the henhouse when you're a bird of a different feather. And there's no merit in being that way or not; things are what they are for a reason."

"But that poor man!"

"Enough of your compassion! I'm telling you, nobody pities you, certainly not him, nor would they knowing the truth. Because normal people despise *us*."

And she fell silent. All at once, that *us* brought us together and opened an uneasy silence between us. She climbed up the garden wall, arranging the honeysuckle.

"The ocean's so blue! It doesn't seem like autumn," she said, hopping to the ground. "Think about what we've said, reflect and take pity on yourself as you would on a stranger. Remember your daily sorrows, looking to them to justify the decisions that lie ahead of you. Think how humiliated you've felt."

"Yes, it's been awful. I always felt I'd given in to an act against nature."

"That's just the right phrase. Against nature, against *your* nature… What more is there to say? We'd better stop. Think long and hard if your current life's worth continuing, and don't tell a soul what we've said here. Words and thoughts are the important things in life, and actions are only a consequence. Sometimes they're less important than we think." By then she was thinking out loud. "Are you going to paint today?"

I was making a portrait of five-year-old Lalín sweeping the burnt autumn leaves with a giant broom. I'd been seduced by the contrast of his blossom-pink face and bright young porcelain eyes with the dead leaves and the promenade of yellow poplars.

One day, seeing him sweep the avenue at the back of the garden, I'd made a sketch in my notebook that Julieta had shown to the maestro, enthused.

"The best gift you could give me," said the boy's grandfather, "is that picture exactly as you've planned it." Then turning to Jorge, "Your wife has the makings of an excellent artist."

Starting the next day, I had everything I needed at my disposal: canvas, brushes, and a shady place in the garden with a view of the poplars. Even Lalín would pose for a minute every day. And Jorge would watch me, half-pleased, half-sarcastic.

"Well, who would've thought!"

With the painting finished and hanging in the hall on the eve of our departure, the maestro and Julieta gave me letters of introduction for some aristocratic families and rich, famous writers whom I simply had to visit.

"You manage to do portraits of their little heirs, as I'm almost certain you will, and your name and fortune are secured," said the maestro.

We certainly needed the money. Jorge's unlucky business deals had made quick work of mother's modest savings, already much reduced between illnesses and trips. That winter we'd given up the house and one of the maids because they were too expensive, forcing me to work in a cramped little flat. Jorge was delighted to watch me help the remaining maid, while I was resigned and melancholy.

Now everything had me giddy, almost feverish: the happy prospect of making children's portraits; the heroic resolution I planned to make back at home, moving my bed into another room; the calm conversation I'd have with Jorge to determine our future relations.

We disembarked at Alicante, where Antonio lived with his wife and their four little kids whom we still hadn't met. We didn't tell them we were coming. Try as he might to hide it, Jorge was in a foul mood during the entire trip. According to him, he was bored to death at Villa Rosina because the maestro was getting senile and, as for Julieta, he found something about her vaguely repellant.

My sister-in-law María was my age, a pale blonde with clear blue eyes and a pure, arched brow. Motherly, docile, and kind-hearted in the extreme, she made for the ideal wife. Perhaps she was smart, but she was so weighed down in childcare, we barely managed to talk. Besides, I no longer had any desire to make friends, knowing myself on the margin of life.

As always, Jorge and Antonio held long conversations after lunch and dinner, staying at the table for several hours. Two days in, the joys of home and family came up in the evening discussion. That's when they talked about Julieta.

"Women that smart are no good for marriage," said Antonio. "Maybe abroad, but the Spaniard is a bit of a Moor and can't stand seeing too much intellectual superiority in a woman."

"If they're so smart, then let them stay single," Jorge grumbled.

"What do we know?" I said, referring to Julieta. "Maybe she loved him at first. I believe he's very smart himself. But love's not eternal, and our affections evolve in many directions. In the best of cases they turn into a calm brotherly love."

Jorge stared at me, hoping my words would be the key to his soul's somber monologue after years of never finding the solution.

"Does that take very long?" joked Antonio, trying to dismiss the significance of my words.

"It depends," I said, determined to make a stand, "but in the end it's inevitable."

"You heard her!" shouted Jorge, in one of his sudden rages. "You heard! After twenty years of marriage, my wife's discovered she doesn't love me. The most she can offer is brotherly love. Well, you can keep it for yourself! I don't need it! What did you talk about with Julieta?" he asked, intuitive. "I already saw she was driving you mad! She's not a decent woman; a divorcee never is. What did she say to you? Out with it! What?"

"Don't shout, man," begged Antonio, seeing the maids listen curiously at the door.

"I'll shout if I please! It's my fault for giving this imbecile wings. This idiot thought she was really something, all because some know-nothings said she was good. If only she'd stayed in the kitchen sewing socks as is every woman's duty. My whole life, what a sorry mistake!"

"Mine too, but I don't complain!"

By that point I was trembling in desperation.

"Yours!" he roared, throwing in my face all the macho's disdain for his mate. "Yours! But who are you to complain? Get out! Out of my sight! I can't take it anymore."

Antonio intervened to keep him from approaching me, and I left the room, where I could still hear him shouting long afterwards. I couldn't think. The shame of being bullied in front of my in-laws and the maids—my dignity trampled, my selfhood covered in scorn—was paralyzing my thoughts. María followed at my heels.

"Don't be angry, dear. Don't be angry! He's good at heart."

The resentment I'd built up over years keeping quiet poured from my eyes and my lips.

"Good? He's a stupid good-for-nothing!"

My sister-in-law widened her eyes and didn't reply.

I hastened to pack my bag, count the money for the trip, and throw on some clothes.

"Where are you going at this time of night? It's already ten. There's not another train till tomorrow."

It was true! I let myself fall into an armchair, hiding my face in my hands. I couldn't cry. So many years of silence, useless! Everything in my life, a failure! I wanted to die, Lord, to rest once and for all from that wearisome farce.

I finally fell asleep by force of exhaustion and prolonged nervous tension. When I woke, I saw Jorge at my feet.

"María Luisa, forgive me! I promise you..."

Then I broke into tears, mad and despairing, overcome with anguish, made into an invalid who could barely stand on her own two feet. Jorge undressed me, carried me to bed, lay down beside me, and hugged me against him. And I wasn't his sister that night, either.

We departed on the first train in the morning. I couldn't stand the looks of my in-laws and their servants.

In a corner of the carriage, over the monotonous clatter of the tracks, the previous day's scene came back to life before my eyes, and the scornful words echoed in my ears. And I cried for hours to Jorge's amazement and that of the other travelers. I refused to eat and didn't stop crying day or night, crying over my lost youth and failed sacrifices, over the abuses I'd taken even after he insulted me, over the act I'd kept up for so many years.

Back in Madrid, the house had been closed all summer long and was full of dust and cobwebs. The doorwoman lent me a maid that very same day, and together we cleaned, beat out rugs, and wiped windows. Jorge looked on with an air of satisfaction, thinking those chores would make me forget what had happened. Once in a while, he looked up from his book to study me.

"You make for a fine little housewife," he said, just as I finished making his bed. "The bustle puts color and life in your face. You look like a new woman!"

"You just like watching me work this way," I replied in quiet indignation.

"I won't deny it."

"And you even think it's all I'm good for. But I know I can do more. This'll be the last time you'll see me in this role you like so much."

Jorge looked at me astonished, not having expected such a determined response, but I was dead set on ending the scene that had started in Alicante.

"As of tomorrow, I'll paint to earn my living and won't have to serve you as women do their husbands—serve you for *everything*, that is. No! That's it! I don't want a thing from you, am asking for nothing. All I demand is my freedom, my absolute freedom. Did you think I forgot the other night? No, sir, I'll never forget! If you want me to stay in this house like a sister, fine; if not, I'll go to an inn. But now you know, I'm not your wife!"

Jorge chalked it up to resentment over what had happened. He approached me with open arms, intent on acting out a scene of definitive reconciliation.

I pulled back in a rage. That morning I wasn't exhausted and anguished like the night I fell into his arms.

"Don't touch me! I said *no*! Think what you want, decide what you want—it's all the same to me. Just remember, I can care for myself, and I don't need anyone else. I'm not looking for anyone's love, nor will I give them mine in return. Not to anyone! Remember, from this moment on, I ask only for my freedom."

Jorge turned pale and went back to his chair.

"Don't shout! What use is it for the maid to find out?"

"Yes, you're right, I won't shout. Never mind that you insulted me in front of other maids, and I'm not even insulting you."

"Fine," said Jorge, pausing to think, but as always uncomprehending. "Fine, then. You can change bedrooms here or go somewhere else. You can do what you want, but you'll regret it. It's fine by me, whatever you decide."

BAR DUBLÍN

My exhibition of children's portraits opened in early November in a little gallery on Carrera de San Jerónimo.

Some recent artist acquaintances helped me hang the canvases and gave me good advice about lighting and invitations, from which I deduced there's either less envy in the world than people say, or my friends were exceptional. Since then I've realized that both things were true, if only in part.

Thirty minutes after the opening, the invited guests and photographers had left, and two young women stood whispering their impressions in front of a picture.

"Are they painters?" I asked.

"No, the taller one's a violinist, and the other accompanies her on the piano. They've given concerts in the major European courts. People say they're … too close."

"Really?"

"But the taller one's unfaithful. I'm sure of it, I know them well," said Carmenchu. She was a middle-aged girl, the daughter of aristocrats, whom I'd met at one of the homes to which I'd been recently to make a child's portrait.

I watched with interest while my friend greeted the other two women. The tall one was a blonde: pretty golden eyes, small mouth, distinctly mannish appearance. The other was a petite brunette: almond eyes, broad cheeks, something exotic in her build and features. Later I found out her parents were Peruvian, and she probably had indian blood... Ah, my forgotten Guanche!

Her memory was gone from my heart and my lips, but not from my head, which brought her to mind when I saw the Peruvian. For two whole years I'd been absolutely free and was earning enough to live comfortably and paint at a leisurely pace. I'd made new friends, and once in a while Cupid even winked at me from the corner of my studio. I only saw Jorge for lunch and dinner, and our relationship was limited to a few words at the table.

At seven, Carmenchu and I went to take tea at Bar Dublín, a cross between a bar, a brasserie, and a tearoom where my friend had her evening get-togethers.

"I'll introduce you to my friends. Wait and see, they're a real bunch of characters."

They were waiting in a corner of the bar around two tables that had been pushed together and were loaded down with tableware and ashtrays. Carmenchu introduced me, and at first I didn't catch their names or think anyone was especially interesting. To be honest, they greeted me coldly, with a slight bow of the head, then went right back to talking as if I didn't exist.

Over the following days I went about cataloging and organizing them in my thoughts and realized Carmenchu was right: they were quite the characters. The first one to catch my attention and stand out from the others was Júpiter, a man of around sixty with gray temples and a healthy, even aggressive, look of youth. His name was Hernán Cortés and he claimed to descend from the famous conquistador, but everyone called him Júpiter after his pen name as an art critic. Like the mythological god, he hurled his lightning bolts this way and that, and woe to the wretch who roused his anger, for he was sure to be struck. He did me the courtesy of overlooking me as an artist, for which I silently thanked him.

At times I came to think he really didn't know what I did, but no, that wasn't true.

"Here in Spain," he said one day, not looking at me and addressing the group as a whole, "nobody paints children. My father tried his hand at it, but nobody else."

And nobody came to my defense! True, Carmenchu wasn't there that day.

Next to Júpiter sat Rosalía, a beautiful *señora* well over fifty who wasn't an artist, knew nothing about art, and had no right to be there apart from her looks and her foolishness to match.

"Bet you can't guess what happened to me on the street," she'd come in saying.

Júpiter would cast her a sidelong glance of pure disdain and answer violently.

"How should we know if we weren't there with you? What a stupid thing to say!"

"You could guess," she countered, a little wounded by his tone.

"I don't know how."

"Well," she continued, "I was walking down the street when a man planted himself in front of me and said, 'Look what a lovely lady.' Ha, ha, ha! So I go and tell him, 'But pray, kind sir, let me go on my way.' 'Never!' he replied. 'You won't move an inch till you give me a kiss!'"

"And you gave it to him, didn't you?" asked Júpiter.

"Sure! As if I were going to kiss him right then and there… So I go and tell him, all serious, 'Get out of my way or I'm calling a police officer. Don't you know to whom you are speaking? The wife of Don Juan Manuel Hernández Pérez, that's who! And you need only ask at the National Library; they'll tell you exactly who he is. But go in the morning, as he leaves in the evening.'"

"Naturally! Tomorrow he'll go straight to the library and ask about your husband," said Júpiter, looking sarcastically at the rest of us.

Rosalía runs out of things to say before long, for the instant the conversation strays from her beauty, she contents herself with smiling to show off her lovely teeth.

Beside Rosalía sits my friend Carmenchu, a romantic, something of a painter and something of a poet, but actually a medical doctor. I see that everyone likes her, and all of them owe her a favor, but Júpiter throws her the occasional gibe.

Next to my friend sits Leonarda, the violinist I met at my show, who also directs the sextet that livens up evenings at Bar Dublín. And next to her is Lupe, the dark-skinned indian, quiet, indistinct, and apparently ordinary, but intelligent, observant, and opportune. Her words are full of wit and fair beyond dispute.

Since their seats are empty during the sextet's performances, we must defend them from casual interlopers. The most insistent of the lot is Jaimito, a theater critic of uncertain age, skinny and weak, envious and sly, who only comes two or three times a week and is always late.

"Darlings, why go so silly over saving their places? Nobody paid for a spot here," he says, taking a seat. Then leisurely stirring his tea, he comments offhandedly, "Yesterday my father jumped off a balcony in Palencia and killed himself."

Carmenchu jumps in her chair.

"How awful! And that's how you say it!"

"How else?" asks Jaimito between sips of tea. "Sometimes we sensitive souls seem coldest on the outside."

Júpiter looks at him out of the corner of his eye and signals his disbelief.

Beside Lupe sits a blond young man with small blue eyes, a German or a Scandinavian, a revolutionary anarchist, which doesn't prevent him from living in something like luxury and wearing a magnificent leather coat. He's extremely intelligent, cultured, and well-read, but who knows how he makes his living, and he lashes out at anyone who writes.

"My dear children," he begins with a thick German accent. "One must possess a great deal of culture to have the right to put pen to paper. Here in Spain you don't know a thing, nobody studies…"

Strangely enough, Júpiter refrains from destroying him with one of his lightning bolts. Nor does Leonarda have anything to fear from Júpiter, and at times it's even he who must endure her truths.

Carmenchu fills me in on what's not in plain sight, warning me to keep it a deep secret. Even though everyone knows it, nothing ever leaves the confines of the group. Júpiter's in love with Leonarda, his companion at the theater and the movies, but he'll never tell her because he knows about her abnormal inclinations. Meanwhile he, who always makes himself out to be a normal man and has clashed with Leonarda more than once on the matter, feels a certain weakness for the young German.

A few days later I discover that the lovely Rosalía isn't nearly as good a wife as she makes herself out to be. Many nights, there's a car waiting for her at the door of the bar, and in it a man in boots who's not her husband.

Lupe's suffering a great deal these days, Carmenchu replies when I ask some questions to finish getting to know the group. Haven't I seen that bitter expression tugging at the corners of her mouth? She's been with Leonarda for years, despite knowing about her affairs.

That tall, slender girl is Juana, half-French, half-Basque, divorced from a painter, an indiscriminate flirt. She's been Leonarda's fling for over three years now. Poor Lupe!

She knows it, I observe, but there's nothing Juana could need for herself or her friends that Lupe's not swift to provide. The Peruvian's love is worthy of being carved in stone.

Among the group's occasional members are José Juan, a caricaturist and friend of Leonarda's, a self-avowed invert who claims he'll even say so on his calling cards; big-bottomed, quick-witted María Pilar, ambitious and vain, complete with a shawl and red carnations; and little Lolita, with the gray hair and face of an old person, and the gestures and build of a girl on her way to school, imitating her father's walk.

One way or another, they all have something to do with art, as artists, writers, critics, or librarians. But apart from me, Leonarda, and Lupe, none of them make a living off their art. And even so they all ignore me.

At first, this amuses me, and I don't say a word or take part in their arguments over works of art or literature. It's always the German who's holding forth, with Júpiter's absolute acquiescence.

After a few days, I feel hurt by their snub and start to doubt my work. They must've gone to my show and discussed it before I got to the bar. They probably thought it was awful. Still, I keep making money and some critics I don't even know wrote glowing reviews. The show closed two weeks ago without anybody in the group saying a word to me. In that group of artists and semi-artists, I'm the hazy figure accepted almost out of obligation.

"Would you like to come over and make a portrait of my little grandson?" asks Júpiter one afternoon.

I'm surprised by the offer and start work the following day on the portrait of a pale, scrawny boy. I give it to Júpiter as a gift, free of charge.

"Your work is a hit with the public," is all he replies before changing subjects.

But it's enough for me to feel grateful.

"Promise not to tell," says Carmenchu around that time. "I trust you very much, but promise not to tell. Have you noticed anything strange about Juana?"

"No."

"Well, something's up. I heard Leonarda's head over heels for a girl from outside the group. Another pianist, I think. To be honest, I don't know what she is, but Juana's throwing a fit, and I think Lupe's happy."

Leonarda treats me warmly, though she's another one who hasn't said a word about my show. She's more interested in something else about me, I can tell from her questioning eyes.

"Yesterday I saw you on the street with a slender *señora*…"

"Yes, an old friend."

"That's all?"

My life has her rather intrigued, and she'd like to know something about me. It's the typical desire of the abnormal for meeting others of their kind.

Lupe barely ever looks at me. Why not? Her keen sense of perception hasn't alerted her that her high cheeks, almond eyes, and the color of her skin, dark as ripe grapes, hold a strange attraction over me. In matters of love, we tend to be faithful to a single type, and Lupe has much in common with Florinda, with an added advantage: she's not an archaeologist.

Leonarda keeps asking about the slender *señora*.

"Did you go out with her today? That's why you're late, isn't it?"

"Yes."

"Really, dear, it bothers me not to know. Don't go denying to me that…"

"I'm not denying a thing to you."

Secret by secret, I end up knowing much more about Leonarda than about Carmenchu, but only as a good friend, for Leonarda's madly in love with a lady pianist.

"And what does Lupe say?"

"Lupe? But there's nothing between us. Nothing, I swear! Many years of camaraderie, over fifteen years working together, but that's the extent of it."

"And Juana?"

"Juana, she's worn out on me. Love's not eternal; in the end it runs out. I've never been in love for more than two years. Right now I'm at the end of one love and the beginning of another."

We can't make many asides before Carmenchu protests and Júpiter shows his bad mood. Besides, the sextet's breaks are short, and Lupe and Leonarda go straight back to their places on stage with the other *señoritas*.

Incidentally, all of them are blondes. They go from platinum blond to Leonarda's deeper bronze. Lupe alone is a brunette. I see her in profile, with a wavy lock of hair falling over her eyes and a tragic frown on her mouth. I don't know why, but it moves me to look at her.

One night I dream about Lupe. She's sitting beside me, listening to my affectionate words and looking somewhere else. I feel an immense pain seeing myself spurned.

The next day I tell Leonarda, who eyes me curiously and seems puzzled.

"Well, you know what Freud says. Dreams let us act out and fulfill wishes we haven't yet formulated in our waking thoughts, despite them being latent there."

We both fall silent. Seated on a velvet sofa in the café, we gaze at a table where a horrible, potbellied old toad has his beady eyes on a little girl.

"Lupe's much smarter than she seems," says Leonarda all of a sudden, as if she were reading my thoughts. "She's got lovely eyes and a beauty all her own, and she's good at heart, as are you."

"Me?"

"Yes, you. I know you already much better than you can imagine, and I believe you and she would be happy going through the world together. In many ways she completes you; she's more practical than you, more reasonable."

349

From that day on, I notice Lupe gets nervous when I look at her, averts her gaze, loses her usual quiet composure.

Right now, I'm busy purchasing a small automobile. Ever since I saved a few thousand pesetas, it's all I think about, a small car to go every day and see the sun go down among the Pardo's oaks. But I don't want to go alone. That would mean continuing my sad past life!

Two days later, I have the car but don't know how to drive. A happy coincidence! Lupe can drive! They had a car, too, though they sold it a couple of months ago. So the day after the purchase, Lupe and I take our first drive down Rosales, descend into Moncloa, pass the Puerta de Hierro, and finally reach the Pardo.

The cold winter evening lights up with the last glimmers of the setting sun. Lupe stops the car in an avenue of leafless trees, and we contemplate the twisted oaks against the violet stripe of sky in the twilight. Lowering a window, we're greeted by the perfume of thyme and of icy pure gusts of mountain air.

I find Lupe's hand in mine, tiny and smooth, with pale, square nails like a little boy's.

"Do you love me?" I ask.

Lupe stares into the distance and doesn't answer.

"And Leonarda? Do you love her very much?"

"Yes, very much."

"But Leonarda has other loves."

"I know it," her voice trembles. "I know it all too well. It's over between us, but I keep on loving her."

We stop talking for a moment to swallow the bitterness of her words.

"I'll love you just as you do Leonarda, even if you don't love me back. For now, it's enough for me that you let yourself be loved."

"All right."

That's all it takes as far as I'm concerned. I squeeze her hand, and she squeezes back affectionately.

"Shall we? It's almost five thirty."

Yes, yes; we've got to go back. The concert starts at six.

Entering the bar, all the regulars are already around the table. Júpiter ignores us, as usual; Rosalía laughs, recounting one of her adventures from the street; and Leonarda looks at us inquisitively.

"Well?" she asks on her way past me.

"Nothing," I reply, "you're the only one she loves."

"Bah! She'll end up loving you, I'm sure of it! Just keep at it."

Back at home for the night, I find my brother-in-law Antonio talking to Jorge. They fall silent seeing me come into the office. We eat dinner and talk about María and the kids. They've gotten so tall, and they think of us often. Antonio's only in Madrid for twenty-four hours. Before going to bed, he signals me over.

"I've got to talk to you."

"Go ahead, talk."

"No, tomorrow. Didn't you say your studio's on this street? What time can I drop by?"

"Whenever you want. By nine I'm there working."

"Till tomorrow, then."

The next day he shows up at my studio looking serious.

"I had to tell you. Do you know how stupid it is for a woman to abandon her duties?"

"For a woman, yes, but not for me. My duties are different."

"Look," says Antonio, ready for anything, "you and I have always gotten along."

"We have, very well."

"Well, now I'm telling you, you've got to win back your husband. Don't you see what a beautiful task I'm proposing? Just think, you've left him alone with his pain on the brink of old age. Turn back your sights on him, María Luisa! Win him back over, fall into his arms."

The flowery masculine rhetoric has no effect on me, but hearing those last few words, I rise up in fury.

351

"Fall into his arms? Is that what you said?"

"Yes… But woman…"

"I'd rather jump out of a balcony! And you can feel free to tell him so."

HER

She calls me every day on the telephone.

"Where to today? There's snow in the pass, but we can go half-way up. Do you want to?"

"Of course, I'd go with you to the ends of the earth."

A snicker on the other end of the line.

"Then it's decided. I'll pick you up early, since we've got to hurry back."

"I know, dear, I know. You needn't remind me."

All our outings inevitably end at the bar, where the concert starts at six. And besides, how could we go an afternoon without Leonarda?

Still, now she loves me. She tells me so every time I ask her, some fifty times every evening.

"Do you love me?"

"Yes, of course. I wouldn't be here if I didn't."

Here is my studio, where she comes to see me less often than I'd like, always with an indulgent smile portending mockery.

"Oh, my lovely one. Thou art dark like the Shulamite!"

The Song of Songs springs to my lips like a fervent prayer.

Lupe never answers. She looks at me and emits a sound from her throat, half-acquiescent, half-teasing. Sometimes I fall speechless under those gazing eyes, which seem to look past both my love and the present, and one day I see them fill with tears at the sound of me speaking.

"Right now, Leonarda's with her new girl friend. Yesterday she told me she invited her over."

Lupe cries silently in my arms, and I too cry heartrending sobs, resting on a shoulder that's not trembling for me.

Alone again, I think back bitterly. How stupid I am! To go and fall in love with the one woman I shouldn't have, the one woman who'll never really love me! The sensible and dignified thing to do is to end it. Tomorrow, a new life. I'll tell her I can't go out evenings, that I have to paint while there's still light. And then I won't go to the bar.

But the next day the telephone rings, and her sweet, serene voice comes back to me.

"Where to today?"

Oh, Pardo paths, mountain roads, long winding routes to Alcalá and Aranjuez! Almost always I saw you through a veil of tears. Lupe speaks as slowly as she drives, leisurely as if she were reminiscing out loud.

"One time, *she* told me, 'I won't go out tomorrow. Don't bother coming, we're expecting a visit.' But I couldn't go the whole day without seeing her. So I went to her house, and she'd gone out with a girl friend! Nothing, just a new fling. I went home a mess, crying in the street... Another time, it was in Vienna, and we were playing that night in a palace. And *she* got there late because right at the hotel..."

And she goes on telling me about another affair, another thorn in her heart.

"I don't know how you love her!"

"Because other times she loved me most out of all of them," she

354

answers, sounding triumphant. "Yes, she had twenty other women, but I was the other woman to all twenty of them. And there were times when we were so happy! Coming back from concerts, late at night, arm in arm on the way to our room, we'd see sweethearts huddling in corners and say, 'That's the normal thing. But, oh, are we happy!'"

Lupe doesn't realize the martyrdom to which she's subjecting me till a badly contained sob bursts in my chest. One day, the pain grows so unbearable, I shout.

"Stop the car! Stop, for God's sake. Let me out. I can't take it anymore, I don't want to see you anymore! Let me out."

She doesn't stop, for she's good above all, but nor does she spare me any jealous torture recalling a past that's still present and renews its wounds daily.

And I can neither hate Leonarda, the very embodiment of charm, nor stop loving Lupe, because every atom of my body and soul is turned towards her, she who sometimes looks at me with a mother's worry.

"Why are you getting so thin? Are you eating too little? Do you feel all right? Nothing's hurting, is it? I get the sense you're hiding something."

It's just that I want to forget her, to make an effort to stop loving her. My days and my nights go by planning a life I never start living.

One day I argue with Leonarda over a social question. It's the kind of argument that's over in an instant because we're very polite and know it could turn personal and sour. I content myself with making a mild insinuation to which she responds in turn in front of everyone.

"Leonarda told me to warn you," says Lupe the following day, "she won't consent to you making another allusion like last night's."

"It's not up to her to grant me permission or not. We'd better not go back to the bar. You know, I've been watching Leonarda, and she's terribly selfish."

"She'd be the first to admit it," says Lupe, slightly wounded. "She's selfish, all right, very selfish. But she's larger than life in every regard!"

And the most absolute admiration echoes in her impassioned voice.

Her exclamation is a blow to the gut, and I shut my mouth and feel sad. I've got to cure myself of this love!

Spring has come, and with it the end of concert season at the bar. The evenings are long, and we could take drives in the country till the stars come out if Lupe weren't always in a hurry to return.

"Lupe," I tell her over the phone, "this evening, I'm going straight home. To stay out of trouble, I won't go to the bar."

"Okay," she answers, unperturbed.

We drive up the mountain road, get out to pick poppies and cornflowers, and snack on some cakes that Lupe packed just in case, with her usual motherly foresight.

"You know I'm going home today, don't you?"

"Yes, that's why I wanted you to eat."

"You, too, then."

"No, I'm going to the bar for a while."

I was hoping she'd pass on the bar today, but I don't dare ask her to stay home. I know she'll go either way.

She drops me off at my doorstep when the sun's still shining on the streets. Instead of going up, I walk slowly in the direction of Bar Dublín. How bitter it is to be alone! I walk by the door and can't work up the courage to look inside. Then I walk by again and look. As always, Lupe's sitting next to Leonarda, and just beyond them is a lovely young woman.

"Yesterday Rosa María came to the bar," says Lupe the following day. "Leonarda's pianist friend. She's really pretty! I'd like you to see her."

And she says it giving no sign of hatred or envy. Maybe, deep down, she's proud such a beauty yielded to the violinist's love.

The get-togethers have moved to a spot on the Castellana, and I barely ever attend. I've got no idea how Lupe spends her evenings and only see her at night for an instant. She's always complaining about the heat. There's no escaping to the country until summer ends and the evenings get shorter. A sad summer, too sad to forget; it leaves in my soul a bitter deposit of humiliations!

Lupe likes to go out for an aperitif in the morning, just at the time when I'm working. All the same…

"I'm going out this morning," I say over the phone. "You hear? I'm leaving now."

"Ah!"

"What about you?"

"*We* have a date at Chicote with José Juan and a friend of his."

There's a pause. Maybe Lupe's thinking that she ought to go out with me. But Leonarda's expecting her! Her thoughts reach mine over the phone line: "I can't sacrifice a morning that's going to be so happy!"

My voice grows weak in the long wait for a reply that will never arrive.

"Fine, then," I say sadly. "See you this evening!"

My place in Lupe's life is very small. Her heart, like her telephone, is almost always busy. I meet her family, and one day they invite me to lunch. That's when I discover she's nearly always on the phone with Leonarda. They ring each other up about everything and nothing. The thought of it makes me moan.

"You barely ever need me. One call in the morning, and you've done your duty for the day."

"Who are you to complain?" she answers, astonished. "I've got friends I never call. Ángeles, for example. Lifelong friends! Well, it's been a month since we last spoke."

"I thought I was more to you than Ángeles."

"And you are. That's why I call you every day."

If only I could rip this love out of me! I'm losing weight, growing sadder by the day, and I'm always upset, at myself, her, and everyone. And I'm making scenes that leave both of us angry.

September has come, the days start getting shorter, and the temperature drops at night. The car's in the shop, and Lupe and I are walking down the Castellana, arm in arm, waiting for the tram that will take me home. It's almost cold out, and we shiver a little under our lightweight dresses, a holdover from summer.

"Go on," I tell her. "Go home before you catch a cold. You already said you don't feel good. Unless you prefer to see Leonarda at the refreshment stand," I add, struggling to sound indifferent.

"No," says quickly, "today they're not there. They went to Café Roma, right around the corner."

"Well, go on, then. Go on, if you're cold."

I pray she doesn't go, holding out the vague hope she'll prefer to wait with me for the tram. If only!

Just then a graceful figure crosses the avenue. It's Rosa María, who's also headed to the café to meet Leonarda. Lupe breaks free of my arm and runs after her, fascinated, irresistibly attracted, forgetting she's leaving me behind.

I see the two of them disappear and feel the air around me grow dense and cold, as if it were trapping me in a block of ice. I take a few steps and repeat without knowing what I'm saying, "How awful! How awful! How awful!"

What's awful? Since then I've thought about it. What's awful is the seduction of a love that takes Lupe away from me, the way she abandons me without looking back, all the love I've bestowed on her without putting a dent in her memory-hardened soul.

I start walking towards the café but stop before reaching the street corner. I just pictured the scene I'll make walking past the door, spying through the curtains on the group, where Leonarda will be sitting between Lupe and Rosa María. And the blood rushes to my temples, mak-

358

ing them pound and covering my brow with shame. No, I won't go! How far am I falling? I think about other loves, about a little voice that comes to me some days over the phone: "María Luisa, are you okay? I'm not asking you for anything. I just want to know you're okay, that you're happy."

I've got to seek a new interest in life and stop seeing her altogether! It's a matter of dignity, of finding myself and redeeming myself in my own eyes. And I need the cure quickly; blow by blow, the wound's becoming impossible to close.

I reach Colón and go back to waiting for the tram on the edge of the sidewalk. How sad and bleak is the summer night with gusts of autumn air! What's keeping the tram? From the shadow of the street emerges a figure who hurries down the slope of Calle de Goya, almost at a run. It's Lupe!

She scans the avenue and rushes to meet me.

"I thought you'd gone! It was just that... Rosa María told me... And then, I... We went up together because Leonarda had to tell me... And they were already leaving the café. I said, 'María Luisa's waiting for me,' even though I didn't know if... Seeing as how I didn't say anything when I left... I didn't say goodbye to her, either."

She's pale and sick, with purple rings around her eyes, and the mad dash really exhausted her.

"Poor Lupe," I say, bitterly tender. "The hardships it brings you to love Leonarda!"

"Love her? I don't know why you say that. She even told me, 'Come with me,' and I refused."

"It wasn't worth the effort. She was with Rosa María!"

"No, no; you're wrong. Rosa María was walking ahead of us with Jaimito, and we were walking behind them. You see?"

Lupe won't ever suspect the barbs of her excuses and the excruciating pain they cause me.

"Fine, you came back because your conscience was bothering you. Thank you for that."

359

She frowns and denies I have any reason to be upset with what happened. Then two times she calls me the love of her life. On the tram, I reflect coolly and feel debased, trampled before a rival I cannot hate, and I cry out of shame and humiliation.

Getting back home, the maid informs me, "Señor Medina said for you to proceed to his office. He's got to talk to you."

I enter his room without removing my beret. Jorge rises from his table when he sees me.

"Take a seat. I had to tell you... Are you in a hurry?"

"No, say what you want."

"Well, I had to ask, has it ever occurred to you that one day— not that it's already happened, but...—that one day I might meet a woman?"

I realize what he's trying to tell me.

"Yes, it has, and I find it only natural."

"Ah!"

We're silent for a moment. Deep down I keep pondering the evening's pain and abasement and almost forget I'm with Jorge.

"Well, imagine I'd met her. What would you think?"

"Very good," I reply, as if the deal were done. "It's fine by me. I just hope she makes you happy and that she's good and honorable."

"She is," says Jorge. "She's very good."

"I'm glad. I assume you'll want to get married. Luckily, the Republic has sorted that out for us. I'll look into it and tell you what I learn. I'll talk to Rosarito Alonso, my lawyer friend."

"No, don't get ahead of yourself. We've got time."

"Was there anything else?"

"No, nothing."

I stand up and end the conversation. On my way past the telephone, I take the receiver off the hook. I don't want Lupe to call me, don't want to see her again. That's the end of it.

The next day I start painting very early, not thinking, almost happy, for art has the power to make one forget everything personal, as if in order to create, the individual's soul must dissolve into the eternal and infinite soul of the universe.

Lupe arrives at the studio after lunch, pale and flustered.

"What happened to your phone? It's not working, and today I had to talk to you."

"What is it?"

Lupe's shocked to see my appearance so changed by the previous day's humiliation.

"And you? What happened to you?"

"To me? Nothing, nothing ever again."

"Good grief! Are you still mad about last night? I promise, you've got no reason to be. I had to tell Leonarda…"

"That's what the phone's for. Don't you call her twenty times a day? One more time, and you'd have said it all."

"Over the phone? Yes, phones are just great for…"

"You could've told her today in the morning. Surely you went out together as usual."

"Really, dear! Don't you know what happened? They offered her a contract for twenty concerts, which always wind up being more. And they're going away."

"Going away? Who?"

"She and Rosa María. She's a good pianist, but I don't know how they'll manage. Leonarda's used to me being her accompanist in concert. I believe they've been rehearsing for several days, because they knew about it, but they didn't tell me until … until last night. Today I haven't even seen them."

"But you must've talked ten times on the phone."

"Not even once. What's gotten into you? How do you expect them to have time for that right before their trip? They're going to Sweden and Norway, Germany, Belgium… In short, the usual itinerary."

"Is she happy?"

"Well, it certainly beats giving lessons in Madrid and directing the sextet at the bar. They'll bring back money to live for two years worry-free."

Who's unhappy is Lupe, try as she might to hide it. As for me, I'm quite pleased, because this changes all the decisions I've made since last night. Leonarda's long absence will show me what I can expect from Lupe. My doubts are coming to an end, my constant jealous brooding, my life in perpetual wait.

"And is Rosa María happy, too?"

"Yes, but she says she didn't sleep a wink last night."

I see right away that Lupe can't know whether Rosa María slept if she didn't talk to them all morning, but I keep my observations to myself. Why cause more trouble if it's all about to end?

"I don't understand why she couldn't sleep last night but could sleep others."

"Because they signed the contract this morning."

"Ah!"

We keep on talking. I see Lupe's immense sadness in her eyes and in the frown on her mouth, bitterer now than ever. She clings to me seeking refuge from her misfortune, and I caress her like an unhappy child. And she, not looking at me, starts to think out loud, oblivious to the pain her words can cause me.

"One day, years from now, she'll stop flitting about. She'll find herself alone and exhausted. She'll have no one, and then she'll come back to me."

"What are you talking about?"

"You heard."

"And why would she return to you in particular?"

"Who else is there? She wouldn't go to Juana, nor to Rosa María, who's married, nor to the others who loved her but are married with children or loaded down with siblings, nieces, and nephews. She'll come back to me, so I can care for her and spoil her. I'm sure of it!"

To those words, so dreadfully unbearable for me, I don't know what to reply.

AUTUMN'S END

OCTOBER

Just like every morning, I get to the studio and ask over the phone, "Would you tell me how Señorita Lupe's doing?"

"A little better," comes the voice of the maid. "She's asking what time you'll come over this evening."

"At six. Give her my best."

I hang up the receiver. It's already been a month since Leonarda went away, and Lupe hasn't felt good for even a week. I dial again.

"Señorita Alonso?"

"Yes, she's in."

"I need to know if she can see me this evening."

"Wait just a moment."

I hear the secretary's footsteps fading into the distance, only to be replaced by more vigorous steps and my lawyer friend's voice, slightly husky.

"Who is it?"

"María Luisa Arroyo."

"Oh, it's you! Is something wrong?"

"Yes, I've got to speak with you about a professional matter. What time is good for you?"

"Come at five."

"Until this evening, then."

"Until then."

The rain's pounding on the studio windows in a furious fall downpour, and I'm looking out at the street. The trees are still covered in leaves, but the glistening wet sidewalks and the people rushing past under umbrellas give the city the appearance of a winter's day, like a sad foretaste of the season to come. I'm shivering in the studio, still without heating or carpet. In my blood and my bones, I too feel the coming of somber days and long, frozen nights.

In the evening I get dressed to go out in a wool suit fresh from the tailor. A faint ray of sunshine, filtered through the rain, wrests sparks of light from the bottles on my vanity. How thin I am! Until now I've always smiled at the ambiguous image looking back at me from the mirror, something of a boy, something of a woman. I believe before long, I'll look like a man once and for all, a skinny, ugly man.

Rosarito greets me in her office like someone attending to business.

"Tell me."

"Nothing much... I want a divorce."

"Do you have justified motives, or justifiable ones?"

"No."

"So why?"

"Well... Maybe we ought to have a long talk, so I can come clean to you a bit about my own faults and misfortunes."

"There's no need. I already know."

I look at Rosarito and see in her eyes that she knows everything. I practically jump.

"But I didn't think I was flaunting or giving any reason to believe..."

"That's what you all think. In the first place, your appearance... Besides, I've known you for five years, I know your girl friends. I've crossed paths with your car more than once on Cuesta de las Perdices, whether you saw me or not in your excitement over your company. And not long ago I ran into your husband in a café with a younger woman. And seeing how one's a lawyer and goes through life connecting the dots... *Voilà.*"

"Yes, but you must think I'm a madwoman. You know nothing of my struggles, the mistake of an entire life."

"Let's go out. Did you bring the car?"

"No, it's Lupe who drives, and she's sick."

"That's okay, we'll take mine. We'll take a drive and talk, if you want."

Rosarito has her car beside the gardens in the plaza, parallel to others that also sit waiting for their owners, windows closed and washed by the rain. She unlocks the door, I sit down beside her, and she starts the engine.

The Retiro is solitary and sad on this rainy day. I talk without looking at Rosarito, nor does she look at me. This gives me more courage to talk and her, more freedom to answer.

I give her a brief account of my life, concluding that it's not my fault if despite all my efforts, I haven't been able to adapt to a normal life.

"And you've jolly well wasted your time," replies Rosarito. "You really are a special case. Because being children of a man and a woman, sometimes the part of the brain our father handed down works best, but other times our mother's full femininity takes over."

My friend has some unique ideas on the matter that aren't entirely my own, but I don't dispute them.

"Yes, yes," I continue. "All that to say, after the scene of our separation from bed and board, as you'd say in your professional jargon, he's never gotten anything in *that* department."

"Bah," scoffs Rosarito in disbelief.

"Really, I swear. He's another exceptional case. Naturally, he saw he was alone and found himself another woman. And since one day I asked him for my freedom, now I want to grant him his."

369

The car is parked next to the Ángel Caído, and we study the trees as they start turning yellow and the ground carpeted in wet leaves.

"Are you cold?" asks Rosarito. "Because if not, we could roll down a window."

She does so, and the car fills with the smell of autumn, a smell of clay and of moisture fermenting in marshy spots where the last summer roses are dying.

"The afternoon's poetic," says my friend, "but it seems to me that you're sad."

"No, it's the season. It's always the same for me. The flowers sprout inside me in the spring, I think, and part of me dies every autumn. As it happens, I feel the impact of autumn more every year as it comes into tune with the course of my age."

"But you're very young!"

That's what they all say. But I looked at myself in the mirror this afternoon… I glance at the time. A quarter till six and it's almost dark out.

"Tell me what I must do."

She explains the steps to take, and I agree to return to her house the next day. We quickly leave the park, and it's not two minutes before she's dropping me off at Lupe's. I get there on time, and her mother greets me shaking her head in disappointment.

"She's the same as before. Got dressed, then got back in bed. She never quite gets better!"

I find her sitting in bed, with a wild lock of hair strewn over her brow and her mouth's bitter grimace even more pronounced than usual.

"How are you feeling?"

"Better. There's been a letter from Leonarda. One success after another: Oslo, Berlin—now they're off to Vienna."

The room is dark, barely illuminated by a small reading lamp on the bed. I talk about my divorce, about Rosarito, who already knew, who'd seen us in the car.

"See?" says Lupe. "I don't like that one bit. Surely you said it was a lie. You've always got to deny it, then all the rest is gossip."

"How little you love me," I say sadly.

"Little? Much more than I'd like to! All that love stuff never pans out for me. There's so much suffering!"

We circle back to my divorce, and Lupe lies down in bed to listen. She only sits up when I say I'm leaving.

"It's eight, and dinner's always late because of me."

Lupe's sitting on the bed and studying the floor, somber and sad.

"Listen, has she ever told you if she loves me?"

"Who?"

"Leonarda. She must've told you something. Tell me, did she tell you she loves me, or that she doesn't anymore?"

There's an absence in her gaze, a stubbornness on her brow, and such a look of anguish in her eyes, I don't have the courage to say what I'm thinking.

"I don't know. She hasn't said a word to me."

"Yes, she must've said something. Tell me! Or else she's completely stopped loving me!"

I go back home. All the fall leaves just turned yellow in my heart.

Jorge and I talk for a moment at the table.

"Rosarito told me a divorce by mutual consent would be easiest and most discreet. There's no need to make allegations, no need to blame one another. It's quicker and less unpleasant."

He doesn't answer and slams a door hard on the way back to his room. Well, what did he expect? Or does he not know what he wants?

The rainy days keep coming, and once again I've decided not to see Lupe. I paint non-stop, burning the candle at both ends, smoke cigarettes, and wait. For what? For Lupe, whom I haven't seen in two days; for her, though I'd never admit it. On the contrary, I don't want her to come! I never want to see her again! The experiment is over. I wanted to know what Lupe would be for me far from Leonarda. Now I know.

Another fall day. But this one is cheery, washed clean by the rain of the previous days, cool, golden, and happy, like a memory of summer. Seated on a sofa in the studio, I enjoy the day's peace. One more day… If I can make it through a week without seeing Lupe, I'll know I'm cured.

The maid comes in and hands me a letter. New York! It's from Carmenchu, who went there in the spring on a scholarship.

"Come spend a couple of years here. It's the perfect scene for you. You'll paint like in Spain and earn ten times more. I spoke to some families, and they can't wait for you to come and immortalize their youngsters in childhood. Make up your mind!"

The phone rings. Rosarito. We talk.

"If your husband is intent on keeping quiet and slamming doors, it's time for a trip."

"Just now I got a letter from Carmenchu. She says I ought to go."

"And I say so, too. Get out of here. Abandonment of domicile is more than enough to justify a divorce, and since you're turning down his financial support…"

I'm rereading Carmenchu's letter when the doorbell rings. It's Lupe! All the bells of my soul ring in glory.

Cheerful and doting, Lupe drops down beside me, snuggles up close, and starts talking with our faces nearly touching.

"No, don't say a word. You're right! I shouldn't have asked you … the question I asked. I shouldn't ask anyone, but least of all you."

As usual, the tone of her apology wounds me more deeply than its cause in the first place.

"Enough talk about that. You'll just make me suffer like always. No, we're going to talk about something else."

"About what?" she asks, startled and fearing reprisals.

"Nothing bad," I answer, stroking her curls. "What would you think about us going to America?"

"What? To America? Not me. Just think, I'd really like to go with

372

you, but it can't be; I've got my family, my parents... Impossible! I wouldn't leave them for anything in the world. You don't know how close we are at home. I could never live so far apart from them... But who gave you that idea?"

I tell her what Rosarito said and show her Carmenchu's letter.

"I don't dare give you advice. You know I'll be sad to see you go. But you've got to go alone! As for me, I won't try to influence you."

"In any case, I've got to go. It's the only way to get the divorce. I need to spend a few years away from here. Besides, it would be good to make a name for myself in America, to earn some money."

"But why America? Why not Paris? I'd go with you to Paris! Leonarda's going there soon for three concerts. Then they're off to Brussels and next month back to Paris."

I realize the case for me to go to Paris is too overwhelming to be open to dispute. And Lupe talks all afternoon about Paris, the Latin Quarter, the boulevards, her and Leonarda's favorite spots when the two of them went to give concerts.

The studio lights up with fall sunshine and happy memories. Lupe's forgotten all about the family she couldn't leave behind just moments earlier.

"And your family? Would they let you go without a good reason? How will you live without them?"

"Really, dear. It's different to stay in Europe, the same as it was back when Leonarda and I would go on tour for three or four months at a time."

We drink tea and make plans. I accept what she says without arguing. She's happy, and the sun of her laughter has shone on my poor cold-prone heart. Paris, yes, Paris! We'll go to Paris because Lupe wants to. We'll live like bohemians, dining with Leonarda and Rosa María in Latin Quarter dives. An evening full of hopes and memories. The memories belong to Lupe alone, but I adopt them as my own like the children of the woman I love!

373

NOVEMBER

The days are fleeting, the wind blows strong, the sun brings little warmth, the evenings are cold and harsh.

Lupe tells me another letter came from Leonarda. She's going to Brazil! She just signed a year-long contract.

"This time she's not coming back," says Lupe, in a craze. "At least, I don't think she's coming back. I was at her house this morning. I opened the closets, and I just don't know... There were little things that seem to prove she doesn't plan on coming back for a long time. On the other hand..."

I talk to her about our trip to Paris.

"Oh, no! You must be kidding! Life's so expensive there, we'd barely make it a week."

My husband's mood too is gloomier than usual. He doesn't go out. The good and honorable *señorita* stood him up. I talk to him affectionately, trying to smooth out this rough patch, and don't speak again of Rosarito Alonso. Encouraged by my attitude, he asks me some questions.

"Did you sell the car?"

"Not yet, but I have it in the shop to sell it."

Then he wants to know how much I got paid for my latest portrait.

"Not that it matters to me. It's your money, but I have it in my head you're letting yourself be exploited by those shameless fathers."

I tell him the price, and he thinks it's far lower than what I should charge.

"It's stupid to devalue oneself like that. If you can't handle the public, you'd be better off sticking to your needlework."

I raise my eyebrows, logically surprised at what I perceive as the irony of his words, and Jorge erupts into one of his rages.

"Keep making that face, and I'll slam you into the wall," he howls, then runs off to lock himself in his room.

I'm starting to feel weak in the head. I've lost so much weight in so little time, many people see me and don't even recognize me. I'm not sleeping. Nights give me lots of time to think, and my thoughts are like thread winding on a bobbin. Do I go? Do I stay? How the wind blows in the mountains! Rosarito's right, I've got to get out of here, and now it won't be to Paris. Unless it means spending a day with Leonarda, Lupe doesn't want to go there. Do I accept Carmenchu's offer? By the end of the night, I've wound all my thread around a decision. I'm going to request a passport for America.

I go out in the morning and get my picture taken. Waiting for the photographs, I stop by my car in the shop. There's already a buyer, but the offer is low. It doesn't matter; let them have it for whatever. I need the money right away. Now to the tailor to order two suits, then to the hairdresser.

Back at home, they tell me Lupe's been calling all morning.

"Lupe," I call her. "Lupe, what's wrong?"

"Were you out? You sure did go early and take a long time!"

"I went shopping."

"Why didn't you tell me yesterday? We'd have gone together. Just when I've got to talk to you…"

"We'll talk this evening. Where should we meet? Dublín or my studio? Dublín?"

I hang up the receiver. What's going on with Lupe? Her voice sounded happy.

It's another evening of projects and hopes. A letter from Leonarda, from the ship that's taking her to America. Why didn't we go to Brazil?

"You see? She's suggesting it. We're not the ones trying to intrude on her life. It's she who can't stand to be alone with Rosa María. She'll pave the way for us. You'll see, she'll have everything waiting on a silver platter."

Lupe has some savings, and if I sell the car, I can take several thousand pesetas, enough for us to hold out till I get paid for my first commission. We're off to Brazil! *Viva* Brazil!

I gaze out at the street from the windows of the bar and see people bustling past, whipped by the wind of the cold, dreary evening. How come this time Lupe says nothing of her family?

Another night of reflection. How clearly I see in the bedroom's darkness! The same Lupe who couldn't go to New York is able to go to Brazil, and she could go to India or Japan if Leonarda were there. Tomorrow I'll ask for the passport.

More raw autumn days. Short, cold evenings in which Lupe and I walk quickly down the avenues of the Retiro, where the wind toys with dry leaves, whisking them this way and that. I too feel caught up in the gale of a passion.

"Don't you think," I ask my friend, "that sometimes the leaf knows more than the wind, and lets itself be taken because it wants to?"

"The things you come up with!"

DECEMBER

All my time goes by in preparations. I moved my books and my clothes to the studio, and everything's already packed in two big suitcases. Where am I going? To Brazil? To New York? My passport's good for either place, and I can choose right up to the very last minute.

"Tomorrow I leave for Alicante," announces Jorge at lunchtime after several days of silence. "José María and Consuelo just got there with Juanito, who's going to enroll in the naval school. I don't know if they'll come to Madrid. I don't think so, but just in case, have the maid prepare rooms for them, your studio if need be. If you'd like to go with me…"

"No, I've got a lot to do now."

Lupe didn't call me all morning long, and at three her voice comes over the phone line, hoarse like she's talking through tears, but sounding triumphant.

"María Luisa, can you hear me? Leonarda's here! She came back alone. Rosa María stayed behind in Lisbon. I'll tell you more later; I'm with her at her house. And *she* called *me*! Today I can't see you."

"Okay."

I hang up, and my arms go slack. But now I know what I must do.

I go to the travel agency and jot down the name of the boat. A telegram to Carmenchu: "I depart on the Normandie."

I dine alone, for Jorge already left to see his brothers. I don't doubt for a second that within a week they'll all be in Madrid. My two sisters-in-law will put all their good will into making us hug in their presence.

Before going to bed, I write to Lupe. I can barely make it past the first line with the tears that are blurring my vision.

"I too am ill with abandonment, and I too am calling you. I leave tomorrow on the nine o'clock express to Cadiz, where I catch the boat on Thursday. Come! I need you!"

And I write the date: December twentieth.

Tonight, I sleep. I'm so tired, I fall into a deep sleep from which I don't emerge until the maid wakes me up. Then, still in bed, I write to Jorge.

"They've made me magnificent offers to make portraits in America, and I'm going. I'll write to you the moment I get there. I hope you'll be happy, that you'll make a resolution to be happy. As you know, I love you like a sister."

The day is so dark and the dawn came so late, I turn on the light to bathe and get dressed. Under the light of the mirror, I study myself severely. I'm starting to get old! There's gray in my temples and wrinkles around my eyes like petals wilting after so many burning tears.

In the station I look around with a faint sense of hope. If only Lupe were to take pity on me! But why would she? Does Leonarda take pity on her, by chance? Do I on my husband? We're all alone in this selfish world, where the one triumphant love is our love of ourselves.

I take my designated seat in the carriage and look out over the platform. Not many travelers. It's cold out, it's almost Christmas, and nobody leaves home if they can avoid it. I glance at the clock. There are still five minutes. Who knows?

My need for Lupe is physical and spiritual. Ten years younger than me, she's given me months of motherly support, the sweet relief of knowing I'm protected, a practical outlook on the present, a prudent hand to save me from rashness and folly. And now what's to become of me? What am I to do, a bohemian with no common sense, no love of life or care for the future?

The train whistle blows and we're off. She didn't come!

I wrap my leather-lined coat around me, over my wool skirt and comfortable blouse, and I close my eyes to block out my vision, to sink into a slumber made uneasy, almost delirious, by the speed and clatter of the carriages.

When my in-laws hear I left, they'll say it was an escape!

I hear my brother-in-law Antonio waxing poetic: "Come back to your home—woman, wife, queen of your household. Come back to your duties and your people."

No! You all despise *my* people: Joaquinito, Fermina, Lolín, Rafita, the pariahs of a normal society whose only aim is to keep on reproducing; the people you threw out of your honorable homes, your homes full of lust and wailing children and smelly diapers. They walk with me, and I with them.

I was dreaming, and I think I just shouted. I open my eyes and peer at the gentleman sitting across from me, who doesn't look up from his book.

The frozen fields rush past us, the trees clamoring towards the heavens with their branches bare, the houses shuttered, no sign of life save the smoke from their hearths. And it's starting to snow…

TRANSLATOR'S NOTE

In a memorable scene towards the beginning of *Hidden Path*, María Luisa recalls her ten-year-old self watching two elegant young ladies ascend the marble staircase at a fancy hotel. The adult narrator, recreating her perspective as a child, describes the hotel's upper stories as a magical space hidden from view, a "marvelous world that I couldn't see and perhaps never would." The unseen rooms hold out a promise that the young María Luisa does not fully grasp but that propels her along the winding path that comprises the rest of her narrative. In the final pages, María Luisa is still traveling, and we as readers are left to ponder whether and to what extent she will gain access to everything represented by the space at the top of the stairs.

But what exactly does that space signify? What is its promise? There is no single answer, but in the context of the story we might associate the hotel's upper floors with a life dedicated to the pursuit of art, beauty, self-determination, and love between women. The twin forces of sexism and homophobia seek to prevent María Luisa from leading such a life, yet she keeps on striving. In light of the novel's publication history, as detailed in Nuria Capdevila-Argüelles's foreword, we might also read the hidden world as a figure for Fortún's manuscript, which remained out of sight for over seven decades prior to its release in Spanish in 2016. Finally, as a translator, I like to think of the longed-for space as a fitting metaphor for the English translation, the book that you are reading now.

The first few times I read *Hidden Path* in Spanish, the sounds and shapes of a potential English-language translation called to me like an invisible presence behind Fortún's words. After numerous twists and turns, the translation is now out in print. But as is always the case of a literary translation, publication is not a definite end point. Just as María Luisa continues her journey in the final chapter, translation as meaning-making must continue in the form of further acts of reading, interpreting, and critiquing. And just as María Luisa's path is marked by loss and triumph, the work of translation means negotiating that which is rendered different in the process of transferring meaning and form across languages.

This translation aims to give readers the chance to experience *Hidden Path* in English in much the same way they might do so in Spanish. That means attempting to recreate the signature characteristics of Fortún's style: flowing prose, more concerned with meaning and rhythm than syntactical precision; natural dialogue, finely attuned to the psychology, socioeconomic circumstances, and regional dialect of each character; and frequent, often jarring shifts between the lyricism and sensuality of María Luisa's private thoughts and the mundane banter of her milieu. It also means capturing the self-aware quotations—some satirical, some sincere—of the genres of discourse that pervade the narrator's life: panegyrics to the traditional Catholic family and the perfect wife, Spanish Golden Age honor plays, fairy tales, romance and adventure novels, medical theories of inversion, and early twentieth-century homophile defenses of sexual diversity, to name a few.

There is also a need to register the stylistic shifts that accompany the changing seasons of María Luisa's life and narrative. Looking back as an adult, the narrator reconstructs her perspective at different ages and the attendant evolution of her experience of time. As she gets older, the days seem to slip by more quickly, such that the sixteen chapters of Spring linger on several years of girlhood and early adolescence while the remaining twenty-two chapters cover a full two and a half decades of youth and adulthood. The pace of the prose matches the pace of time passing as the writing quickens into the rapid, dialogue-driven encounters in the last chapters of Autumn and Autumn's End. Narrated in the present tense, these final chapters read like a diary, a swiftly penned account of events as they happen or shortly thereafter. The translation aims to convey these varying textures to evoke the feeling of reading *Hidden Path* as Fortún wrote it.

Inevitably, the movement between languages comes with losses and gains. The complexity of translating two chapter titles gives a sense of the choices I faced while bringing the novel into English. "Sweetname" and "The Ancient Elder" are my solutions to the challenges posed by "Dulce Nombre" and "El sauco centenario," respectively. The former's difficulty arises from the strangeness and layered allusiveness of the name of an older cousin whom María Luisa meets at Tía Teresa's palace. The narrator and her cousin agree that Dulce Nombre is not a name in Spanish. There are women named Dulce but not typically Dulce Nombre (literally, Sweet Name). Yet the latter does reference a common women's name in Spanish through its connection to the Catholic festivity of the Dulce Nombre de la Virgen María, celebrated on September 12 in honor of the Most Holy Name of the Blessed Virgin Mary. The name's Marian dimension is apt since María Luisa's cousin promotes the traditional feminine virtues of obedience, humility, and sweetness.

There were several worthy contenders for translating Dulce Nombre into English, and I thank the many individuals who helped me think them through. Of the fine alternatives, the name Marigold preserves Dulce Nombre's allusion to the Virgin Mary, fits nicely with the gardens where María Luisa meets her cousin, and is relatively rare in contemporary English. However, because Marigold and comparable options are recognizable as women's names, they do not align with Dulce Nombre's assertion that her name "isn't a name but the description of a name that other people have to guess and whose secret rests with me," a statement that recalls the late nineteenth-century invocation of homosexual love as "the love that dare not speak its name" and underlines María Luisa's vaguely romantic attraction to her beautiful older cousin. My rendering, Sweetname, plays down the Marian reference in the English but captures the mystery and oddness of Dulce Nombre in Spanish. The one-word version is purposefully strange but plausible given the existence of compound words such as *bittersweet* or *sweetheart*.

In the case of "The Ancient Elder," English has a greater potential to enrich Fortún's title. A more direct translation of "El sauco centenario" might yield "The Hundred-Year-Old Elder Tree" or "The Centennial Elderberry," multi-syllabic mouthfuls that lack the alliteration and sonorous vowel sounds of the Spanish. "The Ancient Elder" recuperates Fortún's brevity while sacrificing some of her precision concerning the tree's age. Further, the word *elder* introduces a degree of ambiguity not found in the Spanish word *sauco*, a straightforward name for bushes and trees in the genus *Sambucus*, commonly known in English as elders or elderberries. As a homonym, *elder* can refer to these plants as well as to a forebear, ancestor, or senior family member.

Fortunately, the word's various meanings dovetail with the content of the chapter, wherein María Luisa draws connections between the elder tree and her older relatives. First she imagines that the tree witnessed the infancy of her recently deceased uncle and the lives of his parents. Later she relates the felling of the tree to her father's death, which ends her childhood by depriving her of "the protective shade of his arms." In this instance, a felicitous coincidence of the English language makes the title "The Ancient Elder" a suitable means of foregrounding the parallels between human and botanical life that are present in the chapter but absent from its Spanish-language title.

There are many other subtle differences between *Hidden Path* in Spanish and English, but in the end something more essential remains the same for readers of the two languages. In the last chapter of the Spanish, the final word *nevar* leads into an ellipsis and a space white as the snow that María Luisa is observing from a train. The ellipsis and the space remain in the English, a passage from language into silence that, far from putting an end to meaning-making, raises numerous questions and possible responses. Does the snow signify old age and death? A wiping clean of the past? Hope for the future? The work of translation continues indefinitely in the blank space of the page as we are invited to imagine the next steps for María Luisa, and for ourselves.

***

In the novel's final paragraphs, the narrator is traveling alone but takes strength in the thought that others accompany her from afar. Similarly, I owe a debt of gratitude to the institutions and individuals that helped make this translation possible, even during the social distancing that accompanied the last stages of its completion in the midst of a global pandemic.

Nuria Capdevila-Argüelles, María Jesús Fraga, and Editorial Renacimiento supported the translation from the start, with Nuria and María Jesús generously responding to numerous queries concerning the nuances of Fortún's Spanish. Together with the scholarship of Marisol Dorao, their research and editorial work have expanded Fortún's legacy, bringing *Hidden Path* to light in the first Spanish edition and revealing another facet of Celia's creator. Thanks as well to Michael Ugarte for his advocacy on behalf of this translation and to David Rade at Swan Isle Press for his keen attention to all aspects of its publication. I am grateful to the Spanish Ministry of Culture and Sport for awarding a generous grant in support of this translation.

The Office of Research and Sponsored Projects at the University of West Georgia also provided a generous grant. I am indebted to Denise Overfield, Janet Donohoe, Robert Kilpatrick, Shelly Elman, Yvonne Fuentes, Julia Farmer, Betsy Dahms, Muriel Cormican, Nathan Vargas, Holly Garner, and Darlene McDaniel for their help and encouragement. I also thank the College of Arts and Humanities under the leadership of Pauline Gagnon for providing time and space to complete the manuscript during an AIR Serenbe artist's residency in Chattahoochee Hills, Georgia.

Many individuals offered valuable feedback on early drafts: Kathy, Frank, Jake, and the Terrific Translators under the tutelage of Suzanne Jill Levine at the 2019 Middlebury Bread Loaf Translators' Conference. Thanks to Rhonda Buchanan for her enthusiasm and expert guidance and to Dolores Romero López for her support. Nathan stands in a category apart for being the first person to hear each chapter in English and a constant source of inspiration. You are the artist in my life. Finally, thanks to the students in my Spring 2020 seminar Elena Fortún and Modern Spanish Women's Culture: Anna, Evelyn, Giezi, Lauren, Lyndsey, Mayra, Patricia, and Stacia. May you be among the first of many *afortun*adas and *afortun*ados beyond Spain.

Jeffrey Zamostny
MAY 2020
CARROLLTON, GEORGIA, USA

Swan Isle Press is a not-for-profit literary and
academic publisher of fiction, nonfiction, and poetry.

For information on books of related interest
or for a catalog of new publications contact:
https://www.press.uchicago.edu/ucp/books/
publisher/pu3430685_3430697.html

Hidden Path
Designed by Marianne Jankowski
Typeset in Adobe Jenson Pro
Printed on 55# Natural Offset Antique